BRIGHTER DAYS AHEAD

War pulled them apart, but can it bring them back together?

Molly lives with her repugnant father, who has betrayed her many times. From a young age, living on the streets of London's East End, she has seen the harsh realities of life. When she's kidnapped by a gang and forced into their underworld, her future seems bleak. Flo spent her early years in an orphanage and is about to turn her hand to teacher training. When a kindly teacher at her school approaches her about a job at Bletchley Park, it could turn out to be everything she never realized she wanted. Will the girls' friendship be enough to weather the hard times ahead?

BRIGHTER DAYS AHEAD

BRIGHTER DAYS AHEAD

by

Mary Wood

Magna Large Print Books
Long Preston, North Yorkshire,
BD23 4ND, England.

British Library Cataloguing in Publication Data.

A catalogue record of this book is
available from the British Library

ISBN 978-0-7505-4685-0

First published in Great Britain in 2017 by Pan Books,
an imprint of Pan Macmillan

Published in Large Print 2018 by arrangement with
Macmillan Publishers International Ltd.

Magna Large Print is an imprint of Library Magna Books Ltd.

Printed and bound in Great Britain by
T.J. (International) Ltd., Cornwall, PL28 8RW

To my friend Stan Livinston – RIP.

Loved and much missed. Stan helped me in my self-publishing days, editing my work and advising me. He was a man who gave to others, and became my dear friend. May you find a thespian group and a huge disco hall in heaven that you can enhance with your wonderful talents.

1

Molly

The Other Side of War

Molly stiffened. Beery breath, soured by a recently smoked cigarette, wafted over her shoulder. The weight of her dad's body crushed her against the pot sink. His hand, taking a forbidden trail, slithered around her waist and travelled upwards.

With all the strength she could muster, Molly hunched her body and pushed backwards. The sound of a chair crashing to the ground caused her to draw in a deep breath. Angry and yet fearful, she turned to see her dad tottering on unsteady legs, the chair he'd bumped into now sprawled on the floor behind him. Unable to steady himself, he lost his balance and landed with a thud on his backside. Molly winced. The cracked lino that covered the concrete floor of the kitchen wouldn't have cushioned his fall. His cry spoke of his pain, but Molly felt no sympathy for him, nor did she attempt to help him.

From a slackened mouth that leaked spittle, his slurred words held no apology. 'You little bastard – push your old man over, would you?'

'You should leave me alone, Dad. It ain't right, touching me like that!'

'Like what? I thought for a minute you were your mum, that's all. I meant no harm, girl.'

'Mum's been dead eleven years, so you can leave out that excuse. You should stop drinking. You don't know what you're doing when you're drunk.'

'Yer old dad gets lonely, Molly. It wouldn't hurt you to give him a bit of comfort.'

'Comfort! You're disgusting. What man would want that kind of comfort from his own daughter, eh?'

Fighting back the tears, Molly felt desperate to escape his presence. The back door stood open, but she turned from it and stormed out of the kitchen and into the hall instead. She hesitated at the parlour door, and again at the bottom of the stairs, but her need to get out of the house made her reject these sanctuaries and make for the front door. She didn't relish the thought that she might encounter passers-by on the street, but she preferred that to going into the yard at the back.

The yard connected with the rear of her father's butcher's shop and held the fear, for Molly, of bumping into Foggy Fieldman, so-called because he constantly had a cigarette hanging from his lips and smoke curling up his face.

Foggy worked for her dad in the preparation shed that ran from the end of the shop along the full length of the yard, forming an enclosure with the buildings that housed the coal shed, the out-house and the outside lavatory. With the short-ages that war had forced upon them all, Foggy had little to occupy him now. The huge carcases he used to cut into roasting joints, chops and steaks were a rarity, and he spent his time bagging up the offal that her dad had managed to get hold of, and making sausages out of the poorer cuts of meat that were more readily available.

'Idle hands find trouble,' her old granny used to say, and this was certainly true of Foggy. Having witnessed her dad's lack of respect for her, Foggy seemed to have the idea that he could behave in the same way. He'd changed from the person she'd trusted into a leering predator who lusted after her.

She lived in fear of going to the lav in the back yard, and even of being in her own home at times. Not that her fear was all down to her dad's and Foggy's antics, because now there was the threat of air raids to contend with – and they had her scared out of her wits.

The soft, warm breeze caught her skirt as she stepped outside. Paying no heed to the chafing of the bricks through her white cotton blouse, Molly leaned heavily against the wall and lifted her face. The late-August sun blistered down, giving off an intense heat, though it failed to reach the cold place where her heart sat.

The scene before her compounded her misery, as she gazed at the ruins of a house across the road. Her ears still zinged with the high-pitched noise caused by the explosion, and her body trembled with the shock of the reality of the first air raid experienced by London.

Almost a week had passed since that day – 24th August 1940 – when one of the many sirens that Londoners had become used to throughout the year had actually meant something. A week during which everyone's nerves had become frayed. Yes, it was thought the bomb that had destroyed the house and other buildings nearby had landed in the wrong place, but now the news was full of more to come, after Churchill's reprisal in bombing Berlin. But no one knew when it might happen.

Mr and Mrs Hopkins, the tenants of the bombed-out house, had ignored the warning siren. Though badly injured, they had escaped with their lives. Only one wall of the house remained standing and, as if in defiance, the collapsed bedroom floor clung to it. Wedged at an angle against the ground, a double bed spewed from the gap. A wardrobe lay beside it, smashed into shards of wood – its hanging rail, still attached, revealing clothes doing a haunting dance in the breeze, as smoke from the smouldering embers curled around them.

Molly swallowed the urge to cry as she watched the workers clear the rubble. One of them stood near the corrugated-iron air-raid shelter that would have saved the couple from injury. He smiled as she looked across at him. Then he heightened her sense of humiliation as he let out a low wolf-whistle.

The gesture nearly undid her, but she fought the tears that prickled her eyes. Londoners didn't show such emotion on a whim. Never mind being frightened – or being treated as an object, and not a person – you had to carry on, and you had to keep others going, too. If you gave in, you would be lost, and Hitler would have won.

With this thought, a new determination came over Molly. She had a job to go to and, at this rate, she'd be late back after her lunch break. Returning into the house to collect her purse, she became worried by the sound of her dad snoring. He should have his butcher's shop open by now. As it was, she knew they were losing business and things didn't look good.

Not wanting to chance going to wake him, as she feared facing her dad's wrath again, Molly slammed the door hard as she left. The action gave her some satisfaction. The noise it made would have scared him out of his slumber.

They had always been the affluent family in Sebastopol Road in Edmonton. She remembered that her mum had wanted them to move to a better area, but her dad wouldn't have it. He'd said he needed to be amongst his own, as half of his business came to them because their neighbours all knew him as one of them.

Cancer had taken her mum. At ten years old, Molly had watched the ugly, slow deterioration of a beautiful, buxom woman into a skeletal, unrecognizable one. She could still feel the agony of her loss.

Everyone said she looked like her mum did at her age. She could see this herself, when she dusted the lovely brass-framed wedding photo of her mum and dad, which stood on the piano in the parlour. Her mum had been beautiful, and Molly had inherited many of her qualities: the same sleek black hair and dark, flashing eyes. It wasn't these features that attracted men to her, though. It was her shape – something else she could attribute to her mum. With a small frame and over-large breasts, she'd always been teased that she'd been in the front of the queue, when they were dished out. How often she'd wished she hadn't been. Her breasts were a curse, as far as she was concerned. Most men leered at her, in one way or another. If not openly, then they did so with a sideways glance, giving her a wink if she caught them looking, as if they thought she wanted what they offered.

Nothing could be further from the truth. Losing her mum at such a young age had taken away her confidence, and though she'd done well at school, being naturally clever, on leaving school she hadn't wanted to do anything that might entail going away from home. Not that there were many opportunities for girls to do so, although her brains would have got her into college to become a secretary or something. Instead, she chose to work in a shoe shop in the town centre because, like her dad, she felt safe amongst her own people. How often she'd regretted that decision.

As she was about to turn into Osmond Road, Molly looked back. She wasn't surprised to see her Aunt Bet, her mum's sister, lifting the latch to their home. Widowed in the last war, Aunt Bet adored Molly's dad. The thought of them together repulsed her. But it also left her with no one to turn to who might be able to help her, as Aunt Bet was her only relative and wouldn't hear a word against her dad. A deep loneliness and a yearning for her mum seared through her at this thought, and Molly thanked God for her friend Hettie.

Hettie lived on the same street, just a few doors down from the corner where Molly's house and the butcher's shop stood. They'd grown up together and had a special bond. She could talk to Hettie, though shame prevented her revealing everything.

The sound of a vehicle slowing behind Molly stopped the morose thoughts that had threatened to overwhelm her and replaced them with a feeling of trepidation, as the kind of car not usually seen in Edmonton pulled up beside her. Black and sleek with white-rimmed wheels, it reminded Molly of those cars she'd seen in American films. A woman leaned out of the window. Molly looked up and down the street – no one was about. Her trepidation deepened as the woman called out to her, 'Here, lav, you know of an Alf Winters? He has a butcher's shop round here somewhere.'

The surprise of being asked for directions to her dad's shop, by this heavily made-up woman with a shock of bright-red hair, rendered Molly speechless.

'Cat got your tongue, eh? I asked you a bleedin' question.' Stark blue eyes stared into Molly's, before travelling the length of her body. Sniggers came from the fat male driver and from a man sitting in the back seat, but they stopped when the woman bawled at them, 'Here, you two, pack it in. Can't you see she's like a bleedin' rabbit in the headlights?'

The back window opened slowly. A blond-haired man, whom Molly thought to be in his forties, put his head through and grinned at her. The evil that emanated from him stopped Molly thinking of him as handsome, even though he had chiselled good looks that gave him a certain magnetism. His eyes travelled from her face and lingered on her breasts. She watched his gaze turn from curiosity to lust. Repulsion shuddered through her.

With a smirk, he lifted a half-smoked cigarette to his mouth, took a deep drag and then threw the butt-end at her feet. Molly jumped, but couldn't take her eyes off him. He kept his gaze on her, squinting as the smoke slowly escaped from his mouth, before blowing a cloud towards her in a deliberate action. The menace of this made her gasp.

'You're a good-looker, girl. You could turn that figure of yours into a fortune.' His voice didn't match his looks. The tone was high, effeminate even.

Molly froze at the woman's words: 'Leave it out, Gus. Can't you see she's a virgin? Ain't that right, lav – you've never had a man up yer, have you?'

Loud guffaws mixed with the high-pitched cackle of the woman's laugh. Hot colour flooded Molly's cheeks; sweat-beads formed on her forehead. She wanted to run for all she was worth, but fear kept her rooted to the spot.

'I'd like to be the one to change that. What's your name, girl?' The fat driver bobbed his head to look at her as he said this. The woman slapped his thick thigh in anger. 'Keep your mouth shut, Lofty. It'll get yer inter trouble, one of these days. You're the bleedin' driver, not the mouthpiece.'

Everything about the redhead, whose fleshy

breasts oozed from a figure-hugging black-and-white-spotted frock, intimidated Molly. She twitched her nose against the overpowering smell of cheap perfume that wafted up her nostrils. The woman's lips curled, showing even teeth smudged with her thickly applied red lipstick. 'What yer looking at, eh?'

Molly looked down at the pavement. She had an idea who the two men were, and this compounded her fear, making her voice shake. 'I – I'm sorry, I can't help you. I have to go, me bus will be in at any minute. I'm on me way back to work.'

'You ain't going nowhere, Missie, and we ain't got all bleedin' day. If you're catching a bus from here, that means you live round here and probably know of the butcher we're looking for. So start talking, or else.'

The back door swung open. Jumping back, Molly lost her balance. Groping for something to save her from falling, she cried out as a hand grasped her, digging painfully into her arm. 'No... No, let me go!' Her scream died as, in one movement, the blond man twisted her arm up her back and propelled her towards the open car door. His knee shoved her forward. Her head jerked on her neck, and her face was squashed onto the leather seat. His body thrust at her from behind. 'Stop – don't. Please, don't.' Tears choked her as she felt his hand lift her skirt, but thankfully the woman stopped him.

'Not in broad daylight, you thick-headed geezer! Get her in the car, and let's get going.'

Pain shot through Molly as Gus yanked her

19

head back by her hair and landed a stinging slap on the cheeks of her bottom. Terror gripped her as she realized they were kidnapping her and she could do nothing to save herself. Frantically she looked out of the window, this way and that, but the street was deserted.

'Now, Miss Goody-Two-Shoes, if yer know what's good for you, you'll talk to us. Like Gus here says, you could earn us some money, and that's what you'll be bleedin' doing. But first, answer me bleedin' questions. Do yer know this bloke I'm looking for or not?'

'The b-butcher is me dad.' As she said this, defiance came over Molly. 'You only had to drive a bit further and you'd have seen our shop. It's on the corner of the next street, Sebastopol Road. It's not hard for even you to find.'

For a moment Molly thought she'd gone too far as the woman's eyes narrowed, but then she was surprised, for instead of receiving a further threat, the woman ordered her release.

But Gus wasn't giving in that easily. 'What're yer thinking of? Christ, Eva, she's prime meat.'

Molly held her breath, but Eva didn't waver. 'There's time enough for that. She says she's Alf Winters's daughter. In which case, we don't want to upset him by abducting her. We can cash in later, when we have him in the palm of our 'ands.'

Not daring to look back, in case they changed their mind about letting her go, Molly stumbled away from the car, desperate to put some distance between them and her. As she rounded the corner, the bus she thought she'd missed pulled

20

up. She hesitated for a moment, torn between going back to make sure her dad was all right and carrying on to work. Still angry at her father, she climbed onto the bus. Whatever those people wanted, she'd leave it to him to deal with and would hope he got rid of them.

Her mind didn't register anything that the bus passed on the way to her workplace, or the usual discomfort of the wooden seats, as she mulled over what had happened. The whole episode had frightened her more than anything else in her life, but hearing the first names of the two men had intensified that fear. Molly felt certain they were Gus Williams and Lofty Tyler – two gangsters who had once been notorious around the East End, which lay within spitting distance of where she lived. A long term in jail had seen younger men take over and Gus and Lofty losing their territory. She'd heard they were reclaiming it, as the war had forced conscription on the younger thugs.

Phyllis, a loud sort of girl who worked with Molly and seemed to know everything, had gossiped about Gus and Lofty, saying they dealt on the black market and headed a gang that stole from the ships docked at Wapping and at other docks along the Thames, as well as from the warehouses that lined the docks.

As the bus swung into Church Street, the conductor rang the bell to announce Molly's stop. The sight of the shoe shop gave her other things to think about. Something had changed since she'd left an hour earlier. Sandbags that hadn't been there previously, but were long awaited, were now piled high on the edge of the pavement. War was becoming a reality. It had brutally visited her street, and now people everywhere were ready to believe Hitler's threat to set London ablaze. The row of shops presented a hive of activity, as shop owners dragged the bags and stacked them against their windows under the direction of the Air Raid Precautions wardens. Her own boss wasn't one of them. *He'll more than likely get me and the girls to do that.*

This thought was confirmed as Phyllis came into view. Her wave was followed by holding her head to one side and nodding, in a knowing way, at the sandbags. The movement catapulted Molly's thoughts back to her fears caused by the encounter with the gang, as Phyllis had looked just like that when she'd told them about Gus and Lofty's other activities.

'They're pimps as well, you know,' she'd said. 'They work for a madam called Eva.' Phyllis had gone further and had told Molly of the plight of one of the street girls. 'They dragged me mate in, making her believe she would have a good life with them. She hadn't had much going for her up to then, as her dad and her uncle took what they wanted from her, when it suited them. Now she works the streets. She's in a bad state, but won't hear of me giving her any help, as she says I'll be putting meself in danger.'

The words trembled through Molly as she recalled them. Her stomach churned. Her fear of Hitler's wrath descending on London paled into insignificance, as the implications of what had been said about her earning money for the gang suddenly took on a terrifying meaning.

Not one for putting much faith in prayers, Molly crossed the road begging God fervently to help her, as the sensation of Gus thrusting himself at her revisited her. *Please, God, don't let what happened to Phyllis's mate happen to me... Please!*

2

Flo

An Unknown Future

'Eeh, Mr Godfern, have you heard the news?' Flo shook her raincoat out the door as she spoke to the owner of the chemist's shop – her boss and benefactor for the last seven years.

'Whatever it is, close that door, Flo. The rain's coming inside.'

The door shut after a moment of scraping on the flagstone floor. Wet weather always made it stick. 'They're putting out warnings to Londoners to take any siren seriously and to seek shelter. They say Biggin Hill's been attacked, and that London's going to be next. By, I feel sorry for the poor folk, if that happens.'

'Aye, so do I. But to listen to them Londoners caught up in that bombing a few days ago, they know Churchill bombed Berlin to avenge them, so they're not putting the blame on him. I heard some of them being interviewed on the wireless.

23

They talk of standing against all Hitler can throw at them. You have to admire them. They say as we're tough up here in Leeds, but we have nowt on them lot. Taking it on the chin, they are, and all helping each other. Makes you proud, but I fear what'll happen.' His head shook as if in despair. But then he smiled. 'Mind, it's not all doom and gloom, thou knaws, lass. There's a letter come for you, and it's a brown one at that.'

For a moment Flo caught her breath. Excitement, mixed with worry, churned her insides. 'Is it from them?'

'How many brown letters are you expecting then? I reckon as you'll have to open it to make sure, but I'd like to bet you a florin it is.'

Laughing with him, Flo took the letter being held out to her. There, printed in bold letters above the address of the chemist's shop, she read: 'PRIVATE AND CONFIDENTIAL, Miss Florence Kilgallon'. Once again her nerves jolted and longing flooded through her. *Please let me have passed me exams.*

Finding that she had, and in particular her maths exam, with a mark of 100 per cent, she let out a loud 'Whoopee' and did a little dance. The clanging of the doorbell sobered her, as did the voice of the hypochondriac Mrs Hardacre: 'There's a war on, thou knows, and some of us have nowt to sing about. Me legs have given me gyp all neet. Eeh, I wish I had your legs, Flo, but me dancing days are over. What's made you so happy, lass?'

'Oh, sommat and nowt. Now, what can I get you, Mrs Hardacre? Sommat to soothe your aches and pains?'

'If only you could, but...'

As Mrs Hardacre droned on, Flo let her mind go back to the letter. Now she had a chance of gaining entry to the teacher-training college to fulfil her dream. She had Mr Godfern to thank for it all. It had been a good day when she'd gained the position here. She'd seen the advert in his shop window: *Wanted, an assistant of reasonable intelligence and of good manner.* Well, she had both of those qualities, but the first hadn't been proven, as of then.

Born at the back end of 1918 and now almost twenty-two years old, Flo had experienced the death of both her mammy and her pappy within six months of her birth. Her dad had been run over by a truck and killed instantly when she was six weeks old, and they said that her mammy had been brought so low that she was taken by a fever against which she had no resistance. They had been Irish immigrants and had lived in an area known as The Bank, near Richmond Road in Leeds. The Mount of St Mary's Convent Orphanage stood there too and had become Flo's home until she'd turned thirteen and had been put out to board with Mrs Leary.

A kindly Irish lady, Mrs Leary had taken many a young lass in after they'd reached the age of having to leave the convent. Flo had heard good things about how well she'd treated them and they'd all proved to be true, though she'd been shocked on the second day when Mrs Leary had said, 'You're all settled in here now, Flo, so I'm for thinking that we'll be after taking a walk around the town and getting you a job today.'

Flo had expected to be carrying on at school until she was fourteen, but had known that if you had a job to go to, once you were in your last year, then the school released you. Mrs Leary couldn't see any benefit in those of working class getting an education and, no matter how much Flo protested, Mrs Leary was having none of it. 'You've to work and get yourself set up, and then you'll be ready to take all that life has a mind to throw at you.' She'd gone on to say, 'Isn't it that the Good Lord rewards those who take care of themselves? And that is the aim of this house – to get you standing on your own two feet – so it is.'

As it had turned out, Mrs Leary had been right. Another year at school couldn't have given Flo what she'd gained by working for Mr Godfern.

Mrs Hardacre's nudge and her comment, 'Eeh, it's okay for some, daydreaming away,' brought Flo out of her thoughts.

'Oh, sorry, love – you were saying about your legs?'

'Too late. Mr Godfern's seen to me. By, lass, you'll have to look lively. Folk want attention, thou knows.'

Smiling and apologizing did the trick. Even though Mrs Hardacre still admonished her, Flo could hear a lightness and fondness in the woman's tone that belied what she said.

'And there's no use in flashing those lovely Irish eyes at me, either! Go on with you. You're your dad all over. You even look like him.'

This had been said to her many times. Flo wished she had a photograph of her mum and dad to compare herself to them, but all she had to go on was what the Irish folk in the community told her. 'Your mammy was a good woman, small and gentle and kind; and your pappy was for being a good man, too. A fine-looking man. You have his looks, with your chestnut-brown hair and Irish-blue eyes. You're as tall as him. Is it nearly six foot that you are? And your nose, me bonny lass, is just the same as his. He'll never be gone whilst you draw your breath, so he won't.' Flo longed to have known her mammy and pappy.

Reflecting on what folk said about her likeness to her pappy, her hand went to the bridge of her nose. With her finger she traced the slight bump. Some said she had a Jewish nose, but knowing nothing of her ancestry, she didn't know if this reference had any substance to it or not. Not that her nose bothered her; apart from wishing it was straight, she didn't think it that bad, and actually thought it quite cute. This made her lift her head, as if defying anyone to say otherwise. The net holding her hair brushed her neck and allowed a few of her curls to escape. She always contained the back of her hair in a net for work, but allowed those at the front to frame her face.

'Go on then, lass, how did you do?' Mr Godfern's impatient tone brought Flo's attention back to her wonderful exam results.

Sharing the good news with Mr Godfern, she finished by saying, 'Eeh, it were your help with all those complicated equations that did it. And – and, well, I'll never be able to thank you. You paying me fees to attend night-school and, these

27

last weeks, giving me a day off to study for me exams is what got me this far. I'll pay you back every penny it cost you, I promise.'

'Naw, I'll have none of that. Your determination to succeed was all the payment I needed. But, Flo, I – I'm sorry, but your ambition to become a teacher ain't going to be easy. And ... well, you always knew that my Elizabeth was in university, training to become a pharmacist.'

'I know. She'll be qualified soon and will be here to help you, and then you won't be in need of me any more. You've prepared me for when that happens. And it's all worked out well, as with me qualifications I can look at going to college, as we've allus planned. Me tutor, Mr Dinkworth, will help me find one that trains teachers.'

'Look, as I see it, that will be costly, and you won't be able to work and earn money while you study, as you'll have to attend college full time. I reckon as you'll be better served thinking about finding a well-paid job for a couple of years. That'll set you up, so that you can support your-self. Besides, becoming a teacher ain't every-thing. I reckon as you should try a few things first.'

This shocked Flo, for there'd been an under-standing that Mr Godfern would continue to support her through college. Her heart sank as she asked, 'Is there sommat as you want to tell me, Mr Godfern?'

She saw his body shift in a way that told of his discomfort. Turning from her, he adjusted a few bottles on the shelf behind him. His voice held regret when he spoke. 'Things change, lass. You see, Elizabeth left university at the start of summer and has been taking a break, but she's home now and needs to begin working here, with a view to it being hers one day. I – I could keep you on for a bit, though. Until she learns the ropes, that is.'

'While I look for more work, you mean?' Though he hadn't admitted it, Flo thought that more had changed than simply Elizabeth being ready to come to work immediately. What Mr Godfern was saying didn't sound like the plan to see her through college and then for her to pay him back whatever it had cost him, once she had a post as a teacher.

'Aye. I'm sorry, lass. But things haven't worked out financially for me. The recession hit me hard.'

'Don't ever be sorry, Mr Godfern. What you've done for me I'll allus be grateful for. I'll be reet. I can get set on at the munitions factory.'

'Naw, that wouldn't do at all. It's well paid, I'll give you that, but it'd stifle you. That's happening here, as it is. You're a clever lass and you need something that will stimulate you. Leave it with me. I'll ask around and see what I can come up with.'

Though Flo had faith in Mr Godfern and knew he would do his best for her, as she cycled home that evening she couldn't lift the heavy feeling inside her. The dream she'd held for the last five years of studying now lay in tatters. But then she'd been a fool to think the likes of her could ever make it to being a teacher. Weren't they all middle-class and well spoken, with dads who worked in offices or had a profession? How was it that she'd ever aspired to such a thing, or to think it would be open to an orphaned girl living in the poorest part of Leeds?

Well, she had to face reality and get used to letting go of her dream. Because she was certain Mr Godfern had only been trying to make her realize that she'd gone as far as she was going to go. Maybe he *could* afford to sponsor her, but had known that hers was a lost cause, and that she would never have been accepted in a teacher-training college?

Without her bidding them, tears brimmed in Flo's eyes. Brushing them away caused her to wobble. A hooter blasting as loud as a blooming siren increased her wobble and caused her to lose control. Crashing to the ground, she found her leg twisted under her bike. Her gas mask hit her in the face and pain shot up her thigh.

'You idiot! You shouldn't be on the road – you're not safe. You were riding like a novice. You should keep to the path... Flo! Oh God, I didn't realize it was you. Are you all right?'

As she looked up into the shocked face of Mr Dinkworth, Flo's attempts to smile turned into a sob. Embarrassed and feeling like a child, she could do nothing to stop the flood of tears that prevented her from answering.

'I'm so sorry. I did try to avoid you. Look, wrap this round you.' He removed his jacket and placed it around her. The lining, warmed by his body, comforted her as it touched her skin, as did the smell of the Old Spice aftershave that clung to it. A familiar smell that had been with her throughout her years in the shop, and had always hung around the schoolroom where she'd attended Mr Dinkworth's upper-maths group. He was the only one who bought Old Spice, as most men around here barely took a shaving brush to their chin, let alone pampered themselves with aftershave.

'I'll nip to that phone box over the road and ring for an ambulance. You'll be fine, don't worry – and don't move.'

'Naw! Naw, I'll be reet, ta. Anyroad, I'm only suffering from shock, and that'll soon pass.'

Mr Dinkworth produced a huge, startlingly white hanky and handed it to Flo. 'Here, wipe those tears away. Then, if you're sure you're not badly hurt, we can see about getting you back on your feet. Though I don't see your bike taking you anywhere. You're going to have to have a new wheel fitted, by the looks of things.'

Drying her tears gave her clearer vision. She could see that one or two people had gathered around her and were helping to pick up her bike. Pieces of advice started to come at her. Most thought she should go to hospital, though some were saying she should be more careful, and that the roads were getting too dangerous for cyclists. They all seemed to be talking at once, and in high, squeaky voices. Confused, Flo looked around her.

Mr Dinkworth took charge. She heard him ask everyone to stand back and give her some air, then arranged with a man who'd come out of a nearby house to take in her bike and look after it, until they could come for it; finally, he asked another man to help him to get Flo into his car. 'I'll see that she's taken care of. I know her well. I'm her night-school tutor.'

Though all this was done with the efficiency he always displayed in the classroom, Flo saw that Mr Dinkworth's immaculate self had deserted him. His dark, Brylcreemed hair, usually sleeked back, was dishevelled, giving him a more approachable look than the groomed teacher she'd known him to be.

Glancing over at Flo, he told her, 'I'm taking you to my home. My housekeeper used to be a nurse. She'll make sure you're all in one piece and will put my mind at rest as to whether or not you need a doctor.'

'But Mrs Leary...'

'Your landlady? I know, she'll be expecting you. Don't worry – I've thought of that. There was a boy amongst the crowd. I gave him a penny to take a message to Mrs Leary to say you had been in an accident, but weren't badly hurt, and that your tutor was taking care of you and would deliver you back there later.'

What boy? I didn't see a boy! A feeling of trepidation filled her. 'Please, just give me a lift home, Mr Dinkworth. I only live around the corner from here. I told you, I'll be reet. I–'

'You have nothing to fear, Florence. My intentions are honourable. I couldn't possibly let you out of my sight until I am sure you haven't suffered any ill-effects that may require medical care.'

Feeling silly for having even thought this man would mean her any harm, Flo relaxed a little. As she did, the full force of the pain in her ankle shot up her leg, causing her to gasp.

'I think I'll take you to the hospital after all. That wasn't a sound I'd expect to hear from someone who wasn't badly hurt.'

Limping out of the hospital an hour later, with her ankle bound up and leaning heavily on crutches, Flo was grateful for the steadying hand of Mr Dinkworth as he held her arm.

'How is it now? Do you think you could manage to get to the cafe across the road? They don't close until eight, and I think a nice cup of hot, sweet tea is called for.'

'Aye, I'll have a good try. And a pot of tea is just what I'm needing. I may only have a sprain, but by, they gave me some gyp, pulling and pushing me ankle.'

As they made their way across to the tearoom, Flo thought what a different side of Mr Dinkworth she was seeing. He'd always been distant and yet a gifted teacher, and a non-judgemental one, who saw the best in her and strived to encourage her. She'd been stupid to think he had any motive other than concern and kindness, in wanting to take her to his home. He was just one of life's nice people. The thought came to her that it was funny he wasn't married. Though she guessed he was in his forties, he was still a very handsome man. Tall and maybe too thin, he had a nice face with high cheekbones; and a real professor-look about him, with his striped suit and little round glasses, which – far from detracting from his good looks – suited him and enlarged his lovely brown eyes.

'Now tell me: what had you wobbling like that? I thought you and your bike were going to land under my car. I know you are an experienced rider, so what happened?'

She'd taken a sip of the lovely steaming tea and now licked her tingling lips. 'I – I were upset. And I went to wipe away the tears that were blurring me vision and that led to me losing control.'

When he asked what had upset her, Flo told him, between blowing the steam of the tea away from her, how she'd suddenly found herself without a job and having lost the prospect of taking her education any further.

'Well, maybe another job is the right thing for you, as I did wonder about your ambitions and whether you would make it into college. I mean – well, I'm sorry, Florence, and it shouldn't be like this, but ... everything is decided on the class of person you are. For instance, even though you have twice the brains and ability of Penelope Harris, her father is a bank manager and has influence. He sent her to me to improve her prospects. If both you and she applied to the teacher-training college and they only had one place, then she–'

'But that ain't fair.'

'Life isn't fair, Florence. It lifts you up and then kicks you in the face. One day – maybe after this war even – things will change. People from all walks of life will have the same opportunities and won't be penalized because of their standing in life, their colour, their religious beliefs or their sexual persuasion.'

Already shocked at what he'd said about her

not having the same chances in life, despite getting an education, this last comment saw Flo's cheeks reddening. She kept her eyes on her tea as she brought the cup to her mouth again. *Eeh, fancy him saying a word like 'sexual' – and in here, an' all!*

Looking around the pretty tearoom, with its round tables draped in white cloths and adorned with silver sugar bowls and salt-and-pepper pots gleaming in the light of the low evening sun, she saw that none of the other customers – four in all – had heard. But then if they had, they might be like her and not have an inkling what he meant by 'sexual persuasion'.

'I'm sorry – I've upset you, haven't I?' His head shook. 'Dear Florence, you're so innocent of the world. But you are the very essence of what I am talking about. You, and others like you, will be the ones to bring about change. You haven't accepted your lot. You have striven to better yourself, but the barriers that are in place are foiling you now. Don't let them. Keep your determination to lift yourself from your allotted place in life. You can do it. And you should take advantage of the war to help you.'

'I can't see how the war will help me. War or no war, I can't afford to do owt other than get a job. And, as I'm not trained at owt, that will have to be in the munitions.'

'No, that's not an option for you. Look, I could help you. I have a friend – well, he is more than a friend. We went to university together, and we became very close... Do you understand what I mean?'

Why her face reddened even more, she didn't know. But she thought Mr Dinkworth seemed to be hinting at sommat that was a secret, and yet he expected her to know what it was. She shook her head, unable to find the words to answer him.

'We ... we are a – a couple. We love each other and see each other as often as we can. Though that isn't easy, with the distance between us. He lives and works down south, in a village called Bletchley. His work is hush-hush, but like you, he is a brilliant mathematician and what he does is helping the war effort massively.'

If she could, she'd run out of here and away from him. As it was, she didn't know what to say. Mr Dinkworth and another man loving each other? Oh, aye, she'd heard tell of such things, but never thought to meet anyone who was like that. She thought it were sommat as folk who lived down south did. Not her own tutor! A northerner, even if he did speak posh. Finding her voice, she asked, 'What – what does he do ... I–I mean, in his job?'

'To be honest, I don't know. And you, young lady, should know better than to ask. All I know is that Simon's work is very secret, but highly important.'

'Eeh, he's not a spy, is he? I couldn't do that work.'

'We none of us know what we are capable of until we are faced with doing it, and you – more than most – would be capable of rising to the challenge, should it be put to you. But whatever it is that Simon does, and it may be spy work, I

36

know it is very important to the war effort.'

'And you reckon as I could do this work?'

'I do. I think you have the right qualifications, as you have what Simon has: a mathematical brain. You would need to join the WRNS or the ATS, as they only take on military personnel and civil servants.'

'Oh? But how can you be sure they would send me where Simon is?'

'I know because that is how they build their staff teams. It's nepotism, but it works. Someone knows someone who can be trusted, has the right qualifications, is of the right calibre, and they recommend them. Joining the forces can come after you are chosen, so you would still keep your options open. What do you think? Would you like me to discuss it with him? Simon is a lovely person. You would like him. And he will be fascinated by you. If it works out, you will move to a new area and begin a new life. I think it is the very thing for you.'

Unsure, but with her interest tickled, Flo nodded. 'Aye, I'd like to know more about it. And I'm thinking a new start is what I'm needing.'

She couldn't say that the prospect of meeting his 'friend' scared her, as that would hurt Mr Dinkworth, but she did feel scared. The world these two lived in was alien to her. *Aye, and criminal, an' all.* Her knowledge of such things had come from the newspapers. Mrs Leary had pointed the story out: two men had been caught engaging in homosexual activities and had been jailed. Mrs Leary went on to tell Flo that there was a rule that men of that kind were refused entry to the forces. 'Nancy boys', she'd called them. Flo had been shocked to hear of such things, but she hadn't seen why they should be imprisoned or banned from the forces. Mrs Leary was of that mind too, and she'd stood up for them. 'It's not for being right, putting them in jail. It is as folk should live and let live. I've a friend back in Ireland whose son is that way inclined. A lovely boy he is – was, I should say, as he'll be a grown man now. He had the kindest nature and looked after his mammy, but he was ridiculed by others and took himself off to America to start a new life. Broke his mammy's heart, so it did.'

Mr Dinkworth cut into her thoughts. 'You've gone very quiet, are you sure about–'

'Oh, aye, I'm sure. It's just a lot to take in.'

'Well, let's get you home. I'll be in touch. I'm seeing Simon this weekend.' Then, as if the thought had suddenly struck him, he asked, 'Would you like to meet him? He is coming up on Friday and staying till Sunday. He'll be bringing his half sister; sh-she acts as his girlfriend – oh, I don't mean... Well, just for show. Look, I'm sorry, Florence, this has all been a shock to you. Not just being run over by me, but learning all of this about me. I shouldn't have told you. I'm sorry.'

'Naw. I'm alreet with it. I'm not used to such things, but, well, I – I'm not...'

'Repulsed? You're not disgusted or anything?'

'Of course not. "Embarrassed" is more how I'd put it. And that's because it's all new to me. I don't see as you're any different because of it. But, I – I just don't know how to handle it.' She was tying herself in knots and feeling even more

38

ill-at-ease as she tried to explain her feelings. 'Look, you're still Mr Dinkworth... I mean–'

'Thank you, Florence. That means a lot to me. Yes, I am still Mr Dinkworth; nothing about my private life changes that, though I would like it if you called me Roland.'

Thinking to lighten the tension between them, she laughed. 'Only if you call me Flo. That's me name, as I'm known by. "Florence" is too posh for the likes of me!'

He laughed with her. 'Flo it is. And yes, that does suit you more than Florence does. Though I do see you as a pioneer of sorts, just as your namesake was. You've to change the world, Flo. You and others like you. No accepting your lot. Get out there and show them that women can do as well as men, and that those women who were born disadvantaged by poverty have brains, just the same as the posh lot do. And, Flo, spread your accepting nature far and wide, too.'

'Eeh, I don't know about that. But I'll do me best in this job you have in mind for me. Thanks, Roland.' It surprised her how easily the use of his name came to her. 'I were reet in the dumps as to me future, but now you've given me sommat to look forward to and some hope and ... and re-spect. Aye, that's it – respect is what you've given me, by you seeing me potential. I've only ever had the like of that from me boss before. If this works out, I won't let you down, nor will I let your Simon down, either.'

As he drove her home, chatting about this and that, Flo found she was really relaxed in his com-pany and looking forward to what seemed like a much more exciting future than teacher training. And, as Roland had said, she would change things – well, her own expectations, and hopefully those of others. One day her class would know a different time, and she'd be ready when that time came.

3

Molly

Friends and Dreams

'Help your old dad with his tie, girl, there's a good 'un.'

Molly felt sick as she looked up at her dad. He stood in front of the parlour fireplace, grooming himself in the mirror above the mantelpiece. The reflection of the sun hindered his view. He looked better than she'd seen him look for a long time. His best suit had been pressed, no doubt by Aunt Bet. His hair was sleeked back and his white shirt gleamed – and all for the benefit of that gang from the East End.

This being a Saturday, Molly would normally have been at work, but there had been a shock announcement during the week that the shoe shop was to close immediately. The Jewish owners were afraid that the Germans would invade England, so they had booked a passage to America, where they thought they would be safer.

The closure had upset her for more than the fact that she no longer had a job, as it also meant she might not see David, the boss's son, ever again.

During the time that she'd worked at Gould's shoe shop she'd fallen in love with David. It was a secret love that only she and her friend, Hettie, knew about, as David had never even noticed her on his visits to the shop. Whereas for her, David's visits to see his dad were the highlights of her life, and of her dreams. Now her dreams had been shattered and her life changed completely, as she found herself at the beck and call of her dad.

Once she'd taken in the shock of the shop's closure, Molly thought she'd have to look for a job in a factory, as she wasn't qualified to take up any other work. But her dad had other ideas, and said she was to stay at home and take care of him and the house for the time being. He also said it looked as though he would need her around to help in his butcher's shop in the not-too-distant future. A prospect that she dreaded, as she knew it was linked to the visit of the gangsters he was expecting today.

She fiddled with his tie for him, undid what he'd done and started to reknot it. 'What do you want to get mixed up with that lot for, Dad? It'll come to no good. They're criminals. They steal and kill and–'

'Shut your mouth, girl. They say that careless talk costs lives, and where Gus Williams and Lofty Tyler are concerned, it's true, so watch your tongue.'

'I'm scared, Dad. They can only bring trouble

to our door.'

'More like a lot of money. It's watertight, what they're proposing. No one will ever guess. The shop is a good front for their business, and I'll get a decent cut. What can go wrong, eh? I've had Foggy clearing out the back of the preparation room. He's scrubbed it up like a new pin. What goods we can't get in there will go into the cellar. So, if Eva, Gus and Lofty like what they see when they come today, we'll be in business with them. From what I know, goods will be delivered in my own truck, so as not to raise suspicion. Customers will be sent to us by Eva. Or we will deliver orders to the nobs who wouldn't be seen dead around here and will only place their orders by telephone.'

'But it's black-market! Stolen! Those goods, as you call them, are meant to feed our forces and our people. How can you even think of getting involved in it? You should call the police... No, D-Dad. No!'

Though she'd cringed away from his raised fist, Molly couldn't dodge the blow that her dad aimed at her. The punch landed on her arm. The force of it knocked her backwards. She landed heavily in his armchair next to the fireplace. Hot tears sprang to her eyes. In that moment all she'd ever known deserted her. Her dad wasn't her dad any more. She'd dealt with him being amorous towards her; even taken it as a sign of his love at times, as she'd nothing else to measure his love by. But now he'd severed the last thread that had held them together.

'I HATE YOU!'

42

For a moment she thought he was going to apologize, as he lowered his face to within inches of hers. But his teeth gritted in anger and his spittle sprayed her face. 'Look, Miss Stupid! I'm nearly broke. Do you know what that means, eh? I stand to lose this house, me shop ... everything. Eva and the boys have given me a way out. And not just that, but a way of making a lot of money. We're going to be rich. And you're not going to spoil it for me, do yer hear me?'

A sob escaped her and, with its release, more sobs followed. Soon her whole body cried, and it seemed tears dripped from every pore.

'Pack that in. That was your mother's way. Well, it didn't wash then and it won't wash now. Get yourself busy. Eva and the boys are staying to play cards later, and I want a decent supper presented to them. Right?'

She could only nod. Every fibre of her felt drained, as if someone had tipped her up and emptied her out. Somehow she stood up, steadied herself and crossed the parlour, feeling shocked to the core that her dad showed no remorse for what he'd done.

'And you can bloody well dress yourself up a bit and look presentable. Then I want you at that piano, playing for them. You had enough expensive bleedin' lessons, and you hardly touch the thing.'

Once in the kitchen, Molly ran the cold water and splashed her face. Lifting her head, she caught sight of herself in the small mirror hanging from a nail knocked into the wooden window frame above the sink. Her eyes were red and swollen from crying. She rubbed her stiff and bruised arm. *My own dad did this to me. My own dad!*

Well, she wasn't going to stand for it. She'd find some way out of all this – and she'd start now, by going to her mate's house. She'd not stick around here and play host to that floozy and her two henchmen.

'Eeh, Molly, I saw yer coming across the street. What's happened to yer, eh? Come in, love.'

The note of sympathy in Hettie's voice made Molly sob all the more, making it difficult for her to speak. Not that she wanted to tell all that was going on. 'Me – me dad. He got mad at me and punched me!'

Hettie steered her towards the kitchen. 'Blimey. Your dad? Here, let me take a look at yer. Where's he hurt yer?'

Molly indicated her arm.

'Take your cardi off and I'll bathe it for yer. Me mum swears by putting some vinegar on cotton wool and dabbing it gently on bruised areas. It seems to work, when me dad gives her a wallop.'

'I weren't going to get upset, Hettie. I'm sorry, I cried me eyes out in our kitchen, but I thought I'd composed meself. You've enough on your plate, with what you witness your mam going through.'

'Well, at least I'm used to it. But I've not known your dad to be violent before. What's happened to change things, eh?'

Not ready to share the reason with Hettie, and glad that as yet the gossipmongers hadn't heard what her dad was up to, and with whom, Molly

44

shrugged. 'He'd had too much to drink. Look, let's forget it. I don't want to talk about it.' A sudden thought zinged fear through her: *What if me dad comes after me?* 'That's fine now, thanks, Hettie. You're a pal. Look, if you're not doing anything, d'yer fancy a walk out? We could go to Pymmes Park. I could do with some fresh air.'

'Ha – fresh air, me nelly. More like yer want to be where you might be seen by that David yer always on about. Blimey, you've got it bad. But I don't think it will get you anywhere, Molly. Didn't you say he was a Jew? Well, he ain't going to be looking at the likes of you, is he?'

This hurt. Though Molly had to admit to herself that David's being an orthodox Jew might pose problems.

'Well, a girl can dream, can't she? Go on, Hettie, come with me. We can buy a cup of tea from the kiosk and sit on the bench and drink it. We don't have to be out long. I'll have to be back soon, anyway.' Hindsight gave Molly the feeling that perhaps she'd better be home in time to see to her dad's guests. She didn't relish the idea, but she was afraid of the consequences if she wasn't.

'Ain't you scared there'll be one of them sirens going off? Since them bombs dropped, I only feel safe at home or at work, as I know where the shelter is.'

'There's one in Pymmes Park. You remember, we saw them digging it out. Besides, we can't stop inside for the duration of the war. You know what they say: stiff upper lip.'

'Not a fat one like yours, then?'

Molly giggled. 'I haven't got a fat lip. Me face is

45

a bit swollen with me crying, that's all. A splash of cold water will soon sort that.'

'Go on then. And after you've swilled your face, I'll do your hair for you. You look a mess, and you need to look presentable, just in case.'

'Ta, Hettie.'

Having just turned twenty-one, Hettie was the same age as Molly but she was also as fair as Molly was dark. She had a lovely face, rounded and dimpled, with large blue eyes. She worked as a hairdresser and her hair was always immaculate. Cut into her neck, it had a side parting and a fringe. She was maybe a little too plump, but it suited her and went with her kindly, motherly nature.

'Have you heard from Larry, Hettie?'

'Yes. He'll be home in four weeks. He'll be finished his training then. He says he'll have a few days' leave, then he'll be sent somewhere else. He don't know where, but he thinks it will be overseas, to fight. He wants us to get married while he's home. He'll be lucky. I bleedin' told him that everyone'll think I've got me belly up, or sommat. I said we'd get engaged and then think about marriage on his next leave.'

'Oh, Hettie. Who knows what's going to happen! You should marry him – you're made for each other. Besides, I could be a bridesmaid.'

Hettie was quiet for a moment, and Molly could have cut her tongue out. She shouldn't have made a reference to what might happen, for it always brought into focus all they didn't want to think about. At the sound of Hettie swallowing hard, Molly felt even worse. She could think of nothing to say. She was desperate to get their mood back to what it had been. Hettie's next words gave her that chance.

'I do miss him, Molly. I miss him like mad.'

Instead of sympathizing, Molly pretended that Hettie was being too heavy-handed at brushing her hair. 'Ouch! No need to take it out on me.'

'Sorry. I'll just twist the back up for you, then I'll be done.'

Molly turned, afraid that Hettie's muffled voice meant she was crying, but she was relieved to see that the cause was a few hairpins clasped between her teeth.

'Hold still. There, you'll do. It looks lovely. Put a bit of me lipstick on, it'll suit you.' Hettie passed her a bright-red Max Factor. Molly wasn't sure; she'd always thought it looked common to wear make-up that was as obvious as this.

'There's a mirror over the sink – go on, it'll look good on you. I put some on my cheeks and rub it in; it saves me buying rouge. You don't need to do that, though, as you've got a lovely complexion, Molly.'

Seeing her reflection cheered Molly. 'Ooh, you've made my hair look like Gloria Swanson's did in that film, *Music in the Air*. You know, when she wore that beautiful gown with the frills on? I love it.' Touching the rolls of her hair at the nape of her neck, Molly stretched her head this way and that. 'We should go to a film. How about on Tuesday? That's your half-day, ain't it?'

'What, after Hitler's lot flattened the Alcazar Picture House?'

'The Regal's still standing. Besides, you're not

47

going to spend the whole of this bloody war being a scaredy-cat, are you?'

'Okay, then. But I'm telling yer, any time we're out and that bleedin' siren wails, we're down the nearest shelter quicker than you can say "Hitler".'

Laughing at this, Molly waited while Hettie fetched her purse and cardigan. They didn't carry handbags these days as it was too much, with the cumbersome gas masks they had to take everywhere they went. The new hairstyle and the wearing of the lipstick had given her confidence and an eagerness to get going. *Please let David be in the park, please!*

As they stepped outside, Molly glanced back at her house. The sleek black car hadn't arrived yet. She linked arms with Hettie and compelled her to move faster.

'Bleedin' 'ell, Molly, are you afraid your dad will come after you?'

'Yes, quick, let's get out of sight.'

Hettie didn't answer her, but hastened her step. Molly knew she would understand. She'd hidden Hettie many a time, when her own dad had been on the rampage.

As they hurried along, Hettie held her close. The feel of her soft body gave comfort to Molly and, with it, some of the fear seeped out of her.

When they reached Fore Street, Molly said, 'Let's turn right onto Victoria Road at the bottom of Park Road, then we can turn into Park Lane. I'll show you where David lives.'

'Oh, all casual, you mean, as if we just happen to be walking along there. Honestly, Molly! We'll look foolish if he comes out of his gate – he's bound to recognize yer.'

'He won't. He's never looked at me. Besides, it's a free country. Well, it is at the moment anyway. We're just out for a walk, that's all.'

'What, with your hair all done and your lipstick on? You should've nipped home and put on that nice frock you have. The patterned one with the lilac flowers. I love that one. It would complete the Miss Film Star image.'

Molly laughed, but the comment had made her aware of her clothes. She pulled her cardigan around her, wincing as she felt the soreness of her arm. She looked like a plain Jane in her pink blouse, straight grey skirt and grey cardigan. Still, it wasn't as if she'd planned to go out.

Hettie talking about the lilac-flowered dress seemed to set her off on the subject of clothes. She talked for the next five minutes about a girl who had been into her hairdressing shop that morning in the prettiest of frocks, before moving on to how much her legs ached from standing.

'I usually rest up on a Saturday afternoon, Molly, so you're lucky. I hope we get to see loverboy. And if that bleedin' tea stall isn't open, I'll murder yer.'

Molly didn't much care if the kiosk was open or not, as they were turning into Park Lane and her heart rate had quickened. 'There it is, Hettie, that white one with the sloping roof.' As she said this, David came out of his front door and walked towards his car.

'Say hello then. Go on. We've not come all this bleedin' way for nothing.'

'No, Hettie. I can't – it would be too forward of me.'

'I will then... Hey there, as you live around here, can you tell us if the park kiosk is open on a Saturday afternoon?'

Molly felt her cheeks burn as David looked at her and recognition showed on his face, and in his question: 'Don't I know you?'

They walked towards him. How she managed to speak, Molly didn't know. 'Yes, I – I worked for your dad.'

'Oh yes. I'm sorry about what happened. I couldn't take over and keep the shop open, I'm afraid. You see, I'm a lawyer and I couldn't give up my job. I tried to persuade my father to let Phyllis manage the place, but he wouldn't have it.'

'Yes, it was a shame it closed. I miss working there.' Humdrum conversation, when inside her heart was thumping and all sorts of longings were assailing her.

'Well, I have to go. I hope you get a cup of tea. I think the kiosk is open.'

'You lawyers exempt from being called up, then?'

Molly blushed at this forthright question. The subject was a touchy one for Hettie. She tackled any young man she saw who was still in civvies. She imagined they were all conscientious objectors.

'Not all of us, but I'm working in government, so I am exempt for now. I can't tell you any more, but I'm doing what is needed of me. But I'll gladly go and fight, if I get the opportunity.'

'You're not a conchie, then?'

'No, I'm not. Not that it is any of your business, but I'm far from being an objector. How can I be, when I hear the reports of what's happening to my people in Germany and Belgium?'

'Come on, Hettie. Leave it there.'

'Don't worry, Miss...?'

'Winters – Molly.'

David nodded. 'Well, I have to go. I hope you get another job, Molly.' He bent down and cranked his car. The engine jumped into life, belching exhaust fumes into their path. Molly felt acute disappointment as David got into the open-topped car and began to reverse it slowly out of the drive. But then he waved to her, causing her legs to feel as though they had turned to jelly. She clutched Hettie's arm.

'I think you're in with a chance there, Molly. Come on, I'll race yer to the kiosk.'

The fun of running after Hettie, who'd taken off and given herself an unfair start, settled Molly's excited nerves, and the laughter the chase caused lifted her spirits.

As they came to the shed-type building that was known as 'the kiosk', they slowed down and their laughter quietened. Aggie Blayburn was sitting on the bench near the kiosk. Aggie's son, Trevor, had been killed in France. Molly guessed that Hettie felt the same as her: that their behaviour was irreverent in the face of Aggie's grief. They'd known Trevor. Aggie lived in their street and had brought up a family of seven there. Trevor had been the youngest; his older brother was still serving overseas. The rest of the family were girls:

51

three of them worked in the munitions, and two were young mothers who had moved back in with Aggie when their men had been called up.

There was nothing in Aggie's eyes when she looked up at Molly and Hettie, and the tone of her voice was flat as she said, 'Don't mind me. You enjoy life while yer can, the pair of yer. It's soon taken away from yer.'

'I'm sorry about your Trevor, Aggie. He were a good bloke.'

'He were, Molly. He had an eye for you, yer know. If he was here now, he'd have been chasing yer round the park. He loved a bit of fun.'

Molly blushed. She didn't know what to say, but Hettie, who had a word for every occasion, spoke up. 'Yer must be proud of him, Aggie. I know I am. I'm always telling me customers what a hero he was. He were one of the first to go. And he didn't have to be bleedin' asked.'

Molly cringed. She wished Hettie wouldn't swear every time she spoke, but it didn't seem to bother Aggie, who smiled up at Hettie. 'Ta, Hettie.'

'I'll tell yer what, Aggie. Why don't yer come into me shop on Monday, eh? I ain't got many customers. I'll give yer a nice perm. That'll cheer yer up a bit. Trevor liked to see yer looking nice. Last time I saw him, he said, "Keep me mum's hair curled while I'm away, Hettie."'

'Did he?'

'He did.'

'I will. Yes, I will. I'll see yer first thing Monday morning. Ta, Hettie.'

'Right, and it's free. Free to the mother of a

local hero.'

'Oh, Hettie. You're a good girl.' Aggie wiped a tear away and then got up. 'Well, I'd better go and get tea sorted for my lot. I've sat here long enough with this Rosie Lee. It's gone bleedin' cold.'

Molly laughed; she hadn't heard Aggie swear before.

As they watched Aggie go, Molly put her arm around Hettie. 'That was nice of you, love.' Hettie was like two people at times: ready to take up the fight with anyone she thought wasn't toeing the line, and yet kindness itself to anyone who was in need. She was the very best friend you could have. Molly squeezed her a bit tighter, before turning away. 'I'll get the tea. I won't be a moment.'

As she came back from the kiosk, her mind went over the excitement of actually having spoken to David and of him waving to her. That was something she'd been dreaming about and had longed to happen. Seeing him had made a good day out of a rotten one. A shudder went through her. The encounter with David might have cheered her, but there was still what was happening at home to contend with.

'That was a big sigh, Molly.'

'I know. I was just thinking that we'd better drink this quick and get back. I have to face me dad sometime. He's having some people over, and he wants me to make some supper for them.'

'I feel sorry for yer, love. I'm used to trouble, but you're not.' Molly's silence must have alerted Hettie. 'You can always talk to me, yer know.'

'I know. Thanks, Hettie. But you'd be shocked if you knew half of it.'

'Try me. There's not much that can shock me. It doesn't do any good to bottle everything up.'

If only she could tell Hettie. But what good would it do? *Hettie can't stop me dad thinking he can abuse me, or make him protect me from Foggy, or from...* Molly's heart sank at the thought of that woman and her two cronies. A picture of the one called Gus, and of how he'd shoved himself at her, came to her mind. A deep dread settled in the pit of her stomach.

'Molly?'

'I'm sorry. I'm fine. Come on, let's go, or I won't be.'

'I'll come home with you, if yer like. I've got nothing to do tonight.'

'No! I – I mean, thanks. Sorry, I didn't mean to snap, but me dad wouldn't like that. He's going to be talking business.'

'Where the hell have you been? Don't think for a minute you can defy me.'

'Don't, Dad. What's the point of hitting me? What's come over you? As if pawing me weren't enough, you think you can be heavy-handed as well. I'm a person, not an animal. Leave me alone.'

To her surprise, her dad softened. 'I'm sorry about earlier, love. Me nerves are all over the place. If this lot don't come through with the deal they're talking of, I've had it. Everything I've ever worked for will go.'

It was on the tip of Molly's tongue to say he deserved no less, but at the end of the day he was her dad, and she didn't really wish anything bad to happen to him.

'They're in the parlour. See if you can rustle sommat up for them. Foggy cooked off a bit of gammon, and there's that loaf you queued for this morning. Make some nice sandwiches for them, eh?'

'All right. I'll do me best. But, Dad, I don't want to be drawn into anything. I'm scared of them. I'll serve them, then I'll go to me room.'

He didn't object to this. Molly thought he must have forgotten about the piano-playing. *Thank goodness.* She hadn't relished the prospect of being in the company of the gang for longer than she had to be.

As she set about the task of making sandwiches, she hoped her dad really was sorry about hitting her, and that if things improved for him, he might return to how he'd been a few years ago. A proud man. A fairly well-to-do man, and one who respected his daughter.

Taking the supper through to the parlour, Molly felt her earlier nerves return and increase in intensity. How she managed to place the tray on the occasional table without dropping it was a miracle.

'Your daughter's a good-looker, Alf. She could be a good earner.'

Molly stiffened at Eva's words. Her dad laughed – a fawning kind of laugh. Molly looked at him, putting into her gaze all the contempt that she dared show.

'Don't look like he's got her bleedin' tamed, Eva. But I'd soon get her in line, if that's what yer want.'

A look of shock passed over her dad's face, and Molly felt a ray of hope enter her. But he didn't challenge them, just lowered his eyes.

'Shut yer bleedin' mouth, Gus. Sorry, Alf – boys will be boys, yer know.' Eva's laugh cackled around the room, but her eyes stayed on Alf. Molly watched him melt and grin back at her.

A victory smirk spread across Eva's face. Her eyes travelled over Molly's body. 'Yes, very attractive. I don't think you know your own worth, girl.'

It took only a moment for Molly to get through the door and into the hall. Laughter followed her, her dad's laugh just as loud as the others. A sinking feeling made Molly clasp her stomach, but a noise as if someone was coming to the door got her running for all she was worth up the stairs to her bedroom. With an extreme effort she pulled the chest of drawers across the door, afraid that she would be heard as it scraped along the lino. Once it was in place, she relaxed, though her body didn't stop shaking. *Oh God!*

Her instinct was to fall onto her bed and sob her heart out, but instead she took a deep breath and began to search in the top drawer of the desk. Finding and holding the form she'd been looking for gave her courage. She'd found it weeks ago, on the bus seat on her way to work. Someone had left or discarded it. She would fill it in and post it tomorrow. Then she would wait and hope that the Auxiliary Territorial Service would accept her. She had to escape somehow.

4

Flo

A New World on the Horizon

'Eeh, are you sure you're after doing the right thing, lass?'

Flo smiled. Mrs Leary's Irish accent was always lovely to listen to, but when she peppered it with northern dialect, it sounded funny. Looking up from where she sat at the kitchen table, shelling the peas they'd managed to buy in the market, a feeling of love for this kindly woman seized her. It was easy to love someone who took care of you in a good way, but Mrs Leary was much more to Flo than that.

'Aye, I think so. I hope so, at any rate. I don't knaw owt about the work, it's top-secret, and I don't knaw even if I'm going to be taken on, but I do need a change. And I need to do me bit for the war effort.'

Throwing yet another rejected pea into the pan beside her, she sighed. Getting hold of fresh food wasn't easy, and some of these peas had seen better days. Not that any would be wasted. The good pea pods, mixed with any over-tough peas, would be boiled and then simmered for hours. The resulting stock would form the basis of a delicious stew, when the fatty pieces of mutton they'd also

57

managed to buy were added to it. Especially after Mrs Leary performed her magic on it.

Attempting to change the subject of her possible departure, Flo tried to get Mrs Leary focused on the new girl she'd taken on. 'Kathy is settling in nicely. She went off to school really happy today.'

'Aye, she's for being younger than they usually come to me, but she wasn't for being happy living in the convent. Her daddy hasn't been dead long. Killed whilst doing his army training, God love him. Though you'll be knowing that. Her mammy left when Kathy was a wee bairn. How does a woman do that? It beggars belief, so it does.'

'I don't knaw. By, it's bad enough when your parents die, but I can't imagine what it would be like to have them leave you. Eeh, poor lass.'

A knock at the door stopped their chatter. When Mrs Leary opened it and Flo saw Roland Dinkworth standing there, her cheeks flushed. As much as she didn't mind knowing about his personal life, she still felt embarrassed that she did.

Before Mrs Leary could ask who he was, Flo jumped up and went to the door. 'Hello, um...' Still she stammered over what to call him. After five years of calling him 'Mr Dinkworth', she suddenly felt shy about calling him 'Roland'.

'Are you for knowing this gentleman, Flo?'

'Aye, I'm sorry, Mrs Leary. This is Mr Dinkworth – R-Roland.'

'Be Jesus, the man who has been for changing your life? Come in, come in and make yourself at home. I'm honoured to have you. Though it would be fair to say I'm cross with you, at the same time. I hear you're after taking me Flo away from me.'

Flo held her breath. She doubted Roland had ever had such a greeting. But he took it in his stride and laughed as he stepped into the kitchen. His first words set him up as a friend to Mrs Leary. 'Well, what a lovely kitchen. It feels homely and welcoming, and it smells delicious. And is no more than I would expect, from a woman of your calling. Flo often speaks of you.'

Mrs Leary looked as though she would burst with pride. 'That'll be me steak-and-kidney you're after getting a whiff of. It's cooking on me stove, as I'm to be making a pie, so I am.' She wiped her floury hands on her pinny and half-nodded at Roland. 'Though I must say, the Good Lord Himself knows there ain't much steak in it, but the bones it once clung to are. So I'm hoping He will do as He did when He turned the water into wine, and make me pie seem as though it is full to the brim with meat.' Winking, as if they were both part of a conspiracy, Mrs Leary lowered her voice. 'I'll be at giving Him a helping hand by putting plenty of beans in it, though.'

Roland laughed again, a genuine laugh, one that made Flo relax. She too felt proud. Proud that Roland would come calling on her; proud of the little place she lived in; and proud of Mrs Leary.

The kitchen was the heart of the sanctuary that Mrs Leary offered to waifs and strays – Flo included. Spotlessly clean, the room was homely and warm. The cooking range took pride of place.

59

Blacking it and polishing its brass rail and handles each week was a chore that Flo gladly took on. It always rewarded her for her effort, by shining back at her and looking grand. As did the copper pans that hung above it. The red quarry-tiles on the floor gleamed from the mopping and red-leading of them. And the big wooden table was scrubbed on a daily basis and covered with a cloth at mealtimes, though Flo liked to see it in its bare state with a bowl of flowers in its centre. Suddenly she had an overwhelming feeling of love for this – her home – and knew she would miss being here; and miss Mrs Leary too, with all her heart and soul.

'Well now, can I get you a drop of tea, Roland?'

'Thank you, Mrs Leary, that would be very nice.'

'You be putting your gas mask on the side and be off into the parlour with Flo then, as I've a mind you have a lot to talk about. I'll fetch it in to you, so I will.'

Once in the parlour, Roland stopped any shyness that Flo might feel by saying how good it was to see her.

'You look very well and rosy-cheeked, not like the last time I saw you.'

'Happen that'll be the fire. I were sitting too close.'

Roland didn't comment on this, but changed the subject. 'Maybe I shouldn't have said yes to the tea. It must be difficult enough for Mrs Leary to get supplies for you all, without strangers coming and partaking of them.'

Flo loved the way he spoke, though it did put his station above her and made a little of her shyness stay with her. 'Eeh, don't worry. Mrs Leary has her ways. She has a good stash. Oh, I mean, she's not hoarding or owt. She just...'

Roland laughed out loud. 'Don't worry. I'm not going to be reporting her. She has a right to what she can get, when she gives so much to those in need. Is there a Mr Leary?'

'Aye, there is. By, he's a lovely man. He don't say much, though, but he knaws a lot. He works for the Post Office. He often helped me with me homework when I were studying.'

'*Was* studying... Whoops – sorry, I slipped into teacher-mode again. Forgive me. It isn't as if I'm for saying everyone should speak the King's English. I love accents. Ignore me.'

'Naw, I think you're reet. I should try. Especially as I'm thinking on about that job you suggested for me.'

'That's why I'm here, Flo. I spoke to Simon about you, and he is coming up north again later today. We would love you to join us for dinner. He wants to meet you. That's if your leg is better and you're up to coming out?'

'Me leg's fine. I reckon it were just badly bruised, as I can get around as normal now. Surely a sprain wouldn't heal, in just a couple of weeks?'

'Well, the doctor did say it was difficult to know how bad it was. Now, about that dinner?'

'Eeh, I've never been asked to dinner afore. I wouldn't knaw what to do. I–'

'Ha! You eat, of course, you goose.'

Flo laughed with him. But inside, her shyness

61

of him deepened. He and his Simon were different from her. Above her station in life, and she still didn't know how to handle what he'd told her about their relationship. 'I – I'm wondering what it would look like: me being with two men. I'm not even used to being with one.'

'Oh, don't worry. Simon will be with his half-sister, Lucinda. Remember, I told you about them? She's a jolly good sort and makes everyone believe they really are a couple.'

A jolly good sort! This seemed to widen the social gap between them. But something in Flo wanted to accept. 'You'll not take the likes of me to anywhere posh, will you? I haven't got owt to wear to them places, and wouldn't know how to go on with all them knives and forks.'

'Oh, Flo, you're so funny. I miss you in my class. Actually dinner is at my house, so you can come in your pyjamas, if you like.'

Flo couldn't help giggling. Somehow she knew that dinner being at his house had been a snap decision, to make her feel at ease. But in the five years of her being his pupil she'd never known him to have a sense of humour, and he'd been someone she was in awe of. Now Roland seemed human. She liked him. She liked him a lot. 'I might just do that. But, aye, joking apart, I'd love to come.'

The moment she said this she regretted it. *Eeh, I'm getting above meself, going to a dinner party. By, whatever next.*

'As God is me witness, you're after being the prettiest girl I've ever seen, so you are.'

Flo laughed. 'You're bound to say that, Mrs Leary. Eeh, I wish it were true.'

'It is true. And that frock looks a picture on you. Get yourself away and enjoy yourself, and don't be worrying. You're for being beautiful, inside and out.'

Looking at herself once more in the hall mirror, Flo did feel that she looked nice. Her yellow frock with little pink daisies on it had a full skirt and a nipped-in waistline. The collar was trimmed with lace, and the neckline was cut so that it met just above her cleavage. She twirled round as excitement mingled with her nerves.

She'd rushed out, after Roland had left, and used some of her last wages to buy the frock, after admiring it for weeks in the window of Rose's Gown Shop. It didn't matter that she couldn't really afford the cost; the frock gave her confidence, so it was worth going without for.

Alighting from Roland's car, Flo looked up at his house and felt her already-jangled nerves rise to fever pitch. It was a grand place. Three storeys high, it was one of a row of houses with gloss-painted doors and brass handles in the Roundhay Park area of Leeds. The steps leading up from the pavement were scrubbed till the stone almost shone, and the little garden on each side of the path leading to the steps looked beautiful with the late-summer roses still flowering.

'It looks lovely, Roland.'

'Thank you, and welcome to my humble abode.'

Once inside the hall, the rest of the house wasn't

to Flo's taste. It was a little over-ornate, she thought; the type of house you would expect a wealthy old lady to own. Rich shades of reds, golds and purples were everywhere. The upholstery and soft furnishings were velvet, and the carpets were thick to the tread. The smell of polish vied with that of the fresh flowers adorning every windowsill and sideboard. The whole impression wasn't what she had imagined Roland's house to be like.

'Let me take your coat and then we'll go through. Simon and Lucinda are probably still in the garden, where I left them.'

As Roland helped her with her coat, Flo experienced a moment of acute embarrassment as he whispered, 'Don't mind the decor. I inherited the house from my grandmother and haven't got round to changing anything. I loved coming here so much that, although this is stifling to live with, I can't bring myself to make the changes needed.'

'Oh. No, it all looks lovely, I–'

'Don't worry – your reaction when you came in was the same as everyone's. And Simon nags me constantly to redecorate and refurbish. Now, what can I get you to drink?'

'Oh... I – I don't know. D'yer mean a pot of tea?'

'No. Gin, rum, a cocktail? Look. Let's get you seated with the others, then I'll choose something for you.'

Simon greeted Flo with a peck on her cheek and complimented her appearance. There was something about him that she liked immediately, as if somehow he was a best friend. It was the same with his half-sister, Lucinda, though Flo would never have guessed them to be relations. Simon had blond hair; he was tall and handsome, with green-blue eyes. And even if she didn't know anything about him, she would have said there was something effeminate about him. His mouth in particular – the full lips framing small, even teeth, and the way his hair flopped in an untameable, boyish way. His smile was warm, and it was this that had given her the feeling that she had found a friend. Lucinda was the opposite in looks, but gave out the same warmth. Petite, graceful and dark-skinned, with long black hair that she wore tied back from her face, she was lovely.

'Here we are. A gin and tonic.'

'But I'm not a drinker. Eeh, you'll have me rolling all over the place.'

They all laughed, but she didn't mind. She knew it wasn't *at* her, but because they found what she said funny.

'Sit next to me, Florence...'

'Flo – I'm no more a "Florence" than the next one. I've nowt about me that fits that posh name.'

Simon laughed again and hitched his body up on the bench, patting the place next to him. 'Roland told me you were funny and would have us laughing. I like you, Flo. You're my type of girl. I've heard a lot about you from him.'

Roland calling from inside the house that it was all true, and addressing Simon as 'darling', felt so natural. Flo was surprised not to feel embarrassed by the endearment.

'And it was all good, too, so I'm very pleased to meet you at last. I believe Roland has told you I am involved in work that might interest you.'

'Simon, let the poor girl get to know you first, before you try to recruit her to your secret service, or whatever it is you do down there in Bletchley.'

'Sorry, Lucinda, old girl, but I've taken to Flo and I'm eager to know if she is interested.'

'Aye, I am. I knaw as you can't tell me owt about it, but that don't bother me none. I knaw what I need to knaw. Roland has said it will involve me using me maths ability, and it's for the war effort. There's nowt more as need be said. If you'll have me, I'll start tomorrow.'

'Well, that's good to hear, though it can't happen that quickly. I need to recommend you to my superior, then he will invite you for an interview in front of a panel. They will decide, but don't worry about that. With my guidance and me being keen to have you, it should all go well. Would you mind if I gave you a little test to do, before we all have too much to drink?'

Lucinda sighed. 'You take the biscuit, Simon. I'm going to chat to your *better* half.' She smiled and winked at Flo as she made to leave them.

Flo felt more and more at home. 'Eeh, I hope I come up to scratch.'

'My brother should have more manners than to make you prove yourself, when you have only just met us.'

'Naw, I'll be glad to show what I can do.'

With this, Lucinda left them, giving an impatient sigh.

66

'Sorry, Flo. I suppose Lucinda is right, in a way, but I do need to know you can handle what will be asked of you, before I recommend you.'

Flo just nodded. She didn't say so, but she felt glad to have a chance to show that at least, in the brains she possessed, she wasn't inferior to these folk. Though she couldn't help thinking that the panel Simon mentioned sounded daunting.

The equation he wrote out for her posed her no problems. 'Well done, old girl. You're the one for me. I'll be pulling strings the minute I get back.' Simon kissed her cheek again. The more she was with him, the more he felt like a lovely older brother.

'I told you she was good.' Roland came back out to the garden, followed by a relieved-looking Lucinda.

'She is, she is. Now, Flo, raise that glass. You haven't taken a sip yet.' The sound of the glasses clinking together in a toast to her made her feel accepted. 'Go on, you have to take a sip or the toast will be wasted.'

She laughed at Simon. His expression held an appeal. To please him, she took a small sip, then coughed as if she would choke. Simon's antics at this didn't help, as he skipped around panicking and flapping. This made her laugh as well as choke, till she thought she would never take a breath again. Lucinda slapped her back and spoke crossly to Simon, telling him to calm down.

At last Flo caught her breath. 'Eeh, were that bloody fire-water?'

The laughter that followed seemed to Flo to bond all four of them together in friendship, and

67

she had a nice feeling about it. Her next sip went down a lot more easily, and the warmth she felt travelled from her head to her toes. She could get used to gin and tonic.

Relaxed now, and with excitement for her future settling in her, Flo enjoyed every moment of the meal.

'Let's leave the men to their brandy and cigars, Flo. There's a nice fire glowing in the front room. We'll take our sherry in there and have a girlie chat,' Lucinda suggested, once they'd finished eating.

Feeling a bit light-headed, Flo refused the sherry. 'By, I could no more put another drop of alcohol inside me than dance with the King himself.'

'Oh, Flo, you're so funny. But you're right. If this is your first time drinking, then we should go steady. I'll see if there is any coffee going.'

'I'm reet sorry, Lucinda, but I've never tasted coffee and am not sure if I'll like it. I'll just have a glass of water, if that's alreet with you.'

'Of course, and easily done, as there's water on the drinks tray. I'll join you.' As she sat down again, she looked at Flo. Flo sensed something was worrying her. 'Is everything alreet, Lucinda?'

'Yes. Well, no. Not really. I'm concerned about my brother. You know about them, don't you? Simon and Roland, I mean.'

Flo wished Lucinda hadn't mentioned the subject. She was happy just to accept it, but didn't feel right discussing it. Unable to speak, she nodded her head.

'Well, I'm fine with it, and I cover for Simon all

the time – pretend to be his girlfriend, that sort of thing. But if ever they are caught... Well, it frightens me. Simon would never survive in prison. And the shock and shame would be terrible for our mother.'

'I'm reet sorry for you. I wish I could help, but–'

'You can. When you get to Bletchley. Oh, I know it isn't certain, but I'm sure, as Simon wants you there, it will happen. Will you watch out for him, for me? Caution him about being reckless when Roland comes to visit him. Go out with him to meet Roland, so that you act as a sort of cover. Try not to let them be seen alone together. I know I'm asking a lot, as you've only just met us, but...'

Shocked, but understanding this lovely girl's concern, Flo agreed. 'I knaw as I've only just met Simon, but I like him. He feels like the brother I never had. If there's owt I can do to keep him safe, I will. I promise you.'

Even though Flo had learned these rich types were very demonstrative, she didn't expect the hug that Lucinda jumped up and gave her. But it felt good. These were nice, genuine folk, and they made her feel happy.

'Come on. Let's rejoin the men. I thought we might play a hand or two of rummy. Do you play cards?'

'Naw, but I'll soon learn.' They'd reached the dining room and Lucinda opened the door. The sight that met them stunned Flo for a moment. Simon and Roland were locked in a passionate kiss. She recovered quickly, helped by the matter-of-fact way Lucinda dealt with it.

'Hey, no smooching – we have a guest and it's not polite.'

The two broke apart. Both stared at Flo, a look of fear on their faces. Feeling sorry that this should be so, she sought to put them at their ease. 'By, you've got it bad. The moment our backs are turned, you're at it.' As soon as she said the words she wanted to take them back, as the silence left her feeling embarrassed and confused.

Roland was the first to react. His laughter was so loud and hearty that it was impossible not to join in, and soon they were all mopping their eyes.

Flo found herself in Simon's arms. 'I love you, darling. You're like a breath of fresh air. You're just what I need. I can't wait to get you down to Bletchley with me. We'll have some fun, girlie, you and I.'

To her, Simon could do no wrong. She hugged him back. The feeling she felt for him was like nothing she'd ever felt before. It wasn't anything to do with being attracted to him, but it had a lot to do with love. Yes, she'd look out for him. She'd do everything she could to protect him.

An unexplained shudder rippled through her. Like Lucinda, she couldn't bear it if he went to prison. She hoped with all her heart that would never happen.

5

Molly

The Blitz Begins

'He's hit yer again, hasn't he, love? Oh, Molly, what's got into him? Come in – let's get that eye sorted. It looks awful.'

Molly couldn't talk for sobbing. Her dad was drunk again and it wasn't even dinnertime. 'He wanted me to help Foggy with something, and I refused.'

'There's rumours flying around, yer know. They say yer dad's mixed up with them bleedin' lot who terrorize the East End.'

'Well, everyone must know it's true by now. That car's never been away from our doorstep this last week. Me life's changed, Hettie.'

'What's going on, then?'

'Don't ask, love.'

'I can guess. Yer dad's been getting a lot of stock delivered these last few days. He'll get into trouble if he's caught, whatever he's doing, as it won't be anything legal with them lot. He's in sommat he should never have started, if yer ask me.'

'Hettie, don't say anything. Keep denying it, if you're asked. Just say that a business in Church Street went bust, and me dad's got all their busi-

71

ness and taken over their stock. Or anything you can think of. But don't let him think you know anything. You'll be in danger, if you do. And I'll be in big trouble.'

'I won't, love. But folk are bound to put two and two together. The talk's rife about who your visitors are.'

'I'll tell me dad to sort it. He's got the means, and he won't want to see his old customers get into any bother with those gangsters he's mixed up with. But if he thinks it's come from you, he could well let the gang take whatever revenge they want to, just to show an example. He'd think of it as getting at me.'

'How did it come to this, eh? Bloody war. I think I'll keep Larry waiting and apply to do war work. I've got to get out from around here. It's like we're being hemmed in. And we don't know when the bleedin' Germans are coming to drop more bombs on us. It makes me nervous. I'd rather put me hand to sommat to fight back, than sit here waiting for them to come.'

'I've filled a form in for the ATS, but I lost me nerve and haven't sent it in. I'd like to do something, though. Perhaps we'll get some ideas from the newsreel at the flicks today. They're always showing some aspect of the war and what folk are doing.'

'You're right. Let's bathe that eye for you, love, then we'll get going. But the same bleedin' rules: if the siren sounds, we run like bloody hell.'

'Ha, a lot of good you'd be in the firing line.'

'I'd be fine. It's just the thought of them Germans dropping bombs on us. It makes me feel that I'll have no chance. But if I were in the voluntary service, or the Wrens, I'd feel as though I was doing something about it all.'

As they descended the magnificent staircase of the Regal, Molly was still chuckling over the scene in the film *His Girl Friday* that had made her laugh the most. Cary Grant had played the boss of a newspaper who was trying to convince his ex-wife to return to him and, more importantly, return as his best reporter. When the telephone rang while he was pleading with her, he acted as if the caller was one of his reporters who had to go off work on sick-leave – and the interaction with the poor man on the other end, who had no idea what was going on, was hilarious. At that point, Hettie had nudged her and whispered, 'You don't 'alf look like that actress, yer know.' This enhanced the temporary illusion that she was the leading lady, an illusion that Molly was always left with after seeing a film.

The stairs of the Regal perpetuated this, as they added glamour to her usually dull life. She swept down them in the manner Rosalind Russell – the actress Hettie had referred to – would have done.

It was still light as they left the cinema. Always a stark reality moment. She wasn't Rosalind Russell any more, but plain old Molly Winters. *Oh well...*

The nearby church clock boomed out its count of the hour. It had only reached four of the five chimes she was expecting when the moaning wail of the siren drowned it out. For a split-second, she and Hettie and all of the emerging film-goers stood stock-still, their reaction different from the complacency they'd always felt previously. The reality of what had happened, the last time they'd heard that wail, had changed all that.

People began to gather family and friends close, and to mutter and shout in frightened tones. Then, as if all propelled into action at the same moment, they began to run. Hettie grabbed Molly's hand. 'Hurry, Molly, come on – the nearest shelter is that one in Pymmes Park that you told me about. Quick: run!'

Panic set in around them. The crowd of forty or more people surged forward. Someone fell in front of them. Molly tried to stop to help, but the force of bodies pushed her onwards. How she and others missed trampling the poor lady to death, she didn't know.

As they turned the corner into Silver Street an elbow dug into Molly's side. Winded for a moment, she stopped. Gasping for breath, she leaned against the railings of the park. Hettie hadn't noticed that she'd dropped back and was now a hundred yards or so ahead.

She wanted to shout after Hettie, but could only keep her head down to ease the pain in her side.

'Can I help you?' Despite the need to speak loudly, the velvety tone of the man's voice was still discernible and very familiar to Molly. The sound overrode the pain in her ribs and sent her heart racing.

She looked up into David's face. The usual feeling, whenever she was near him, zinged through her. He had the handsomest face she'd ever seen.

She wanted to reach out and touch the lock of hair that fell from each side of the bowler-type hat he wore.

Looking down and breaking the hypnotic aura, she raised her voice to thank him and told him how she'd been punched out of the way.

'I have my car. I was just passing when I saw you. Come with me. There's a shelter in our garden, which a barrage of bombs wouldn't be able to—'

The drone that spoke of many aircraft bombers coming closer and closer drowned him out and had her shouting, 'Oh God, they're here!' Looking in the direction in which Hettie had run, Molly saw her lone figure hurrying back towards her. 'That's me mate ahead – will yer pick her up too?'

Before David could answer, terror ripped through her as the shadow of Luftwaffe planes turned the blue sky grey. Looking up, she felt she could almost touch them and shake the hands of the pilots in their cockpits. Only she wouldn't; she'd sooner slap their faces.

As this thought died in her, her whole body froze. The bellies of the planes opened and what looked like a hundred or more bombs descended towards them. She felt David's body huddle up close to her, and tasted his fear as it mingled with her own.

Seconds ticked by in slow motion, then her eardrums felt as though they would burst, as explosion after explosion wrapped her in a cocoon of screams and thrust her body into the road, brutally ripping her clothes from her and

75

scraping her skin on its rough surface.

A hand grasped hers and a voice cut through her ringing ears. Though it was muffled, she could detect its terrified, desperate tone: 'Help me, help me!'

Trying to clear the dust from her eyes and to cough away the smoke that clogged her throat, Molly clung to the hand, feeling its pull. 'David! David...'

The ripped surface of the road scraped her skin as she crawled towards him on her belly, using his hand to help her get closer to him. What she saw, when she did so, tightened the grip of fear that enclosed her, until she could hardly breathe. Part of David's tangled car had him trapped. The blast had whipped it onto its side and at any minute the car could fall either way – if towards him, it would crush him.

Where she found the strength from, Molly didn't know, but she managed to stand, put her back to the swaying car and force it to fall towards the pavement.

Still the bombs kept coming, but the sound of them exploding diminished as they flew over towards Wapping and the docks. Shaking her head, Molly tried to clear her ears. David's moans of pain merged with the sound of a house collapsing across the road, and the piercing screams that split the air. The world was on fire. Flames turned the normally tranquil scene of a parkside road into an inferno from hell.

The light that blazed in the trail of the fires showed figures running from building to building. *Air-raid wardens!* Determined to get their attention, Molly took a deep breath. Her throat stung and a fit of coughing seized her, but somehow she forced the words out: 'Here. Over here.' But the clanging of the fire brigade's bells and the crashing sound of bomb after bomb exploding in the distance made her cries sound like whispers.

'David, lie still. I have to fetch help.'

He moaned. Her heart tempted her to stay with him, hold him, protect him, but she forced herself to move.

On legs that wanted to collapse under her, she made it to where some figures were digging out the rubble. She tugged at the arm of one.

'What the devil? Here, come on, Miss – you should be in a shelter.'

The reprimand felt so normal. Many a time she and Hettie had been told off by one of the wardens, if they'd caught them riding their bikes with a light on as they made their way home from the Alcazar Picture House. The cinema that was no more. *Oh God, Hettie ... Hettie! Where is she? Please, God, don't let her be hurt.*

'Please come. Me boss's son – h-he's hurt and – and I don't know where me mate is.'

'You look injured yourself, Miss. Make your way to that ambulance over there; they will help you. We'll see that the young man is taken care of. And you say there's another one over there?'

'Yes, me mate, Hettie. I don't know where she is. Sh-she was running towards me when the bombs started to fall. I – I'll come with you.'

'No, you won't.' Taking his jacket off, he wrapped her in it, then shouted over to his colleague and ordered him to take her to the ambulance. Molly could do nothing but obey, although she desperately wanted to go to David and find Hettie.

The shaking of her body from head to toe was a different feeling from any that Molly had ever experienced. She couldn't control any part of herself, nor could she speak. Her sore, grit-filled eyes could only stare, unblinking, into space.

'She's in shock. Shirl, get her wrapped up warm. There's some sweet tea in me flask – see if you can get some of it into her. They're bringing the young man over, but the other one's copped it, poor girl. She's impaled on the railings.'

Molly opened her mouth to scream, but nothing came out. The interior of the ambulance began to spin around her. Vomit rose in her throat and projected out of her mouth. Then a blackness closed in on her, leaving her isolated and unable to hear anything, before a nothingness shrouded her and she went into a deep faint.

When she came round, it was to feel her body jolting from side to side and her hand being held. She opened her eyes and saw that she was inside the ambulance, and that David lay beside her. Realizing it was his hand in hers, she tightened her grip and clung on to it as if somehow the comfort it gave would take away the pain of what she knew. She tried to speak, but her mouth seemed full of dust.

'Here, lav, have a sip of this. Come on, it'll help yer.'

'Hettie? Where's Hettie?'

'Was that the name of the other girl?'

Molly could only nod. Her mind screamed against them confirming what she dreaded to hear, but at the same time she had to know.

'Sorry, lav. Was she a mate of yours?'

'Y-yes... Is she–?'

'There was a fatality. A young woman about the same age as you, but we can't say if it was your mate until we have identification.'

Molly sank back. In her desperate heart, she knew it was Hettie.

Sensing a movement next to her, she looked towards David. He lay on a stretcher on the floor by her side. His face was a mass of dirty-looking scrapes and bloodied, gaping wounds. In a voice that spoke of a parched throat, he said her name. She said his back to him. His smile wasn't a real smile, just a tight attempt at one, but he squeezed her hand a little harder.

The calmness this brought cleared her mind a little. With this clarity, the enormity of what had happened hit her with full force. *Hettie can't be dead. She can't.* 'No... No, *nooo!*'

'Now, now, young lady, we know you've had a massive shock, but there's some really badly injured people on board, and they don't want to listen to you shouting. They're scared out of their wits as it is.'

She wanted to say she was sorry to the man who'd spoken, but couldn't. She clamped her lips together to stop them doing as they pleased and letting out her despair. At that moment, someone above her groaned. A hand flopped from the side of the upper stretcher. Looking around her, she saw there were four stretchers – two of them suspended above where she and David lay on the floor of the ambulance.

The sound of one of the nurses saying, 'He's gone, poor soul,' had Molly wanting to scream once more, but she remained with her mouth clamped tightly shut. No living nightmare had ever given her the terror and shock she was going through at this moment.

Suddenly her anguish increased as she thought of her dad. 'D-does anyone know if there's been any damage on Sebastopol Road?'

'We don't know, lav. It's all over the area, and it ain't finished yet. We–'

Another blast took away whatever he said next. *Oh God, the planes are circling back towards us!*

'Hold on, everyone, we have to stop.'

With this instruction, the ambulance came to a halt. The doors opened and what looked like a raging inferno met their eyes. 'Come on, lav. You have to get out. These wardens will take care of you. We may not be able to fit you back in.'

'What about David?'

'He has to stay, but we need you out of the way, as you appear to have only minor injuries. Here, give me yer hand.'

'Molly, come and find me... Please f-find me.'

'I will. I promise. Hang on. You'll get help soon.'

Once outside, Molly pulled the blanket around her more tightly as she watched the crew remove the dead man. She heard them tell the wardens who must have flagged them down to keep the body covered, and they would see that a van came to pick him up.

'How many injured have yer, then?' the female nurse asked the warden.

'We only have one. There's more inside, but it'll take us a while to get them out, so if you could come back.'

Once this was decided upon, and the injured person was put on the stretcher the dead one had vacated, Molly was told to get back into the ambulance, as there was still room for her.

David's hand immediately sought hers again. It felt right. To her, it was as if he'd always done this, and she never wanted him to stop.

The doors slammed, shutting out the blazing world. The ambulance trundled away once more, shaking her body. Lulling her.

Trying to block out the moans of the new patient, she shyly asked David if he felt all right.

'I've been better.' She could see this was a throwaway answer and didn't reveal what he was really going through. Then he shocked her as he said, 'You're beautiful, Molly. You saved my life. The first-aid man thinks my leg is broken. The pain is bad, but I am alive, so am thanking God – and you – for that.'

Feeling flustered under his gaze, Molly just smiled. *He called me beautiful! And he spoke of God, too. Do the Jews believe in the same God that we Christians do?*

David's small laugh surprised her and interrupted her thoughts. 'You know, even Hitler can't take away your beauty, though he's had a good try. You have a black eye coming, and your lips look bright red, poking through your mucky face.'

She laughed with him, though to do so hurt her bruised stomach. He can't have noticed her swollen face when he stopped to help her. Funny that they could still laugh, despite the fear, the pain of loss and the worry about family and friends. Not to mention seeing their beloved London crumbling and burning around them. But that was Londoners for you. No matter what creed or persuasion they were born into, they always found something to be cheerful about.

As they became serious again, she looked into David's eyes. In their dark-chocolate depths she saw something that jolted her, just as it had the first time she'd looked at him. And she knew what he meant about Hitler not being able to block out beauty, because he was beautiful too, despite the injuries to his face and it weeping blood.

To her, he was the most beautiful person she'd ever looked on.

A week later, Molly called at David's house. She hadn't seen him since the air raid. It had been a time of hell visiting the earth night after night. Mostly the Germans were concentrating on dropping their bombs around the docks, but a few found their way to the roads near her street.

The destruction was something Molly thought she could never get used to. Always she felt as though dust clung to her. It cut her throat, and everything she ate or drank tasted of it, as buildings had their hearts ripped out of them. Displaced people walked the pavements, carrying what was left of their belongings. The WRVS and the Salvation Army had set up soup kitchens in vans, and had taken over halls and churches to provide stations where people could go for help. Many people were beginning to take up residence on the platforms of the underground rail network. But despite it all, there was a prevailing spirit of 'They won't beat us.'

Molly didn't feel like that herself today. She felt beaten on all fronts. This morning she'd attended Hettie's funeral, such as it was. Already there was a shortage of decent coffins, and Hettie had been lain to rest in what looked like one of the crates that were always arriving at her dad's shop.

David opened the door to her. Molly wanted to rush forward and be held by him, but he was struggling with his crutches. Shyness overcame her as she looked into his pale, drawn, bruised and patched-up face.

'Molly! Come in. I'm glad you came. I didn't know how to get hold of you.'

Stepping inside caused her a moment of doubt as to whether she should have come. The hall spoke of wealth, and almost shouted at her that she didn't belong there. A thick red carpet accepted her tread as if it would swallow her into its deep pile. Rich, dark-wood occasional furniture and a hat stand lent it an air of elegance, and a grandfather clock gave a peaceful feel as it steadfastly clicked off the seconds.

Molly followed David's slow and unsteady progress through to a beautiful room furnished in blue and gold. The legs of the embossed-gold velvet-covered sofas sank into a deep-pile royal-blue carpet. Her breath caught in her lungs.

'My mother's taste, not mine. She comes from regal stock. Her parents are related to royalty, though I doubt anyone of that blue blood would recognize my mother's status now. She is a Jew and is tainted with Hitler's brush.'

'Oh no, surely... I mean – well, that ain't here, is it? Not that I know a lot about what's going on, but there has been some news on at the flicks about Germany, Poland and Belgium, and how the Germans are stopping the Jews having any rights and are taking their businesses.'

'I believe there is a lot more than that going on. Anyway, we won't talk politics or war. How are you? I've been so worried about you. And your friend – please say it wasn't her that–'

A tear found its way down Molly's cheek. Others, unshed, stung her sore eyes.

'Oh, I'm sorry. I don't know what to say. Poor girl–'

'Me and Hettie grew up together. We lived opposite each other all our lives. As kids, we had a big falling-out over a doll that I had. Hettie never had anything like that and she took mine home with her, then didn't want to give it back. Me mam said she could keep it. I loved that doll, so I wouldn't give it up. I was a selfish thing, being an only child, and didn't know how to share.' By now the tears were wetting Molly's face.

'It's funny how something little comes back to haunt you at these times. Look, just a moment, I have a daily helper. I'll shout to her and get some tea brought to us. I know you like tea – you and Hettie came all the way around the park to ask me if the kiosk was open.' He smiled and his face lit up.

Molly couldn't help but respond and a little giggle escaped her. But then she laughed out loud at his next joke.

'I imagine you got lost; it's easy to do so around the park. You only have to turn the wrong way and, well, it's a maze.'

Drying her eyes, she responded in the same light-hearted way: 'All right, the game's up. No, we didn't get lost. I made Hettie come this way because I knew you lived here.'

For a moment she wished she could take this back, but then she saw a change in the expression on David's face. 'I hoped that was the reason. I haven't been able to stop thinking about you since that day, Molly. I was driving around in the hope of seeing you, the evening we were caught up in the bombing raid. I guessed you couldn't live far away.'

She couldn't speak. The moment didn't need words. Something invisible had passed between them. They still stood feet apart, and yet it was as if she was in his arms.

'Oh, Molly. I've had feelings for you for a long time.' His beautiful velvety voice took on a much deeper note. 'I – I wish I could hold you. Would you let me?'

'Yes...' This was said in a whisper as she moved towards him. But for David to hold her was an impossible feat, if he wanted to remain standing.

She was so near him. Their eyes held each other's.

'Let's sit down.'

The sofa he chose hadn't looked inviting, when

85

Molly had first come into the room, but she found as she sank into it next to David that it accepted her like a huge pair of soft arms.

He gently pulled her to him.

It should have been a moment of extreme happiness, but Molly's desolation hadn't left her. A feeling of being where she was meant to be overwhelmed her, and it broke the fragile veil she'd been able to bring down temporarily to mask her pain. Huge sobs racked her body. David didn't speak, but just offered her his hanky and held her to him. His hand stroked her back.

It took a while to reach a calm place. When she did so, she started to apologize, but David hushed her. 'I'm here for you, Molly.' His fingers followed the trail that her tears had taken, wiping away the remnants of them.

The grandfather clock broke the spell, and the three chimes it gave brought Molly down to earth. 'Oh, I'll have to get back. I – I look after me dad, and he thinks I'm still at the funeral. He'll see others who attended from our street returning to their homes, and he'll start wondering where I am.'

'Have that tea first. Tell him you got chatting or something. Don't leave yet, Molly.'

She didn't want to. She never wanted to leave David's side again, but by now her dad would be drinking, and if his cronies were coming round to play cards, he'd want her to make supper. The last thing she wanted was him in a foul mood tonight.

'I'm sorry, I really have to go.'

'Will you come again?'

'I'll try, but I can't get out that often. I'll do me best to come in a few days.'

As she went to get up, David pulled her back down. His face came close to hers. His lips pressed gently on her mouth. Molly had never experienced a feeling like the one that trembled through her.

'Oh, Molly, please come as soon as you can. I can't get out yet, but I'm interviewing a handy-man-cum-driver in the next couple of days, so then I'll be able to come and see you. Where do you live?'

'Sebastopol Road, but don't come there. Me dad would kill me. Look, he doesn't get up very early. He drinks a lot and stays down in the cellar, even after the air raid has finished. He had some straw-filled mattresses delivered, and we shake them out and try to sleep on them while the bombs are being dropped. He's sometimes down there till after ten in the morning. I do a few chores, then walk out to see if there's anything I can do for folk. I could stand at the top of our road where it meets Fore Street and then, if you can get out, we could meet there.'

David's expression showed that he found this strange. But he didn't protest. 'All right. Let's say three days from now. I should have a man employed by then, and I'll drive round at about nine in the morning. But do your best to try and sort something out so that we can go to dinner; or if you can come round here before then, that would be wonderful. I'm beginning to miss you already.'

She giggled at this, unable to believe how everything was turning out. She loved the way David could suddenly turn things into a joke by giving a quirky look as he said something ordinary. Kissing him gently on the cheek, she said, 'I'll see meself out. Don't try and get up again.'

When she got to the door, she turned and waved. His little-boy-lost look tugged at her heart, but also made her smile again.

Her mood had lightened. Outside, everything looked different, brighter. She'd walk across the park; it would be quicker. And she'd try not to look at the spot where the railings were twisted and broken. This thought made her heart feel heavy once more. *Oh, Hettie. Hettie.* But then the sound of a bird tweeting made her lift her head and look into the sky. The bird's excrement landed on her shoulder. A smile curved her lips. 'All right, Hettie, there's no need for that!' A giggle bubbled up inside her, and her sadness lifted. Hettie was watching over her. That would be Hettie's way of telling her off. Molly could almost hear her: 'Bleedin' hell, Molly. Yer got yer man, and all yer can do is mope!'

A part of her knew she'd always mope when she missed Hettie, but a big part of her knew that Hettie was happy for her, and that helped. She was to go forward. How it would all work out at home, Molly didn't know, but she would put a brave face on things and keep battling on. Hettie would help her. And so would David.

Ooh, I just can't believe it. I have my David at last.

At this moment, nothing else mattered to her.

6

Simon

Spiteful Talk

'He should never be allowed in uniform. It's a disgrace!'

'Oh, shut up, Kitty. Simon's the best code-breaker we have. We wouldn't crack half of the codes without him. Besides...'

Simon tried to step back and go out of the door again without being seen. He'd heard the comment and felt the pain of it, but Jane Downing, a decent sort, had spotted him and stopped in her tracks while defending him, embarrassment burning her cheeks. He smiled at her as he walked through the corridor and within sight of the dozen or so women in Hut 6, the hub of operations at Bletchley Park, where the Enigma messages from the Germans' army and air force were decrypted. Some of the women looked up at him, but most dropped their heads and looked busy. Simon decided to make light of the situation and try and make them giggle.

'Girlies – *darlings* – who are we gossiping about today? Do tell!' A ripple of nervous laughter gave him a feeling of relief. He was sure he'd managed to make them think he didn't know it was him they had been discussing. Turning towards his

89

own office, a small room at the top end of the hut, he hoped that would be the end of the conversation, but Kitty had other ideas.

'We were talking about you, actually. Your kind are not fit to wear His Majesty's uniform!'

Not wanting this to deteriorate into a slanging match, Simon decided to pull rank. 'Please address me as "sir" or "Officer Fulworth" when you speak to me, Wren Hamlin. And please refrain from speaking about me to others.'

'Huh, you have to earn respect. It's not–'

'Kitty!'

Her name, spoken in a warning tone by Jane, did nothing to stop Kitty Hamlin from voicing her hurtful remarks. 'Well, everyone knows what he is...'

Unable to hold his tongue any longer, Simon asked, 'Oh? And what are you, Wren Hamlin? Wasn't that my colleague, the married officer John Perry, I saw you with last night? Giving you a good humping against the wall, wasn't he, darling? Screaming like a stuck pig, you were, and I wasn't the only one to see or hear you.' Wanting to bite his tongue out, he turned away.

The moment's silence that followed his remark was broken by a yell that would have made a fishwife proud. 'What? What are you talking about! I was out with my mum last night – she came to visit me, didn't she, Jane?'

'Yes, she did, and I did see you go out with her.'

This was just what he'd wanted to avoid: getting the girls on the side of Kitty Hamlin; especially Jane, who had tried to stand up for him.

With as much dignity as he could muster, he marched towards his office, but the giggles and the whispered word 'Faggot' undid him. Once he was in his office, tears filled his eyes.

Leaning against the door, Simon gave rein to them for a moment, allowing them to run freely down his cheeks. Their salty taste had him wiping his eyes. What's the use? *Oh, Roland – Roland, if only we could run off somewhere. To a mountain hideaway in a hot country and live in peace.*

Thinking of his visit at the weekend to Roland, the love of his life, Simon pulled out his wallet and took out the photo he carried of him. Kissing it made him feel better and quelled the fear that always clogged his chest when people referred to his homosexuality. No matter what his rank, or his standing here at Bletchley Park, if he was proven to be in a relationship with another man he would go to prison. And so would Roland. It was the main reason for them living so far apart. No one knew him, when he visited Roland. To all intents and purposes, he was just a friend from school days and, in public, they always had Lucinda in tow. And no one knew Roland in London, where Simon had an apartment in the house that his mother had made over to Lucinda and him. They had converted it into two dwellings; Lucinda occupied the five rooms upstairs, while he had the bottom half. It was an arrangement that worked well.

Unlike the North, where Roland lived, people in London didn't take much notice of each other's comings and goings, which made it easier for them to enjoy more private times together, going out to dinner or to the theatre. Precious, snatched time that Simon dreaded this war would take away from them. The recent news of the conscription age-limit being raised had worried him, although, at forty-three years old, Roland had just missed being called up. Nevertheless, there had been talk of that limit being raised again in the future. *Oh, God, I couldn't bear it!*

With his head reeling from a particularly difficult code that it had taken him hours to come up with a formula for, only to find it wasn't correct, Simon bent over his desk and ran his fingers through his thick blond hair. His back ached from standing, jotting down equations on the huge board that occupied one wall of his office.

A legacy of his childhood, his back pain wasn't helped by being a tall man. Six foot two in his stockinged feet, he towered above most people he knew. His back had been injured at the age of twelve, when he'd been a boarder at Rugby school. On one of his visits to the town centre, a gang of boys had set upon him. They had called him a 'nancy boy' and had beaten him up. When they'd finished with him they threw him down the embankment of the railway line and that had resulted in one of his discs being ruptured. His back had been weak ever since.

Straightening himself some time later, he realized it was already dark outside. *God, what time is it?* A glance at his watch told him it was almost nine-thirty. He hadn't been out of his office since the incident that afternoon, or had a cup of tea or anything to eat. A sudden pang of hunger and thirst seized him. He'd go to the bar for a drink and then call at the canteen and bring something back, so that he could continue working. He didn't feel like company, and knocking off wasn't an option. He had to break this code!

Using the window as a mirror, he tidied himself up. Flattening his hair as best he could, he donned his jacket. As he fastened his belt, he examined his face. What was it about him that gave away what he was? His full, effeminate lips didn't help. Or his soft blue eyes, framed by long, dark lashes. Or his high cheekbones or his oversmooth skin. He hardly ever had to shave, and when he did it was only to scrape away what would be termed bum-fluff. He had to admit he was the epitome of a *pretty boy*. Even his slim figure and delicate bone structure had something of the female form about them, though they belied his strength. When he stripped, his torso was strong and muscular. He had great stamina and was athletic. His saving grace at school had been his running ability. He'd brought the championship cup home for the school three years on the trot, and had been in line to be part of the Olympic team. But he'd been sidelined and had always suspected that the rumours about his sexuality were the reason why.

Giving a sigh that released some of the tension his thoughts had brought about, Simon put it all out of his mind. Outside, the late-evening air had a crisp feel to it. Breathing in deeply, he walked towards Bletchley House and the room that had been converted to offer a comfortable area, much like a gentlemen's club, for the officers to relax in.

93

The usual babble of voices hushed as he walked in. Sensing an atmosphere, his heart thudded against his chest. Looking around, he asked, 'Anything wrong?'

Someone coughed, and a voice from one group said, 'Only that a faggot has walked into the room.'

'Oh, not that old hat. Just found out what one is, have you, Jones? Being one is nearly as bad as being a sheep-shagger–'

'Why, you...'

'Now then, that's enough. I reckon as you deserved that, Davy. As for the rest of you, if any of you want to stoop to name-calling, like a lot of schoolboys, then do it when I am not around. Come and sit over here, Officer Fulworth, you look like you could do with a cup of tea.'

Grateful for the general's intervention, Simon went over to the table in the far corner of the room where he sat partaking of a glass of wine. He felt relieved that, as he did so, the others began to chat to each other again and the atmosphere eased. 'Thank you, sir, but I thought to take some refreshment back to my office. I've a particularly sticky problem that I cannot get to the bottom of.'

'Have a break, old chap. All work and no play...' A puff of smoke from the general's pipe produced a pleasant smell of Old Holborn tobacco. Where the general got his supply from, no one knew or questioned, but the aroma aroused a yearning in Simon to have a smoke himself – something he'd been trying to give up, after finding he was getting more and more out of breath on his morning run.

Out of habit, he patted his pockets, even though he knew he didn't have any cigarettes on him.

'Want one of these, Fulworth?'

The voice surprised and alarmed Simon, but he nodded and took a cigarette from the packet that John Perry offered. Perry's eyes locked on his with a steel-cold look that held a warning. Confused, Simon looked away. A heat crept up his neck and flooded his face. Fear tickled his stomach muscles. The click of Perry's lighter made him jump. The flame from it danced menacingly in front of him. There was no doubt that Perry knew what had happened between him and Kitty that morning. *Damn!*

'Sit down, Fulworth. You're shaking like a leaf. You're working too hard, man.' This, from the general, broke the frightening spell that held Simon. Drawing the smoke deep into his lungs calmed him. He nodded his thanks and sat down, grateful to be off legs that he didn't think would hold him up much longer.

'Are you experiencing any problems with the rest of the men, Simon?'

'N-no, sir. No, everything's fine.'

'Good. Let me know if you do. We don't want you upset, for we need you to concentrate. Oh, I hear things, but you never give any hint that they are true and your behaviour is impeccable. I rather like to think these rumours are because of a certain look you have, and I hope they are unfounded. You have a girlfriend, I believe?'

Hating having to lie to this man he so admired, Simon nodded. Then he made a joke to cover his discomfort. 'Sort of, but we hardly ever see each

95

other; maybe that's as well, though, as she's a fiery lady and this way we remain friends.'

'Ha, I know what you mean. Absence may make the heart fonder, but it helps to keep the peace, too. You must miss her, though. Where does she live?'

Wanting to talk about anything but this, Simon shifted in his seat. Passing his half-sister off as his girlfriend didn't sit well with him. But needs must, and luckily Lucinda wasn't known to any of his set, as she had been brought up by their mother in India.

A couple of years after his father's death, his mother had remarried and Lucinda had come along within the first year of the marriage. Simon had been ten at the time and already in boarding school. His grandfather had taken it upon himself to bring him up. Simon shuddered, as memory reminded him of the abuse he'd suffered at the hands of this man who should have loved him.

'Are you all right, man? You seem very distracted.'

'I am, sir, sorry – always like this when I have a problem on my hands. Forgive me, you were asking about my sis... girlfriend. Lucinda lives in London, so not far away. She's a journalist. Harbours an ambition to become a war correspondent, but I try to persuade her against it. Seems very dangerous work to me.'

'You were going to say "sister"? Have you a sister or any family, Fulworth?'

'I – I, yes, a younger sister; she lives with my mother in India.' *Oh, how the lies mount up.* 'She's

96

a half-sister. I haven't seen her for years. I've been thinking about her a lot lately, hence my mistake. Look, there's something I want to talk to you about, sir.'

'Go ahead.'

'It's about the meeting we had concerning an assistant for me. I have someone in mind. She's a northern girl from the lower classes, but she's had the benefit of a good education and excels in maths.'

'Not our usual type, then. How do you know her?'

'Through a friend. He and I were at university together. He runs evening classes in Leeds, where he lives. Poverty is rife there and although, as I said, the girl is from the lower classes, she had a benefactor who paid for her lessons. She excelled in everything, but in maths in particular. She passed her exams with very high marks. Apparently she was hoping to go to university to become a teacher, but the gentleman who has sponsored her thus far has run short of funds. In any case, it is thought that she'd stand little chance of getting a place. Not that she doesn't deserve one, but ... well, you know. Keeping the lower classes down and all that. My friend recommends her highly. Of course he doesn't know what my work is, but he does know that I'm looking out for a good candidate to assist me.'

'Hmm, I'd like to see her. Turing and Welchman are already beginning to murmur that we will have to break ranks at some point and recruit from the lower classes. We are very short-handed and are running out of what have always been considered "suitable people" to draw new candidates from. Problem is, we simply don't have the budget to employ the number of hands we need. It's my guess that Welchman, in particular, will eventually cause a ruction and force the government's hand. If your girl fits in and does a good job, she will prove that there is a bigger pool for us to fish in. Approach her, and I will put a panel together. We'll interview her, but no promises.'

'Thank you, sir. I was introduced to her in person last weekend. My fiancée and I went to stay with my friend and he invited her to dinner. I liked her very much. I took note of her good points, and they were many. I also found out as much about her as I could, by asking questions without being impolite. You know the kind of thing: what her interests are, does she have a boyfriend, what does she think of the war? I wanted to get a true picture of her. She came up trumps in everything. And she astounded me by solving the very difficult equation I set her. She knows that I am recommending her, but not what for, of course, and yet she is very keen to join us. I asked her to solve the equation to satisfy myself of her ability and, as I think my friend is more than taken with her, to make sure his judgement isn't clouded by his feelings for her.' Simon sighed; always he needed to draw the scent away from what having a male friend might conjure up in others' minds. 'Anyway, she amazed me. She came up with the right answer in just a few minutes. A very clever and nice, level-headed young woman.'

'In that case, we'll do this quicker than usual. Come and see me tomorrow. I'll sort out a date to interview her and you can telephone your friend to arrange it. I'll have the train passes ready, so that you can send them to... What's her name, by the way?'

'Florence Kilgallon, sir.'

'Irish? Southern or northern?'

'Neither. Her parents were from Ireland, but she wasn't sure from which part and displayed no allegiance to the country whatsoever.'

'We'll have to make sure on that. The southerners are not with us in this war, as you know.'

'Right-o, sir, but I don't think there will be a problem. She can't even remember her parents, and is a northern girl through and through.'

'Well, let's get the ball rolling and we will see.'

'Thank you, sir. Now I beg your pardon, but I really would like to get back to my office. Would you excuse me? I'll just get a sandwich from the mess to take back with me.'

'Yes, of course. Do you think you will crack this one? It is vital, you know. They are using this code more and more, of late. Very important that we get a tag on it.'

'Will do, sir. I'm nearly there, as it is. A bit of burning the midnight oil should do it.' Stubbing out his cigarette, Simon stood, saluted and made his way to the bar. Upset with himself for doing so, he bought a packet of Senior Service cigarettes. He really had intended to stick to his resolve to give up.

Perry stood near the door. Trepidation clutched

at Simon's stomach muscles as he walked to-wards him. On reaching the exit, Perry moved forward, barring his path. 'Been talking about things you shouldn't, I hear, Fulworth. Well, I'd be careful if I was you. Walls have ears, they say. And if my little bit of fun with Kitty gets out, trouble will come looking for you. Trouble with a capital T.'

'Get out of my way, Perry. I'm not afraid of you. If you want to mess with that whore, it's your business; but if she continues to snipe at me, then you had better warn her, because I will put her on report, and your sordid dealings with her will likely come to light.'

'You disgusting faggot! I'm watching you. One whiff of you getting it off with another man and you'll find yourself in prison. And good rid-dance.'

His trepidation turned to sick fear. Pushing past Perry, Simon just made it outside before he vomited in the bushes. The retching caused the pain in his back to reignite and made him un-steady on his legs. When he got back to his office, he remembered he hadn't bought a sandwich. Not that he could have eaten it now. *God, how did things get as bad as this?*

His colleagues had been fine with him until recently and he'd always had their respect. Now he was the subject of snide remarks, sniggering name-calling and subtle bullying. What had changed? He knew the answer: Kitty Hamlin.

Kitty came from a family in Essex who weren't born into moneyed society, but had made their way by means of her father becoming a rich industrialist. A trained tailor, he'd started a small factory turning out mass-produced clothing for men. The last war had done him a huge favour and his business had mushroomed, as he'd secured the contract for supplying the forces with uniforms. Kitty had attended a private school and turned out to be university material, though somehow the rough edges of her parents' beginnings had never been smoothed out. She was a nasty piece of work, and had swiftly made up her mind about Simon and made no bones about letting her conclusion be known. Before she came into his life, everyone had accepted his story of having a girlfriend, and that had been that. Now they questioned its validity. What was it with Kitty? Why was she so bothered by him? How he wished Roland was here. To be able to hold him and be held by him.

Loneliness threatened to suffocate Simon. But shaking off the feeling, he set about tackling the code once more and soon lost himself in the fascination of the equations he needed to solve, and in the thought that coming up with a formula would provide information that might be instrumental in saving many lives.

It had turned midnight before that happened and he was able to pass on his solution to the main office. He hoped, with all his heart, that the formula would enable the deciphering of the latest batch of intercepted messages.

As he rode his bicycle through the gates of Bletchley Park, dampness cloyed at Simon and chilled his body. The recent warm weather had

101

given way to heavy night-dews. Pulling up the collar of his trench coat gave a little comfort.

Billeted with a local woman who lived about fifteen minutes' ride away, Simon relished the exercise that the journey gave him and looked on this time as a chance to unwind. But tonight the usual sounds – a hooting owl, the flap of a swooping bat, the scream of a small animal as it became a meal for a larger predator, and the wind swishing through the branches – gave a sinister feel to the air.

A rustle behind the hedge, which he couldn't put down to night-creatures, set his heart drumming in his ears. The words 'Right, it's him. Get him!' hardly registered, before three figures jumped out in front of him. His attempt to swerve around them caused him to lose his balance. His body hit the ground, and the bike landed on top of him. Hands grabbed at the frame, jarring Simon's trapped ankle. A cry of pain escaped him, but was obliterated by fear as a shadow that he could only attribute to a giant bent over him. Sour, alcohol-fuelled breath wafted into his open mouth, making him retch. The man's fist crashed into his face, disorientating him. *What's happening?* He tried to call out, but blood filled his mouth and something hard caught in his throat. Choking he spat out the offending object just as a vicious kick sank into his groin, taking him into a sickening cascade of pain.

'Give it to him – go on, you said you would!'

Through the wave upon wave of searing agony that gripped his groin and zinged through his body, the realization came to him that they were pulling his trousers down. Unable to struggle, he prayed: *Please God, no. Please don't let this happen.*

A shout drowned out his pitiful plea. 'Oi, what's going on there?'

His attackers disappeared. Torchlight illuminated him. Shame smothered him. *Oh God, let me die!*

The voice of the torch-bearer held disgust. 'Good God! What's all this then? Men, doing this to you? Were you willing?'

He couldn't answer. How could anyone think him party to what had just happened?

When the light left his face, he could make out the uniform of the man and saw it was a policeman.

'Right, I think some questions will have to be answered. This isn't a good position to be found in. You're under arrest...'

'No, Officer, please! Th-those men, th-they jumped me. They kicked me and then sought to humiliate me.'

The pain from the kick began to subside, but the humiliation was just as hard to bear.

Without touching him, or offering a word of comfort, the policeman said, 'Get up and make yourself decent, man.' The tone of his voice still spoke of his distaste. 'I saw the others running off. Did you know them?'

Simon's body trembled all over with the effort it took to stand. As he bent to pull up his trousers, his stomach rolled over. Dashing to the verge, he vomited on the grass. This involuntary action deepened his shame.

'You're in uniform! Bloody disgrace.'

Simon cringed. But what the officer said next gladdened him. 'How dare they attack one of our serving officers? I'm sorry for my initial assumption, sir, but if you could see your way to coming to the police station, I would like to take a statement. Then I and my men will do our utmost to find out who they were.'

'Thank you, Officer. Thank you. But I've had a very long day. What they did to me has left me in a lot of pain. I need to get home. All I can tell you is that I think they were local. Farmers, or something like that. They smelt as if they had been putting in a hard day's labour and had then drowned it in beer. And they spoke with a local accent. I can think of no reason why they should attack me.'

'Right-o. I've an idea who it might be, from what you say. There aren't many young men left around here after the call-up, but farmers are exempt and I know three farm labourers who would fit the bill. But call in at the station tomorrow. If you remember anything in the meantime, jot it down. Now, let me just take your name and where you are staying.'

Wanting to get away and disappear into his own misery, this was an irritation to Simon, but he obliged. It did hearten him that the officer's whole attitude seemed to have changed.

'Now, sir, will you be all right getting home on your bike?'

Simon felt as if he would never be able to ride a bike again, but he so wanted to be alone. 'I'll make my way back into the Park and rouse one of the drivers. They'll take me home. I'll be fine, thank you.'

Wary of every little noise coming from the trees that lined his way, Simon somehow made it back inside Bletchley Park.

With familiar buildings around him, he felt safe again, but couldn't contain his emotions. Sitting on the grass outside the front of Bletchley House, he felt tentatively inside his mouth. A gap that wasn't there previously told him that one of his front teeth had gone. Being proud of his smile, this devastated him. He pulled up his knees, leaned on them and rested his head. Huge sobs racked his body. As these subsided, he thought again of Roland, and longing coursed through him to be with him up in the North, in his hideous house, and to be loved and comforted by him. This thought led to Flo coming into his mind. Somehow he felt he had a friend in her. He hoped with all his heart that she would pass the interview. Life wouldn't be so lonely with the jolly Flo by his side.

7

Molly

Life Changes

Molly stood on the corner of Sebastopol Road and Osman Road waiting anxiously for David's car to appear. The morning had a cold feel to it. Rain threatened, but she didn't care. She was rejoicing because the overnight bombings had missed her street for three nights in a row now. But she was mindful of those who might have suffered elsewhere in London. Each day brought news of horrific losses, but also of tremendous courage.

She just needed to know if David was safe. Every morning, since a couple of days after the time she'd ventured to his house, the handyman he'd employed had driven him this way so that he could reassure her.

Five weeks had passed since that fateful night that had brought them together. Now her life centred around the times she could meet up with him. David had filled part of her with a happiness that somehow made life bearable.

Though his leg was still encased in plaster, the rest of his injuries had healed. Not those inside him, though, and that was the same for her. The trauma they'd experienced and the loss of Hettie would take a long time to heal, if ever.

They spent what time they could together. But every second was fraught with fear, for Molly.

She longed to tell David what was going on at her home, and what she had been forced to be a party to. But she daren't. She knew that David, being a lawyer, would take action against what was happening, and she needed to protect him.

'Say a word to anyone about our involvement, or what goes on here, and you're dead meat, Missy – and that goes for whoever you tell.'

Remembering those words from Eva sent a shiver through Molly. But the real fear had been planted by Gus. He'd come into the kitchen, where she had been preparing supper, and had tried to maul her. He'd picked up the knife she'd been chopping onions with and held it at her throat. 'One day, my girl.' He'd lowered the knife and pressed it into her breasts. 'Like these, don't you? Well, I'd slice them off in an instant and eat them for me tea. You just make one bad move. Just one.' She'd pushed him away, telling him that she'd scream if he touched her again. He'd slinked off back into the parlour, and Molly had known he'd been afraid of Eva finding out what he was up to.

Molly didn't know why Eva was protective of her in this way, but realized from her attitude that there was a hidden reason, and this frightened her almost as much as Gus's persistence. When Molly thought of how Eva constantly threatened to put her on the game, the mystery deepened. If that is what she had in mind, then you would think she wouldn't care what Gus did.

At least Molly had her dad to help her, as whenever the subject came up and he was around, he'd not allow any such talk. She could see, though, that her dad was getting more and more afraid of Eva, Gus and Lofty. He did their bidding now, no matter what. How soon before he gave in and sold her to them?

Molly's life had changed drastically and she missed going out to work, but had decided not to go away to do war work. She wanted to stay near David.

Feeling more anxious as time went on, she looked in the direction that David would come from, but he still wasn't in sight. She thanked God every day for David coming into her life. He'd kept her sane and helped her experience a happiness that overshadowed everything.

Though she had to admit that the happiness she harboured inside her was mixed with a nightly dose of terror, as the sirens droned their warning. People would scramble for shelter. Crashing, ear-splitting explosions would begin. And it would seem that surely this time the world would end. This time one bomb would have her name on it and would take her into oblivion – or, worse, take David from her.

Though times were hard, a feeling of hope mingled with that of hopelessness among the people. It was a strange mixture, but a fair description, as it seemed that there was never going to be an end to the bombardment, and yet the terrifying experience had brought out the best in all the folk of London. Molly found that she no longer walked along the streets outside her immediate neighbourhood with her eyes forward, passing but not seeing anyone she encountered. Now those in the next street and further afield were no longer strangers, and she hoped each time she walked towards their houses that they were all right.

At last David came in sight. His smiling face, as he lowered the window when he came alongside her, lifted her heart. Bending her head into the window at the back where he sat, she gave him a light kiss.

When she looked into his face she saw that his smile was fixed. 'What is it? Has anything happened?'

David opened the car door. 'Get in, Molly. We have to talk.'

Her heart lurched.

Once she was settled next to him, he pulled her to him. Ignoring the cold and unwelcoming feel of the dark-green leather seats of his Wolseley, she snuggled into his warm body.

'Drive around the park, please, Wilson.' The old man obeyed without a word.

'David, what is it? You look so pensive.'

'I've been called up.'

'B-but why? I mean, you haven't been called up before, and yet you are of the right age.'

'My work had an exemption to it. But now more fighting men are needed and there are women lawyers who can take our place. I knew a week ago, but didn't like to say anything until I knew it was final. I went for a medical and, as my leg is healing well, it hasn't barred me. I'm to report for another medical in six weeks. I've decided to opt for pilot training.'

'Oh no, David, I can't bear it.'

His arms pulled her closer. 'Darling, I want you to know that I love you. I know I have said so many times before, but now I want to do something about our love. I just don't know if we can, because of the differences in our faiths. I wanted to give you time before I discussed our future. But we don't have time now. And so I need to find a way to resolve our differences. I want us to be married.'

The strength of the happiness that assailed her was something she'd never experienced in her life. It took away all the fear, pain and loneliness that had been her lot. And it filled her with courage. 'I love you, too, David. And I will do whatever I have to, to be worthy to become your wife.'

'Not "worthy" – don't say that. You are the worthiest woman in the world. It is I who am going to denounce my faith for you. Not the other way round.'

'No, you mustn't. It means so much to you. I am a believer, and so are you. But I don't practise my religion, and you do. I will convert to Judaism and will be proud to.'

His lips sought hers. The pressure of the kiss was gentle and sweet at first, but gradually it deepened and awoke in her a passion that shocked her.

'Come to my house with me, my darling.'

'I can't, David. I have to get back; my dad will be up soon.'

His look held disappointment, and she knew that her response to his words had given him false hope. Until now she had been the one to try

110

and keep their feelings from going too far.

David's next question surprised her, as she'd thought he would try to press the point of her going to his house. 'Will your dad be a barrier to us marrying?'

'Yes, he will. But I will run away. I'm old enough to make any legal decisions myself, so there won't be any problems, but we have to plan it. We'll have to move to another area. Oh, there's so much to talk about. To plan. And I can only get out of the house for a few minutes a day, or for the odd evening.'

'Meet me tomorrow, as usual, and I will have worked something out. I don't understand why your father has such a hold on you, but I can see you are afraid, my darling. I will put our marriage plans into action as soon as I can. At least a civil wedding. The Jewish one can come later, when you are ready. Oh, my Molly. I bless the day that brought us together, even though it was one of the most horrible days in our lives. I love you beyond anything.'

His lips were on hers again. His tongue probed gently until she opened her mouth. The sensation awoke urges she didn't want to deny, and she knew she wouldn't, the next time they were alone in his house or wherever they went together.

In that moment she also knew that whatever it took, she would follow her David. She would always be his. It took all her strength to leave him, when the time came. Her heart wanted to go with him, right there and then.

As Molly lay later that night in the dank cellar of

111

her home, the silence surrounding her was fraught with fear. Her own fear eclipsed that of the other four occupants of the cellar, whose alcohol-fuelled breath putrefied the air as they lounged around her, sleeping at intervals and swigging drink at others. The presence of Eva, Gus and Lofty in the cellar terrified Molly. The stench of them had her swallowing down the bile that rose to her throat, causing her to release an involuntary cough as the stinging aftermath threatened to choke her.

The candle they kept lit had extinguished itself. The blackness clawed at and disorientated Molly.

She felt for the box of matches she kept nearby, hating being unable to see the others. While she had her eyes on them, she could be ready if they tried anything.

The air raid that had caused them all to descend into the cellar had ended. The bombing had started earlier than usual and had been close by. Too much so for the three people Molly despised most in the world to have made their way home in safety. Her dad had insisted they took shelter with them.

The sound of the match scraping on the flint strip grated on her tense nerves. Its light showed her dad asleep on a makeshift bed.

Lifting the match higher, she saw Gus. The bottle in his hand had very little whisky left in it. His eyes travelled along her body. The knot that held her chest so tight she could hardly breathe threatened to strangle her. It was the burning of her fingers that at last helped her to gasp air into her lungs, and shaking the match vigorously left them in darkness again. The sound of a movement had her scrambling for another match and striking it. Gus was closer to her than he had been. He stopped his progress as the lit match took away his element of surprise.

This time Molly reached for a candle from the shelf above her and lit it. Its flame gave her sight of the smirk on Gus's face. Her fear intensified.

She kicked out at her dad, hoping to rouse him. His body wobbled and his snore rattled around the cold, dank cellar. 'Dad, Dad, come on. It's over. DAD!'

'He's dead to the world, girl. So it's just you and me. And I intend to have some fun.'

'Leave it out, Gus.'

This, from Eva, brought Molly instant relief. When trying to arouse her dad she'd been afraid of waking Eva and Lofty, too, in case this time they might help Gus, rather than deter him.

'What's up, Eva – it's our plan, ain't it? She's wasted here. We need her ready and put to work where she can bring in good money.'

Eva nudged him and gestured towards her dad.

Molly opened her mouth to scream, but nothing came out. Her eyes fixed on the bottle. As Gus raised it above his head, beams of light danced around it, glinting off the remaining golden liquid.

Gus's movement was swift, and the bottle smashed down on her dad's head, his moan releasing a breath she thought he would never draw in again.

'Bleedin' 'ell, Gus. I didn't mean that hard. Yer could have killed him.' Eva scrambled over to Alf,

113

pawing at him in her distress. Molly felt disgust as she thought of the growing relationship between her dad and Eva. It had repulsed her to see them fawning over each other these last few weeks. More than once she'd met them coming out of his bedroom.

Aunty Bet had moved up to the Midlands and was working in a munitions factory. Her last words before leaving had been to tell Molly to get out. 'Come with me, me little darling,' she'd said. 'We can be happy together. I don't like leaving you here with him and those new cronies of his, what with these air raids going on.'

If it hadn't been for David, Molly knew she would have gone, and willingly.

Eva was feeling for her dad's pulse. Molly held her breath and could only stare at the trickle of blood seeping from his forehead.

'He'll be all right, Eva. If I'd wanted to kill him, I would have. He'll be useless for a couple of days, but he'll survive.'

'You can count your lucky stars that his pulse is still strong, mate – that blow were too bleedin' heavy. As it is, he's sleeping like a bleedin' baby. Come on, get her out of here, but you can forget having your fun. I've got a good customer who's looking for a virgin. He pays high, if I get him one.'

'No, Eva, I'm having her. I've wanted a piece of her since we first saw her.'

'You can bleedin' want on. Yer not going near her.' Eva's voice held authority before she sneered, 'Besides, the size of you, no virgin can take you. On top of which, you've caused me to put more of

114

our girls through abortions than I like to think of. You've got no control, and she's got no protection in place. I promise you can have some fun with her, once she's broken and she's fixed up with a Dutch cap.'

'And me, Eva. I wanna do her, too.'

'None of you are touching me.' Molly had been searching for and found the bread knife that she'd hidden beneath her sack-bedding. Wielding it, she rose to her feet and backed towards the stairs. Climbing them backwards, she kept her eyes darting from one to the other of their shocked faces, swishing the knife in front of her as she went.

When she reached the cellar door, she groped behind her with her free hand and found the latch. Every limb shook as she turned to open it, but the door didn't give when she pressed the latch and pushed. She tried again, shoving with all her might. Anguished tears ran down her face and a screeching noise came from her as she drew in a fearful breath. Her body became weak; her arm fell to her side. The knife slipped from her grasp, echoing as it hit the step. Hands grabbed at her. Her legs scraped on the stone steps as Gus dragged her back down. At the bottom, he lifted her onto her feet, then twisted both of her arms behind her.

'Get up there and open that bleedin' door, Lofty.'

Forced upstairs now, Molly tried to struggle free, but the pain of twisting against the strength of Gus's grip was too much to bear. She begged them to let her go. Spittle ran down her chin and

115

her tears of despair mingled with her snot.

'Take a look outside, Lofty – see if the bleedin' car's still in one piece.' Eva rummaged through the kitchen drawers as she said this. Finding some string, she held it aloft. 'Help me to tie her up, Gus.'

Molly kicked out. 'No ... no. Leave me alone. Me dad'll kill you all.'

'Ha, he might not see the light of day again, let alone come to your aid.' Gus tightened his grip on her. Terror seared Molly more deeply than the burning feeling that rasped the muscles of her shoulders.

Lofty came back in. 'We're good to go, but there's a lot of folk milling around. Looks like there's been a hit in the street. Someone shouted about me taking a bloke to hospital in me car.'

'Bleedin' 'ell. Right, we've got to make it look as if me and her are injured and need to be taken to the hospital. Otherwise they could come at us like a bleedin' lynch mob. Lofty, you'll have to carry me out. Gus, make her unconscious and then carry her out. Right, let's go.'

Molly fought for all she was worth, but made no impact. Nothing she could do would stop Gus. She felt the pressure of his fingers on her neck. Saw the room go into a shadowy place, as the voices and all noise around her faded. She tried to hang onto the thought that had brought David into her head, but she couldn't. The last things she saw were the licking flames where a bomb had struck, and the last things she smelt were the smoke and dust that enveloped her street.

8

Flo

Pulled Both Ways

'What did it feel like when your dad died, Flo?' Kathy sat on Flo's bed, watching her putting on her make-up. Her own bed was on the other side of this large bedroom, which housed three beds in all, in readiness for any child needing a place to lay her head.

Whilst Flo had been living here there'd only been one other, a girl of sixteen. Eunice, her name was. By, she'd been a handful when she arrived. She was a hair's breadth from being sent to an approved school, but Mrs Leary's love and understanding turned her around and she was now living in a nurses' hostel in London, training to be a nurse. Flo had the occasional letter from her. Thinking of this, she decided that she would look Eunice up, if she did get the position at Bletchley.

'I don't remember, me little lass. I was just a babby. But, eeh, I can imagine it's a deep pain as you're feeling.'

'It is. Sometimes it stops me from swallowing, it's that tight.'

'By, Kathy love, you shouldn't have been put through this at your age. I don't know what to

117

say. I reckon that no matter what anyone says, it don't make it any better.'

'Naw, sometimes it makes it worse, as if they think I should get over it, but I can't. Me dad were a-all I – I had.'

Flo gathered the sobbing child to her.

'W-will you always be here, Flo?'

Flo hesitated, but couldn't be less than honest. 'I'm not likely to be here for long, but I'll allus be your friend. This war is taking loved ones away all the time, and I'm no different. I have to do me bit. It's possible I will go very soon, but I'll write to you. I promise. And you write back, an' all, or I'll be upset.'

Kathy's arms tightened around her. Flo stroked the mass of soft, dark curls. An overwhelming feeling of love swamped her for this lost little ten-year-old.

'Would you like to come with me, eh? I'm off to the shops. I've a few things I need. Then we could see if there's a suitable matinee on at the flicks. What d'yer reckon, eh?'

'Oh, yes please.'

'Reet, go and get yourself changed. Put that nice red frock on that you were wearing when you arrived, there's a good lass.'

Kathy's head dropped.

Flo used her forefinger to gently tickle under her chin. 'Eeh, what's that look for? Have I said sommat wrong?'

'I hate that dress. The welfare bought it for me to wear to me dad's funeral.'

'Well then, I bet he looks down on you with pride every time you wear it. If I were you, I'd wear it specially for him as often as you can, afore you grow out of it.'

Kathy brightened. 'D'yer really thinks as he looks down on me?'

'Course he does. He's not going to stop watching over you, and you can talk to him, an' all. I do, to me mam and dad. It makes me feel better, even though I didn't know them. Have you a picture of your dad?'

'Aye, but it hurts to look at it.'

'To my mind, you wouldn't be any kind of a daughter if it didn't. But that's no reason to hide him away as if he were never here, is it? Get it out from wherever you keep it and give it pride of place on that dresser there. Then I can get to know him, an' all.'

'I wish you'd known me dad, Flo, and I wish you were me mam, an' all.'

This touched Flo. She had to swallow hard to compose herself. Fussing over applying her lipstick helped. You couldn't cry with your mouth wide open. Once that was done, she felt more composed. 'I can be your big sister, lass. Will that do?'

'Aye, that'll be grand. Can I tell folk?'

'I don't see why not. It's none of their business anyroad. Reet, get dressed afore I go without you. Now, where's your dad's special dress?'

'I like it being called that. I'll get it.'

'Good. Once you have it on, I'll try to sort out that mop of yours. You look like you've been pulled through a hedge backwards.'

This had Kathy giggling. Then she became serious again. 'Why don't you have a picture up of your mam and dad, Flo?'

'I haven't got one, lass. By, if I did, it would be up there like a shot. Folk have told me about how they looked, and it appears I take after me dad. I have his nose anyroad.'

'I like your nose. It makes you special.'

'Ta, lass. Now, are you going to talk all morning, eh?' Flo threw a pillow at Kathy. She dodged it, but her squeals of delight warmed Flo's heart.

Coming out of Timothy White's on New Market Street, where Flo had bought a suitcase and had handed in Mr Leary's prescription, she saw Roland. On spotting her, he waved his arms. 'There's a friend of mine, Kathy. I won't be a minute. You wait here for me. But don't move, there's a good lass.'

'Hello there. I've been to Mrs Leary's and she said you were in town. I thought I'd come in on the off-chance of finding you, but I didn't think I'd be this lucky.' Roland caught hold of Flo and kissed her cheek. 'You look lovely. Going somewhere special?'

'Ta, I do me best. Naw, nowhere special, just shopping and maybe to the flicks, if there's a suitable film on for me little friend over there.'

'Oh? I might join you. But first, I have news. There's an interview arranged. Simon telephoned me. Shall we go for a cup of tea?'

'Yes, I'd like that. I'll just pop over and get Kathy. I don't know if I mentioned her to you before, but she lives at Mrs Leary's with me.'

'I see you are preparing for leaving.' Roland nodded at the suitcase Flo had bought. The three of them were sitting at a table in a teashop next to the Odeon.

'It was on offer. A real bargain, so I snatched it up. I wanted to be prepared. Thou knaws, even if this doesn't come off, I'll still have to think of moving. I'll look for some kind of work to help with the war effort.'

A little hand came into hers. She squeezed it and wiped a crumb from Kathy's cheek, smiling down at her. 'By the way, Roland, Kathy don't just live with me, she's me new sister now.'

'Lucky Kathy, I say.'

Kathy grinned. It didn't take much to lift the little lass's spirits.

'Really though, Flo, I do think this is going to come off. As I said, I've heard from Simon, and the interview is a week on Wednesday. Is that all right?'

'Aye, it's grand. Eeh, I can't wait, and yet I'm scared out of me wits.'

'You'll be fine. Simon will brief you. Though I'm worried about him. He insists he's all right, but he sounded funny. He put it down to a couple of visits he's made to the dentist, said he's had to have a tooth out and a new one put in on a denture, and he can't talk properly at the moment. But there was something else. I can't put my finger on it. Anyway, I'm going down to London at the weekend. He can get a little time off, but said he doesn't feel like travelling up here, so I'll stay in his apartment with him. We wondered if you would come?'

'Oh, I don't knaw what to say. Where would I stay? Eeh, London – by, I'd be lost down there. And what about the air raids, won't you be scared?'

'Lucinda has an apartment above Simon's and she'll put you up. She's happy for you to stay until after the interview. Simon's staying at home until Tuesday, and he'd like to spend some time with you, help you to prepare. As for the bombing, Simon's area has been badly hit, but his street, Guildford Road, has mostly been untouched. Life has to go on, and he has a great air-raid shelter. And if we are in the local pub, there's always Vauxhall Underground, which is under a mile from there. It's super-fun getting around in the dark during the blackout, and there's plenty of warning if there is an air raid.'

'If you're sure, then I'd love to come and it would settle me some, to spend time with Simon afore the interview.'

'Jolly good. Simon will be thrilled. I'll pick you up at eleven on Saturday. The train leaves at eleven-thirty. We have to change a couple of times, so won't get down to London till about three in the afternoon. It'll be a good experience for you. Especially on the Underground, as you will no doubt use that quite a bit if you work at Bletchley.'

Two days had been and gone since she and Roland had met in Leeds, and now Flo couldn't believe how quickly the four hours it had taken to get to London had passed. Roland was good company. They did a crossword together on the

122

journey – something she'd never done before, but she found the cryptic clues easy to solve. The moment they met up with Simon, Roland was full of her talent. 'Simon, you just have to swing it for Flo. She has a brain that can cope with everything that yours can. I bet even you won't beat her in solving crosswords.' His jolly greeting landed like a heavy brick as they both took in Simon's appearance. 'Whatever's the matter? My dear fellow, you look... Hey, is that – have you had a black eye? What happened?'

'It's a long story.' Simon shook Roland's hand, holding it longer than was necessary, then he hugged Flo to him. Her concern for him stopped her feeling embarrassed as she hugged him back. As they came out of the hug, he said, 'Let's go to the pub, and we can go back to mine after. I have something to tell you.'

Flo could feel her temper rising as she listened to what had happened to Simon, and how he thought a girl in his office and her lover were responsible. 'Eeh, Simon, how can folk act like that towards another? It beggars belief.'

'It does, to nice people like you, Flo, but I've been the brunt of Kitty Hamlin's spite all week and it's beginning to get me down.'

For all the world, Flo thought Simon was about to cry. She could see that Roland was longing to hold him but dared not, so she took Simon in her arms.

'Is this your floozy then, queer-boy?'

Simon let Flo go and jumped up. 'Kitty? What are you doing here?'

Flo stared at the young woman and had the

impression she was looking at a cat, even down to the green eyes. She was small for someone who could spit venom, very fashionable and held a cigarette in a long holder. She blew a lungful of smoke towards Flo. 'What are you staring at?'

'I've not got words to describe it. We don't have things like you up north.'

'Cheeky bitch, I'll have your eyes out.'

'I don't think so. If you make a move to hurt my friend, I will report you to the MPs for unseemly behaviour.' Simon's voice shook as he said this, but recovered and sounded authoritative as he nodded, adding, 'Now, what are you doing here – have you followed me?'

'Think a lot of yourself, don't you? Why should I follow you? Unless you're up to something you shouldn't be. I just happen to be here with my friend.'

Flo was shocked to realize this woman probably *had* followed Simon. But why?

'Well, if you'll excuse us, we're moving on. Goodbye, Miss Hamlin.' Simon took hold of Flo's arm and steered her away. Roland followed them out.

Once outside, Simon released a telling sigh. Flo could tell that all the worry in the world was weighing on him and felt glad she'd agreed to come to London with Roland. She dreaded to think what would have happened if the woman had seen Simon greet Roland on his own. As it was, Flo had seen them touch hands under the table. She prayed Kitty hadn't seen that, too.

For a moment Flo thought Roland was going to put his arm around Simon as he raised his arm, but he lowered it again without touching him. Flo felt pity at this. They were afraid even to express their concern for each other in public, but she could hear the feeling in Roland's voice when he spoke. 'Don't worry, Simon, she saw nothing that she could use against you. Come on, don't let her spoil our couple of days. Let's go to your apartment. Is Lucinda in?'

'No, not yet, Roland, she'll be home later. She's had to work.'

Roland looked disappointed. Flo realized that he wanted time on his own with Simon and had hoped Lucinda would take her to her apartment, out of the way. He obviously hadn't expected Lucinda to be working. Though, as a journalist, she did work long and unsettled hours. Thinking to ease the situation, Flo offered to make herself scarce.

'Look, take me back to the apartment with you, so that I can leave me case and know where it is, then I'll explore a little. Eeh, I'd love to see a bit of London. Didn't you say as there were a bridge over the Thames that's not far from Simon's, Roland? By, it'd be grand to see that.'

Flo saw them both visibly relax for a moment, though Simon constantly looked over his shoulder as they walked towards his apartment. She wondered how they lived like this. Always afraid. To her mind, it wasn't fair. They were who they were and, to her, what they did in private was their own business.

Flo stood in wonderment looking over the bridge, gazing down at the water. When she looked up,

125

she could see boats of all shapes and sizes, and cranes that looked like giraffes lining the banks of the Thames. But her enjoyment was tinged with sadness. The destruction she saw all around tore at her. And she wondered, what must it feel like to have your house bombed out and all your possessions destroyed?

A woman came towards her pushing a pram loaded with what looked like household goods. Flo could see a battered saucepan hanging from the side and towels balancing on top. Two young, scruffy-looking boys trailed behind her, each lugging two heavy bags. They looked a picture of dejection, and Flo's heart went out to them. 'Hello, Missus. Can I help you with sommat?'

'Where you from? You don't sound like a Londoner, lav.'

'I'm visiting from up north. Me name's Flo. You look worn out. I were thinking you could do with a bit of an 'and.'

'Ta, but unless yer can bring me man back from France and build up me bombed-out house, I don't see what you can do, lav.'

'Where are you heading for? Eeh, that's a load and a half. If it's not far, I could perhaps take a bag off each lad and carry it for them.'

'I'm going ter me mother's – that's if you can call her a bleedin' mother. Swilling the drink back from morning to night, she is. Gawd lav us. How we're going to manage in her one-up and one-down, I don't know, but it's all I have. And beggars can't be choosers.'

This shocked Flo, but touched her at the same time. 'I'm sorry for your plight, lass. We've had

126

no bombing where I'm from. But we're sending down what we can, to help you all. They collect stuff at the church on a Saturday afternoon. Then it's sent to the Sally Army down here.'

'That's kind of yer. I've 'ad stuff from the Sallies. Well, nice to have met yer, but I have to get on. And you should get back to where you're staying. They say it's going to be a clear night, so they'll be over with a few more bombs for us. I'm only a couple of streets away now.'

'I'm staying in that direction. Let me give you a hand. Eeh, I've never seen the likes of what I've seen around here. I'm reet sorry for you all.'

'Ta, lav. Me name's Pauline. And if you're going in the same direction, I'd be grateful if you would take a bag off each of me boys; poor mites are done in.'

'I'm Flo, pleased to meet you.'

To Flo, Pauline looked around forty years old, but judging by the age of her boys, one probably about six and the other seven or eight, she thought Pauline was more likely to be in her early thirties. Small and with untidy, greasy hair, which Flo assumed was not as dark as it looked, she wore a long brown coat that was several sizes too big and was held together by a piece of string.

The bags Flo took from the boys held clothes. A smell of smoke came from them and she could see those on the top were charred.

They walked a little way in silence, passing bombed-out homes with folk rummaging amongst the ruins looking for whatever they could salvage. A couple of times they had to walk in the road, as rubble blocked the pavement.

Pauline told Flo that they'd hardly had any respite from the bombing for weeks. 'It's hell when it starts, so make sure you get to a shelter, lav.'

Flo's throat constricted. She'd been daft to come. But then this woman and her lads had no choice – they were here, and that was that. She had to show as much courage as they did. Besides, Roland had said Simon had a good shelter, so she'd be safe.

These thoughts went through her mind as they passed by the end of Simon's street. Not many yards further on, Pauline turned left into a road that could have been a million miles away, as the contrast between Simon's house and this little house, which stood on the end of a long row of similar cottage-type houses, was stark.

Flo looked at the torn nets, dirty windows, overgrown path and paint-peeling front door and her heart filled with pity. She turned to Pauline and asked, 'Would you let me give you some money, Pauline? I haven't got much, but I don't need it. Me ticket home's paid for. It might help you a bit.'

'I couldn't, I–'

'Eeh, don't say that. I want you to have it. Here.' Taking from her purse the five bob she'd brought with her, Flo pressed it into Pauline's hand. Pauline closed her fingers around it, before looking up at Flo. Silent tears ran down her face. Flo hugged her impulsively. 'I have to go now, lass. Will you be all right?'

'I will, and ta. You don't know what you've done for me, lav, cos me mum won't have anything in, and this'll feed me kids, till I get sorted.'

'Can I come and see you if I visit me friend again? I'd like to see how you're getting on, and I could bring sommat from the church collection of clothes and stuff for the boys.'

Pauline just nodded. Her hand reached out to take Flo's. Flo held the cold, small hand in hers and looked down into Pauline's tired dark-brown eyes for a moment, before saying goodbye. When she got to the end of the street, Flo turned. Pauline was still looking towards her and raised her hand to wave. Flo had to swallow her tears as she waved back. Pauline looked so forlorn. Flo wanted to run back to her, but she knew there was no more she could do, so she made herself turn the corner and walk towards Simon's street.

She'd been gone a good hour, so Simon and Roland should be expecting her back now. The warmth she'd felt from helping Pauline stayed with her, and she vowed that she would try to find a way of helping more of these Londoners. If she got the job at Bletchley, Roland had said she could easily get a train here. Well, that's what she'd do in her spare time – she'd volunteer to help the victims of the bombing. Feeling better, she quickened her step. It was beginning to get dark. Her heart pounded at the thought of being in a bombing raid herself. But, as she'd thought before, if Londoners could do it, then so could she.

Not two hours had passed before Flo thought she would eat her words. They were enjoying the lovely meal that she and Lucinda had cooked and had brought down to Simon's apartment.

Lucinda had got hold of some scrag-ends. They'd scraped the meat from the bones and minced it, before cooking the meat in a saucepan. Lucinda had added all manner of spices and herbs, some of which Flo had never seen or heard of before. They'd topped the mixture with fluffy potato and had managed to make a delicious gravy, by making stock from the bones and adding a cornflour paste and gravy salts. But what gave it a special touch was how, when Lucinda carefully portioned it into the white bone-china bowls, she put a sprig of parsley from the garden on top of each portion. Flo had never seen anyone do anything like that to food, and it looked lovely.

Simon's apartment was bigger than Lucinda's, as the ground floor of the original house extended further out into the garden than the upstairs. Simon had two bedrooms and what he called a sitting room, but Flo would have called a parlour, plus a dining room. Lucinda also had two bedrooms, but her sitting room and dining room were all in one. Both apartments were decorated and furnished with a lot more taste than Roland's house, with cream being the main background colour, and nothing garish – just soft blues and golds, with beautiful carved furniture in highly polished mahogany. But, to Flo, nothing could beat the luxury of taking a bath without the hassle of fetching in the tin tub from outside, filling it with kettles of boiling water and pails of cold, then erecting the partition by slinging a huge sheet over the clothes horse to give her some privacy. *Eeh, how the other half live!* She was loving it all.

But her enjoyment deserted her with the wail of the siren.

'Bugger! Oh well, here we go – nothing to worry about, Flo. Go with Lucinda and get yourself some blankets. Did you put some flasks up, just in case, Lucinda?'

'Yes. Now come on, Flo. Hitler waits for no one.'

Fear had rooted Flo to the spot. Roland lifted her physically, before she could move. *Oh God, it's really going to happen. The Germans are coming!* She wanted to scream her terror, but the practical way the others just got on with it prevented her and reassured her.

It was cold in the Anderson shelter in the garden, but they huddled together and Flo soon began to feel warm. The chatter was lively, and Simon had brought a bottle of whisky with him. Flo took a big gulp, when offered, even though it made her choke. She needed some Dutch courage.

'Don't be afraid, Flo. It will get very noisy, but we're safe in here. Even if the house takes a direct hit, the roof of the shelter has been reinforced, so the rubble will only bury us and not flatten us, and the air-raid wardens will soon have us out.'

None of what Lucinda said comforted her. How could they all take this in their stride? But expecting the raid was nothing like experiencing it. Flo had never known such noise. Her ears hurt with it. Every wind-whistling bomb took an age to land, and she thought each one would hit them. But worse than that were the screams of agony. Every fibre of her wanted to run to help

131

those stricken, and yet she knew she wouldn't be able to move a limb. On and on it went, till she wanted to beg them to stop.

Lucinda's arm came through hers. Somehow there was more comfort in Lucinda showing fear than there had been in her stoic courage. Disengaging her arm, Flo took Lucinda's hand with her left one and put her other arm around Lucinda's shoulders. They huddled like this with their heads down for the rest of the raid. Flo had never felt more bonded with anyone in her life than she did going through this hell on earth with Lucinda.

When all had been quiet for half an hour, Simon lit his torch and put his head out. 'Well, the jolly old house is still standing. Come on, let's get inside.'

'Eeh, Simon, shouldn't we try to help those as have been hit?'

'Not a good idea, Flo. We would only hinder things. The volunteers are well trained and organized.'

'But surely we can offer hot drinks or sommat?'

'I've never thought of that. I suppose we can. Wait here, while Roland and I go along to the nearest bomb damage and ask the wardens.'

To Flo, the next hour was the best and the worst she'd ever spent in her life. She loved giving help and comfort, distributing drinks that she and Lucinda made with the many kettles of boiling water Simon and Roland ferried from the house. Everyone who could help did so, supplying cups, teaspoons and some even a packet of tea, a precious possession. Most of the tea was

132

served black with little sugar in it, but it didn't matter. It was as welcome as it could be.

But though all of this warmed Flo's heart and made her feel needed, the extent of the damage, loss and injury cut her in two. She hoped the job Simon had lined up for her really would help the war effort. But more than that, she hoped it would help to bring the war to an end.

9

Molly

A Worse Fate

Molly never thought she'd be so glad of the many air raids happening night after night as she had been these last couple of weeks. The man she was being saved for hadn't been able to get away. From what she could glean from the conversations held in front of her, he was a doctor in his middle years. The thought of him repulsed her, and each day she prayed that somehow David would find her and rescue her.

She was in a flat above a tailor's shop in Soho. But she knew, from what the other girls told her, that the shop was just a cover for the real business that went on here, and enabled gentlemen to look as if they were buying clothes or having a fitting, when instead they slipped through the curtains at the back of the shop and up the stairs to the flat.

There were five girls in residence. They slept in one room they called 'the dormitory', with two double beds in it. Being the new girl, Molly found that she had to sleep at the bottom of the bed, with the feet of the two at the top digging into her and kicking her throughout the night. Not that she would sleep anyway. That came in the daytime when the others were active, having been sent out to tout for business or entertaining clients in one of the other four rooms she'd been shown. These were called 'boudoirs' and were decorated and furnished in rich creams and purples and hung with mirrors. Each housed a huge bed and had a washroom of its own.

She dreaded the day she would have to go to one of the boudoirs.

At first she'd spent her days and nights weeping and begging to be released, as well as hoping that her dad or David, or even Foggy, would come. But there was only so much crying a body could do and only so much the others would tolerate, before they showed they'd had enough by telling her to 'shut the fuck up'.

This had been a turning point for Molly. She realized that her companions were all she had, and she didn't want to alienate them. Making her mind up on this made her stronger.

Hope lived in finding out which girl was Phyllis's mate. The last two days had felt special, as she became close to Ruby. As Phyllis had said, Ruby was in a poor state – thin, so that you could see her ribs and her shoulder bones sticking out. She was often dirty and unkempt, with blackened teeth. Ruby was sent out into the streets on a daily basis. She never entertained in the house, as the other more wholesome girls did, and when she returned she incurred Eva's wrath if she didn't have anything to cough up.

Molly felt overwhelming pity for her, but also saw in Ruby a possible way of getting a message out. They sat together on the bed, the only two left in the dormitory now. 'Ruby, would you help me?'

'I can't. I'd get me bleedin' neck wrung. I'm sorry for yer, but don't ask me to be a party to getting yer out of here.'

'Please. Me boyfriend has money. His name's David. He'll pay you. He'll pay you enough so that you can get away from here. He'll help you. We're unofficially engaged, and he must be desperate to find me.'

'I'm sorry. If you knew what them lot were capable of, yer wouldn't ask me.'

'Well, do you ever see Phyllis while you're out and about?'

Ruby cringed away from her. 'Are yer a spy for them, eh? How come you ain't working yet? What're yer doing here, anyway?'

'No. I told you, I used to work with Phyllis, and she told me about you. She's desperate to help you – you could go to her. She knows David; she'd take him a message. Please, Ruby, I beg of you.'

Ruby was quiet for a minute.

'Wouldn't you like to get out of here, Ruby? I promise you, if you help me, I'll help you.'

Still Ruby didn't speak.

135

The sound of someone coming had them both looking towards the door. Caught as if in a trap with no escape, they remained still. As the door knob turned, Ruby said, 'I'll see what I can do.'

Relief mingled with Molly's fear. Eva stood in the doorway, and her face showed her pleasure. 'Well, Missy, yer time has finally bleedin' come. Get that nylon gown on that I hung in the cupboard for yer, and be quick. The doctor is about to make you into a woman, and I'm about to have a big payday.'

The door slammed shut. Molly looked at Ruby, and her fear must have shown in her face.

'Don't struggle, lav. It ain't worth it, and it makes it hurt all the more. Besides, he cuts up rough if yer do. He's even been known to slash a couple of girls, thinks he's doing a bleedin' operation. But if yer sweet to him and let him have his way, then he can be good to yer. Act the baby-girl with him. Tell him yer afraid – he likes that. He likes to coax yer, win yer over, but not fight with yer. That makes him mad.'

'I – I can't. Oh, Ruby, please help me. I can't let him.'

'Yer bleedin' have no choice, girl. Pull yerself together and get it done. We all 'ad to, and you're no different.'

Resigned to her fate, Molly got off the bed and went to the cupboard. The pure-white gown mocked her. Flimsy and sheer, it would hide nothing. With it there was a pair of white silk, long-legged pants with lace frills around the edge of the legs and a snow-white bra. Molly shuddered.

'Come on, I'll help yer get ready. I promise yer, if you act all shy but willing, it'll be all right. Yer might even enjoy it, as he has some tricks, does the doctor. He's an artist in making love, as long as you don't make him lose his temper.'

Ruby made it sound as though Molly was in for a treat, but her heart was full of dread.

'He might even seduce yer by offering yer some opium. Take it. You'll love the effect and nothing will matter to yer – you'll be floating in a lovely dream. There'll be no pain, just wonderful sensations.'

Opening the door to the boudoir, Molly noticed a sweet, pungent smell of smoke. Part of her felt glad about this, for maybe she was to get the opium treatment, something she'd been hoping for since Ruby had told her about it.

Her heart banged against her chest at the sound of his voice. 'Come in, my dear.' There was a tone of aristocracy about it, as if the King himself was waiting for her. This increased her shyness. She didn't dare look up. Didn't want to see the hateful man who had bought her and would do to her what she'd only ever wanted David to do.

He was close now. She could see his bare feet, his calves and the bottom edge of his paisley dressing gown. He had nice feet. His toenails were manicured and shone with cleanliness.

His hand lifted her face. 'Let me look at you. Don't be afraid.'

Molly looked up into eyes as dark as David's. A surprisingly handsome face, with a gentleness about it that she hadn't expected. He looked a lot

137

younger than she'd thought he would.

'There, I'm not so bad, am I?'

His smile showed even, white teeth. He smelt of the sweet smoke and his eyes glazed over as he gazed into hers.

Molly wanted to claw at him and say that he was bad, evil and that she wanted to kill him, but his face changed in an instant as if he detected this in her. 'I'm not going to have trouble with you, am I?'

The evil in his tone frightened her. Suddenly Ruby's advice seemed her only path. No one was going to save her from this. Ruby had even intimated that some girls had ended up dead. She wanted to live. 'N-no, I'm just frightened.'

His arm came round her and he pulled her close. 'Don't be, my beautiful one. I will look after you like a daddy would.'

This repulsed her. The last thing she wanted to think of was her dad. But there was some comfort for her in the way he cuddled her as if she was a little girl. She leaned on him as a feeling of acceptance came over her. Tears cascaded down her face and yet she wasn't consciously crying.

'Now, now. You can sit on my knee, and I will make you all better.'

Bile rose to her throat. She swallowed it down. Coughed as it rasped her throat with its acid taste.

'Here, baby, have a drink of water.'

Molly took the crystal glass and drank the refreshing cold water.

'Good girl.'

Within a few moments, something had changed.

138

She felt relaxed and went willingly with him to the huge red velvet chair that stood next to the bed. Sitting on his knee, she felt the hardness of him. But somehow it didn't matter. Her head felt light. Her stomach muscles clenched with pleasure and expectation.

'Good girl.'

The doctor's hands began to roam over her. The sensation was nice and she wanted to respond, but through the haze she remembered Ruby's words: 'Act all shy but willing – he'll love it.'

Molly knew at that moment she did want him to love it. But why? Why did she want this? What was happening to her?

When his hand pulled up her gown, her fear came back. She clutched the hem in an attempt to prevent him from being able to get his hands further up her thighs. He slapped her hand away. 'Naughty girls are punished.' His face became ugly, his eyes evil. Ruby's words came to her again: 'Don't struggle, lav. It ain't worth it, and it makes it hurt all the more. Besides, he cuts up rough if yer do.'

As his hand rose above her, Molly pleaded, 'No, please. I'm sorry – I'm scared. I've never done it before. They say it hurts. I don't want to be hurt.'

The doctor softened and his face relaxed again. 'Don't be afraid. I'll be very gentle.' He stood back up and then sat down in the chair. His hand reached for the hashish pipe. The air intensified with the scent she'd detected when she'd entered the room. 'Come back on my knee. I have something for you.'

Relief came to Molly. Ruby had said she would not really know what was happening, if he gave her the drug.

When she sat on his knee, she didn't feel him this time and wondered if her refusal had taken away his ardour. She hoped he wouldn't get it back.

He took a long drag of the pipe. A bubbling sound came from the bowl beneath it. Releasing the smoke, he lay back, before handing it to her. 'Now, have you ever smoked a cigarette?' She nodded. 'Good, right, suck in a little. Breathe it in deep into your lungs.'

Molly did this willingly, hoping it would take her into a world where she didn't know what was happening. The first intake made her cough, but the next lifted her, as if taking her soul from her body. The sensation was one of euphoria. The fear that she'd felt left her.

Molly's head felt heavy, but not painful. Her body, she knew, had been through sensations that she'd loved and wanted to experience again. Relief made her want to cry. Through the fog that clouded her brain she justified what had happened. *I had no choice.*

But as some awareness seeped into her, her mind showed her the true horror of it all. She'd been coerced into consenting to behave in a way that was alien to her. A sob escaped from her, but she swallowed hard. She mustn't disturb the doctor.

The weight of him leaning on her body told her

he must still be asleep. Fighting against a still-fuzzy and tangled sense of not being able to coordinate or plan what to do, she eased herself away from him. The only thing registering was that she had to get out of here.

Once off the bed, she turned to look at him. Shock smacked her fully awake and aware as she stared into the unseeing eyes, registered the slack mouth, saw the waxen, unmoving face.

A scream erupted from her that hurt her own ears and rasped her throat.

The door opened and Eva came through. 'For Christ's sake, what the bleedin' hell's up with you, girl, eh? You were having the time of your life – we all heard yer. What's happened?'

Shame washed over Molly at this, but was replaced by fear as Eva's voice rose even louder. 'Christ! H-he's d-dead. DEAD! What? What have yer done, eh?'

Molly couldn't react. A violent tremble shook every part of her.

'Gus! Gus...'

Gus appeared as if he'd already been on his way. Lofty was just behind him.

'Bleedin' Norah, he's dead, Gus – he's gone.'

Gus didn't react. Eva's voice took on urgency. 'Do sommat, Gus, do sommat!'

As if someone had cranked up his mental capacity and given him authority, Gus strode over to Molly. 'Get out of here.'

She scampered away. As she reached the landing she heard Gus order Lofty to dress the doctor, then wrap him in the bed sheet.

Eva's shrieking voice came to her: 'I want his

141

wallet first. From what we all heard, he had a bloody good time with her. Dead or not, he's bleedin' paying for that.'

Gus laughed, a sick sound that turned Molly's stomach. His head appeared round the door. Molly gasped at the raw anger she saw in his face, but as he neared her, this slipped into a mask of lust.

His tongue moistened his dry lips as he approached her.

Molly cringed away, her nakedness exposing her vulnerability. Gus's sour breath wafted over her as he leaned towards her. 'Later, girl. My time is coming. I'll make you squeal louder than you did for the doc. I'm bleedin' telling yer, you ain't had nothing yet.'

She pushed him away and ran into the dormitory. Ruby was still there, fear etched on her face, but she opened her arms. Molly went into them and sobbed her heart out.

When she'd calmed a little, Ruby helped her to the bathroom. While she washed Molly and helped her to dress, she talked of everything and anything.

Molly eventually found her voice. 'Ruby, please help me. Please.'

Ruby was silent for a moment. When she spoke, some hope trickled into Molly. 'I ain't promising anything. But give me the address of your man.'

'Oh, Ruby, thanks. Thanks. You won't regret it. I promise you. He'll get this place closed and those monsters brought to justice.'

'He won't. And you shouldn't let him try. They have people in their pay – people you'd never

142

dream of. No one can touch them. Not even the King himself would try. Your man needs to get us out of it, take us somewhere we can't be found. That's the only way.'

Molly's stomach clenched as a thought came to her. 'Do you think they would hurt David, if they caught him?'

'Course they would. Slit his bleedin' throat soon as look at him, they would. I'll make him aware of the danger.'

'No! No, he'll come after me – you won't be able to stop him. I couldn't bear him to be hurt. Look, go and see Phyllis. Get her to go and see me dad.'

'But I thought you didn't trust your dad. Anyway, that'll put Phyllis in the firing line.'

Molly didn't trust her dad, but for one moment she thought he might help her. He'd refused to let them take her, hadn't he? They'd had to knock him out, in order to get her away. He might just be angry that she'd gone missing. These thoughts left her as quickly as they'd come. Despairing now, she sat heavily on the bed. 'It's hopeless. I just can't see a way out.'

'Look, it were obvious that it weren't as bad as yer thought, now were it? Everyone could hear 'ow much yer enjoyed it. If you play yer cards right, you could have a decent life in the future. You've got what men want, and Eva ain't going to let that get spoilt. She was standing outside the door practically rubbing her hands together. You could almost see the pound signs rolling around her head. She'll keep the likes of Gus off yer. Your best bet is to make up to her. If you're to get a ticket to anywhere, it's got to come from her.'

Molly nodded, for she could see the truth of this.

'Let them do what they have to, to get rid of the body. Be pliable when they tell you the part you have to play, if there's any questioning from the police. Though I doubt that'll happen. With Gus wanting the doctor dressed, I'd say that he wasn't planning on dumping him in the Thames, but meant to take him back to his own home and let him be found there. He probably copped it with a heart attack or sommat. Anyway, once it's all sorted, let Eva think you're ready to do things her way. She'll be your best mate. You'll have her eating out of yer bleedin' hand.'

Something about all this made sense to Molly. Ruby knew these gangsters better than anybody. She'd already learned herself that no one did anything without Eva's say-so. She also knew that no one escaped here, or if they did – according to the talk of the girls over the last week – their bodies were found floating in the Thames. She didn't want that. She wanted to survive, to go to David. To live happily with him, if he'd still have her, and forget all this ever happened.

Feeling resigned to her fate helped to settle her. 'Thanks, Ruby. I'll do what you say. And if it's ever in my power to help you, I will. I promise. Even if it's just getting you some extra food to build you up. Let's see how it goes, eh? Somehow I'll turn all this to me advantage. We're Londoners, girl. Never say die, eh? After all, a bomb might get you tomorrow and you could end up as worm pie.'

'What? Well, I've never heard that one before. Ha, you're a funny one. But you know, I've got faith in yer, Molly. You've got brains. You've been educated. Yer can tell that, with how you speak. God gave you that advantage for a reason. It's time you put it to good use and bettered yourself. Even if it is in a whorehouse.'

Molly couldn't answer this. She felt both acceptance and determination. And in that moment she made her mind up that she would beat Eva, Gus and Lofty at their own game.

Standing up and going to the window, she felt a moment of doubt. Everything she'd wanted to give to her David had been taken by another man. And she'd been willing. No matter that she'd been under the influence of hashish, she'd enjoyed it. She'd learn how to do it well so that she became sought-after, and she'd then be able to pull some strings with Eva.

There was nothing about her plan for Molly to relish, unless it was to think of it as a way out of this hellhole. Going back to Ruby, she asked. 'Have you ever been good at sex, Ruby? Can you give me some tips?'

'I was one of the best. A long time ago, before I got badly beaten and left for dead by a punter, then Eva lost interest in me. She treats me like a dog, but I have no choice. I have to warn you, Molly, once they have you, it ain't easy to get away. They'll hunt you down and kill you. I'll teach you all yer need to know, girl. Use that, and your brains, to make everything better for yourself.'

It didn't seem something to thank Ruby for,

but Molly did. While doing so, she wished with all her heart that she didn't have to take this path, and she wished it was her David she was asking to teach her. But that wasn't going to happen, and thoughts like that would only undo her resolve. She'd put David out of her mind. Out of her life. She had to, but maybe one day... Maybe.

10

Flo

A Baptism of Discovery

With six weeks of training behind her, during which time she'd had a crash course on touch-typing as well as physical fitness, Flo walked tall to the station in Glasgow with Wren Belinda Harper, her friend and companion, to begin the next leg of her journey.

Flo loved her uniform and felt a sense of importance and pride as others greeted them and looked at them in awe. Men dubbed their caps. Old ladies made remarks such as 'We'll beat them, with lassies like you hens on our side.' Children told them they looked lovely. And other military personnel saluted them, and they returned the formal greeting. Some of the salutes were accompanied by a wink of appreciation, until Flo felt like a heroine who had single-handedly won the war.

But the war wasn't won and, though she still didn't know what her part in winning it would be, all of this was reinforcing her feeling that she would carry it out to the very best of her ability. Her next step was special training in London. A two-week stint and then, if that went well, she would finally go to Bletchley: to do what? Her imagination gave her the role of a spy. What else could it be? Secret work carried out in a remote mansion? It had to be that.

Belinda pulled her out of her thoughts: 'Penny for them?'

'Oh, I were just wondering what we were being trained for, and though the thought terrified me at first, I was hoping we are to become spies.'

'Yes, I rather fancy that. Clandestine operations behind enemy lines. I'd be good at that.'

'Eeh, it'd be grand.' But as Flo said this spontaneously, worry surfaced in her. She really must try to drop her northern sayings. Her way of speaking had grated on the nerves of her training officer more than once, and it had almost landed Belinda in trouble for speaking up for her.

It had been on a particularly difficult day. A cross-country run in wet, cold weather. Trying to cheer everyone, Flo had chatted away until the officer had criticised her: 'For goodness' sake, how many times? It's up *the* mountain, not "up mountain".'

Belinda had become indignant and in a loud voice had said, 'Up mountain, or up *the* mountain, what does it matter? Girls from north, south, east and west are doing their best in the war effort, and Flo is doing more than most!'

Flo had feared for Belinda when the officer had said, 'Are you talking to me, Wren Harper?' But then her tone had softened and she'd said, 'As you were, both of you.'

A few minutes after resuming their trek up the hill the officer had caught up with them and, in a much softer tone, had told Belinda, 'Actually, I agree with you, Wren Harper. Wren Kilgallon is putting in a really good effort – well done, Kilgallon.'

When later on the officer had sent for Flo, her nerves had jangled like church bells in her stomach as she'd waited outside the office, thinking that she'd blown it and that Simon would be disappointed in her. But the interview had been a pleasant one.

'I want to apologize, Wren Kilgallon. I've been rather hard on you. It may have seemed that I was singling you out. I was, actually. You have excelled in everything, and several times I had to put you under pressure as part of testing not only your ability, but also your temperament, as you are required for a special type of work. I don't know what that is, but I had a remit to work to. I will be sending an exemplary report to my seniors. You have passed all I could throw at you, in a commendable way. Well done, and good luck. You leave tomorrow for London.'

Thinking of this, Flo asked Belinda, 'What d'yer suppose the next step is? Eeh, I'm finding it all grand.'

'I wouldn't agree with you on it all being grand, as you put it, Flo, but I must confess I'm curious myself.'

'By, Belinda, I wish I could talk like you. I knaw as it were a test, but that constant picking up on me vowels and sayings did unnerve me. What this lot down in London'll make of me, I dread to think.'

'I think they will love you. Besides, I'm sure they will be more interested in your knowledge and aptitude, so just be your lovable self.'

It felt strange to be hearing this, or even to think of herself as mates with someone of Belinda's standing. Belinda's father was a scientist, but Flo suspected that her family were related to royalty or some such, with the way she spoke and the things she spoke of – like owning horses and having maids. Belinda had also told her that the family's 'pile', as she referred to her home, was in Kent and that part of their house had been requisitioned by the government to be used as billets for those training to be pilots. She'd made Flo laugh with the way she viewed this: 'Trust me to have left home by then, to study mathematics at Oxford. Imagine living in close proximity with all those males!'

Belinda was here now because she'd had a sudden urge to give up her studies for the time being and do something towards the war effort. She chose the Wrens because she wanted to go to sea, but it didn't seem likely that she would. If Flo knew anything, Belinda was heading for the same place as her, Bletchley Park. *Eeh, I hope so; it'll be grand to have her with me.*

Around them people jostled for a better position on the platform. A mother with young children tried to quieten them, but her efforts were lost as

149

the baby showed the good set of lungs she had. Trains chugged into the station, clouding them in smoke that stung Flo's nostrils and made her eyes run. A soldier clung to his girlfriend, while a tearful woman, probably his mam, patted his back. Flo longed for him to take just one arm from his girl and put it around the little woman.

At last the disembodied voice that echoed out announcements said the word 'London', after listing what sounded like a hundred other stops for the train now standing at platform one.

'Eeh, that's us, Belinda.' Flo's excitement increased as she picked up her rucksack and surged forward with the rest of the crowd, but they didn't make much progress and found themselves with no seats. 'So much for being polite – they're like a herd of cattle!'

'Ha, I know I told you not many minutes since to be your lovable self, but I didn't mean to the point of letting everyone get on the train first, you goose.'

They laughed together as they settled down to sit on their rucksacks in the draughty corridor.

Flo's stomach rumbled almost as loudly as the train as it pulled out of the station. Standing up and rummaging in her rucksack, she found the sandwiches and flask that had been put inside for her.

'Don't eat it all at once, Flo. I know you have a huge appetite, but it's a very long way to London. That has to be your lunch, dinner and supper.'

'I'll just have a bite. I were that thrilled, and yet sad, to be leaving the camp that I couldn't eat much breakfast.'

'I know. It was sad to say goodbye to the others. I wonder where they'll all land up. Or where we will, for that matter. Special training in London. Sounds like it's a real possibility that we could be sent overseas as spies or something. That'd be top-hole.'

Flo just nodded. She'd long realized that she should say nothing about what she knew, which, though it was very little, was enough to make listening ears curious. She didn't want that to happen. Whatever took place at Bletchley, she knew it must be something very important, so she thought it best not to mention that the place even existed. She'd never even mentioned her friends Simon, Roland and Lucinda, in case knowing that she had friends of their standing had led to questions. This thought caused her to think of any free time she might get over the next two weeks. *It'd be grand if I got to see Lucinda while I'm in London. And Eunice – I wonder how Eunice's nurse's training is going; she were struggling when she last wrote.* Pauline came to her mind, too, and Flo thought of the day she'd met Pauline and helped her to her mam's with her pram and her young 'uns. She'd often worried about Pauline and decided she'd go along and catch up with her, if she got the chance.

Belinda cut into her thoughts. What she said felt as if she'd read Flo's mind. 'What are you thinking of doing if we have some free time in London, Flo?'

'I – I don't knaw.'

'I have a cousin who lives in Holland Park, she's a bit of a social animal, but great fun. I thought we could go and stay with her. She would love you, and she would certainly take us to the best shows.'

'No, ta. It's good of you, but I couldn't intrude. I've been to London afore, thou knaws. Me ex-tutor took me... I – I mean, a few of us. He wanted us to broaden our horizons.' She hated fibbing like this and decided to tell Belinda the truth about visiting Simon and Lucinda, if Belinda ever found out about Bletchley. But for now it was better not to mention anything that might lead her to slip up and mention it. 'Don't even say you've heard of the place,' Simon had said, and she couldn't let him down.

Bending the truth, Flo told Belinda about meeting Pauline during her free time on the trip with her tutor, and how she worried about her; and about Eunice, who'd been a handful at Mrs Leary's, but had turned out really well, once she was shown love. 'Anyroad, I intend to look them both up and see how they're faring.'

'I'll come with you. Meeting someone like Pauline, who's experienced the Blitz first-hand, and Eunice, who's changed her life around, will be top-hole.'

Her fear of not getting the chance to see Lucinda, if Belinda tagged along, and her indignation for Pauline and Eunice made Flo snap, 'They're not a sideshow, Belinda! They've both been emotionally hurt. Pauline had hardly owt left of her belongings, besides not having her husband to support her, as he's somewhere in France. And Eunice had been abused for years. She didn't trust anyone, and didn't know what it were like to be loved until she came to the house

152

where I was being looked after.'

'Oh, Flo, forgive me. I meant nothing like that. I did sound heartless, didn't I? I'm so sorry, old thing. You have the right name, you know: Florence. You take after your namesake in how you care about the less fortunate. It's part of why I love you.'

'Aw, I shouldn't have yelled you out. I'm sorry. I am a bit fierce, when it comes to defending them as have nowt. Of course you can come. But you have to be prepared for what you see, where Pauline's concerned; she don't exactly live in Buckingham Palace.'

'I think it best that I don't. I'll go and see my cousin and you can go on your mercy mission. How's that?'

Not wanting to protest, Flo just nodded.

The first few days in London flew by. On the evening of the third day Flo met up with Eunice. She'd managed to get a message to her, and Eunice had phoned the digs where Flo and Belinda were billeted in and arranged the visit.

'Eeh, Eunice lass, it's good to see thee. You look well, an' all.'

For a moment Flo felt worry enter her that all wasn't well for Eunice, as her response was a tight, forced smile. But within seconds Eunice widened it to her usual dazzling smile, which lit up her face. On seeing this, Flo relaxed.

'It's good to see you, an' all, Flo. Look at you: that uniform really suits you. You're here in training, aren't you? Anything you can talk about?'

They were sitting in a cafe across the road from

the hospital in Endell Street. 'Afraid not, as I don't knaw meself yet – probably some boring office job or another. I've had to learn to touch-type in double-quick time, so that tells you sommat.'

'How's life treating you, other than the war? Any young men on the horizon?'

'Naw. What about you?'

Again Flo had the feeling Eunice was skirting around something and keeping the conversation light. For a moment there was an awkwardness between them, until Flo brought up some memories of their time with Mrs Leary. Once more Eunice's smile lit up her lovely round face and put dimples in her cheeks. Her hair, always unruly, fell across her face. She brushed it back and the sunlight caught it. It wasn't a dissimilar colour to Flo's chestnut locks, only a little more ginger. 'They were the happiest times of my life, Flo. At least when I settled down. I gave you and Mrs Leary some hard times before then.'

'You did. But Mrs Leary understood, and she helped me to, so we got through it.'

The chatter went on and on in this vein. Flo became increasingly uncomfortable. 'Look, lass, there's sommat not reet with you. What is it?'

'Oh, nothing. Just tired. Air raids night after night, and a workload more than I'm trained for as yet. I just feel out of me depth. I'm having to catch up with schoolwork on the run, too, as I need qualifications in English... Oh, I don't know. Bitten off more than I can chew, I suppose.'

Happy with this, as she could relate to the feeling of being plunged into a strange world, Flo

154

suggested that they walk a little way in the direction of Flo's digs. 'That's if you have the time, of course?'

Once outside, Eunice linked arms with Flo. 'You know, although I made trouble, you were like a sister to me, and still are.'

'Ta, love. That's a compliment I've been paid twice now.' She told Eunice about Kathy.

'Bless her. I know how it feels, as you do, to be suddenly thrust into a home like none you've known and to try to settle. It's as if you're not worthy of it and someone will take it away from you.'

'Is that how it was for you?'

'Yes. I came from hell. Me mam didn't care about me. She knew what me dad was up to, but she was just relieved that he didn't want to bother her, once he started on me. And then there was the baby...'

This shocked Flo. 'What baby? Eunice? Oh naw.'

'Yes. Me dad made me pregnant. It was taken from me. Well, I was only a kid meself. But I saw it, and loved it. A little girl. She'd be ten now. I pray every day that she went to a good and kind couple who love her.'

Flo put her arm around Eunice and pulled her to her. 'Eeh, lass. I don't knaw what to say.'

Eunice straightened up and dried her eyes. 'There's nothing you can say. But *I* can. I want to thank you. Since knowing you, I've loved you deeply, Flo. And you've never let me down. Not even when I was a pain in the backside. Keep safe, Flo. And keep in touch.'

155

'Of course I will.' It was there again, that feeling Flo couldn't put her finger on. And the look that Eunice had given her when she'd told her she loved her. It was intense. *Oh, I don't knaw, nothing's like it was. I'm most likely imagining things.*

Once back in her digs, there was no time even to think about her meeting with Eunice. The siren sounding reminded her of what Eunice went through – as did all Londoners – night after night, and had been doing since early September. How did they cope? *How?* Gathering her things, Flo didn't relish another night in the cellar, even though the people who ran these digs had made it very comfortable. It felt, somehow, like a tomb to Flo. It was the not knowing what was happening above that caused this feeling, though Belinda kept her sane with tales of her life when she was a girl at boarding school. It seemed that Belinda got into all sort of scrapes, and most of them had Flo splitting her sides with laughter.

It was the following weekend, after a very strange but interesting week of learning about codes and methods of breaking them, and how messages were intercepted, when Flo stepped off the train at Vauxhall station and into the arms of the waiting Lucinda. Strange because nothing was said about why they would need the knowledge that the training centre had made them take on board. Nevertheless, Flo had found it all fascinating, as had Belinda. They'd even practised making up coded messages for each other to decipher.

'Come on then, tell me all you've been doing, old thing.' Lucinda held Flo away from her.

'Eeh, I wish I could. I'm bursting with information, but none of it is for anybody's ears. Just to say I'm enjoying every minute.'

'Well, that's something we can tell Simon. He's ringing tonight. He's really mad that he can't get time off to come and see you, but I'm not. I need you all to myself.'

This wasn't said in a jovial way, and Flo was hit by the same sensation she'd felt about Eunice. 'Are you all reet, Lucinda? You sounded a bit – eeh, I don't knaw, but you weren't yourself when you phoned. Is sommat up, lass?'

'Well... Look, let's go into the Victorian Tea Room. We can have a chat.'

Sensing that Lucinda had something to get off her chest, and that it might take some time, Flo worried they might not make it to Pauline's.

'Would you mind if we talked back at yours, Lucinda? Only I hoped I could make a call on the way. You remember that lass I told you of, the one I met on the bridge that day? I wanted to drop in on her and see how she were doing.'

'Yes, of course. Sorry, I'm so desperate to talk to someone. Look, I'll leave you at our street and go home and make us some tea there. I'll take your bag with me. Take your time... No, I mean be as quick as you can, or I might lose my nerve and not tell you.'

At this, Flo regretted putting Lucinda off, but if she didn't call on Pauline now, then her chance would be gone, as she had to catch a train early in the morning. She and Belinda only had twenty-four hours of freedom, and both had so much to pack into that time. They planned to meet at

157

Westminster tube station in the morning and take a taxi from there back to their training office to complete their training, before they were thrown into the wide world to do their war bit.

As she walked to Pauline's mother's house, Flo couldn't get Lucinda out of her mind. It worried her how poorly Lucinda looked. *By, what with her and Eunice, I feel as though I'm being torn in two.* She made her mind up to make her visit to Pauline a short one. Just as long as she knew how Pauline was and whether she needed anything, that's all that mattered.

Around her there had been further destruction: piles of rubble where once a building had stood, and other buildings with their guts torn from them, now looking for all the world as if they were begging her for help. Broken windows reflecting the sun gave the impression of tear-filled eyes. Blackened walls stood as if their spirit wasn't completely destroyed, even though smoke curled from their insides. The stench of broken sewage pipes mixed with that of the smoke and sulphur. Flo wriggled her nose against the foetid air. Her heart went out to those who were suffering so much.

How she'd become used to the air raids was a wonder, but in just a week of spending half of each night down the cellar, she had. Although one night had been different. She and Belinda had gone out to the pub just down the road, thinking they'd be back in plenty of time, but the raid had begun early and had caught them out. They'd run to a tube station and found they had a hundred or so Londoners for companions. A sing-song had started up and they'd joined in. She'd learned songs like 'Show me the way to go home' and 'Daisy, Daisy, give me your answer do'. *Ha, I can't remember the last time I enjoyed meself like that.*

The Salvation Army workers were down there with their huge lidded milk churns full of hot soup. The thought came to Flo that she'd never tasted anything so delicious in all her life, though part of her felt disloyal to Mrs Leary even for thinking this.

With Mrs Leary coming to her mind, Flo felt an ache in her heart. How she missed her and Kathy and Mr Leary. But it wouldn't be long now and she would be able to spend a couple of days with them. Her hand went to her pocket and felt the crumpled letter she'd received. She'd been given a PO Box-number address and had been told that all mail should be sent to it. She'd been warned that it would be opened and read, before it was passed on to her, as would her own mail to others, which had to be sent to the same address before it was forwarded.

Mrs Leary's letter, and one from Kathy, had been the first she'd received up in Glasgow, and that had been two weeks after they had been sent to her. Mrs Leary's had begged for news and told Flo how worried they all were about her. As soon as she could, she'd telephoned Roland and asked him to assure them both that she was fine and was really enjoying herself, and that she would write as soon as possible. She'd since written the promised letters. Both long, and both full of fibs. She'd woven a whole lot of funny tales around a pretend existence in an office where she said she processed orders for military clothing. She'd even made up colleagues she worked with, and told stories of their goings-on. Roland had been shown a letter by a laughing Mrs Leary, and the next time she'd phoned he'd told Flo that she had a gift for telling tales and he thought she should take up writing. 'Your imagination is quite something, Flo,' he'd said. 'You could write a book.'

'Eeh, stop taking the rise out of me,' she'd told him, but he'd become serious and told her he meant every word.

'Your letter to Kathy read like a children's story. You have a talent for it.' This had pleased her; she didn't know why. Thinking of Kathy now, she just wanted to run to her and gather her in her arms and felt pleased that the girl sounded settled and happy. Her letter was full of her school life, her friends and how she wanted to be a Wren, too, when she grew up. Mrs Leary had worked her magic once more.

Turning into Pauline's street, Flo was met with an astonished 'It ain't... It *is* you. You're back again then, girl? And look at you. That uniform suits you.' Pauline was standing leaning on her gate. Although she was alone, she didn't present a picture of sadness, which lifted Flo.

'Aye, I told you I'd come and look you up. I've been wondering how you're managing?'

'I'm doing all right. It's nice to see yer. Come in and have a cup of tea, girl. I've got me mum's place all shipshape, and she's been sober since I moved in, an' all. It's working out fine – we're company for each other.'

'By, that's good to hear. I've no time for tea, though. Sorry. Me mate's making me some, as we speak, and I promised her I'd not be long. I'm just glad as you're all right, lass.'

'Well, I ain't saying as it's a bed of roses, but we're muddling through, like the rest of them. And I heard from my Fred; he's doing fine. He misses us, but he has some good mates. Here, look, he sent me a photo of them.' Pauline fumbled in the pocket of her pinny and pulled out an envelope.

Flo looked at the group of soldiers in the photo, relaxing with a cigarette, and particularly at the one Pauline pointed out. 'By, he's a handsome fella – you must miss him. Are the kids doing all right, Pauline?'

'They are. They're as ragged-arsed as ever, but happy. We've had no hits in this street and that's settled them a bit. I wouldn't let them go away, like most did, but I've regretted it. Little one is a nervous wreck, but I couldn't be without them.'

Flo wondered at this. She thought of Kathy and knew she wouldn't want her to experience a bombing raid just so that she could keep her near, but then she hadn't given birth to her, so she didn't know how strong the pull to keep her with her might feel. 'Eeh, with how it's been, I can understand you regretting that. But young 'uns are resilient, they'll cope.'

'I know. I wish I could take them out of here, but stay with them – not leave them with strangers. A lot fetched their kids back, but some haven't seen them in over a year. I just couldn't bear that.'

'I'll ask me mate if she knaws of owt like that. There might be a scheme or sommat. She's a journalist and deals with all sorts. Anyroad, I'm sorry this was a short visit. When I'm here again, I'll come and visit you.' Putting her hand in her pocket, Flo brought out the five bob she'd been saving. 'Here, I've got this for you, as I've not been able to get the clothes and other things I promised. Get the kids a treat.'

'No. And I mean it this time, Flo. I took it last time because I was desperate, but me man's allowance is coming to me regular now, and with what me mum can tip up, we're doing all right. When I said me kids were ragged-arsed, it was just a saying we have for them getting themselves in a state. Not that they have much choice, when their playground is a bombsite. Now, give us a hug before you go.'

Hugging Pauline reminded Flo of being with Mrs Leary. The two women smelt the same: of baking, fresh washing and love.

'Oh, I nearly forgot. Here's a few sweets for the kids. They say everything made with sugar will be rationed so tell them to make the most of them.'

'Ta, love. I bless the day I met you, Flo. We always think of you up in the north as being a bit slow and behind the times. Digging coal out of deep holes and drinking all you earn, but you're not like that. You're caring and loving.'

'Aye, well, we're only a small country, by others' standards, but we have this north–south divide. We think of you lot as posh and having plenty of money. By, I've had me eye opened to the truth of that myth, an' all.' They laughed

162

together and hugged each other tightly.

'Till next time then, Pauline.'

The happiness and relief Flo felt at finding Pauline so well made her want to skip along the road. The haunting look had gone from Pauline's eyes and she seemed really settled, if still afraid for her kids.

That feeling soon left her, as she listened to Lucinda not an hour later.

Feeling hungrier than she'd felt in days, Flo was on her second butter-less spam sandwich when Lucinda both frightened and shocked her.

'What I have to tell you isn't easy, Flo. But I want you to know that I wouldn't do anything to jeopardize the safety of the country, or of you and Simon.'

'I don't understand; of course I knaw you'd not do that. What's wrong, Lucinda? You've got me worried now.'

'I – I'm in love, and the problem is: he's German.'

'Naw!'

'I can't help who I fell in love with, Flo. Please try to understand. I'm not seeing him. I – I mean, not at the moment. I only write to him. Oh, I'm sorry. I've frightened you now, but I had to tell someone. I'm going out of my mind.'

'Eeh, I knaw you can't help falling in love, lass, but a *German*. And you're writing to him! How?'

'He has a French aunt. He sends his letters to her, then she posts them to me. He speaks French, so he writes in French and talks as if he's a Frenchman and as if that's where he lives. We met up in France once, before Germany invaded. We spent a wonderful week together.'

'And he was a student here? At your university?'

Lucinda laughed at this, a nervous laugh. 'Yes. Cambridge was full of every nationality going. That's where our love began. But when Hitler started to mobilize, he went back home. He feared that if things escalated, he might be held prisoner here. We both studied to become journalists.'

'Eeh, Lucinda, I don't knaw what to say. I – I wish you hadn't told me. You knaw as I'm training to join Simon. How...? I mean what will happen, if this is found out?'

'That's why I had to tell somebody. I'm at my wits' end. Simon would go mad if he knew. And yet I don't like deceiving him. I'm thinking of moving to the South of France. That's where Aldric's aunt lives. I can live with her as her companion. I speak French, I could get away with being French.'

'But, I – I don't knaw. I mean, will you be safe – what about the occupation? And, well, how can you keep this from Simon?'

'That's why I'm telling you, Flo. I want you to tell him for me, but not until after I've gone. I'll give you my address in France, and you can write to me and tell me how he takes it. But don't worry; the South of France is under the Vichy government, a French organization. Oh, they work with Germany, but things there are not so bad or as frightening as they are in the north.'

'How d'yer expect him to take it, Lucinda? His own sister fraternizing... Eeh, I'm sorry. I – I meant...'

164

'I know what you meant, Flo. I – I thought you would understand: I'm not fraternizing, I'm not.' This came out on a sob, and Flo felt immediate remorse. She jumped up and went to Lucinda.

'Eeh, lass. I knaw as it's hard for you, but you can't do this. We've all had to make sacrifices, and you have to give up this Aldric. You have to, Lucinda. You could be arrested as a spy. God, Simon would lose his job! Besides, it is like fraternizing, ain't it? As ugly as that sounds, it is like that.'

'No, it isn't. Oh, Flo, try to understand. It's just two people who love each other. We can't help it that our countries decided to go to war with one another. We can't switch off our feelings. Besides, I – I haven't told you it all … Aldric was here.'

'What!'

'It was four months ago. He travelled with his aunt. He had another aunt who lived here in England. He lodged with her when he was at university. Well, she died and Aldric, who passed himself off as French, and his aunt were given papers to travel to her funeral. Aldric looks more French than German. His mother was French, and Aldric takes after her. He has a French passport, as he is entitled to. He keeps it at his aunt's.'

'Naw. Oh God, Lucinda. And you didn't report him?'

'No. I couldn't. I was so happy to see him, and it won't happen often, even with me living in France. He's been called up. He won't be fighting, he'll be a war correspondent and... Anyway, he asked me to marry him. I said yes. Oh, Flo, I *do* love him. I can't live without him. We ... we slept together. I – I'm pregnant with our child.'

'Eeh, Lucinda love.'

'So, you see, I have no choice. I have to go. I'm not wicked. Aldric and I didn't start the war. We fell in love long before we thought there would ever be a war between our countries. I must go to him, I must.'

Flo was silent for a moment. Whatever Simon was doing at Bletchley – and she thought she now had a good idea – it couldn't be compatible with him having a sister who was married to a German.

'You have to let me talk to Roland, Lucinda. I knaw that, like me, he'll stand by you. But you have to give up Aldric. By, you could be imprisoned for writing to him. And him being a journalist makes it even worse. Your letters are bound to have something in them that he could use. Your whole life is war news, and we share our news with loved ones. Look at how much you knaw about what Aldric is doing. Well, he must knaw the same about you. It can't go on, Lucinda, it can't.'

Lucinda's whole body sank into Flo. 'Help me, Flo. Help me.'

'Aye, I'll do that. I promise. Now, let me get on to Roland. He'll knaw what to do. I'll telephone him. But I won't tell him owt on the phone. I'll just say you need help and he isn't to tell Simon about it, but to come down next weekend. I were planning on going up to see Mrs Leary and Kathy before I go to Bletchley, but that will have to wait now.'

166

'No. You must go up to see them. I'll come with you and stay with Roland. Oh, I hope he knows what to do.'

'He will. And ta, Lucinda, I really do want to see me folk. Well, I knaw as they're not that, but they're the closest I have to a family. I'll stay here with you tonight, if you like. What d'yer reckon?'

'Thank you, Flo. Thank you. You know, I have friends as well as many acquaintances in my set, but I don't count any of them as close as I do you. I know we haven't known each other long, but you're a special person, Flo.'

This warmed Flo and went a little way towards dispelling the enormity of everything she'd heard. Getting up, she crossed over to the telephone. Somehow, between them, she and Roland would help Lucinda, though at this moment she didn't know how.

11

Molly

Chances Stolen

Soaking in a warm bath, Molly allowed the tears to weep from her body. Every part of her cried: her soul, her heart, poured out her desolation.

The encounter she'd just had wouldn't leave her. The titled, so-called 'gentleman' had been anything but. One of the richest men in England, he paid well in order to vent his depraved needs on the girl of his choosing. Today, he had picked Molly.

He'd called her a slut and a whore, besides other things that were so abhorrent to her she couldn't even think about them, and he'd slapped her with a hairbrush each time he'd uttered an expletive.

She'd begged him to stop, but had found that his pleasure increased with her every plea, until at last he sank back onto the bed and felt a completion of his lust.

Cringing in the corner of the bedroom, she'd watched him. His screams of ecstasy rang in her ears as if they were bells pealing a joyful announcement to her: 'It's over... It's over!'

As he cried like a baby, calling her 'Mummy' and asking her to forgive him, promising he'd never be a naughty boy like that again, she'd felt like taking the brush to him and swiping him to kingdom come with it. But she'd soothed him and helped him to clean himself up, playing the role she was paid to do.

She'd been shocked at how much that was. Thirty pounds! The shoeshop had only taken that amount in a month! It was more than she would tell Eva about.

She'd put one of the ten-pound notes into the lining of her dressing gown to squirrel away in the tin tea-caddy she kept behind a panel under the bath. She'd found the hiding place by accident. Her foot had kicked against the panel one day and she'd realized it was loose. With her tweezers, she'd been able to unscrew it far enough to put something behind it. Her heart raced with the possibility this opened up to her, and she'd immediately thought of the tea-caddy. It had been a gift from one of the punters that Eva, in a very generous moment, allowed Molly to keep. She'd emptied the precious tea into a bag and began to use the caddy to store the odd pound note that she could siphon off her earnings.

Molly's nerves tingled as she thought of what she'd done today. She'd been motivated by revenge for what Eva had put her through. The punter had handed over the money, saying that she'd pleased him more than any of the other girls he'd had and she deserved double what he gave them. The ten pounds made her hoard up to fourteen pounds. Enough to allow her to take a chance on escaping. But how she would achieve that she didn't know. And it couldn't be just her. She'd have to take Ruby, as she couldn't bear to think of the reprisals Ruby would suffer. From the moment Eva had realized how close they were, she'd threatened many times to take it out on Ruby, if Molly did anything out of line.

But fourteen pounds was a lot of money, wasn't it? If she went soon, she could get two train tickets to Birmingham and go to her Aunt Bet. The thought cheered Molly a little, though the hopelessness of putting her plans into action soon dispirited her again.

There was only one positive thought she could hang on to, to cheer her: her bruises had to heal before another man would look at her, and that would take at least two weeks. Two weeks' respite from being pawed by old men. From having them do things to her that repulsed her, and forcing her

169

to do things to them.

Her mind went back to the first man. Was it just a few short weeks since that time? Seven, in all. She'd never been questioned by the authorities about the doctor's death. Ruby had found out that Gus and Lofty had taken him back to his home, as she'd supposed they would. Molly's heart went out to his wife. She'd been told that if she opened her mouth, then the biggest scandal would be unleashed about her husband's activities – and not just on the night he suffered his fatal heart attack. Molly had seen the official story in the newspapers: *The eminent doctor passed away suddenly at his home.*

In a strange way, Molly knew she'd never forget him. Nor could she let go of the hazy, beautiful and sensual world he'd taken her to. More tears flowed from her. Tears for him, but mostly tears brought on by the thought that David should have been the one to introduce her to that world. Where was he? What did he think of her? Brushing him from her mind, she stood up on shaky legs.

The door opened before she had time to wrap herself in a towel. 'Bleedin hell, you got away light. Poor Jean's still suffering, and he had her two weeks ago.'

'Light! You should stop having him here, Eva. He'll kill one of us yet. A couple of times he went for me head, but I managed to duck. One blow of that brush, with the force he wields, and it'll be curtains, I'm telling yer.'

'I'll warn him. Now, what's he tipped up?'

'It's in me top drawer. He gave me a score.'

170

'Blimey, yer must've been good. You have a rest now, and if you feel up to it tomorrow we'll go to the flicks and then maybe on to a show. 'Ow's that sound, eh? I'll get yer dad ter come, if yer like.'

'No, thanks. I don't care if I never see him again. But if I feel up to it, I'd like a night out.'

'It won't be a night – at least not in them places, it won't. I don't fancy spending time down one of them Undergrounds when there's a raid. We'll go around noon. There's an early matinee. Then catch the late matinee of a show. After that, we'll go down Mac's cellar. Have yer heard of it?'

'No.'

'It's great down there. I'm thinking of running something along the same lines. I've got me eye on a place that's got a huge cellar. I might buy it and live in the top half, and convert the cellar into a strip club and gambling den, with a couple of rooms for pleasure. That way, even if Hitler bombs the rest of the building, punters can be safe and enjoy themselves. I'll take you to see it tomorrow.'

Molly nodded.

'Now, take that miserable look off your face. Your eyes'll take days to lose the swelling your cry-baby antics have caused.'

This was said in a motherly tone and marked the way her relationship with Eva had changed. But not inside. Inside, Molly hated the woman and would sooner kill her than look at her. Outside, it was different. These last weeks she'd done just what Ruby had counselled her to and had nurtured Eva's friendship. It had been easy

171

to do. Eva had shown that she craved another woman to like her. It was pitiful how she trusted Molly, really. Especially as the first chance Molly got, she would do her utmost to do the woman down.

These occasional treats of going out with Eva were valued by Molly. Just to see the outside world and to breathe fresh air – that's if you could call it fresh. A lot of Soho was flattened now, and the air was putrid with the smell of burning buildings, and death.

In the dormitory Ruby greeted her with, 'All right, love? Here, I've made you a cup of Rosie Lee. We're running out of tea, though, so we need to get some from somewhere.'

Molly smiled at Ruby. A weak smile that told of her pain. As Ruby smiled back, Molly noticed how much better her teeth looked. They were almost white. Molly had taught her how to brush them each day with bicarbonate of soda. Or, if that wasn't available, then the soot from the back of the fireplace did the job.

Ruby had put weight on, too. Molly had encouraged her to eat more, and to wash her hair more often, counselling her that if she looked better, she might get more work in the boudoirs, which was infinitely preferable to the streets. Out there any Tom, Dick or Harry – clean or unclean – could take Ruby up an alley for a couple of bob or less, then knock her about if they felt like it.

'Bad, were it, Molly? Well, it's over with now, love. I doubt she'll let him have yer again. Most of the girls can only stand it once, and he knows that. He accepts that she has to get him someone new each time. Sometimes she pulls in one of us street workers for him.'

'I think she might let him have me again, Ruby. She never said she wouldn't. I think he'll ask for me, as he tipped up more than he does for the others. I managed to get some for meself.'

'Shhh ... walls have ears, remember?'

Flopping down onto the bed made Molly wince, but it felt better to be in a semi-lying position. The tea tasted sweeter than usual. 'You get some sugar from somewhere, love?'

'No. It's saccharine, but a new brand. One of the girls from Peggy's house got them for me. Trixie, her name is. She's a good sort. Me and her watch out for each other on the street.'

This worried Molly, as Ruby would get into trouble if she was found to be mixing with Peggy's girls. Eva feared the girls might leave her to go and work for Peggy, if they found out how much better they were treated there. They got plenty to eat and were kept clean. Which is more than could be said for Eva's street girls.

'Trixie gets me the odd punter, if she's got too many waiting. Or, if they won't have me, she gives me some of her pickings, so I don't come back empty-handed. But me trade's picked up a bit since you took me in hand.'

Molly didn't know whether to be pleased about this or not. But a part of her felt glad that Ruby's lot had improved. She loved Ruby like a sister. She reminded Molly of Hettie. Abrupt in her manner, kind and a salt-of-the-earth type.

The queue outside the Victoria Palace Theatre for

173

tickets to the matinee of *Me and My Girl* stretched around the corner. Being early, Eva and Molly were near the front. They'd been into the cinema, but had come out after half an hour of the film. Molly had been uncomfortable on the bench seats, which had very little padding. During the part of the film they'd seen, her attention had been taken trying to pluck up the courage to broach the subject of her disappearance from home, in an effort to find out if David had ever called round to her house, asking for her. As the conversation between her and Eva had dried up, she took all of her courage in both hands, though she dreaded the answer. 'Does anyone ask where I've gone to, Eva? Y'know, like Foggy, or some of me neighbours? Or does me dad ever ask after how I am?'

Trying to look as if her question was just idle curiosity, Molly looked up at the grey stone building, concentrating her gaze on the pillared balcony, then bending her head backwards, so that she could study the dome on top of the building.

'Yer dad does ask and he says a couple of the neighbours have, but he tells them you went off without telling him, but he's since heard from you and you're in the forces. He's coming to terms with what happened now, and enjoys the odd bit extra that I give him from your earnings. Gives him a bit to spend with the bookie's runner.'

Molly was surprised by how much this hurt. But what Eva said next turned the hurt into a deep pain. 'Last time I saw him, yer dad said

174

sommat about a fella calling round your house, asking about yer. Who would that be? You never said you had any friends, other than that Hettie.'

David! Molly almost said his name out loud. She hoped nothing of what she felt showed in her face.

'He were in uniform. Air force, your dad said.'

'What did me dad tell him?' It took all her effort to keep the trembling of her body from her voice.

'Dunno. Why? Who were he?'

'No one special' – *only my life.* 'He was caught up in the same bomb attack as me and Hettie. He told me he was in the forces, and that he'd look me up one day to make sure I was all right. I gave him me address.' Changing the subject, she made herself sound disinterested. 'I'm tired, Eva, and I'm hurting all over. Can we come to see this show another time? I just want to go to bed.'

'Bleedin' hell, Molly. I've wanted to see this for ages.'

'Well, why don't you? I'll go back on me own. You can trust me. I'll be truthful with you. I would go off, if I had some money and somewhere to go, but I've got neither. All I can do is go back.'

'You bleedin' do go off and I'm telling yer, that Ruby as yer so fond of will cop it. One move from you as to leaving me, and she's dead! You're me best earner, and yer know too much.'

'Christ, you're an evil woman, Eva.'

'And don't you forget it. Now, I'm at least going to get tickets while I'm here, so we can come another time. We'll go back, once I have

175

them. On the way we'll call in at that new place I told yer of. See what yer think. I've put in an offer for it, but it were as bleedin' low as I dared go. I'm nervous now, and I need someone with a bit of intelligence to tell me if I should up me offer.'

This was the last thing Molly wanted to do. The soreness of her body had been joined by the pain of missing David and renewed fear of the trap she was in.

She tried to concentrate on David. So he is now in the air force. *Probably he'll still be in training, but where?* Why hadn't she asked him more about it? But then, what use would knowing be to her; she'd known where he lived, but had never contacted him. She could have done. Ruby would have posted a letter. But she'd had to think of David's safety, and she still had to. Eva's gang was capable of anything.

Once Eva had purchased tickets for the following week, her mood changed a little. 'I'm looking forward to that, and I bet you are, an' all. Right, come on. We'll get a cab. If we can bleedin' find one.'

The journey in the green-and-black Morris cab was far from comfortable, but the mile and a half they had to travel was done in a relatively short time, and Molly was glad of the respite when they stopped off at the office of the agents who were handling the sale of the building Eva was interested in.

Ebury Street in Chelsea looked just as sad as the rest of London. Burnt-out shells of buildings still bled water. Some of the leaks, Molly imagined, were from the firefighters' attempts to douse the fires, others from broken pipes. Debris danced in the gutters as the wind flicked charred paper along.

The building they now stood in front of looked forlorn. Its windows were smashed, and some of its window frames blew backwards and forwards in the wind. At any moment the precarious screws or hinges holding them could give way and turn them into dangerous missiles.

'Well, what d'yer think, then?'

What Molly thought was that the intention to turn this once-beautiful house into a brothel-cum-illegal-gambling-and-drinking-house was despicable, but she didn't express this. She looked up and down the street. She knew this area was near the King's Road, a busy thoroughfare, although for Eva's trade punters would travel to wherever and wouldn't care if it was in the middle of a desert. 'I like the look of it, but it needs a lot of work.'

'Not as much as you'd think. What you can see is blast damage, but the rooms are all intact, and the structure is safe. The owners have even left all the furniture, and I can tell yer, a lot of it is classy stuff. The agent told me it's Georgian. It'd look good and give a good impression of me club. The nobs like that sort of thing. That's if there's any of it left. Bleedin' looters could have been in. Come on, let's take a look.'

Once inside, Molly felt a sense of sadness. Water ran down the walls, leaving the beautiful mahogany furniture standing an inch deep. High ceilings with decorated cornices gave an air of grandeur, and the doors were heavy and ornate.

'Did the agent say your offer had been accepted?'

'No. They want a few more bleedin' hundred quid.'

'Pay it. I don't know what the amount is, but if you were happy with your first offer and they only want a bit more, I'd go for it and get this place dried out and secured as quick as you can. Else everything will be ruined.'

'Right. That's all I wanted to 'ear. We'll call back there, drop off the keys, pay a deposit and get the agent to get workmen in, pronto. I'm on the up, Molly. And you can come with me. You can be me manager. You've got brains.'

The walls of Molly's nightmare closed further in on her.

'You're not saying much.'

'I told you, Eva, I'm tired and in pain.' How Eva could even think of discussing business with her, when she'd been instrumental in selling her to a sadist who had inflicted so much pain on her, Molly didn't know. She did know that she'd had enough. Sucking up to Eva hadn't helped. It had only drawn her in deeper and given Eva fancy ideas. It was time to take her destiny into her own hands – she had enough money now. The time had come for her and Ruby to get away.

They hadn't been back at the brothel long when Molly stiffened with fear. Eva's screeches came to her as she lay on her bed. 'I'll kill the bleeder!'

Somehow Molly knew Eva was talking about her. Footsteps stomped along the landing, coming towards the dormitory. The door flew open. Eva stood there, her face screwed up with evil. In

178

her hand she held Molly's tea-caddy. 'You bitch! You've been stealing from me.'

Molly stared into the piercing eyes. Smudged with mascara, they gave Eva the look of the monster she was. A sense of doom weighed down Molly's heart.

Her terror deepened as Gus pushed past Eva. 'You slut, you!' His hand grabbed her and yanked her off the bed. Unable to get her footing, she landed on the floor. 'Get up.' A vicious kick sank into her kidneys, taking Molly's breath from her. An indescribable pain creased her. 'I said, get up!' Once more Gus yanked at her, almost pulling her arm from her socket. 'Yer going ter pay fer this. No one crosses Eva.'

'And that Ruby, an' all. She must have known. I want her to get it as well, Gus.'

This forced Molly to find her voice. 'No! No, please. Please. Ruby didn't know – no one did.'

As Gus shoved Molly towards the door, a shadowy figure jumped back into the first boudoir. She thought she knew who it was, but what she heard as she was shoved into the second boudoir confirmed it. 'Now, will you let me have another girl, Eva? You wouldn't have known, if I hadn't told you that I saw her put ten into her gown.'

'You can have that bleedin' Ruby just as soon as I locate her. And do what yer like with her. Don't worry about me warnings about not going too far. Have yer fun. I don't care if I have a bleedin' body to get rid of. But you'll still pay, and as much as you gave to that bitch. Only from now on, all punters hand their money in to me or Gus.'

Molly heard no more. She'd been sure the hairbrush-man hadn't seen her take the money. But even if he had, how did they find her tin?

The answer lay in a look from Delilah, a bitch of a girl who hadn't liked Molly taking more than her fair share of those she considered the 'best' punters. She sidled out of the second boudoir, gave a satisfied smirk towards Molly and let out a little giggle. *She must have overheard a conversation between me and Ruby.*

Gus pushed Delilah out of the way as he manhandled Molly into the room. Once he'd kicked the door closed, he threw her onto the bed.

'First, yer going to have a taste of a real man.'

Molly didn't fight. What would it matter? She'd just look on it as servicing another punter. They were all different, but however Gus liked to do it, she could take it.

Undressed, he lived up to what she'd first heard about how big he was. None that she'd had could match him. His weight crushed her while he tried to enter her, but once he'd achieved that, he lifted himself and looked down at her. 'You're good.' His words went into a moan as he began to thrust at her.

Molly tried to block out the pain he was causing her bruised body.

When he stopped for a moment, she wondered why. She turned her head to look at him. His face twisted into a scowl and his hand whipped her cheek. 'Don't just fucking lie there, bitch! Give me what yer give the punters. I've heard yer moaning and screaming out.'

Afraid of what he might do, Molly arched her

back in pretence. She moaned as she did so. She could act out pleasure. She'd done so many times. Thankfully, he just seemed to want normal sex. Nothing fetishistic. Well, she could give him that, couldn't she? Any whore could give him that. *And that's what I am. A whore. A nobody.*

12

Lucinda

Chasing Elusive Happiness

Lucinda waited as the operator tried to put her through. She'd received an urgent hand-delivered message that her editor wanted to speak to her. It seemed she'd missed two calls from him. This hadn't surprised her as she'd been out walking as often as she could, trying to make sense of everything, seeking a tiredness from the exercise that would make her sleep. And even when she'd been in, she'd ignored the telephone, thinking it might be Flo or Roland and she'd have to lie to them.

At last she heard the American drawl of her boss at the *Daily News,* one of London's most popular papers. 'Lucinda! Great to hear from you. How are you? Feeling a whole lot better, I hope. Have you made your mind up about taking the correspondent's job?'

Lucinda bit her lip. Everything in her screamed against her doing this, and yet she knew that common sense couldn't win over what her heart desired of her.

Making her voice sound as normal and decisive as it usually did, she answered, 'Yes. I would love to do it. When do I go?'

'Is tomorrow too soon?'

Her heart jolted. No time was too soon, but could she really just run out on Flo and Roland? She heard herself answer, 'No, that'll be fine. Where and when?'

'I knew you'd say yes, so in anticipation I had all of your papers prepared. And I've got press clearance for you with both the English and German governments, and that phoney government in the South of France. That's where you will go initially – just the other side of Paris to Vichy. You will stay there for a week, before you are to join the forces in Belgium. Though be careful of the Germans; they say they will give you press immunity, but they don't play fair. Dickie Peterson was taken in last week as a suspected spy. We haven't heard anything of him since. But we're onto it. And that's why we need you out there. Things are happening that are not being reported on. You'll fly out in a supply plane. It'll be a bit hairy, as they're carrying cargo for the Resistance workers. You may have to jump if they can't land. You've parachuted before, haven't you?'

'Yes, I told you. Me and a few others from university took a course. It was all for fun, but I enjoyed it and did a few jumps.'

She felt momentary fear for her unborn child, but she knew that things rarely went wrong on a jump and there should be little or no risk if it went smoothly. She had excelled in her training and had perfected the landing; in the end, it had felt no different from rolling on the grass, and never jarred or bruised her. *Yes, I'll take the chance... I have to.* 'I'll set it up, then. You'll only have a makeshift seat next to whatever it is they're carrying. There'll be a camera on board for you. I want pictures of the drop. So take all that you can, then leave the camera on board to be delivered back to me. We'll decide what we can get clearance to use. Get over to Harwell in Berkshire, wherever that is. You'll pick up your papers at the post office and report to the commander on the air base there. Everything you need will already be at the base waiting for you. And good luck.'

'Before you go: how do I get news back to you?'

'There'll be other correspondents with you to show you the ropes, and the Resistance will take you to the world news office. The army will also be part of the chain. They take the film and your written report to the airfields and make sure they are loaded onto the transporters coming back to Britain. There's various means.'

As she replaced the receiver, Lucinda had a moment when the deceit she intended to practise – not only on her dear brother and friends, but also on the newspaper – gave her a feeling of intense shame. But she had to do this. There was no other way she could get to France. Flo would explain why she'd gone. Along with Roland and Simon she would find a way of covering for her absence. Now all she had to do was write a note for Flo and Roland.

Flo had found that she hadn't as much time off

as she'd first thought, and so Roland was coming down to London instead of Flo and herself going to Leeds. The plan was for them all to meet here in her apartment on Saturday. Guilt visited her as she wrote that she'd taken a job in France. She didn't say that she wasn't intending to return.

With her only experience of flying being in a small aircraft, from which she and a few other students from Cambridge engaged in the sport of parachuting, Lucinda wasn't sure if the sick feeling she was experiencing was air sickness or due to her pregnancy. But cramped up as she was, sitting between two huge bales of she-knew-not-what, she had the devil's own job to keep from vomiting.

The pilot had kept up a running commentary about where they were, so she knew they were over France. 'In five minutes we will be landing, ma'am. You know that you will be met by Resistance workers, I presume?'

'Yes.'

'Well, get your parachute ready to put on, just in case. And don't be alarmed, for whichever way you reach the earth, the Resistance workers will grab you and hurry you into the bushes. Extreme secrecy is their thing. If we're able to land, we need you to go down the chute as quickly as you can. We will then take off and drop the cargo from the air, as we can't stay on the ground long enough to unload manually. So please do everything with the utmost speed. No hesitation. Understood?'

'Understood.'

A few minutes later Lucinda wanted to scream that she hadn't understood they would have to dodge enemy fire. The ack-ack of ground-fire terrified her, as did seeing what looked like sparks shooting past the window.

The shout of, 'Gunner, north-west twenty-nine degrees: fire!' had Lucinda cowering and covering her ears. She bit hard on her lip, as terror streaked through her. After a moment she saw an almighty explosion on the ground beneath them. The pilot's shout of joy brought a small amount of relief to her.

'You did it! Well done, gunner. By the looks of things, the Resistance are engaging what's left of the unit. We'll have to turn back.'

'No. Please, I have to get down there.'

'You can't parachute from this height – we would be dropping you into unknown territory. Good God, woman, you could land anywhere.'

'Well, now that the Germans have been stopped, surely we could at least get over the landing strip and I can jump there. I have experience. I used to parachute for sport, when up at Cambridge, and carried out a lot of jumps.'

The pilot was silent for a moment. She could see his bent head; he was scrutinizing the terrain below. Probably checking whether the activity was still going on. His radio crackled. A French voice came over the air. It appeared to be from the men on the ground. The second pilot left his seat and tuned in. Lucinda couldn't understand a word, even though she spoke excellent French. She assumed it was coded.

'They have the way clear, Squadron Leader;

they're saying the mission can complete as per schedule.'

'I don't like it. Tell them we will drop the supplies, but won't come in. Tell them the person will parachute in.'

Once this was done, the second pilot took hold of the parachute. 'Here, I'll help you on with this. I'll just unhook it. Leave it with the Resistance group, and they'll return it to the next shipment. Even if it's damaged, parts of it can be recycled.'

Lucinda breathed a sigh of relief as she donned the parachute and checked that she could locate the ripcord. But her relief soon dissolved into fear as the hatch was opened. Beneath her lay a mass of blackness. No light could be seen anywhere.

'Wait for it. Right, give them the signal.'

Another radio message was sent and below her Lucinda saw a runway of flames light up.

'Go!'

As the rush of air caught her breath, she felt a moment of panic. She'd never jumped from this height before. She had no idea when to release her parachute. She'd been reckless, as she wasn't trained for this kind of jump.

Her body swirled and descended. She tried desperately to judge how near the flames below were. When she thought she had free-fallen long enough, and the flames looked as near as she remembered the ground looking in her previous jumps, she pulled the ripcord and prayed.

Within a few minutes, pain jarred her shins as her feet smashed against a solid mass. Intending to use the rolling technique, she tried to break the rest of her fall, but something prevented her from moving. Agonizing pain ripped through her body, as what felt like a thousand sticks stabbed into her. Voices came to her from below. Reaching out, she felt the rough bark of a tree. Her body slipped, and something tightened around her neck. *Oh God ... help me!*

Her body shifted again. Torches shone on her. She couldn't breathe. Her legs dangled. Judging by the tightness of her jacket, she knew it had caught on something. Terrifying clarity about the horrific danger she was in came to Lucinda. If the bough that her parachute was caught on broke, or the material gave way, she would hang.

A desperate voice shouted in French, 'Grab that branch to your right. Henrique is coming. Quick, hold on to it – take your weight.'

Reaching out, Lucinda tried in vain to find the branch they were talking about, but then a tearing sound and the sinking of her body took all her strength. The pain in her neck zinged through her. She had no air. The thought came to her: *My baby, my baby...* Then a blackness overcame her that she knew she would never come out of.

Roland pressed the bell for a third time. 'There's no answer. Wait a minute, I have a key to Simon's flat. We'll go in there, and up to Lucinda's flat that way.'

Flo felt her heart begin to race. Trepidation settled in her. *Lucinda, please be in. Please.*

A shiver took hold of her body as they entered Simon's cold, empty apartment. There was a silence clothing the whole house that spoke to

Flo of doom.

Inside Lucinda's apartment, Flo's eyes were drawn to the note leaning against the clock on the mantelpiece. For a moment she stared at her name, beautifully written on the white envelope.

'You'd better open it. Then I think you'd better tell me what this is all about – what trouble Lucinda is in. I've been worried sick all week. I called Simon to tell him I was coming here to meet you, but he couldn't make it. I almost told him Lucinda had a problem and that she wasn't answering her phone, but decided not to worry him until I'd got to the bottom of things.'

'I knaw. I managed to get to use a phone and tried calling her.'

The ripping open of the letter gave Flo a feeling that she was about to read something that would change all of their lives: *Dear Flo & Roland, Forgive me…*

Flo handed the letter to Roland and listened as he read it out. 'Oh, dear. This is the last thing we needed to hear. I knew she wanted to be a war correspondent, but why go now, when she is in trouble? Look, sit down, Flo. I'll put the kettle on. While we drink some tea, which I'm surely in need of, you can tell me what all this is about.'

The tea tasted good. Roland must have found some sugar. It had been a long time since Flo had tasted its smooth sweetness, so different from the bitter saccharine they were forced to use, if they wanted to sweeten anything.

Roland was quiet for some time as he scrutinized the letter once more. It was as if he thought there was more than he'd initially read. Flo waited.

188

'She seems to have gone three days ago, but she says nothing about the trouble you spoke of. What is it, Flo? What trouble had Lucinda got herself into?'

The telephone ringing prevented her from answering. She jumped up and ran to it. 'Simon! Simon? Simon, what's wrong?' Flo's whole body turned cold. Goosebumps stood up on her arms. Roland took the phone from her. His face drained of colour.

Something terrible had happened, but Flo didn't want to know what. Simon's sobs told of something so painful that she didn't know if she would be able to stand it.

'Oh God, no! No... Oh, my darling. Look, I'm here with Flo. We'll come to you. I'm in my car, as I – well, I'll explain when I see you. Have they given you compassionate leave?... Good. We'll bring you back here. Hang on, Simon, my darling man. Hang on.'

The ring of the phone as it disconnected brought Flo the realization that the moment was upon her. She wanted to cover her ears with her hands. When Roland did speak, the shock in his voice was so deep it cut into her.

'He – he ... Simon, he said, Lu-Lucinda is dead. Dead – oh God!'

Flo's world – the wonderful new world these people had given her – tumbled out of all understanding at these words. Her lips opened to release the scream that threatened to strangle her, but instead she sank under her own body weight and landed in the fireside chair that Lucinda had said was her favourite. A big, comfy chair that

189

seemed to wrap its arms around you, but which today had no impact on Flo.

But then she saw how Roland's every limb trembled. His eyes stared blankly and his mouth hung slack. His need spurred her to get up and go to him. 'Sit down, Roland. Please. Sit down.' As she spoke she tried to be a source of strength to him. She coaxed him and rubbed his back – natural comforting actions – and yet nothing around her was natural, or even familiar any more, for it had all been scarred by the impact of the horrific words Roland had uttered. *Lucinda ... dead? No... No!*

Gradually Roland was able to tell her what had happened. When he'd finished, his voice was a desperate plea. 'I need to go to Simon. We both do. We need to bring him back here. Oh, poor man. Poor, poor Simon. And Lucinda. Darling Lucinda. How could such a thing happen? Why did she go? Did you know she was going? Is this what the trouble was: did you want me to stop her?'

In that moment it came to Flo that she wouldn't tell him the whole truth. She would keep Lucinda's secret about the baby, and she wouldn't tell them the true nationality of her boyfriend. 'She ... she was in love. She had a French boy-friend. She wanted to go to him, and this was the only way. I begged her not to. I – I... Sh-she had agreed to come up to Leeds for a few days to be with you. Until I had to change our plans.'

'That can't have been all. Flo, you said she was in trouble. Having a French boyfriend isn't trouble. Sad, yes, as they would have to be apart so much, but not trouble.'

190

Weighing up the lesser of the two evils – fraternizing or ... – she blurted out, 'She was pregnant.'

'No!' This came out on a gasp, and it was a long moment before Roland spoke again. 'We can't tell Simon.'

'But what will we tell him as to why we were here?'

Roland was silent for a moment.

'We'll say that Lucinda had told you she intended to go to France, and begged you not to tell Simon until she was there. So you asked me to try and persuade her not to go. I thought it best to come up and see if I could get Lucinda to come to stay with me for a while, to talk it all over. We'll leave it at that. No mention of the French boyfriend. Though I suppose we ought to try to contact him.'

'She was going to give me an address so that Simon would know where she was. She said to tell him that she would be with her boyfriend and his aunt.'

'See if there's anything else in the envelope.'

'Yes, there's a small card.' Flo's hands shook as she pulled the card out. *Please don't let it have Aldric's name on it.* It didn't, only a French-sounding female name, Mme Bonheur. *She must be Aldric's aunt.* Flo handed the card to Roland.

'Do you know the name of the boyfriend?'

Afraid to say, in case it was an obviously German name, Flo lied again. 'No. Lucinda did mention it, but – well, I can't remember. I... Oh, Roland, I can't believe she's dead.'

His arms came around her. 'I know. Poor Lucinda.'

191

'How did she die?'

'I – I don't know. Simon couldn't tell me. Look, we need to get to him. Leave this other business with me. I can speak French. I will take it on myself to write to this lady. I'll tell her we are sorry that we don't know her nephew's name. But I'll ask her to kindly inform him.'

Flo had a moment of misgiving. What if Aldric didn't believe that Lucinda was dead? What if he thought her English family had found out about him and had made up her death? He might try to come over again! But then, surely he would realize that they didn't know he was German, so they would have no need to lie. This thought settled her mind. But another dread replaced it. How was she going to face Simon?

13

Molly & Ruby

Forming a Sisterly Bond

Molly leaned against the wall and the bitter wind chilled her bones, making her teeth chatter. The flimsy skirt she wore flapped in the breeze, whipping her bare legs as if with icy fingers.

Ruby huddled up to her, her thin body allowing her protruding bones to dig into Molly's side.

Neither of them had eaten for days. Both had been given only a week to recover from the backlash of finding Molly's tea-caddy. Gus had beaten the already injured Molly after satisfying himself on her, and the hairbrush-man had been let loose on Ruby. Only the screams of horror from the other girls in the house at the time had brought the onslaught to a halt. Since then, Molly and Ruby had been put out on the streets every afternoon to tout for business. If they failed to attract any customers for themselves, or to send any punters to the house, they were left to starve.

Molly prayed that Trixie would come along today, as she had done once before this week. Trixie hadn't had any spare money to give them, but she had taken them for a cup tea.

The prayer had hardly died in her mind when the chirpy Trixie came round the corner. 'Look at you – you'll freeze to your deaths. Let's go to the Kettle and Tea Pot. I'll treat you to a Rosie Lee and a bun. I've made a bleedin' killing today.'

Molly moved stiffly. Ruby sank even more heavily onto her. 'I need help with Ruby, Trixie.'

'It ain't bleedin' right how that cow, Eva, treats yer. She wants stringing up, mate. Yer should come to Peggy's and work for her. You're a good-looker and have the figure for it. At least, you *were*. Look at you, Molly, you're not half the girl I saw a few weeks ago. You were walking out with that bitch who owns you, and you looked lovely. I was glad you weren't working the streets then, as you'd have been real competition. Does Eva keep you clean, down below?'

Trixie had hold of Ruby's other arm, and together they managed to get her to the small cafe in a back alley.

193

The warmth of the place, and the stench that permeated from it, hit Molly – stale body odour and cigarette smoke, mixed with that of the food bubbling on the stove behind the counter, made her stomach churn. Her body swayed.

'What you dragged in now, Trixie girl? You're a bleedin' do-gooder, and you can't afford to be. Some of these whores'll take yer purse just as soon as look at yer.'

At this, Molly recovered. Trying to muster what dignity she could, she stood straight and, in her best voice, spoke up for herself. 'I beg your pardon, Missus. I may be down on me uppers, but I'm not a thief.'

'What were you and her doing the other day in me back yard then, eh?'

'We were only looking for any scraps you might have thrown out. We're starving.'

'Give them a break, Dolly. Here, love, come and sit here with me. I'll buy you a pot of Rosie Lee, but you'll have to open your legs to pay me back.'

'Shad up, Mikey. You're not funny.'

'Sorry, Trixie. I was only joking. You don't think me, or anyone in their right mind, would put our old man into either of them two, do yer?'

Everyone laughed. The sound brought Molly lower than she'd ever been. Her instinct was to run, but the pull of a hot drink and a bun was too much for her.

'Take no notice, girls. Let's sit over there by the window. I want to keep me eye open for any of our lot who might tell on me. Peggy's all right, but if she's crossed, she can be a tartar. Besides,

194

it won't do me standing any good to be seen with you, so if I see a potential customer coming, I can move away.'

Molly had never dreamed the day would come when a known prostitute would think it below her to be seen sitting with her.

'Look, don't take umbrage at me saying that. It's only a business thing. I'd always look out for you girls. You're me mates, and I don't let mates down.'

Molly understood and thought that, although she'd never had a sister, the bond she had with Ruby and Trixie must be how it felt between sisters. She wondered if Trixie felt the same, and tested the water by asking a favour. 'Trixie, would you try to get a message to me dad for me?'

'You have a family! Blimey, how did a girl like you come to get this low?'

'It's a long story. But me dad's me only hope of things changing for me.'

'Where does he live, then?'

'Edmonton. Sebastopol Road. He has a butcher's shop on the corner.'

'Not him as Eva's tied up with?'

'Yes, and that's how I'm like I am. They kidnapped me and forced me into this life. He can't know how low I've become, as I'm sure he'd do something.'

'I doubt it, lav. Here, get this tea down yer.'

Dolly had slammed the huge pot down on the table, with three chipped and cracked mugs. Trixie poured the steaming liquid as she spoke. 'There ain't any sugar, and you two could do with some of that to give you a bit of energy.'

'We're used to it. Let's get some into Ruby first. Here you are, Ruby. Sip this.'

Ruby let Molly hold the mug for her. The tea dribbled out of her mouth.

'Ruby, take some in, love. You'll feel better then.'

Ruby opened her eyes and looked around her.

'She needs help, Trixie. You know what you asked out there: about Eva keeping us clean? Well, she does have a quack round sometimes, but he's never looked at Ruby. What if she's caught something? She's feverish.'

'It could be, but she just looks to me like she's got flu. Them sores around her mouth are from the wind drying and splitting her lips. I've got some Vaseline in me bag. I don't always use it for me lips, though.' Trixie laughed her common-sounding laugh, and Molly couldn't help grinning at her.

Taking some of the Vaseline on her finger, Molly applied it to Ruby's dry, cracked lips. 'Let your tea cool a bit, love – it'll smart them sores. Eat some of your bun.'

'Have you got any family, Ruby?'

Perking up a bit, Ruby answered Trixie. 'Not so yer'd bleedin' know. I left home at fourteen. Me dad were killed at work and me mam married this drunk. He had a son older than me, and this so-called stepbrother started to rape me. Me mum wouldn't listen to me. I reckon she were scared of her old man. I got out, came to London and got picked up by Eva's lot. That were when it was the younger gangsters who ruled, and you didn't cross them bleedin' lot. War took them off the patch, so Eva hooked up with this lot.'

196

Each girl fell silent as they went into their own thoughts. It was Trixie who spoke first. 'Bleedin' men. I had the same, but with an uncle. Me dad's brother. He was having it off with me mum, an' all, bleedin' cow as she were. Me dad tried to help me, but he were weak-minded and opted for the quiet life. So I hopped it. I was sleeping rough, when this girl took me back to Peggy's one night. I took to the life as if I were born to it.'

Molly told them what happened to her.

A hand stretched out and took hers. She looked into Ruby's face and saw a love there that touched her heart. Trixie, too, extended her hands across the table and took Molly's and Ruby's other hands. 'We'll be all right, girls. You two have to get a bit canny, that's all.'

'Canny?' Molly asked.

'Yes, it's a word me granny used to use. She was Scottish. It means to get a bit wise, play the game in your favour. You cross Eva, you get punished. You please her, you get looked after. First thing you need is food, to build you up. I'll do what I can. We'll meet here every day and I'll stand you a bowl of stew.' Letting go of their hands, Trixie shouted, 'Dolly, two bowls of your stew over here, please. And serve it in bleedin' clean bowls for a change.'

Laughter rippled round the customers.

'Shut your mouth, Trixie. You're a soft touch. Been giving you the sob-story, have they?'

'I bring a lot of custom here, mate. If yer want that to continue, yer'll leave me business alone and make sure there's a good bit of meat in them bowls.'

Dolly didn't retaliate.

'See what I mean? Canny. I work Dolly, she don't work me. I slap her down if she tries.'

'What you two do now is clean yourselves up. There's water in that bleedin' hole yer live in, ain't there? Well, get up early and wash yourselves. And wash your underwear out at night. And pinch some of the other girls' slap. Brush your hair, and put slap on every day. I'll sneak yer some clothes out. We'll meet here at twelve noon each day. You can go round the back to get changed. I'll sort it with Dolly. Then you can hit the streets and start earning some money. You give me a bit of what you earn, and I'll keep it safe and add to it. You'll have to trust me on that. Then, when we're all better off, we'll make plans for our future. I want a house just like Peggy's one day, and you can come in on it with me.'

Molly wasn't sure about it all, but it sounded a lot better than she had at the moment. 'I'm in, and thanks, Trixie.'

'And me, Trixie. You're a real pal.'

'Good. Let's hold hands again. I liked that. It were the first real contact I've had from friends who are just that, and not out to get sommat from me.'

Molly felt the tears come into her eyes. Trixie – the girl she'd thought of as a known prostitute and, yes, had looked down on in a small way – had offered her a lifeline; but more than that, she'd offered her friendship and a sisterly-like love.

Trixie smiled at them both. Molly smiled back, but her smile froze on her lips as Ruby slumped forward.

198

Trixie reacted with a squeal. 'Ruby! Gawd help us. She's got it bad. I thought she was perking up. She should see a doctor. There's a quack I know. Well, we call him that, but he is a proper doctor, just not allowed to practise any more.'

'We've no money.'

'I told yer, I had a good day. And I did yesterday, an' all. It's the business crows. They're all old men, but still want their oats. They know they'll be stuck at home over Christmas, and they're getting all they can before then. Peggy's struggling to find rooms for us when we take them back to hers. She had to put me and a punter in her front room today. We had a giggle, I can tell yer. It's like a bleedin' Aladdin's cave. I've never seen so many ornaments.'

'Thanks, Trixie. You're a good 'un. Is this quack's place very far?'

'No, he's only round the corner. We can lift Ruby round there. But you need to concoct a story as to why she ain't with you, when you go back.'

'She'll have to be with me. If I go back without her, they'll kill me!'

'Leave it out; even Evil Eva ain't got it in her to go that far.'

'She has. She gets that Gus and Lofty to do it. You must have heard of that girl who was dragged out of the Thames a few weeks ago?'

'Were that their doing? Blimey, mate. I'm not so sure now. I don't want any trouble.'

'Please, Trixie. Look, give me the money and tell me where to go. I'll take Ruby along there. I'll never tell them that you helped me.'

Trixie passed over a pound note and ten bob in change. 'Watch these bleedin' lot in here – they'd take that off yer as soon as look at yer. If any of them follow you, stand still and scream your heart out. They'll soon run off. The place you need is along there, down Dean Street. It's called Winnett Street. It's a cobbled lane.'

'I know it. I had a punter there just as it got dark the other day. The siren went and he never finished. He scarpered, leaving me with nothing.'

'It happens. Anyway, the geezer's place is the fourth door on the right. A red one; well, it was red, once upon a time. It's peeling now. Take no notice of what the place looks like, just ring the bell three times. Three quick rings. Tell him I sent yer and you've got money. Good luck, girl. Oh, and here, take this change; I reckon there's about ten bob there. Give it to that cow, Eva. It might save yer from a beating and get yer a meal later.'

Molly's eyes filled with tears.

What should have taken ten minutes took half an hour. The final stretch seemed just too much, but a lad with a barrow – the type with four wheels – stopped and asked if she needed a lift with her friend. Molly had known she could go no further, so she decided to trust the boy.

'Cost yer a florin, though, mate. I don't run a bleedin' charity.'

'I'll give it to you when we reach our destination and the man I need to see opens the door. I don't want you snatching me money.'

'I don't reckon as you've got that much, Miss. All right. I'll have to trust yer. She looks as though she'll keel over, if I don't.'

Together, Molly and the boy helped to get Ruby into the barrow. The boy kept his word. Molly liked him. He told her he went around the streets with his dad's barrow, trying to earn a shilling from folk who were salvaging their shops or homes. He offered to take their chattels wherever they wanted them to go. 'Me dad's fighting this bleedin' war, and I have to help me mum keep some food on the table for me brothers and sisters. I have a good name, I don't lie and I don't cheat. More than me bleedin' job's worth.'

'How old are you?'

'As old as me tongue, and a bit older than me teeth.'

Molly guessed he was around thirteen.

When they reached the house, Molly did as Trixie had said and rang the bell three times. After a moment the door opened just enough for Molly to see a wizened old man peering out at her.

'I – I need help for me mate.'

'What sort of help, young lady?'

The boy butted in before Molly had time to answer. 'Here, pay me first, and let me get on me road. I'll be losing custom.'

Molly found a florin amongst the coins that had made up the ten bob Trixie had given her. 'Here, and thanks, I couldn't have got here without you.'

'You're welcome. Now, Mister, can I unload me cargo or not?'

The man peered down at the boy for a moment and then asked Molly, 'Have you the money for whatever treatment she needs?'

'I have a pound.' *Please let that be enough! I can feed me and Ruby for a week on the rest.*

'Who sent you?'

'Trixie.'

'Bring her in.'

The boy helped her to lift the near-unconscious Ruby out of his barrow. 'I should have charged you more. I would have done, an' all, if I'd have known you had a pound on yer.'

'I need it for me mate. But if I see you around and I've got more on me, I'll give you some extra. You've been a good help. Thank you.'

The boy left muttering, 'Can't bleedin' spend any thankyous.'

Molly couldn't help smiling. She hadn't asked the young chap his name, but she hoped their paths would cross again and they would become friends.

Stepping inside the building gave her a feeling that somehow she was in the wrong place. Nothing about the grand entrance hall matched the outside. Flock wallpaper in red and gold gave an impression of riches. The deep, carved-mahogany bannister curved up to the landing above and framed a gold carpeted staircase. Oil portraits of men and women of a bygone age lined the hall, and a beautiful grandfather clock stood in the corner, gently ticking the seconds. The sound gave Molly a feeling of peace and homeliness.

'Help her through here.'

'Come on, Ruby love. Make one last effort. I can't hold you.'

Ruby rallied a bit and took some of her own

202

weight. Together they managed to get into the room indicated, where a different atmosphere met them. This was a clinic-cum-operating-theatre. Everything was pristine. The shade of the low light gleamed a bright silver, the high bed was covered in dazzling white cloths, and the lino floor had been scrubbed to within an inch of its life.

'Get her onto the bed.'

As Molly did this, she asked, 'What do I call you?'

'Most call me "geezer".' He laughed, a jolly sound. His face creased, giving him a nice gran-dad-type look. 'But "doctor" will do. We have a "no names" policy, so I don't want to know yours, and you're not going to know mine. Don't worry, I know the street people call me a quack, but I'm not. I'm a retired doctor who happens to want to help the less fortunate. Yes, I take money from those who have it, but I have a reason for that, and it isn't about lining my own pockets. It helps me to get supplies of anything I might need to carry out my work. Now, let's have a look at your mate. I'll start by taking her temperature, and then I'll examine the obvious place. I'll need you to undress her, and to wash her down below. In order to do that, you can fill that steel bowl with warm water at the sink over there, while I make the initial checks.'

In the silence, the water hitting the bottom of the bowl resounded around the room. By the time Molly had taken it over to where Ruby lay and placed it on the table next to the bed, the doctor had finished his checks and stood looking down at Ruby with a worried look on his face.

203

'Has she been coughing?'

'Yes. She's had a cough for a long time.'

'Hmm... I'll examine her further, but I think it's pneumonia, though there could be other things wrong, too.'

Molly was surprised at how she carried out the task of washing her friend without any embarrassment. It seemed a natural thing for her to do.

'Have you had any nursing training, young lady?'

'No.'

'You should think about it – you have a way with you.' As he bent over Ruby and began to examine her, the doctor said, 'You don't sound like the type to work the streets. Why are you?'

'I – I don't want to. I mean, it's how things happen, isn't it? Me family hit hard times and this was the only option for me.' Her fear of Eva made the truth out of bounds.

'There's plenty of other options for someone who appears as bright as you do. Besides, your country needs you, as the saying goes. There's work aplenty for those who want it. Women are needed more and more, in hospitals, factories and even manning fire engines. Why should you be any different?'

Molly's lack of an answer got the doctor lifting his head and giving her a piercing look. His blue eyes had a deep, youthful colour to them and his round face showed that he'd once been a handsome man. He still had a full head of thick hair, which was mostly as white as snow but showed a darkening at the temples, giving Molly the thought that it had once been black.

She lowered her eyes. 'Has me mate got a disease, then?'

'No, though she's lucky not to have, and so are you. You girls risk your lives doing what you do. I fail to understand it.'

'We don't do it willingly. Well, most of us don't.'

'I can help you, if you'll let me.'

'No! I – I mean, you don't know the whole story. Look, if me mate's all right, we'll get on our way.'

'I didn't say she was all right. She's extremely ill and is going nowhere tonight. And if you're her true mate, you will stay here too, so that you can take care of her. I'm not up to it, but I might be able to get someone in.'

'She can't... I – I can't. We have to get back. We have to!'

'Will she get care where you take her?'

'I–'

'Look, I'll help you to get back there, but this young lady must stay in my care. If she reaches the climax of her illness and isn't looked after properly, she will die.'

The enormity of what he said hit Molly. She had no control over the tears that flooded her eyes and tumbled down her cheeks. Everything seemed so hopeless. She couldn't bear to lose Ruby; she and Trixie were all she had in the world.

'I'm sorry, young lady, for whatever trouble you are in. Keep your pound and get a taxi back. Come back in the morning and we'll see how the land lies then.'

With this, the doctor began to erect a tent-like

205

contraption over Ruby. Molly desperately wanted to stay and help, but she had to return to Eva's, and she had to think up a story why Ruby hadn't done so.

Taking Ruby's hand, she squeezed it. 'Everything'll be all right, mate. I promise you. I'll come back tomorrow. You hang in there. Don't worry about a thing, love.'

The doctor followed Molly to the door. 'If she does pass away during the night, I will call the police in the morning. I'll tell them that I don't know who she is; that she appeared on my doorstep and I opened up my old surgery room to help her. She will get a pauper's grave.'

His words showed Molly the full pity of her own and Ruby's life. And she knew in that moment that if anything happened to Ruby she would go to the police herself. She didn't care about the danger she might be in if she did. As it was, Ruby wasn't out of Eva's clutches. Eva would find her somehow, and this tightened the fear Molly felt of that evil woman. Only the thought that, for now, Ruby was in the best hands possible gave Molly some comfort and helped her take her courage in both hands, and face going back to Eva without her.

'She collapsed, Eva. I had no say in what happened. Before I knew it, an ambulance arrived and Ruby was taken away. I don't know where to.'

The air stunk of the gin Eva was swigging. Of late she'd taken more and more to drink. This made her even more volatile. Molly waited.

'Just make sure you bring her back here tomorrow. If yer don't, Gus'll find her. I've had enough of the stupid cow anyway. Her days are numbered. If she's as ill as yer say, yer better pray that she dies, cos it'll be in a better way than she will at the hands of Gus.'

Eva's cackling laughter grated on Molly's nerves. It went on and on. Seeing the bottle of gin, Molly picked it up. She raised her hands above her head. Her body shook with power. Sweat ran down her face. But just as she was about to bring the bottle down and smash Eva's head with it, the wailing of a siren crushed the moment.

Molly lowered her arms. A feeling of utter disappointment settled in her, drowning the elation that had filled her body. But within seconds she was overcome by incredulity at what she was capable of.

As the half-dressed men and scantily clad girls came out of the boudoirs, Molly could only stare at them. She was still held by the shock of what had just happened. *Would I really have hit Eva?* Without a doubt, she knew the answer was *Yes*. What that made her she didn't know, but she liked the feeling that, given the chance, she would – and could – fight back. Putting the bottle down, she looked up to see Gus and Lofty appear through the door that led to the kitchen. *No doubt been stuffing themselves.* With the strength still flowing through her veins, she spoke to Gus as if she were his boss. 'Gus, Eva's drunk again. You and Lofty help her to the cellar.'

Gus took this as if he'd always done as Molly

had told him to, and with a gentleness that belied everything she knew about this brutal man, he lifted Eva in his arms.

Chaos broke out around Molly as everyone scrambled for the cellar.

Molly turned away from that direction. For once she wasn't going to hide from Hitler's might. She was going to have a leisurely soak in a bath – something that had been denied her for so long. She was a different Molly now. A stronger Molly. She would find a way out of this life, for her and Ruby. It couldn't be yet, but she'd find a way. She just needed Ruby to get better. The alternative was unbearable.

14

Simon & Flo

Adjusting to New Lives

Simon looked through the hatch of his office in Hut 6 of Bletchley Park. Before him were a dozen or so bent heads. The click-clackety noise of their machines was usually a pleasant enough background sound, but today it irritated him.

Across from his desk, Flo worked on a small table that stood against the dark-green painted wall. Her silence over the last hour reflected her absorption in trying to solve a particularly difficult coding that they were trying to get a handle on. Since Roland had introduced her to cryptic crosswords, she had become hooked on doing them and was a near-genius in the ability she'd shown for mastering even the most difficult clues. This aptitude had been a missing link in his work.

Simon watched her beavering away, scratching out columns of figures and scribbling down more combinations. He had to admit that he felt great admiration for Flo.

No, his feeling for her went deeper than that.

To say she'd replaced Lucinda in his heart wouldn't be correct, but she had soothed some of the ache from the deep gulf in his life that Lucinda had left. The love he felt for Flo was different from that he had for his lost sister, and for his mother too, for that matter. To him, the feelings he had for them were a natural extension of their relationship and all-encompassing. But the love he felt for Flo just flowed from him.

These last four weeks had been a strange time for him. The pain in his heart was relentless. It hung like a prophet of doom. Every morning he woke feeling a dull fear, as if something dreadful was going to happen. It disorientated him. He had to sit up and think things through. *What is wrong? What is going to happen?* Then clarity would kick him deep in the gut: *She's gone. My precious Lucinda is gone forever.*

Each time this happened, he would be assailed with fresh grief. He tortured himself with how she'd died. His imagination gave him her terror. They'd said it was instantaneous, but he couldn't believe that – he wanted to, but he was too intelligent to be fobbed off by the kindness of it.

Hanging wasn't instant. *Oh God!*

'Simon?'

He smiled over at Flo. What he would do without her, he didn't know, though the compassion of the other girls and his colleagues had sustained him, too. There had been a difficult hurdle to surmount. He'd not been able to deny that his sister and his supposed girlfriend were one and the same. The papers had exposed the lie, with pictures of Simon being the only relative in England. He'd explained that because of the impression he gave, and the ridicule his looks always brought him, they'd made up the story of her being Simon's girlfriend to protect him. Whether he'd dug himself a deeper hole for the future or not, time would tell.

Kitty hadn't wanted to let up. In his hearing, she'd said, 'I suppose we'll be told that northern girl is his girlfriend now.'

She'd received short shrift from Jane Downing, who'd told Kitty to shut up and remain shut up, as the subject was now closed. Jane had gone on to say that Simon was one of their own, and they had his welfare to think of.

That telling phrase – *one of their own* – had warmed his heart. He'd felt like hugging Jane, but instead had thanked her in an inadequate way, afraid of breaking the fragile hand of friendship that she'd extended to him.

'Are you alreet, Simon? You've been at staring into space this good while.'

'Oh, you know. Just thinking.'

'Aye, I knaw. I've been thinking an' all, and it don't help none. Look, we've both got two days

210

off next weekend – well, we will have if we crack on and get this last batch sorted. Why don't we go up to London, eh?'

'I can't. I–'

'As Mrs Leary says, there no such thing as "can't" – "can't" means "don't want to". I knaw you don't wish to, but I think you should use all of your courage and do it. I've sommat in mind for us.'

'Oh?'

'Aye. I've been thinking about it ever since we helped out the night we were all caught up in the bombing, and before that, if the truth be known. I'm thinking we could volunteer to help the Sallies or the WRVS.'

'Ha, you're priceless, Flo. You do know that the WRVS is a women's organization, don't you? I think it will have to be the Salvation Army – or the Sallies, as you call them.'

'You're not against the idea, then?'

'No. I really enjoyed helping that night. I'd love it. But, well, *Roland...*' He hated how he'd felt compelled to whisper Roland's name.

'Roland can come an' all.'

Flo had also lowered her voice.

'Oh, I wish, but I'm afraid he can't get away early enough. He's joined the ARP and he has to be on duty on Friday night through till Saturday morning.'

'Reet. I'll go to London then, and I'll get things set up for us. That's if I can stay in your flat? It has to be this weekend, as I'm going up north on Boxing Day, if I can get transport. I've three days off then. It'll give me a much longer break with

211

Mrs Leary and Kathy, and we're planning another Christmas Day for Kathy, so she can open my presents for her.'

'Of course I don't mind. Flo, I was going to ask you, would you help me to clear out Lucinda's flat when we get a couple of days off after Christmas?'

'Aye, I'll do owt to help you, you knaw that. I wish you could hear from your mam, an' all. It'd settle you some.'

'Yes, poor darling, I don't know if she's even received the letter I sent. I know there's no good way to hear the news, but I do keep wishing that I could have gone to India to tell her and Lucinda's father, myself.'

'Eeh, Simon, it's all very sad. I still can't take it in. It don't seem reet, especially as we've had no funeral.'

Simon fell silent.

'By, me tongue goes away with itself sometimes. I'm sorry, I shouldn't have—'

'No, please don't be. I feel the same, as if there hasn't been an ending. As if we've been told what happened, and we have to get on with it. Maybe a memorial service would help, but I'm not inclined to hold one until I hear from Mother. It would be bad cheese of me to finalize everything without her, or without giving her a chance to have her say about how the service should be conducted.'

'How about me, you and Roland go to church next time we are all together? We could ask the vicar to mention Lucinda and ask for prayers for her soul, and then we could plant a rose tree or

212

sommat in a pot and have it stand next to the steps of your house.'

'That sounds excellent. Thank you, Flo. Look, I *will* come with you.'

'Eeh, that'll be grand. I feel as if I've sommat to look forward to now.'

'Yes, I do too. It's a feeling there are things we can do for Lucinda, and that helps. I think I'll get my car out of the garage on Saturday, and we can drive out to the market gardens in Essex. I love the idea of the rose. I have a full tank of petrol, as I haven't had Bells out for a long time.'

'Bells?'

'Ha, that's my nickname for my car. I – it comes from something Lucinda said once when we drove out of London together for a picnic. It was a nice day, I had the roof off and the wind was lifting her hair. As we came to a more rural area, church bells were ringing and she put her hands in the air and shouted, *"Che bel suono!"* It's Italian for "what a beautiful sound!"'

He couldn't continue. Without him knowing it had happened, his eyes had brimmed over and wet his cheeks.

'By, that's a lovely memory. You knaw, I'd love to learn to speak another language – they have such lovely words.'

Simon wiped his huge white hanky over his face. Flo was right; it was a lovely memory. It had referred to the time that he and Lucinda had been in Venice and the church bells were ringing out. He had a sackful of memories of his beautiful Lucinda, and hoped that one day they would give him more joy than pain to revisit them. For

213

now, he was grateful to Flo for changing the subject. 'I'll teach you. We'll start with Italian. I have a feeling about Mussolini. I think he will be trouble in the future and we need to be ready for him. As far as I know, I'm the only one here who can translate from Italian at the moment.'

'Eeh, that'd be grand as owt.'

A small smile curved Simon's lips as he wondered at his suggestion. He ought to be teaching Flo to speak the King's English, not another language, but he knew he would miss her lovely sayings and the sound of her natural accent.

At first it had worried him as to how the staff would take to her, but a lot of them had warmed to her and she had their respect. They showed admiration and trust in Flo's work, even though some of them could be toffee-nosed. Flo wasn't like them at all. They were highborn – the daughters of dukes, lords and the noted wealthy, and extremely well educated too, especially those working here in Hut 6. However, they recognized Flo's intelligence, even if they fell short of actually socializing with her or including her in any of their conversations.

Flo didn't seem to mind. He knew it mattered to her that her ability and the work she did were acknowledged, but she wasn't one for trying to be something she wasn't.

They stood outside Simon's house just over a week later. The cold drizzle of the evening dampened them, but neither moved towards the shelter that going indoors would give them. Flo knew she should take the lead, but the sense of the moment strangled her ability to act.

A gloved hand took hers, seeking comfort. She peered into Simon's devastated face and felt a moment of guilt. *It's too soon for him ... too soon. What was I thinking?*

'Let's do this.'

'Aye, it'll be good to be in the rooms that Lucinda loved so much.'

'She did like my flat, didn't she? I suppose I was selfish to have bagged it. She was here much more than me, once war broke out.'

'Naw, she loved her own rooms more. And she had the run of the place when you weren't here. She told me she often lived downstairs, and used just her bedroom when she was here on her own.'

'That makes me feel even worse.'

'Aw, you're just that way inclined. She only did it as it was better than having an empty space below her in the daytime. She loved that it was yours. She wanted to keep it reet for you.'

'I know. I'm sorry – I'm picking at everything you say.'

His arm came round her. Flo smiled up at him. 'Reet, let's get the blackouts down.'

'Yes, stand where you are, so that when I close the door I don't bump into you. It's really dark in this hall at night.' As Simon said this, she could hear him moving about and knew he was locating the torch he kept on the hall windowsill.

A small beam lit enough of an area for her to follow and adjust the blinds, as they moved around the flat. Once that was done, Simon flicked the switches and flooded the rooms with light.

He stood for a moment in the doorway of the

front room and looked around. Flo's involuntary shiver prompted him into action. 'The fire's laid – I'll just put a match to it.'

'Aye, I'll go through and put the kettle on.'

It seemed to Flo that something other than the lingering spirit of Lucinda was making them stilted with each other. She daren't give her mind to what it might be.

When she came back through to the lounge, carrying the tray holding the teapot and cups, milk and saccharine, she met Simon coming down the stairs. His face looked grim. 'It was always going to be difficult, Flo.'

'Eeh, I knaw. Let's go in and settle down with a cuppa, then I'll make you sommat to eat.'

'That sounds like a good idea. I've fixed the blackouts upstairs, and Mrs Peterson, our daily, has remade the bed and left the fires up there ready. I've put a match to them, so it will be warm enough for you. That's if you'll be all right sleeping up there?'

'I will, if old Hitler doesn't send us any bombs tonight. Otherwise we'll both be in the shelter anyroad.'

'Yes, better prepare for that.'

'I have done. There's a flask of cocoa made. Eeh, where Lucinda got cocoa from, I don't knaw, but I'm glad she did.'

The evening was awkward. Their conversation felt forced. In the end, after a supper of fried potatoes and fried egg, Flo – thinking that coming down here had been a big mistake – excused herself and went up to have a bath and get into bed. She was tired enough to know that she would sleep. And she would find comfort from being in Lucinda's flat.

It surprised her, the next morning, to find that she'd slept right through the night. Why no siren had sounded, she couldn't imagine. Maybe an early warning had thwarted the bombers, or the air force had fought them back. She could think of no other reason why the bombers hadn't come.

'Are you awake, old thing?'

Flo pulled the covers up under her chin. 'By, Simon, don't you knaw it's rude to come into a girl's bedroom?'

'Yes, but I don't care.' He plonked himself on the end of her bed. 'Sit up. I've a cup of tea here for you. It's a peace offering. I was a pig to be with last night. I'm sorry.'

'Eeh, naw. There's no room for "sorry" in them circumstances. We're friends, and I knaw how you were feeling. I'm just glad that I was here for you.'

'I am, too.' The tone of this lit something in Flo. She'd felt the same tension last night, but now it was tangible, as if she could touch the feeling that was passing between them.

Looking away, she sipped her tea, letting the action bring her some composure. 'Reet, skedaddle, I need to get dressed – we've a lot to do today.'

'Yes, we have, and for that we need sustenance. I've been out and managed to get a loaf. We have some home-made marmalade from Mrs Peterson – it's not made of oranges, but of marrow and

217

ginger. It's delicious. I'll make us some toast by the fire.'

Marrow marmalade... Flo hadn't ever heard of that. She marvelled at how resilient housewives were these days. They couldn't get oranges, but what the heck; they wouldn't go without their marmalade and so they invented, or dug into historical recipes and made do.

The delicious smell coming from downstairs made Flo realize how hungry she was. She was dressed in no time, choosing to wear the new pair of slacks she'd bought in a little shop in Bletchley. It had felt good to be able to buy some quality clothes. The salary the Wrens paid her was far more than she needed and enabled her to buy these extra treats for herself.

She topped the navy slacks with a pink twinset. The soft wool of the short-sleeved jumper, with its wide waistband, cushioned her skin from the itchiness of the mohair cardigan that went with it.

As she brushed her hair, the low winter sun shining through the window highlighted the golden strands that peppered the chestnut sheen. After each stroke of the brush, her hair bounced back into curls, so Flo decided to leave it hanging loose. She made a side-parting and held it back from her face with a clip. Applying a light layer of lipstick and hanging a strand of cultured pearls around her neck, she stood back to admire the effect. Would Simon think she looked nice? She shook her head as if to banish the thought, grabbed her gas mask and her coat and ran down the stairs.

'Ready for anything, sir! And reporting for duty.'

Simon turned on his haunches. He was crouched in front of the fire. The flames had put a blush on his face. *He's beautiful.*

'You look stunning, darling. Come and sit down and have some toast.'

The light voice in which Simon said this could have meant he was talking to anyone. He called everyone 'darling'. Why it should matter to Flo, she didn't know. But it did. Making a joke, she said, 'By, I don't think "stunning" is the right word, but as long as I'm presentable... No one with a nose like mine can be called stunning.' She giggled at her own words.

'It's a lovely nose. The best bit of you.' Simon turned back to the flames, only to lose his balance. Swinging his arm up to regain it caused the bread on the end of the fork to plunge into the flames and catch fire. This sent him into a panic. He skipped around the room screaming out, 'Help, help!'

Flo was helpless with laughter. 'Calm down, Simon! You'll have the room on fire. Chuck it into the grate. Eeh, you're an idiot.'

Simon's laughter joined hers. The silly moment put them back once more at the level of their easy friendship. Flo felt relieved it was so. She couldn't understand the undercurrents that had crept into their relationship since they'd arrived here. She didn't want it to be like that. She didn't know how to cope with it, and was glad they could sit together and enjoy the toast with lashings of the scrummy marmalade in an easy atmosphere.

Finding the Salvation Army wasn't difficult. Although there hadn't been an air raid around their part of London during the night, there was work to do every day for the charities that worked in the area.

Just around the corner from the church over near Vauxhall Bridge they saw some activity around a van, the type they knew was used as a soup kitchen. 'I'll pull up here, you go and talk to them – you have a way with you. They might think I'm a time-waster.'

Simon's maroon Jaguar glided to a halt across the road from the van. Most people standing around the van turned and stared. Flo felt an attack of nerves as she walked towards them. One young 'un called out, 'What's the toffs want with bleedin' roadside charity?' A woman Flo assumed was his mother clipped his ear. 'Stop bleedin' swearing, you.'

Flo felt a giggle bubbling up. She smiled at the onlookers. 'Hello, I'm looking to offer help and wanted to talk to the–'

'Flo! Me lovely northern girl. Gawd love us, you're here again.'

'Pauline! Eeh, it's good to see thee. I were going to pop round to yours later. So, you're working with the Sallies now, eh?'

'I am. I've had a lot of help from them, and now that I'm on me feet I wanted to give sommat back.'

Pauline disappeared from the serving hatch that she'd poked her head out of, and then reappeared from a door around the back of the van. Flo opened her arms and then felt that she'd smother the tiny Pauline. Standing her at arm's length, she looked into the face she'd come to love in such a short time. 'By, lass, you're looking grand. You have colour in your cheeks, and your hair – well, I didn't realize it was so blonde. It's lovely.'

Pauline flushed. 'Give over! I've been putting a little bleach in me rinsing water. Ha, gotta keep up appearances. Me man might come home at any time, yer know.'

'Really!'

'I wish. But we live in hope, and keeping busy helps. What was that you said about volunteering then?'

Flo told Pauline her plans.

'So, you're settled now? I'm proud of you, girl. I won't ask you what you do – I've been schooled in the protocol of war by the Sallies, and you warned me last time I saw you not to do that. I'm the same with me customers. No matter who comes to me window, I serve them with a smile and a comforting word, if needed, but I never ask who they are or what's their business.'

'You're very wise. It can be awkward, and dangerous, to question folk these days. I sent you a letter; did you get it?'

'No, not yet, but everything's topsy-turvy, and the post is taking weeks longer than it used to. Except for bleedin' bills. They find their way through, no matter what.'

Flo laughed with Pauline and gave her another hug. 'You knaw, you can always come to me if you need help. I put me address in the letter. Though I never did find out if it was possible for you to be evacuated with the kids. Sorry about that. I explained in my letter about me mate, Lucinda, who I was going to ask.'

'Yer look sad, lav. Is anything up?'

Flo told her about Lucinda. 'No wonder you're down. Well, I reckon as this kind of work will help you, and her brother.' Pauline reached for Flo's hand and squeezed it. 'Don't worry about me and the kids. I've sent them off with me mum. It don't seem so bad, her being with them. They're in Wales. A place called Aberfan. They've been housed in a little cottage together and are loving it. I'm going to visit next week – I can't wait. In the meantime, I do war work three days a week. I work at a factory that makes uniforms. Then I do this, an' all.'

'That's grand. I'm reet pleased for you, Pauline.'

'Right, back to the business of you helping us. There's one question I will ask: how much notice do you and yer mate have, when you have time off? Only that might be a factor in whether they accept yer.'

'Oh, usually plenty, as we have a rota system. But it can be messed with, so it might be difficult to commit to a schedule. If you tell me where to go, I can tell them in charge our position, and see how it goes.'

'I'll take yer, if yer like. Here, Gladys, can yer manage for a while? I'll just be a mo.'

To this there was an answering reply: 'Of course, you take all the time yer need.'

'Right, come with me, Flo. The man who organizes us only lives around the corner and as much as I'd love a ride in yer mate's nice car, we can walk there.'

'I'll see that you and the kids get a ride one of these days. When this lot's all over, we'll go for a picnic. Eeh, that'd be grand.'

'It would. I'll look forward to it, lav. And like yer say, it'd be reet grand.'

Flo let out a laugh that had many heads turning. 'I've nearly got you speaking proper English, lass. Yorkshire English!'

They both laughed at this. Flo sobered first. 'Eeh, it's good to laugh, but I suppose we ought to get to see this boss of yours. I'll just go and tell Simon what's happening.'

Mr Jenkinson was a kindly man, who welcomed Flo and Pauline into his house. After listening to Flo, he nodded his head. 'Of course we would like your help. And don't worry about the rota that we normally run – we won't include you in it. Here's my telephone number. You just let me know when you are coming, then I will stand down someone who is tired or has done a lot of shifts. How does that sound?'

Glad that not being able to give a structured timetable was acceptable, Flo thanked Mr Jenkinson. 'Oh, before I go, will there be any training?'

'No. I'll just leave someone on with you both, for your first couple of shifts. You'll get the hang of it by then.'

'Yer can work with me for the rest of the afternoon, if yer like, Flo. Gladys was saying she was tired and her feet are swelling. I could send her home, then.'

'If Simon's up for it, then I am. Are you busy in the afternoons?'

'Can be. Them as have lost their homes are often salvaging what they can in the mornings. Then they come for sommat to eat in the afternoons. We had a load of sausage donated this morning. I'm thinking of making a big sausage stew, and then keeping some to griddle and serve on a stick.'

'Sounds good. I make a good stew. And Simon can serve at the window while we're busy cooking. He's good with a teapot.'

'Is Simon your young man then, Flo?'

Flo felt the blush sweep up from her core, before it reddened her face.

'Right. You don't have to answer that. I can see you'd like him to be.'

Not wanting to be untruthful, or to come across as ridiculing Simon by speaking of his homosexuality, Flo just giggled. 'Aye, sommat like that, but all will become apparent. Come on, let's get back to him.'

The small confines of the van, which housed two gas rings and a gas boiler, made for a few uncomfortable moments as Flo worked between Simon and Pauline. One thing she was glad of: those two got on like a house on fire, and dropped into a mode of taking the rise out of her on more than one occasion, calling her a cry-baby as she chopped the onions, and nicking her carrots as she tried to cut them into small pieces.

'Give over, the pair of yer. How am I meant to make a stew, if you've eaten half of me ingredients? The next hand to come across me will have their fingers chopped off!'

Simon made a play at a couple more attempts,

on one of them brushing Flo's hand, then holding her gaze for a moment, until Pauline coughed in a meaningful way.

'Mr Jenkinson won't have any carrying-on, yer know.' Pauline said this with a laugh in her voice, but it again prompted a sideways glance from Simon.

A woman at the hatch broke the moment. 'Here, have you that stew ready yet? The smell of them onions frying is getting the whole street going.'

'Now then, Fanny, you don't need to come begging here. You haven't lost your house, and your man's in a job that keeps him at home. We're here to look after the homeless.'

'Oh, I didn't see you back there, Pauline. Sorry.'

'No, I can tell that.'

As the woman walked away, Flo thought it worrying that those not in need might come to the van when she and Simon were in charge. 'How will we know if the folk are needy or not, Pauline? We could be giving food away to crafty folk like that woman.'

'You'll get used to it. Those in need have dark circles around their eyes and a haunted look. Or, if they've just been bombed out the night before, they'll be shook up and obviously upset and in shock. They don't look rounded and well fed, like that Fanny. Ha, she's got a right name as well. They say she offers herself around a bit, even though her man's at home, but then Dick Barker never had much about him.'

Flo exploded with laughter. Pauline looked at her, bewildered, as did Simon. This made her laugh even more. Her sides ached and her eyes

225

streamed with tears.

'What? What's got into you, Flo?' Even though Pauline and Simon didn't see what she was laughing at, they joined in.

At last she was able to say, 'It's what you called them... Th-their names. Oh, help!'

It took a moment for Simon and Pauline to cotton on. When they did, Flo thought they would never stop laughing.

'Well, I'm learning a lot about northerners from you, Flo. I thought us Londoners had a sense of humour, but I've never thought of Fanny and Dick Barker like that before. I'll never be able to look at them with a straight face again!'

The tension that had built up between Flo and Simon melted away after this, and as the van got busier there was no more time for frivolity. A steady stream of hungry, needy people soon demolished the stew and the sausages served on long sticks. Some of the folk tore at Flo's heart and she felt glad that she was able to help them.

Not wanting to dampen the lovely atmosphere they were working in, she didn't mention the idea that had come to her. There were a lot of young women who were shabbily dressed. When it came to the right time, she would suggest to Simon that they brought all of Lucinda's clothes to the Salvation Army. It would be good to see some of the women dressed in something decent.

Simon, she thought, had coped well and looked happier, and she didn't want to spoil that by bringing up the subject, in case it upset him. He'd taken a bit of stick because of his posh accent, but she'd been glad that he'd managed to hold on to his sense of humour.

Only one incident marred the afternoon. It was just as it was getting dark and they were packing up. A group of young lads came to mess about near the van. One of them called over, 'You nancy boys like doing women's work, don't yer? Yer should be fighting, but yer'd probably end up crying like a baby. Yer useless.'

Flo felt her body stiffen. Pauline looked over at Simon as if seeing him for the first time. She soon composed herself and told the boys to bugger off. This made them worse. Their name-calling was now accompanied by the throwing of stones, which bounced off the van with a sound as if a gun had been fired.

Flo was at a loss as to what to do, as the situation seemed to be getting out of hand. After a few moments Simon took off the apron that Pauline had wrapped around him, donned his uniform jacket and stepped out of the van. Flo held her breath. She'd been surprised when Simon had worn his uniform today, but thinking about it, it was like protective armour for him against these situations. A courageous man, he would hate to be thought of as a coward or a conscientious objector.

At the sight of him, the boys quietened down. Simon walked over to them. 'In times of war, a real man will turn his hand to any work that needs doing. There isn't a division of labour any longer. Women are doing what men would normally do, and vice versa. I hope, when you are called upon, you will step up to the board and do your bit.'

A small voice said, 'Yes, sir. Sorry, sir.' The others all joined in. Then one of them asked where Simon was stationed, which led to Simon sitting on the grass verge with them and explaining about asking questions during wartime. He did it in such a way, talking about spies and careless talk, that he held the boys' interest and gained their respect.

It gladdened Flo's heart to watch his confidence growing and to see him managing a situation she knew he'd not coped well with, up to now. She wanted to go over to him and hug him, but instead she helped Pauline pack up the van.

'I think I see the obstacle yer have now, Flo.'

Flo just smiled. Yes, there was a huge barrier to her love for Simon ever being returned in the way she would like it to be, but it didn't stop her being in love with him. *There! I've admitted it to myself. I am in love with Simon.*

An arm came around her. 'Come on, lav. This won't get the pots done. We've to take them back to the depot in those buckets outside and get them ready for stocking the van tomorrow. Let's put our backs into it. There's never a better cure for lovesickness than hard work.'

Flo nodded, then laughed as Pauline called over to Simon, 'Come on, mate. Are yer going to leave all the work to us, or are yer waiting for the Luftwaffe to drop in for a mug of your Rosie Lee?'

The boys and Simon laughed at this. Simon got up and shook each of the lads' hands, then saluted them. The action made Flo realize that if this war dragged on for another couple of years or so, these young 'uns would be in the thick of it. She supposed Simon had realized that too, and that was why he had treated them as if they were already soldiers. But beyond that, she felt proud of him. She knew he struggled with others' perceptions of him, but in this instance he'd risen to the challenge.

When he rejoined them, she smiled up at him. He smiled back. She didn't speak; she couldn't. The tension inside her wouldn't allow her to chat in the usual easy, companionable way they'd always enjoyed. Now there were only small moments of that. Flo wondered if it would ever return. She wished, with everything that was in her, that she hadn't lost her heart to Simon. There was no future in it for her, she knew that. *Eeh, Mrs Leary always told me to expect the unexpected, but how could I ever have prepared meself for falling in love with a man who prefers to have a lover of his own sex?* She had never even thought to meet such a man, but now that she had, Flo knew her life would never be the same again.

15

Molly

No Tinsel for the Wicked

Standing on the corner of Poland Street and D'Arblay Street, Molly watched the sign swing backwards and forwards outside the tobacconist's opposite. 'Craven A', the name of the fags advertised on the sign, stood out in red on a yellow background. What she'd give for a fag right now.

Just past the shop, a team of ARPs were dealing with the aftermath of last night's bomb attack. A pile of rubble was cordoned off and an ambulance stood nearby. Next to it a fire engine spewed pipes that still trickled water. A couple of firemen were reeling them in one by one and rolling them up into neat coils. One of them suddenly called out, 'Eh, look who we have here!' Santa Claus came round the corner, carrying a heavy sack. 'Morning, Santa, yer starting early, I see.'

'Ha, Rudolf dropped me off at six a.m. and he'll pick me back up at four p.m. I've to deliver early, this Christmas Eve, before the Luftwaffe come to wish us all a Merry Christmas.'

They all laughed, increasing the sense of loneliness that enveloped Molly.

'Where you off to then, Santa?' one of the ARP men asked.

'Charing Cross Underground Station. There's going to be a children's party down there this afternoon. Poor buggers.'

'Well, come and have a warm around the old brazier and get a cup of tea in yer. We've got the kettle on and we've a drop of brandy to go wi' it.'

'Brandy?'

'Yes, some toff brought a flask of it over to us earlier. A nice Christmas present, if ever we saw one.'

'Don't mind if I do, guv'nor. Ta, mate.'

As the ambulance drove off, Molly thought she heard the man shout over, 'What about you, Miss? Yer look froze to death – come and have a warm.'

She waited, unsure.

'Come on, Miss, we won't bite yer. Come and share in our Christmas cheer.'

Molly couldn't believe they were inviting her. They knew what she was, for her attire alone would tell them that. Short skirt, high heels and low-cut top. Not that she was touting for business at this hour, but she'd had a customer around the corner who'd chucked her out just before the siren had sounded. When it had, she'd made her way to Charing Cross Underground and spent the night there.

The underground had been packed with families. Most had brought decorations with them and they'd set about getting ready for the party that this man, dressed as Santa, had spoken of. They'd sung carols and drunk home-made beer, but nothing had been offered to her. She'd found out what it was to feel lonely amongst a crowd. She thought they'd have treated a German soldier better than the short shrift they gave her. Judgemental, she'd call them. Though one young girl had spoken to her and shared her mug of tea with her, which had warmed her a little.

Taking up the offer, Molly walked across to them. 'Ta, thanks. I could do with a warm.'

'Here, lav, we've a spare blanket. Wrap it around yer.'

Their kindness plopped a tear onto Molly's cheek. She wiped it away. She could only nod her thanks as the tall fireman wrapped her in the warmth of the blanket. 'Yer working early an' all. Not much business about at this time of day for yer, is there?'

She told them how she came to be there.

The younger members put their heads down in embarrassment. She hadn't thought. She'd become so used to her way of life that it seemed normal. But it wasn't; there were folk, lots of them who, like she used to, thought her way of life was the dregs and the pit of degradation.

Drawing deeply on the fag one of the men had given her, she sipped her tea, and the nip of brandy it contained warmed her inside. She felt a sudden urge to explain herself and make them understand her position. 'I can't help what I am. I got into the clutches of Gus Williams and Lofty Tyler.' Everyone knew who they were – these men included. Molly could tell that by the sharp intakes of breath and the looks on their faces.

The one dressed as Santa was the first to speak. 'So, yer haven't much of a choice then, girl. I feel sorry fer yer. If yer want to get away from that gang, yer going to have to travel to the other end of the country.'

'Or join up.' This came from the tall fireman. 'Women are doing so all over the country, yer know. There's a recruitment office just down the road. It opens in an hour: why don't yer take yerself there and explain yer situation?'

One of the younger ones said, 'I'd go to the police and tell them, if I were you.'

'The cops are hand-in-glove with the gang, or at least most of them are. I wouldn't know how to find one that ain't bent. And if I went to the wrong one, I'd be for it. It ain't worth the risk.'

They were silent for a moment. Molly wondered what was going through their heads, then an older ARP man spoke. 'Look, I only live around the

232

corner. Me missus is the salt of the earth. I'll take you there, and she'll help yer clean yerself up and let yer have one of her frocks. Then yer can look half-decent when yer go to the recruitment office.'

The tears tumbled at this. Kindness always broke Molly more quickly than cruelty. The tall bloke put his arm round her. The young one kicked at a brick and said, 'It ain't right. I always thought you girls wanted to do what yer do.'

Between sobs, Molly told him that there were some who did, but a lot had been forced into it by circumstances or brutality. 'Believe it or not, I was a respectable girl. I didn't know that this kind of life existed, and nor did me mate. Now she's in hospital with pneumonia. Gus and Lofty have been to visit her and have told her they know where her sister lives, and if she breathes a word then she's done for.'

The shock on the men's faces as she said this frightened Molly. She didn't want them to do anything they might perceive as the right thing, like reporting the gang to the police. That would mean dire consequences for her. 'Look, there's nothing you can do. I can take care of meself. I'll get going now, but thanks for your kindness. I'll find a way of going to that recruitment office, but I've to watch out for me mate first and make sure she's safe.'

'I feel sorry for you, lav. If you're near to Charing Cross this afternoon, pop down and I'll see that you get a mince pie.'

Molly wiped her face on the back of her hand and smiled at Santa. 'Ta, mate. And all of you, thanks for showing me a bit of human kindness.

I'm sorry if I've worried you. But I'll be all right.'

'Well, we work in this area all the time, so you can always come and find us. I'll speak to me missus; she works with the WRVS and the Salvation Army. I'll see if she can get the women to extend their charity to you working girls. They knit jumpers, scarves and gloves. You could do with some of them.'

Molly smiled even more widely at this and had a job not to giggle. The thought of prostitutes walking around in woolly jumpers in a rainbow of colours tickled her.

The more the idea took root, the more her restraint cracked, until she burst out laughing. The men looked at her as if she had gone mad, until she gained enough control to share the picture she had in her head. They all laughed with her then. It was a moment like none she'd had for a long time. But it was cut short when a woman pushing a pram shouted over, 'Get away with you, yer floozy. What d'yer think yer up to, corrupting men who have a job to do. Yer disgusting.'

'Now then, Missus, she ain't doing any harm. She's just having a warm, and a drop of tea. Even the devil himself deserves that on a morning like this.'

The woman looked at the tall fireman and scoffed. 'Ha, tickled what yer have in yer trousers, has she? Yer all the same. Men!'

With this, she went off in a huff, and the men laughed. Molly didn't. Inside, she cringed. Inside, she knew that was what she'd become. A floozy that only men talked to.

'Don't let her worry yer, lav,' Santa said. 'She's

only jealous. She'd give her eye-teeth to be you. I mean, look at yer. Hobnobbing with Santa and three strapping firemen, and these ARPs. Oh, aye, the ARPs are old enough to be yer grandfather, but the rest of us are still desirable, and all she's got is a man overseas. Yer have to pity her.'

This set them off laughing again, even though the last bit was probably true, and the poor woman was alone with a baby whose dad had never seen it.

Feeling cheered, Molly wished them all a happy Christmas and made as if to leave.

'Hang on a mo, lav.' Santa pulled his beard down so that she could see his lovely crinkly face. 'Just showing yer what I look like, so yer'll know me another time. I always hang out in the Copper Kettle Cafe, down the road. If yer need a cuppa anytime, come in there and I'll buy yer one. Don't worry about what folk'll think – they'll get over it. Yer might even do me standing some good. "Look at old Derrick," they'll say. "He's still got it, then." Ha-ha.'

With their laughter ringing in her ears, Molly headed in the direction of Eva's place in Beak Street. She had a feeling that she'd found some friends who would help her, and when the time was right she could easily find them again.

As she turned into Regent Street and passed the Quality Inn Restaurant, two girls, dressed in smart grey uniforms, were watering the plants outside. When they caught sight of her, they stopped and stared. One nudged the other. 'Had a heavy night, lav?'

Molly's face flushed, but she held her head high,

ignored them and walked on by. But when she heard the word 'Scum!', her high spirits dampened.

What they were doing was something she should be doing; or, rather, she should be living in a quiet suburb as David's wife. *Where are you, my darling David?* As soon as the thought came to her, Molly banished it. David belonged to a different life, a clean life; she couldn't taint what she had with him by bringing him to mind in this sleazy world of hers where she didn't even have the respect of a couple of waitresses, or of a young mother coping with a baby.

As she turned into the alleyway that would take her up the steps to the brothel above the tailor's shop, her heart dropped even more. But she straightened herself, patted her bra, where she'd hidden the present she'd nicked from under the punter's Christmas tree, and prepared herself to face the onslaught of having been out all night and only earning a few bob. Somehow she'd have to find a way of pacifying Eva so that she could go out and meet up with Trixie tomorrow, Christmas Day. It was now or never, in their rescue of Ruby.

Molly had been given responsibility to put part of the plan to save Ruby in place, and she'd done that. She only hoped Trixie had sorted the rest of what needed doing. Molly didn't know if the plan would work, but they had to try. Ruby couldn't come back here. She and Trixie *had* to prevent that.

They both had some money put by. Last night hadn't been typical of the earnings Molly had managed to make, since she'd cleaned herself up and Trixie had been helping her. Trixie had been true to her word and had brought some decent clothes for Molly to change into each day. And she'd washed and done her hair and cleaned her teeth. Dolly had kept her promise too, and had let Molly change her clothes in a room around the back of the cafe. Though she hadn't been back there to change this morning, none of the girls would be around this early, and even if Eva was, she'd be drunk and wouldn't notice Molly's clothes.

If their plan worked and Ruby was taken to safety, then Molly was going to make her own escape. Now that she had the new friends she'd met this morning, she felt more optimistic about the outcome for herself. The ARPs and the firemen had given her options. She could go to the wife of the kindly older man and get some decent *ordinary* clothes. Then she would go to the recruitment office and sign up. She'd ask the kindly ARP man and his wife if letters from that office for her could be sent to them. Then the moment she was accepted, she'd leave here. The thought lifted her spirits.

As it turned out, getting out of the flat on Christmas morning had been easy. Eva had been vexed that Molly hadn't brought much money back with her, despite being out all night. Gus had slapped her a bit, causing her eye to swell. But by Christmas Day all was forgotten. The absence of a bombing raid on Christmas Eve night, due to the armistice agreed by both sides, which was to last until 29th December, had given them all a respite and had meant that even Gus, Lofty and Eva had been in a good mood. This had increased as they'd drunk large quantities of booze, and shared some with the girls, on Christmas Eve.

Molly had gone to bed early and slept well, until Gus had dragged her out and taken her into one of the boudoirs. She'd endured his long-drawn-out pounding of her until he'd fallen asleep, exhausted.

When they'd all woken this morning, Eva had announced that she, Gus and Lofty were going over to Molly's dad for Christmas Day dinner. All the doors were locked, but this didn't deter the girls. They had a way of escaping through a window that led onto a flat roof. The window had long been fixed so that it wouldn't open, but one girl had been the daughter of a builder and knew how to prise out the glass and replace it with little tacks. If you wanted to use the facility it cost you, but today the girl opened it for nothing.

Thinking of this mode of escape made Molly reflect on what kept all the girls here. Some had opened up about their abused lives, while others had been sucked in by Gus paying them attention. But all were held here by fear. Fear of being killed and dumped in the Thames, or fear for a loved one's safety. In some ways this made for a community feel at times, and today more than at any other time, as they all helped each other. This lessened their fear. Without exception, all the girls were going to Dolly's for dinner, so there'd be no snitches. It was an 'all in this together' feeling.

Dolly had been taking a penny a week off them for months, to pay for everything. Molly and

Trixie were going later, but first they had a job to do, and Christmas Day was the ideal time.

Trixie was where she said she would be, on the corner of Regent Street. 'Merry Christmas, lav. Give us a hug.' The two girls cuddled up. 'Here. I've brought you a gift.'

Molly looked at the little parcel. She guessed its contents by the shape. Unwrapping it, she wasn't disappointed. 'Me own Max Factor lipstick. Oh, Trixie. Ta, love. I won't ask yer where yer got it.'

They laughed together at this. 'Ask no questions, get told no lies, girl.'

'I've got sommat for you as well, Trixie.'

Molly was more excited about giving her present than about receiving the one Trixie had given her.

The punter who had kicked her out last night was married. Molly didn't know where his wife was for the evening, but she'd found out about her existence when she'd gone downstairs to let herself out. There had been presents under a tree by the door. Those she had time to look at were labelled 'To my darling wife'.

There had also been pictures around the room of the punter and a woman. In the most recent ones, the punter and his wife were in their fifties. Molly had seen that the woman still had a great figure. She had a nice face, too. Happy-looking. Seeing this had made Molly feel guilty for a moment. But guilt hadn't entered into it when she'd seen a small present on the edge of all the others and had felt how soft it was. She'd ripped the paper back and had seen a pair of silk stockings nestling in blue tissue paper. She'd immediately thought of the delight Trixie would feel at receiving these.

'Oh, Molly, lav. Silk stockings!'

Trixie encased her in her arms again. Afraid she would cry, Molly eased herself out of the close hug and changed the subject to the reason they were meeting up. 'Right, love, we have to get on. Have you sorted Ruby's sister?'

'Yes. She was glad to get out. It seems the stepdad's brother started to visit her bed, once Ruby disappeared. Her name's Mandy, and she should be up in Scotland by now with me mate. Me mate can take them both in for the winter, but then they'll have to find somewhere. She runs her house as a guesthouse, but at the moment she has soldiers staying, as most of her rooms are commandeered for them because her house is near a training ground. She could do with some help, and has an attic where she can put Ruby and Mandy. I told her they mustn't stay in one place too long, so she'll see about getting them to volunteer, once the weather improves. They can be Land Girls, or sommat along them lines. They'll never be found, deep in the country.'

'I didn't expect that. You never said anything about Scotland. How do you know this mate, Trixie?'

'She was a school friend. She was always a bit better off than us, but not posh. Anyway, her gran died and left her the place. She's run it ever since. She's never married, and never been bothered about men. A proper spinster type, with a kind heart.'

'You should have gone to her yourself.'

'That life's not for me. I'm happy doing what I'm doing. I told yer, I want me own house one of these days, where I can take care of the girls that I'll have working for me, and make meself a packet.'

They were quiet for a moment. Molly didn't have an answer to this, as she didn't understand how Trixie could have such a dream. Eager to put into action the plan to get Ruby safe, she brought the conversation back to that. 'How was Ruby when you went to see her, Trixie?'

'She's not right by a long way, but she's strong enough to make the journey. When we get to the hospital she should be waiting for us. It's up to her to get out of the place. We'll dress her in this coat I've brought with me, and get her to Dolly's. We'll have to keep her out of sight. If that bloody Delilah sees her, all our plans'll go up in smoke. Delilah will do anything to further herself, even if it means hurting her mate.'

Molly shuddered, remembering the time that Delilah had snitched on her to Eva when Eva had found her tea-caddy. There were so many risks in what they were doing, so many things that could go wrong.

'It'll be all right, Molly, don't worry. I've got an ATS uniform for Ruby to travel in. I've even got an army coat for her, so she'll be warm enough – it's all at Dolly's. And Dolly will pack her up some food for her travels. I've got a cabby I know who'll take her to your Aunt Bet's. Are yer sure she'll welcome her?'

'Yes, she gave me her phone number in one of

241

the letters she sent to me, before all this happened. I memorized it, just in case, and I've
spoken to her. I told her everything. She was
shocked about what has happened to me, but I
was able to persuade her not to do anything about
it. She understands. Aunt Bet's had more than a
few run-ins with gangster types and knows the
importance of keeping quiet. She wants me to
come there with Ruby, but I told her that would
be too dangerous, as hers would be the first place
they'd look for me if I went missing. Aunt Bet's
promised that as soon as the trains start running
after the holiday, she will make sure Ruby's on her
way. She'll sort out the route and everything.'

'The beauty of all this is it being Christmas. No
one's expected to get the punters in. The business
folk are with their families. The shops are all
closed, so there's no one with any excuse to come
to London. Any servicemen who are still around
and have some leave will want to go home, so
there'll be no one looking for girls. Talk about a
bleedin' armistice from bombing – we've got one
of our own. Three days' rest from opening our
legs.'

Molly burst out laughing at this, but then
became serious. 'We just need time to be on our
side. We have to hope Gus won't be sent to check
on Ruby for a few days. I don't think he will. I
think they'll stay at me dad's tonight.'

'Well, let's hope that lasts a few days. Come on,
there's me cabby mate. He's all right, is Randy.
He'll do anything for me. He wants to marry me
one day.'

This floored Molly. 'What!'

242

'Ha, I'm still desirable, yer know. Randy finds me so anyway. He knows all about me game and it ain't put him off. He reckons he'll come in with me, when I'm ready to get me own place.'

Molly shook her head. It was beyond her how Trixie could be content with the future she'd mapped out for herself.

Molly looked over at Ruby. Though pale, she looked good in the uniform. She'd put on weight, but her nerves were upset. Her clammy skin told a tale, as did her shaking hands.

The noise from the cafe was deafening, as someone played the old piano that stood in the corner and two of the girls were singing, amidst laughing and shouting.

'Are you all right, love?' Molly asked Ruby.

'Never better, Molly. Thanks for everything. And you, Trixie. Are yer sure that none of the girls will tell, if they do see me? I can't bear you getting into trouble, Molly.'

'They'll not see yer, lav. I promise. They know nothing, lav. Come on, chin up – you'll be leaving in a mo. Yer should be bleedin' happy.'

'Trixie's right. None of them have a clue. Now, hurry, love. We need to get you on the road, and sharpish.'

'Ta, Molly, and you, Trixie. I'll not forget this. You're real pals. Give us a hug.'

'Take that bleedin' fag out of your mouth first, darling.'

They all laughed at this. Just as they did so, the music got louder. 'Quick, get into the broom cupboard, someone's coming.'

243

There was a moment when they heard the music as if all the revellers were in the back room with them, but whoever it was must have changed their mind, as the sound died down to its previous level.

Trixie sighed. 'Bleedin' hell, it's like living in a nightmare. Let's get you on your way, darling, before someone does come in here.'

Randy, the cabby, put his head around the door leading to the outside. 'Trixie, a word, lav.'

As Trixie left, Molly put her arm round Ruby. 'You're going to have to go now, love. Are you ready?'

'I am, but I'm going to miss yer, Molly – both of yer.'

'I know, love. But I'll write. I have the address. And I'll give you an address for me, as soon as I have one.'

'Yer mean it: yer will get out, won't yer, Molly?'

'I will. Just as soon as you're safe, I'll be joining up. It's what I've wanted to do for a long time. Ah, here's Trixie. Take the bag with your sandwiches in, Ruby. And good luck.' Ruby clung to her, and Molly felt the tears prickling the backs of her eyes. She decided, for Ruby's sake, not to break down. Coming out of the embrace, she spoke to Trixie. 'All set, love?'

Trixie didn't answer for a moment, but when she did, she dropped a bombshell. 'Randy can't take yer all the way, Ruby lav. I'm sorry, but he couldn't get enough petrol and can't guarantee he can get some on the way. He's tried all his mates, but with it being Christmas they've all used more than normal. He's only got enough to get him to

244

Leicester and back. You'll get there around three this afternoon. You'll just have to go into a bed-and-breakfast till the trains start up again, then catch one to Birmingham.'

'Oh, Trixie.'

'I know, Molly, but it'll be all right – just a hitch, that's all. Leicester's five hours from here, so no one's going to find her. There's nothing we can do. Bleedin' shortages.'

'I'll be all right, Molly. Don't worry. I'll find somewhere to stay. I'm used to looking out for meself. Anyway, in this uniform I'll be taken in anywhere. If I can't find lodgings, I'll knock on the door of a house and tell them I missed me connection and got stranded. Anyone'll help a girl in uniform.'

'She's right. Let's not put hurdles in places where there might not be any. You've got plenty of money, Ruby, you'll be fine.'

Molly wasn't so sure, but was determined to put a good face on things. 'I'll ring me Aunt Bet in a couple of days, love. You'll be there by then. She'll have a plan of where to get the trains, and the times they go for your journey to Scotland.'

Randy popped his head around the door. 'Are yer coming? I can't keep me engine running much longer and if I stop it I might have a job to start it again. Hurry up, girls.'

'Yeah, we're coming, Randy love. Is the coast clear?'

'There weren't anyone out there when I came in. Let's get going. We've a long drive.'

Molly and Trixie stood a moment looking at the

closed door. 'Well, she's gone. I don't mind telling yer, I'm worried for her, Molly. I'll be glad when yer let me know she's on her way to Scotland.'

'I know. There's nothing to link us to her disappearance. She left the hospital on her own. So staff can't say that we came to get her. And no one here saw her.'

'Just the same, I reckon I'll go out and have a look around, make sure they've got off all right.'

'I'll come.'

Outside the air was damp with the sleet that was falling. The car was visible in the distance, the smoke from its exhaust leaving a smelly trail behind it. The fumes caught in Molly's throat and made her cough. The cough turned to tears. Trixie held her. Her own face was wet, but she made light of it. 'Bleedin' weather, it soaks yer in seconds.'

Neither of them saw a figure jump back into the shadows. Delilah hurried back inside, and out through the back door of the cafe to the yard where the toilet was. No one had noticed her.

Everyone was half-drunk on the cheap whisky that one of the customers had given to the girls. The smell of cooking filled the cafe, and the warm atmosphere hit Trixie and Molly as they walked back inside. One of the girls passed the bottle to Molly. After a swig she began to relax. Trixie took a swig too, then announced that she had a couple more bottles stored at the back of the cafe. Everyone cheered. 'Fetch it through, Dolly, will yer?'

Dolly looked up from the pan she was stirring. 'I ain't got four pairs of bleedin' hands, yer know.

Fetch it yerself. Yer lazy cow – anyone'd think it's Christmas or sommat.'

This set the girls laughing. Molly went over to Dolly. 'I'll help. What d'yer need doing, eh?'

As Molly took over stirring the gravy, others were set the task of laying the tables. Suddenly it occurred to Molly that Delilah was missing. Her heart skipped a beat. 'Have you seen the bitch, Dolly?'

Dolly knew who she meant. 'Yeah, she went out the back a bit ago. She should be back in by now; she's had long enough to do two pees, and anything else an' all. What's she up to?'

'You can never feel safe with her. But Ruby's on her way, so we've no need to worry. Delilah wouldn't have seen anything from the yard.'

'Here she is now. She looks a bit wet. Is it raining that hard out there?'

Molly didn't answer. She left the gravy and went over to Trixie. 'Look at the bitch, she's been out to the bog. How d'yer reckon she got that wet? Christ, if she knows anything, we're done for.'

'She can't know anything. Stop worrying. Yer know yerself how wet we got, and we were only out there a little while. Me cardigan's that wet, I've had to take it off.'

Molly felt better on hearing this. Trixie was right; her own cardigan was still wet and clinging to her. But somehow the niggling worry wouldn't leave her. Delilah was like a snake in the grass. She seemed capable of finding out your deepest secrets. And Molly knew, to her detriment, that Delilah had no compunction about using

247

anything she knew to ingratiate herself with Eva.

A chill ran through her and she prayed to God that Eva, Gus and Lofty wouldn't return to the flat for at least a couple of days. *I hope there's nothing to worry about, but just in case, please God, give Ruby a couple of days' start. And stay with her and protect her.*

16

Flo

Meeting Molly

The hug from Kathy was difficult to disengage from. The child had flung herself at Flo the moment she'd opened the gate of Mrs Leary's cottage. 'Eeh, Kathy love, give over. You're crushing me.'

'Oh, I'm sorry, Flo. I just can't believe you're here. It's grand to see you. I've been at counting the days. Me friend's fed up with me going on about you.'

Ruffling Kathy's lovely dark curls, Flo looked down into her deep-brown, trusting eyes, and a pain of love for this child filled her. 'I've missed you, little one. But it's grand to hear that you have a friend.' She turned to Simon, then back towards the child. 'Friends enrich your life and are always helping you. This is my friend, Simon. Simon, this is Mrs Leary and Kathy.'

'Hello, Simon. I'm Flo's sister, ain't I, Flo?'

'You are, little one.'

Simon greeted Kathy, his face a picture of amusement. 'Pleased to meet you both. Flo talks about you all the time. I feel as if I know you already.'

'And she tells us all about you in her letters, an' all. Are you her boyfriend?'

Feeling herself blushing at this from Kathy, Flo laughed. 'He is a boy and he is a friend, my best friend. Now who's your friend? Do I know her?'

Mrs Leary answered: 'Aye, you do that; at least you may be remembering her mammy. Come in, Flo. It's powerful good to see you, so it is.'

Flo's eyes filled with tears as Mrs Leary gently moved Kathy out of the way and hugged Flo to her. Hugging her back, Flo realized how much she'd missed this lovely Irish woman who'd become like a mother to her.

'Let's be getting you both inside in the warm – for sure you'll be catching your death. I've the kettle making a fair noise at whistling its head off in the kitchen.'

Flo laughed again, and her body filled with the feeling that only coming home can give. The familiar smells assailed her as the heat of the kitchen took her into its welcoming aura. The ever-present stewpot bubbling on the side of the stove, and the baking smells coming from the oven, mingled with the fresh clean smell of the bright, homely kitchen. Mr Leary sat by the fire, the smoke puffed from his pipe spiralling up above his newspaper. He lowered the paper and peeped over the top. 'Hello, Flo. As Mrs Leary says, it is

249

good to be seeing you.'

'Eeh, and you, Mr Leary. This is me friend, Simon.'

Flo had already warned Simon of Mr Leary's extreme shyness, so she was glad to see that he didn't try to engage him in conversation, but just greeted him and shook his hand in a polite but friendly way.

'Well, Flo – and everyone – if you'll excuse me, I'll take my leave now and go and see Roland. I'll see you all tomorrow, for the pretend Christmas Day. I'm really looking forward to that. Two Christmas Days in one year. Excellent.'

Mrs Leary tried to insist that he stay for a cup of tea, but Simon refused, saying he was eager to see Roland. With this, he kissed Flo's cheek and left. She felt bereft. Tomorrow seemed a long way off.

Once the door had closed on Simon, the conversation turned to Kathy's friend, as Flo removed her coat. 'Are you for remembering Mary Ruddles? She was after leaving Leeds when you were just on sixteen, so she was. Anyway, she's back and married and has two wee ones. It is her eldest, Patty, who is Kathy's friend.'

'Can't say as I do, Mrs Leary. Did you meet her at school, Kathy?'

As Flo sat and drank her tea, news came thick and fast of the goings-on in Leeds. It was as if she'd never been away, as she now knew what almost everyone in the area had been up to, as well as their cats and dogs – or at least that's what it felt like. But the best was to come, as Mrs Leary said, 'Now then, you'll never be after guessing who it is will be here in a wee while?'

Kathy looked into Flo's face and gave the news. 'Eunice. She'll be here soon. She came before, and we made friends.'

'Well, that's grand news. How is Eunice getting here, Mrs Leary? We could have given her a lift, if we'd known.'

'Sure, the trains are running, and Eunice didn't want to be bothering you. And she'll take the settee tonight as she can only stay tomorrow, whereas you will be here for a couple of days.'

Surprised to hear that the trains were running on Boxing Day, Flo thought this a good opportunity to let both Mrs Leary and Kathy know that she had to cut short her visit by a day. 'I'm sorry, but I have to leave the day after tomorrow, too. There's nowt I can do about it. Me and Simon are needed in London. I told you about helping the Sallies, in me last letter, didn't I? Well, this being Christmas time, they're really short-handed and they've asked us to work a van on Saturday evening. You see, the truce is over tomorrow night and they're afraid they will be very stretched on Saturday.'

'Oh, that's a powerful shame, so it is. We were planning on having you to ourselves on Saturday, thinking you had to return on Sunday, but we're after being very proud of you. Whatever it is you do for the good of the war, we have no knowledge of it, but this extra work is sorely needed.'

'But I don't want you to go, Flo.'

'Sorry, love. Like I once told you, we all have to make sacrifices. Now, carry one of me bags up for me, Kathy, and I'll carry this one. No, not that one – that has to stay put. Mrs Leary will find a safe place for it under the tree. Have we all we need for tomorrow, Mrs Leary? Only, I've brought a few things with me.'

'That we have, me darling. I've managed to get hold of a chicken, but don't be asking me where from, as I'll only be telling you it came from the little people.'

'Ooh, chicken! By, that'll be a treat.'

'And we have a cracker each, an' all, Flo. Me and Mrs Leary made them. It's a surprise what's inside, and they won't go bang, but they're lovely, all the same.'

Flo thought everything was lovely. The warmth and cosy smell of the kitchen. The love that encased her. The happiness she saw in Kathy. And the thought of having Eunice home, to share in the fun. But even better than that, the fact that Simon would be here tomorrow, too.

She and Simon had managed to get their friendship and working relationship back onto an even keel. Flo hadn't revealed her feelings, and it had gradually become easier for her to cope, as acceptance had settled inside her. It had to be like that. She couldn't allow her heart to run away with feelings that could never be returned.

Seeing Eunice wasn't quite the joy Flo had anticipated. Eunice was a shadow of her former self. *Why didn't Mrs Leary say anything to me?* 'Eeh, Eunice love, what's to do?'

Before she could answer, Mrs Leary said, 'I'll be taking Kathy out for a wee walk. She's to have her tea with Patty, her friend who we were after telling you about, Flo. You girls be taking the time to catch up. Take yourselves through to the parlour – there's a fire lit, so there is.'

It seemed to Flo that Mrs Leary couldn't wait to leave. When the door had closed on them, Flo turned to Eunice and opened her arms. 'What is it, lass? You've lost a lot of weight since I saw you a few weeks ago.' Eunice came willingly into her hug, but holding her increased Flo's concern, as she felt Eunice's bones protruding through her flesh. 'Are you ill, Eunice lass?'

'I'm not feeling right, Flo. And, like you say, the weight's dropping off me. They're doing tests, but I can make a good guess what's wrong, and it ain't good.'

Flo couldn't speak.

'Let's sit down, Flo. I'm out on me feet.'

As Flo followed Eunice through to the parlour, she could see her weakness in her walk. She wanted to scream out her protest at whatever it was that ailed Eunice and had brought her so low in such a short time.

As they entered the parlour, the Christmas tree glittered in the light from the window, but to Flo the beautiful creation of tinsel, with the aged but still-perfect angel on top, now dulled to nothing, in her fear for Eunice. Once they were settled, she waited for Eunice to speak. Shock zinged through her body when she did. 'I think I have cancer.'

'No! No ... no. You can't have! Eeh, lass, you're so young. Oh God, no.'

They clung together.

A feeling of desolation seized Flo. Eunice's young life had been blighted with abuse and the

253

loss of a child; and now to be dealt this devastating blow, just as she was flourishing – it all seemed so unjust.

'Is there no hope?'

'Yes. There is treatment by radiotherapy, but it depends. If I do have cancer, then it has to be caught before it spreads. I noticed blood weeks ago when I went to the toilet, and I immediately reported to the sickbay. The problem is that everything takes so much time, and there's so few resources. Mind, I'm lucky, being a nurse. I get looked after. If I were some poor young woman who couldn't pay for medical help, or to see a doctor even, then it'd be much suffering and curtains for me, for certain. As it is, I still might die.'

'Eeh, love, no. We have to keep thinking that it might be sommat else. There's allus hope, they say. When will you know if you have it, and how bad it is?'

'On Monday, when I return to the hospital. I'm to go to the sickbay and will be given my results.'

'Oh, Eunice love, I'll be at praying so hard that God will find it difficult to refuse me. But, lass, if He does and it is what you fear, I'll be by your side fighting with you. Does Mrs Leary know?'

'I don't think she wants to know. You saw how she rushed out.'

'That will be because of her love for us. She'd not be able to bear it. Not at first; but, by, once she gets used to it, she'll be there with you, an' all. Leave it to me to tell her, but I won't do so until you know for sure.'

'Thanks... Oh, Flo, I don't want to die.'

All Flo could do was hold Eunice close and

allow her sobs to be released. Her own tears dropped onto Eunice's hair. *Why? Why is so much put on one person? Eunice has had more than her share. Much more than any young woman should have to take.*

For Kathy's sake, the pretend Christmas Day went ahead as if nothing was happening other than the need to have a good time. By the afternoon, and after a meal Mrs Leary was rightly proud of, her little parlour was jammed with folk: neighbours and friends, and even Flo's old boss, Mr Godfern, and his family. They immediately cornered Flo and had umpteen questions, but she batted them off well, leaving them proud that she was a Wren and doing her bit. Mr Godfern told her that he had now semi-retired and that his daughter was doing well with the shop. 'She's dragging me into the twentieth century. She's a good lass.'

Before leaving them to return to Simon and Roland, Flo expressed how pleased she was at this. It was a good feeling to be speaking to them, now that she was settled into a new life. She felt she was finally able to put Mr Godfern's mind to rest that he'd done the right thing for her. 'I'll allus be grateful to you, Mr Godfern. You set me on the reet path in me career. By, I wouldn't even have one, but for you.' He beamed at her.

Simon and Roland both welcomed her by moving apart and letting her stand in between them. As they chatted, Flo played with the pink knitted ring, twisting it around her finger. It had been her *surprise,* which had popped out of her cracker. 'I knitted it, Flo, all on me own,' Kathy had told her. Admiring the neat rows, Flo imagined Kathy concentrating and eager to get it done for her, and that warmed her heart.

'You love that, don't you, darling?'

She looked up into Simon's eyes. Found more than a twinkle there and looked away. 'Aye, it's the thought of the time and effort the little lass put into it.'

'And not a small measure of love, too. You're the most-loved person I know, Flo. And you give more love than anyone I know. But I can see there is something troubling you. Can I help?'

'Oh, Simon. It's the saddest thing I've ever dealt with in me life. But I can't talk to you about it now. Will you do me a favour, though? It's me friend, Eunice, she's not well. Will it be alreet if she goes back to London in the car with us?'

'Of course. I'm guessing she is the one on your mind?'

'Aye, she is, and it's bad, but don't say owt.'

Mrs Godfern started to play the piano at that moment, and though even to the untrained ear Mrs Leary's old piano needed tuning, the sound increased the joviality.

'Dance?'

'Eeh, Simon, in here? There's no room.'

'Clear a space, everyone – let's all have a dance.'

Simon's commanding voice had everyone shifting the furniture to the walls and rolling up the rug. Lilly Jordan, whose husband was missing in action and who lived two doors away, shouted, 'It'll have to be an "Excuse me" dance, as there's only five men and all of us women, and we all

256

want a turn.' Laughter filled the room at this, but quietened when Mrs Godfern started to play a haunting waltz. Mr Godfern took his daughter in his arms, while Roland gallantly asked Mrs Leary, and old Mr Burns, who had not long turned ninety and lived along the road, bowed to Lilly and asked for the honour. Everyone clapped her when she went into his arms. No one mentioned the tear they saw glistening on her cheek. Shy Mr Leary took that moment to sneak out of the room and through to the kitchen.

'Well, Flo, that leaves me and you.'

Simon's arm came round her, and his hand took hers. Everything around Flo faded into the awareness she had of him. The strength of his body, the smell of him, the feel of him close. It was as if there were just the two of them in the room. Lulled into the beauty of the moment, Flo leaned her head on Simon's shoulder. A tap on her arm brought her to her senses. 'Someone said this was an "Excuse me" dance. May I?' Roland looked into her eyes.

A blush rose to her cheeks. She went to stammer her apology, but Roland laughed. 'Funny what a couple of sherries can do. Hope they are still working their magic on you, and you'll cuddle up to me like that.'

She laughed with him and the moment passed. 'Aye, it will. You're me first love. Nowt can outdo the love a girl has for her teacher.' They giggled and Roland held her close. So much so that his glasses were knocked off his nose. This sent them into a fit of childish laughter. When they came out of it and sobered up, Kathy was asking Roland to continue the dance with her. Flo walked towards an empty chair next to Eunice. She could feel Simon's eyes on her, but didn't look over towards him. Afraid he'd come and claim her again, she asked Eunice, 'Are you up to doing a few steps, lass?'

Eunice smiled as she stood up. 'I'd have liked it to be a gentleman that asked me, but you'll do.'

Flo held her gently, taking the male role and trying not to let her worry for Eunice show, or to exert her too much. She was rewarded with Eunice's lovely tinkling laughter as they glided around. 'Eeh, this is grand. It reminds me of that social we went to, when we were young lasses. Ginger Small had an eye for you in them days, Eunice. Do you remember when he asked you to dance, and left you with that many bruises on your feet and ankles that you never spoke to him again?'

'Ha, I do. I wonder what happened to him?'

'He's away fighting somewhere, bless him.'

'I'd like to write to him. I treated him badly. He were a nice lad, even if he couldn't dance!'

'Well, that's his mam over there. You'll know her by her hair – it beats yours and Ginger's.'

'Cheeky madam. But I will ask her for his address. I'd love to get in touch with him.'

'By the way, we're giving you a lift back to London tomorrow. It will be less tiring for you – you can go to sleep on the back seat, if you want to. We'll be leaving early as we have to get back; we need to be on the road for nine.'

'Aw, thanks, Flo. It'll be nice to have company. I had too much thinking time on the way up here.'

The music stopped and, as if the momentum had left Eunice, she slumped onto Flo. Simon saw what was happening and was by her side in seconds. Without commenting, he gently helped Eunice to a seat. 'I – I need to lie down ... sorry.'

'Can you give her a hand up to my bed, Simon? She hasn't got a bed of her own tonight and was to sleep on this sofa, but I can take that.'

Simon gestured to Roland, and between them they carried Eunice through to the kitchen. Everyone had gone quiet. 'Carry on, everyone... Too much sherry.' They all chuckled as Flo said this, and the music set up again. A hand came on Flo's arm as she turned to follow Roland and Simon out of the room. She turned and saw a concerned Maisie Small. 'I don't like it, Flo. What's ailing her?'

'Eeh, Mrs Small. All I can tell you is that she's proper poorly. Will you do sommat for her?'

'Aye, owt she needs, of course I will.'

'She wants to write to Ging– I mean, your Gordon. He had a thing for her when they were young, and she's been asking after him.'

'By, he'll be made up. He's never stopped talking about her, you know.'

'Have you a pen and paper, love?'

'Ask Mr Leary. I reckon he's outside having a smoke, hiding away from the dancing. He'll help you. He allus knaws where owt of that nature is. I'll make sure I get it from him and give it to Eunice.'

As Mrs Small turned towards the back door, Flo ran towards the stairs and up to her bedroom. 'Is Eunice alreet?'

259

Simon answered her. 'Yes. Just very tired.'

'Eeh, Simon, I shouldn't have made her dance. You both go downstairs and help to keep the party going for a while. I'll help her to undress and snuggle her down.'

As they approached Simon's house later the next day, having dropped Eunice off at the hospital, Simon asked what was wrong with Eunice. On Flo telling him, his hand came over to her lap and folded itself around her tightly clasped hands. He didn't speak, but the effect of Simon touching her sent a feeling through her that she found hard to control. Latching onto the comfort of the gesture helped her, as she told him how she and Eunice had become friends. 'We're the kind of friends who don't need to see each other all the time to keep our love for one another alive. You know, like family. Which we are, really.'

'Yes, I understand. Though I hope I don't become a friend like that. I want to be in your company all the time.'

Ignoring this, Flo changed the subject: 'We'll have to look sharpish when we get back – there's only an hour to when we have to start to stock the van.'

It hardly seemed so much time had passed before they were at the Salvation Army lock-up and loading up stores, having dumped their cases at Simon's, had a drink of water and a quick swill to freshen themselves.

'There's a lot of supplies already there, as the van has been operating all afternoon. It's on the bombed-out site of St Anne's Church,' Mr Jen-

260

kinson told them.

'I heard the tower of that church was still standing. Is it safe?' Simon asked.

'Yes, that's all cordoned off – the van's just inside the gates. Will yer be able to manage on yer own? I know yer were promised help for the first couple of shifts, but there's no one to call on.'

'We'll be fine, as long as those we're taking over from can show us the ropes before they leave.'

'Aye, that'd be a help. But don't worry, we have helped in a van afore, and with the closing down at the end of the shift,' Flo added.

'I know; I were told, Miss. Nothing like being thrown in the bleedin' deep end, eh? It'll probably be busy, an' all. All the vans and depots have been busier over the holiday. I reckon folk were using the truce to take the chance to socialize around the vans a bit and get sommat that's hot inside them. Not many had what yer could call a jolly Christmas. But it was all happening again last night.'

After telling them where the nearest shelter was if there was a raid, and to drop off any food and the washing up they had left at St Thomas's Church in Regent Street, the man gave them some quick directions.

It didn't take long to arrive at the van. A queue of people stood waiting. The couple Flo and Simon were to take over from had closed the hatch while they cleaned down and prepared some more hot soup. Flo dived in to help, while Simon ferried the man to St Thomas's Church to take the dirty pots and collect more clean ones.

The woman greeted Flo as she stepped inside

261

the van. 'Me name's Rhoda, what's yours, lav?'

'I'm Flo. Pleased to meet you. Looks like you've been run off your feet.'

'We have, and you'll be no different. Look, yer might get a few of the prostitutes. They've worked a bit later during the truce, and we welcomed them for the first time. We used to give them short shrift, but me man works as an ARP and he were talking to one a bit back. What she told him makes your hair curl, poor bleeders. I've put the word out that they're welcome here and if they want any help we'll give it.'

'Reet-o.'

'I've never met a northern girl before. What're you doing down this neck of the woods then, Flo?'

'I'm in the Wrens. I do boring office work. This'll give me a bit of excitement.'

'Ha, I don't know about that. Though it could turn hairy, if there's a raid. But nice to know you're doing your bit. Ah, here's the men. We'll run things through with yer both, then leave yer to it. But mind you move to St Thomas's before it's dark, if you think there's still a need of your services. It'll be all blacked-out, ready. Folk know to enter the door, then close that before they open the inner doors where it's light. Good luck.'

With the rush over, they had done as advised and had moved to the church hall. Once there, they were able to distribute warm clothing from the stored stock, as well as keep up a steady supply of hot drinks and soup. Flo had never been so busy in her life. The cockney crowd had been in high spirits and she'd felt so much admiration for them.

'Well, we didn't do bad for our first time on our own, did we?'

'Naw, it went well. Here, I've poured you a cuppa. Go and have five minutes while I clear up, Simon – you look done in. You've had a long day, with the drive back and everything.'

'Don't mind if I do take the weight off for a mo. Thanks, Flo.'

Flo watched the glow of Simon's cigarette. The hall was quiet now and she was acutely aware that they were alone. Sighing, she began to gather up the dirty pots and take them towards the kitchen. A brash voice stopped her. 'You open, lav?'

Flo turned to see two women coming through the door. As they came closer, she knew they were prostitutes by their clothes and make-up. Why her nerves tightened her throat, she didn't know, but she didn't let this show in her greeting. 'Aye, what can I get you, lasses? We've tea, but no milk and sugar, and a couple of bowls of soup left. Oh, and I reckon I could find sommat nice, an' all.'

The one with the blonde hair laughed out loud. 'Lav your accent, darling. I'm all right, as it happens, but me mate here, she's starving. What's yer name? Mine's Trixie, and this is Molly, for her sins.'

'I'm Flo, and that's Simon over there, having a break. Shall I pour you a pot of tea, Molly?'

'I couldn't drink a whole pot, but ta, I'll take a mug.'

As Molly came nearer, Flo gasped. Her face

was a mass of cuts and bruises. She covered up her distress by making a joke. 'Oh, don't mind me. That's just a saying up north. I should have said "a nice cup of Rosie Lee".'

They all laughed then.

'You make a nice change, girl. The others are all right, but yer get the feeling they think themselves saints to bother with us, if yer know what I mean.'

'Eeh, I'm sorry to hear that, Trixie. Here you are, Molly. Can I do owt else for you girls?'

'Molly'll have sommat to eat, once she's downed that, ta, lav.'

'We have some warm clothes in the store at the back of the church. If you've a mind to have them, you're very welcome.'

'Ha, I don't reckon yer'll have any as we like, lav; but ta, anyway. Are yer going to be here very often?'

'Not sure, to be honest.' Flo told them her set story about working for the forces and how they just did this on odd occasions. She wished with all her heart that she could help the one called Molly. Trixie came across as if she could take care of herself, but Molly looked afraid. 'Eeh, Molly, you look like you fell out with a tram. We have a first-aid kit on board. I could clean your cuts up a bit for you.'

'They should teach you bleedin' lot not to interfere. Molly's all right, ain't yer, girl?'

Simon got up. He ground the remainder of his cigarette into the ashtray. 'It's not interfering, to offer help – that's what we're here for. Flo wouldn't dream of poking her nose into your business, and neither does she deserve to have you talk to her like that.'

'And who are you, when yer bleedin' mother ain't at home, then?'

'Don't, Trixie. Flo didn't mean no harm, and this bloke's just looking out for her, like you do me.'

'Well, I'm sorry, I'm sure. But we came for a cup of tea and sommat for you to eat. That's all, and she wants to play bleedin' Florence Nightingale. Ha, that's funny, as that's her bleedin' name!'

Both girls laughed at this and Flo joined in. 'By, I'm no Florence Nightingale, I tell you. Seeing to a few cuts is me limit.'

'You're all right, you are, girl. Ain't she, Molly?'

'Yes. Ta, Flo, I know you meant well, but we have to be careful.'

'Flo don't want to hear that, Molly. Now, can we have some soup, please, Flo? Not for me, but for Molly.'

Flo dished up a good mugful of soup and watched as the two girls went to sit down on the bench where Simon had been. The one called Trixie lit up a cigarette.

'I don't like the look of that poor girl, Flo. But the one smoking, she's a bit brash and looks like she can take care of herself.'

'Aye, I reckon you're reet, Simon. But I think as she'll take care of her mate, an' all, and that's what made her snap at me. I wonder why she looks so much better off than Molly? Eeh, I wish I could do sommat for them.'

'We can only give what they will take. You've offered, and that's all you can do. Look, go and sit with them a while, have a smoke; you must feel like one, you've been on your feet for hours.'

'By, that'd be grand. I ain't much of a smoker, but at times like this I welcome one.'

The women moved over as Flo approached.

'Park your bottom on there, lav, I've warmed it for yer. I can warm any spot.' Trixie's high laugh accompanied this, and Flo didn't miss the implication.

She grinned at the girls. 'So, if I offer me help, you look on it as interfering – is that a London way? Only where I come from, we all help each other, and I had the impression it was like that down here.'

'No. It ain't that, Flo.' Molly lit a cigarette and blew out a ring of smoke. 'It's just the same as us asking you about your work in that office. There's some things that can't be interfered with. You see, we have certain people – gangsters – that control–'

'Shut yer mouth, Molly, yer can't go telling her that.'

Molly clamped up.

'I reckon I knaw what you mean. The woman I took over from said that her husband is an ARP and he'd spoken to one of you and she'd told him about her life. I feel sorry for you.'

'That wouldn't be you, would it, Molly? I tell yer, girl, yer'll never learn. Look, we're grateful for yer help, but we're all right.'

'You might be, Trixie, but I'm not. I live in fear.'

'Molly! Christ, if yer going to blab to every Tom, Dick and Harry, yer'll be in further trouble. What if Flo calls the police, eh? Where'd yer be

266

then, eh? At the bottom of the bleedin' Thames, that's where. I'll find a way of getting yer out. We managed it for Ruby, didn't we?'

Flo couldn't believe what she was hearing. She racked her brains as to how she could give Molly a way of contacting her. There was something about the girl that had touched Flo's heart and she wanted to help her. 'Don't be at worrying – I won't contact the police. I don't knaw owt, anyroad.'

'Look, Trixie, I have to make a break for it soon. You know that. What if Flo gives me a coat and sommat to sustain me? Then I needn't go back again. Cos I've made me mind up. It's going to be tonight. It has to be. I can't take any more beatings.'

This surprised Flo, but she didn't speak. She waited for Trixie's reaction.

'But what about your stash? Yer'll need that – yer won't get far without money, girl.'

'You're right, of course. What if you keep the coat for me, Trixie? I could go back and get me money and then escape later out of the window. You could meet me with the coat, and I could take me chances from there.'

'All right. If yer sure. Give me the coat and what yer've got, Flo, that'll help her.'

'Where will you go, Molly? By, it's cold out there, lass, and there's the threat of an air raid, an' all.'

'Just get what yer can for her, Flo – the rest ain't your concern.'

Flo rummaged in the box marked 'Coats'. Most of what she found she wouldn't give to a young

267

woman. But then she came across a camel coat that must have been donated by someone with a bit of money. It was the size she'd guessed Molly was, and made of pure wool. Taking it out for Molly, Flo tried once again to offer more help. 'Molly, what if you had a contact number for me, eh? I'd do me best to help you, if you found you needed it. Hang on a mo.'

Hurrying back to Simon, Flo asked how they could be contacted.

'Flo, what are you thinking of? You can't get involved. You'll be in trouble, if anything back-fires on you. You can't make yourself responsible for every waif and stray in London. You have a high-risk job and you have to protect that – and your reputation – with everything you have.'

'I knaw. But, Simon, that girl needs help. I don't see how that can compromise me.'

The sound of a door banging had them both turning round. 'Looks like you don't have the problem any more, darling. They've gone.'

Flo's heart fell. 'Eeh, that's sad, Simon. They're scared to death. Especially Molly. That Trixie said something about her ending up at the bottom of the Thames. You read such things, but you never think you'll meet people who know it as a reality.'

'My lovely Flo. You want to save the world, when it's not possible to do so. Let's get cleared up and get home. There's no one else around looking for help, and if there's a raid I want to be in my own shelter with my own comforts.'

'Eeh, it's a good thing as there's no one else. We've nowt left. I gave Molly the last of that soup. By, I hope it fills a hole for the poor lass.'

'Never mind about them; you need to think of yourself. You've had a lot to take on board, and a hefty few days off. I've been thinking. As we don't have to be back until Monday morning, I'll drive you to Southend-on-Sea tomorrow. It'll probably be cold, but if we wrap up warm we can take a walk and let the sea air blow away some cobwebs, before we go back to that stuffy office and work out what Hitler has planned, now the truce is over.'

'That'd be grand. You know, war is a bad time and brings a lot of sadness, but for ordinary lasses like me who never had much, it's opened up a new world. I thought I would live and die in Leeds; now I find meself hobnobbing with the likes of you and the debutantes who work at Bletchley, and experiencing London. And now I'm going to the seaside. It all beggars belief.'

Simon laughed. 'It works both ways. My life has been enriched by you coming into it, as has the lives of all those girls in Bletchley. But for the war, we would have missed out on that.' He was close to her and now took her hand and looked into her eyes. His voice deepened. 'I'm so glad that I didn't miss out on you, Flo. You don't know what you have given me.'

Flo saw the love in his eyes. Wanted to take hold of what it would mean for her, but knew she couldn't. Forcing a smile, she released her hand from his and turned her attention to the work in hand. She had to accept that the love she had for Simon must always remain a secret. But knowing that didn't help, or stop the ache in her heart.

17

Flo

What a Difference a Day Makes

The wind wrapped Flo's hair around her face, and the salty air tingled her tongue and cheeks. Simon held her hand as they walked along the crowded promenade.

A small hut came in sight, and alongside it a boat. As they neared it, they were assailed by the strong smell of fish.

Flo wrinkled her nose. 'By, some poor souls must still risk their lives to fish.'

'They're not fish; they're cockles and mussels and whelks. Southend is famous for them, and those who gather them don't have to go out to sea, at least not far. It's more wading in to gather them, though they may use their boats to make a large haul just off the coast. Shall we try some?'

They were near the stall now and Flo's stomach turned at the thought of eating what she saw. 'Naw, ta. They look like snails – ugh! I'd heave me heart out.'

'Well, I'd love some. Come on, let's go over.'

The crowds bumped into Flo as Simon pulled her along. Uniformed young men stationed at the local training camp wolf-whistled at her and called out remarks that made her laugh: 'Going for some cockles, Miss? You can be my cockle any day,' and similar harmless banter. Children squealed their delight at this and that, as they were pushed in prams, while older ones ran after seagulls. Sadly, most only had their mothers with them. The elderly walked with heads bent, their walking sticks tapping the pavement as they went. It all created an atmosphere of life carrying on, despite the rubble being cleared from the bombed-out chapel they'd passed, the piles of sandbags, and the rolls of barbed wire and warnings of mines along the beach. Such was the resilience of folk all over the British Isles, and Flo felt pride in her fellow countrymen.

These musings left her as Simon tried to force her to eat a slimy-looking thing that he'd stuck a wooden stick into. 'Naw... Naw, give over.'

'Please, Flo, close your eyes and just taste it. You don't know what you're missing.'

'Eeh, don't make me. Buy me some fried fish. I'd love that.'

Droplets of vinegar dripped down her chin as the steaming-hot fish Simon had bought her from another stall melted in her mouth. Flo thought she'd never tasted anything so delicious. 'Let's sit a mo, Simon. Me fish is sticking to the news-paper, and I can't tackle it walking along at this pace.'

'You look lovely, Flo. Your lips are all greasy, your cheeks flushed with the wind. It's been a grand day, as you would say.'

'It has. Ta ever so much for bringing me. I wish the day would go on forever.'

'Me too, but we'd better make tracks when

271

you've finished eating, or we won't get back till after dark. I want to stop at a market garden on the way and try to get the rose bush you suggested for Lucinda… She'd have loved today. She liked coming to the seaside. We used to have picnics on the beach.'

Flo wiped her hands and face on her hanky, then took his hand. 'Memories are a good thing, Simon. Let them in whenever you can.'

His smile didn't touch his eyes, and she was reminded of his pain and her own.

With the light fading, the house had a forlorn look about it when they arrived home. Flo felt a similar feeling descend on her. How she wished Lucinda would fling open the door and greet them. She could hear, in Simon's tone, that he was feeling the same. 'I'll lay the rose bush in the garden. We'll attend to it tomorrow – there's plenty of soil around the roots. Let's get inside.' Words that dealt with the practicalities, not the pain. It was how they carried on and got through each hurdle.

The sudden shadowy appearance of a man, from behind the bushes that grew just inside the iron railings of the garden, startled Flo out of her thoughts. She swallowed hard. The man stared back at them. In the fast-descending gloom, Flo could make out the towering height of him, but not much else. Simon stiffened, and his arm came across her in a protective gesture. His voice held authority as he challenged the man as to who he was and why he was in the garden.

'Je m'appelle Aldric. I – I mean, I…'

272

'You're French! What is this – what's going on?'

Flo's heart pounded with the fear of her knowledge of the true nationality of the stranger. She felt sick as she listened to his soft, charming French accent.

'I knew Lucinda. I came to pay my respects. I know you are her brother – she showed me pictures of you. Lucinda was my... We met at university.'

'Oh, my dear chap, you were her friend? Come on in. Have you come far? Do you live in England?'

'No, I came over from France. I won't come in, thank you, I haven't much time. I – I was given a short pass – a press pass. I'm a journalist.'

Flo knew the game was up. Faced with knowing Aldric's true nationality and his deception in cleverly covering it up, she could no longer lie to Simon to protect Lucinda's memory. Aldric was an enemy of her country. She had to stop him from roaming England freely under the guise of being a Frenchman. She had to reveal his German nationality.

Thinking quickly through the implications of her options, she decided to try and get Aldric inside the house. If she blurted her fears out here, then Aldric might make a run for it.

Her heart dropped at the disloyalty that she would have to show Lucinda.

'Eeh, you two. I'm freezing me lugs off out here. Come inside for a mo, Aldric. We'll not keep you long, as we know you're in a hurry, but we can't send you off without offering you sommat to drink to warm your insides.'

She walked towards him, effectively blocking Aldric from escaping through the gate. In the dim light Flo saw a look of fear cross his face. For a moment she thought she'd blown her chance. *Did Lucinda tell Aldric about me, and how she'd confided in me? Me voice seemed to upset him, so maybe she joked about me accent?*

It was a relief when Simon stopped any further protest from Aldric. 'Yes, come inside. It would be insulting to Lucinda's memory if we let you go without making you welcome.'

'Thank you. I brought flowers. I was just placing them on the ground when you came.'

'How kind. I wondered why you were crouching down when we arrived.' Opening the door and bending to pick up some letters from the carpet, Simon asked Aldric, 'Do you want to bring them inside? Before we leave in the morning I'll pop them into the church down the road. She loved attending the services there. She sang in the choir.'

'She had a lovely voice.' There was a catch in Aldric's voice. For a moment Flo felt sorry for him, but the feeling passed as she focused on what his real reason for being in London might be.

Simon's easy manner had relaxed Aldric. Flo sought to capitalize on this. 'Eeh, I'm glad you're staying, even if it's just for a little while. It'd be good to get to know one of Lucinda's friends. She told us she had a great time at university, though she didn't tell us the names of her friends. It'd be grand to hear of her antics. She often hinted that she had a whale of a time.'

'*Merci.* I would like.'

Aldric's smile told of his fear having left him. Flo smiled back.

Inside, she hung back, fixing the blackouts in the hall, so to allow Simon to direct Aldric through to the front room.

Looking up the stairs, to where Lucinda's flat was, tore at Flo's heart. *Forgive me, Lucinda. I have to do this.*

'Come on, old thing, we men need a cup of tea...' Crossing the hall towards her, Simon called back through to the front room as he hung up his own coat and Aldric's, 'That is, if you drink tea, Aldric?'

'Normally café, but I did drink tea during my days at university and got quite used to it, so it will be fine.'

At a loss as to how to approach the subject of Aldric being German, without causing a problem that might get out of hand, Flo went through to the kitchen. The sound of the water hitting the bottom of the kettle resounded around her, and the gas ring lit with a greater burst of flame than usual. Her nerves were on edge. Aldric wouldn't just surrender without a fight.

Once the noise level settled to the gentle hissing of drops of water from the side of the kettle hitting the flames, Flo felt better able to think.

There was a phone upstairs. She needed an excuse to go up there, then she could call the police. Walking at a normal pace and with her mind made up, she came to the door of the front room, which although still open didn't give her sight of the two men. She could hear the sounds of Simon

275

lighting the fire and of them chatting. Their conversation sounded normal, friendly and uninhibited. *If only Simon knew!*

'I've got the kettle on. I'm just going to pop up to the flat upstairs. I need to fix the blackouts, in case the light from downstairs reflects up there.'

'Oh, would you like to go upstairs, Aldric? You can see where Lucinda lived.' Flo caught her breath at these words from Simon, but then released it as Aldric refused, saying it would be too painful just now.

As she turned back towards the stairs, a thought occurred to Flo. She crossed the hall and turned the key in the door. She knew this would hinder the police entering the house, but felt it better that Aldric didn't have a means of escape. Once she came down, she would remove the key from the already-locked back door, which led from the kitchen.

After making sure all the blackouts were in place, Flo went into the bedroom, feeling grateful that Lucinda had had the telephone installed in there, rather than on the landing. She'd probably tried to avoid her conversations being heard downstairs, as she must have telephoned Aldric on many occasions. *Oh, Lucinda. Lucinda...*

Flo's hand shook as she lifted the receiver. The ding it made had her standing stock-still. She listened for any sign that the men downstairs had heard it. Dialling zero, she waited for what seemed an eternity for the operator to answer. 'Telephone exchange: what number, please?'

'The police.'

Footsteps hurrying up the stairs had Flo reciting the address as fast as she could and saying, 'Hurry', before putting the receiver down.

'Where are you, Flo? Are you all right? The kettle's whistling away.'

Men! 'Eeh, Simon, you're not incapable. Why didn't you switch it off or, better still, make a pot of tea with it?'

'Sorry, did I scare you? I was worried that you were taking so long up here and might need some help.'

'I do, but not for the reasons you think. Look, don't ask questions – just act normal. I'll explain later. I've rung for the police. Aldric is German, not French. He is a war correspondent. At least that's his cover. I think he may be a spy.'

'Good God!'

'I know. Come on now, let's go down.'

'But...'

Flo hurried away from Simon, but, remembering her cardigan as she reached the top of the stairs, she turned and collided with him. Mouthing that she was sorry, she dashed back into the bedroom and grabbed a bright-blue cardigan that she'd left hanging over a chair and wrapped it around herself. Not the best colour to go with her ruby-red blouse and grey calf-length skirt, but it had to do.

'He's gone!'

'Gone? Where? How? Eeh, Simon, the back door! I was going to take the key out when I came down.'

'I'll go after him; he can't have got far, as there's the high wall to scale. He must have heard us and taken off.'

Unable to speak, Flo held her hands clasped in front of her. Her heart pounded fear around her body, and her mouth dried. *If Aldric's a spy, he could have a weapon. Maybe many of them, hidden about his person.*

A banging on the front door brought Flo to her senses. Letting the three policemen in, she told them why she had called them and what had happened since.

The sergeant turned to one of his men. 'Get back to the ARP depot and get them all engaged in this; we need more manpower than we have.' Turning back to Flo, he asked, 'Can you give us a description of your friend, as well as the man you suspect could be a spy?'

Being as precise as she could, Flo told him Aldric's height and what he was wearing, before giving a brief outline of the same details for Simon. The sergeant went into action once more, barking out orders. The three piercing blasts from the whistle that he blew sent shivers through Flo. Her worry intensified with the terrifying thought that, apart from setting his men to start putting his plan into action, he was giving a clear warning to Aldric that the police were onto him.

Before he left, the sergeant said, 'We'll get him, he has nowhere to hide.'

Nowhere to hide! Flo had been given a briefing on the capabilities of spies, during her training, and to her the whole area presented a labyrinth of hiding places, with all the ruins and the out-of-bounds, broken buildings.

Left alone and in a quandary of fear, she paced the floor. Prayers tumbled from her, asking God to keep Simon safe. She felt useless, for what could she do to help? But with no ideas presenting themselves, she decided that at least she could prepare something for them to eat and make up a flask for the eventuality of an air raid, something that was becoming routine.

As she made sandwiches, using the loaf they'd queued for before they left this morning, and cut thin slices from the ham bone that Mrs Leary had insisted she brought with her, Flo's thoughts remained with Simon. She wouldn't be able to bear it if anything happened to him.

The whistling kettle cut into Flo's thoughts. Steam blurred her vision as she mixed the cocoa she had ready in a jug. The liquid pouring into the flask echoed around the room as if it were a waterfall, but once it was done and the cap screwed firmly in place, the silence that fell oppressed her and increased her feelings of trepidation. For a moment she considered going into the front room and putting the wireless on, but that seemed like a betrayal, as if she could just relax and not care that the man she loved could at this very moment be fighting for his life against a determined German spy!

Deciding to stay in the kitchen, she sat down at the table and placed her head in her hands. Prayers tumbled from her once more, until a noise outside made her sit up and listen. *Simon?*

Even though she was alert, the knock on the door made her jump.

'It's me, Flo. Let me in, old girl.'

'Oh, Simon.'

There was a deep comfort in his arms. His body

melted into hers, giving her the sensation of being held by a man who desired her. Her response was instant. She lifted her head. Simon's lips came near to hers, and his breath wafted over her face. But in a sudden action he jerked his head away. She could sense the control he'd had to call upon. His eyes were fraught with a look that almost shouted his horror.

To cover the embarrassment and the strange feeling that had seized her, Flo took herself from his arms. 'Eeh, I could kiss you, and nearly did. I've been scared out of me wits.'

'And I nearly kissed you, Flo. I – I...' His stance showed his discomfort. She could only look at him and wait as shyness held her in its grip. But what he said next lifted her heart. 'It felt so right.' On the verge of going back into his arms, she was stopped by Simon turning his head away. 'I – I'm sorry. I shouldn't have said that. Please forgive me, Flo.'

'Naw, there's no need for sorry. I – it's fine. It were just a moment that caught us off-guard. Friends in a frightening situation, that's all.' Not feeling that she was finding the right words, Flo changed the subject. 'Did they get him?'

'Yes. Though one poor bloke, an ARP, was shot.'

'Oh God! Is he–'

'It hit him in the leg. Aldric was being held and was struggling, when his gun went off. They've taken the poor chap to hospital.'

'And Aldric, what will happen to him?'

'He'll face interrogation, which doesn't bear thinking about. But we – *you* – did the right thing,

Flo. What I can't understand is why? What was Lucinda doing, remaining friends with him? What was she thinking? And how did you know her friend was German and not French? I have so many questions.'

Shame washed over Flo at the secrets she held and the disloyalty she would now have to show towards Lucinda. 'They will want to question me, won't they? I – I kept a confidence. One that could have put our country in danger. Oh, Simon.'

'Look, tell me all about it first. It may not be as bad as it sounds. You didn't know he would come here, did you?'

'No, of course not. I–'

The wail of the siren saved her.

'Grab your coat, Flo. I'll get blankets.'

'I've everything ready in that bag on the chair: flask, cups and, as we haven't eaten, some sandwiches.'

'Good girl. That's the spirit. It's freezing out there. I'll take them down to the shelter and then come back. I'll take a flask of whisky as well, and we could do with filling a couple of hot-water bottles.'

'Aye, I'll see to that. I left the kettle simmering.'

Mundane things they both knew how to do automatically, but talking about them filled the gulf of awkwardness that had opened up again, with their fear.

Once they were settled in the Anderson shelter, wrapped in blankets and snuggled together, some of the fear left Flo. She would always feel

281

safe when she was this close to Simon.

'You know, Flo, it made me think of Roland, when that ARP was shot. I hadn't considered the danger he could be in, but now I realize there are a hundred and one situations that could pose a risk to his life.'

'Eeh, don't worry – he'll not be chasing German spies in Leeds. There's nowt up there for them to spy on.'

'Oh yes, there is. There's munitions factories and the Blackburn Aircraft company. And factories producing uniforms. All prime sites for bombing, to hinder our war effort.'

Flo couldn't speak. She hadn't thought of the possibility of bombing raids there, and of her beloved Kathy and Mrs Leary being in any danger. Now she realized that no one was safe. As if to confirm this, the drone of hundreds of aircraft filled the space around them, quickly followed by the sound of gunfire and swooping planes. 'The RAF are engaging, and it sounds as though it's right above us. I'll take a look.'

As Simon stood, the sound of an out-of-control engine whining its descent got him outside in seconds. Terror held Flo stock-still as the noise got louder and drowned out the rest of the activity above them.

'It's one of theirs. Well done, our boys! They–'

His words merged into a crashing explosion that rocked the earth beneath them. Debris hit the sides of the Anderson shelter. Flo held her head, screaming to Simon to come back inside, just as more explosions boomed out their terrifying destruction.

'Christ, Flo, London's on fire!'

Flo's heart jolted with the deep fear that took her. She lowered her head and held her ears. This, then, was the way they were being paid back for the ceasefire over Christmas. *Oh God, we're all going to die.*

Simon shouted something else, but Flo couldn't hear what he was saying, for the deafening noise of planes diving, guns shooting and direct hits, added to the screaming sound of spiralling planes as they headed for the ground and erupted into flames. As he came back in, they clung together. The trembling of Simon's body increased Flo's fear. The world was coming to an end.

At last the noise began to fade. Simon looked outside once more. 'Christ, the world is blazing. Oh God, London must be all but destroyed. But our boys are chasing them – look, they're headed north-east.'

'Eeh, Simon, please come back inside. We're not out of danger. They could swirl back; they have done so afore. Wait for the all-clear.'

When he came back into the shelter, he sat down on the opposite bench to her. 'Tell me, Flo. Tell me how it came about that a spy was in my house tonight.'

It was the last thing she'd expected him to say, or that she wanted to do. But she could see, as she shone her torch on him, that it had been on his mind and he needed to know. With her voice shaking, it was difficult to form the words, but as the background noise lessened she told him what she knew. She didn't say anything about the baby Lucinda had been expecting. She thought that was a step too far for him to cope with, and it wasn't necessary that he should know.

'Lucinda was going to Aldric's aunt? She wasn't going to take up the position of war correspondent? But why? She wouldn't have seen much of him, if he was working from Germany. How could she have done this? How?'

'Try to imagine it as if it were you and Roland, and Roland was German. You're happy and in love, then your countries go to war. Would you stop loving Roland? Would you be able to stand the fact that he'd have to leave this country, or be imprisoned? If there were some way you could be with him, I reckon you'd do the same as Lucinda did.'

Again Simon was silent. After a while he lifted his head. 'You're right, of course. And in a way it is like that for me and Roland, even without a war. Secret meetings, not being able to acknowledge each other. Poor Lucinda. It must have been hell for her. She was a patriotic girl. But what if she was so in love and did suspect Aldric? Do you think that's a possibility? Do you think she went, thinking she could stop him spying on us?'

'Naw, I don't think she suspected him. She saw him as a victim of the party that had taken over his country. She said he was anti-Nazi. Anyroad, we don't knaw yet as he is a spy, we only have our suspicions.'

'I'd put money on it. He was armed, for one thing. An innocent visitor doesn't carry a gun. Aldric even being in this country, under the guise of being French... Oh, I know he could hardly

284

come in as a German, but the authorities in France are German and would be unlikely to give a pass to a Frenchman. I can't understand how I was taken in by that. I didn't even question it. Whereas you–'

'I had prior knowledge. Anyroad, Aldric's in captivity now and I don't have to carry a lie inside me, and that's good. But what do you think the police will make of me story?'

'You couldn't possibly know that Aldric was a spy, or that he would come here. I don't think you have anything to worry about. The moment he did show up here, you went into action. I should think you'll be given a medal for your bravery.'

This made her feel better, but something still niggled at her. 'We have to tell Roland the truth about his nationality. I lied to him about that. But I was just trying to protect Lucinda's good name and keep some of the confidence she'd entrusted me with.'

'He'll understand.' Simon shifted to sit next to Flo once more as he said this. 'Come here. Snuggle up to me again.'

As his arm came round her, part of her felt this was where she was meant to be. If things were different – if Simon was different – she could let her feelings for him have their full rein. Because she loved him dearly. No, it was more than that. She'd already acknowledged to herself that she was *in love* with him. But it was all so hopeless.

As if her feelings had been spoken aloud, Simon nuzzled her neck. His whisper was of love. Her heart thudded desire around her body – desire

285

she knew would forever remain unrequited. Sighing, she sat up. She had to address their situation before it got out of hand and ruined everything. 'You've to stop being so demonstrative in your loving towards me, Simon. I have feelings for you. I knaw it's daft. I knaw your situation. But I can't fight them on me own. And you're not helping matters, kissing me neck and holding me so close and – well, your words. They make me believe things could be different.'

'Oh, Flo, there's times when I'm with you that I believe they can be. I do love you. I love you in a way that I've never known before. I even feel aroused by you, which is something I was certain couldn't ever happen with a woman. But it's true. I want to make love to you – with you. Oh God, what a mess.'

Flo's heart sang a joyous song, but only for a moment. Soon it was crying with pain.

It wasn't easy standing up in the Anderson shelter, but if you moved towards the middle you could. She did that now and stood with her arms folded. 'I'd not be able to share you. It ain't in me. I'd have to ask you to choose, and I can't do that. I knaw the love you have for Roland. It ain't that I don't believe it's not possible to love two people – I do; but I don't reckon as it's possible to carry on a relationship with both. This between us has to end now. We have to get over it, and put our friendship back onto a proper footing. I think it may be our grief for Lucinda – and yours in particular – that has made us cling to each other in a physical way, as well as being bound like soulmates. But that will pass. Or at least it'll get easier, and we won't be dependent on each other so much. Shall we make a pact?'

'Yes. We will make a pact. I promise not to show how much I love you ever again. I promise to love and treat you as a dear friend only. I promise... Oh, Flo, it's going to be difficult, very difficult. What's the matter with me? My life was all cut-and-dried, and now you have turned it upside down.'

A tear ran down Flo's cheek. Another followed it and dripped off the end of her nose. Just yesterday she'd found a way to cope, but now the future stretched interminably. A future of being near to Simon, of loving him, and of watching him love Roland. She should be jealous of that, but she wasn't; they were right for each other. She was the one who should bail out, but could she?

The wail of the all-clear siren filled her mind. It seemed to signal not only the end of the air raid, but the end of her dreams.

18

Molly

No One is Who They Seem

Molly shivered uncontrollably. Every limb shook with fear and pain. Hunched up on her bed, she lay still, hardly thinking, hardly functioning. The last beating had nearly finished her. She just wanted to die.

The sound of the bedroom door opening had no effect. No one could hurt her any more than she already was hurting.

'Molly?'

Shocked at whose voice it was, Molly wanted to turn and spit in Delilah's face.

'Molly, I'm sorry, I...'

Through squinting, swollen eyes, Molly saw Delilah slump down on the bed opposite. 'You're vile, Delilah, vile.' The words would hardly form, but Molly put as much venom into them as she could.

'I shouldn't have done it. I know that. I was only trying to make me own life a bit better. But they beat me, too. And the others, as I gave away that we were all out on Christmas Day, when we'd been locked in.'

'Christ, Delilah, why? You'd never have gained from it. And from what I can see, you've had more than a beating.'

'The others set about me, after Gus had finished with me. I want out, Molly.'

'Don't look at me.'

'Please, Molly. I know I ain't to be trusted, as I've done bad things, but I know stuff about this place. There's a back way out. And I have money, an' all.'

This all sounded incredible to Molly. Delilah couldn't be trusted in a month of Sundays. Turning away from her caused pain, but she managed it.

'Think about it, Molly. Two together have a better chance than one. I can't undo all the bad

I've done, but I can make amends, if yer'll let me.'

Molly didn't answer. If she could, she'd get up and punch Delilah, but instead she curled into a ball and closed her eyes. Flo came into her mind. Somehow hope had been planted in her since she'd met Flo. She hoped with all her heart that Flo had survived the terrible air raid of Sunday night. London hadn't experienced anything like it before.

A plan began to form. She'd get better, then she'd leave and try to find Flo. She'd find that ARP first, as it sounded from what Flo was saying that his wife also worked for the Sallies. Maybe she knew how to contact Flo and that bloke. Though *he* wasn't all that friendly. Trixie's fault, for she'd put his back up when she spoke a bit hard to Flo. Funny bloke. He looked like a nancy boy, and yet he seemed more than fond of Flo.

These thoughts led to thinking of David. Would she ever see him again? If she did, would he want her? Her hand brushed away the tear this provoked – she'd cried all she could and it got her nowhere. She had to keep a level head and think about her escape.

'That Trixie were asking after you. She threatened to kill me if anything happened to you, but I told her I was sorry and wanted to help.'

Molly remained silent.

'She believed me when I said I wanted to help yer.'

'Why should she believe you? Everyone hates you, Del. No one trusts you.'

'I can prove it. She said to tell you she has left

289

the coat yer wanted with Dolly, in case yer make a move and she ain't around. But if yer do, then contact her as soon as yer know yer safe.'

'What, Trixie said all that to you! You're a liar. You've found out something and you're testing to see if it's true. Well, it ain't. I know nothing about any coat.'

'Trixie and me used to be mates.'

What crap is this? Trixie would have said, if she'd known Delilah before. She hates the girl. Trixie would never lie. Not to me, would she?

'Look, it was a long time ago. We were at school together, only she didn't remember me. Me name was Martha Gardner. When I told her, she said there was always sommat familiar about me. She was shocked, but understood how I'm like I am. She didn't blame me. She said that she wished you'd be a bit more like me.'

Molly couldn't take this all in. Something in her felt sorry for Delilah, but she knew she could never be like her. 'No, thanks. I wouldn't shop any of the girls in here, even though none of them give me the time of day.'

'Gus kidnapped me as well, yer know.'

Martha Gardner? Of course, I remember when she went missing. It was all in the papers. It was Gus who took her? My God! Molly turned painfully round to stare at Delilah; she hadn't guessed anything like this. Delilah always gave the impression that she was there because she wanted the life. She watched a tear trickle down Delilah's face. Pity entered her, but she cautioned herself, still unsure whether to trust her.

'It was a long time ago, before he hooked up

with Eva. Gus murdered me dad and raped me mum, over and over. I was only twelve. He took me as a punishment to me mum, though I don't know what he was punishing her for. He made me into his own personal slave. He took me so low that I could no longer think for meself. When me mum died, he laughed as he told me, and used it as another reason that I couldn't leave, as I had nowhere to go; and no one who would keep up the pressure to look for me, like my mum had. I still don't know how me mum died, and wonder if Gus murdered her, too. Me name's still on the missing list. Gus set me to spy on the girls they have here. It's the only way I can please him. I've been under threat of death. And I know he would do it, as what I've told him over the years has led to some girls being found in the Thames.'

The tear turned to a deluge.

'I'm sorry for what happened to you, Delilah, but I'm still struggling to understand how you did what you did, knowing it would cause the death of someone you worked here with. I could be next. All of this could be a ploy that you've cooked up to get me to trust you, and then you run to Gus and I'm a goner.'

'No! I promise. I've had enough. I have too much on me conscience. When they started to beat you, and the other girls got a punishment for leaving on Christmas Day, I felt sick to the stomach. I think they are planning on you being next, and I can't take another killing. When the first one happened I nearly took me own life. I swallowed some pills, but I vomited them up. It was then that I realized I didn't want to die. I wanted some

291

sort of a life. The more I told Gus, the better me life became. But I kept it to snippets – nothing I thought would lead to another death. The second one died because she was going to go to the police. I thought she'd just be punished, but they used her as an example. You've taken one punishment, because of me finding your stash, and though it was bad, they didn't kill you because Gus likes to have you himself sometimes. But now you've helped one of us to escape, I'm really scared. I want to help you to get away, but I have to go with you or I'll die, I know it. Please, Molly.'

'You're scum, Del – scum. You don't deserve to live. But if I'm to get out without you blabbing, then I can see that I have to take you with me. We won't stay together. I couldn't have you along with me. I'll talk to Trixie, and we'll get you out and help you to get away, but you'll be on your own.'

'Thanks, Molly. I just need help to make that break. I've always been too scared to do it, and wouldn't know what to do. I might appear worldly, but I know nothing other than a few years with me mum and dad, and then being under Gus's control. I never saw the light of day for years. Try to understand, Molly.'

'I'm trying. And maybe, when I'm free, I'll be ready to forgive you. But me life is in danger because of you. And for what reason, eh? Just so that you could make yourself look good in the eyes of that bastard, Gus.'

Delilah wiped her eyes, then said she was sorry once more and left the room. Molly's stomach clenched. *Is she really genuine, or has she gone to*

292

Gus right now, to tell about me planning to get out? Oh God!

Getting off the bed caused Molly excruciating pain, but she managed it. Feeling her ribs tenderly, she felt sure they were broken, for a sharp pain stabbed her as she gasped in air. She'd hoped to recover for a few days, but now she had to leave – and leave now!

The door opened and Delilah sidled back in. 'Here, if you won't take me with you willingly, then I'm not coming, but I want you to have this.'

Molly stared at the wad of notes. 'You mean it? Really mean it? Will you help me to get out that back way you spoke of?'

'Yes, I will. Eva, Gus and Lofty are out. If you can make it now, I'll help you, but where will you go?'

'I'm not telling you that, Delilah. But I will take you with me. I'll get Trixie to help you get away, using the same route as Ruby did, but we'll not tell you about it, just in case. I still can't trust you. You will just have to follow our directions. I'll have to make a phone call. But this has to be the end of it. Once you're free, you're to go to the police and tell them everything. But you have to wait until Trixie lets you know that I'm safe, otherwise they'll intensify their search for me. I intend joining the ATS. They can't get hold of me then, as I'll be protected. But as soon as you're given the word I'm in the ATS, you have to smash this evil gang. I can't do it, as I still have someone I ... well, that I'm attached to and need to protect.'

Delilah's eyes leaked tears, but she wiped them

293

away. 'Your dad?'

Molly was shocked. 'How did you know about him?'

'I know a lot, Molly. I didn't just tell, I listened. But thanks. Thanks, Molly. I promise you, I'll go to the police once we're both safe. Will you be able to contact me to let me know you're all right? I won't do anything till then, as your life could still be in danger.'

'I will. Now tell me about this back door.'

'There's some stairs behind the door that's marked "Private" and is always locked. I have a key to that, and to the door at the bottom of the stairs that leads into an enclosed yard. I stole them once and had a set cut. There's three, so I think the third one will fit the gate to the yard, but if it doesn't, then there's some crates stacked in the yard. It'll be a matter of climbing onto them to get over the wall, but there's a five-foot drop on the other side. I don't know if you'll make that.'

Molly couldn't believe what she was hearing. 'So why haven't you left before, then?'

'Where would I go? I need you and Trixie to help me, but she won't help me unless I help you.'

'Ah, so we have the truth of it now. You're only doing this to save your own skin.'

'It's a good enough reason, and one you'll believe, so what's the odds?'

Molly acknowledged that Delilah had a point, as it was a reason she could understand and trust. This made her feel better about it all. She eased herself down onto the edge of the bed and thought about everything for a moment. Getting Delilah away shouldn't be much of a problem, for they'd already proved that the route to her Aunt Bet, and then on to Scotland, worked, or at least it seemed that way. She only hoped that Ruby had contacted Trixie by now, so that she would know for sure. There was just herself to consider. In her present condition she wouldn't get far. She needed the help of someone to hide her for a few days. Flo came to mind. Molly felt certain Flo would do anything to help her. She hadn't spoken to her much, but there was something about her. A caring nature and courage. But what if she couldn't find Flo?

Admitting she might have to do this by herself was frightening, but she couldn't let the fear take root. She'd have to hide out on her own until she was well. There were plenty of boarded-up places. Yes, most were condemned, but that would suit her, as no one would go near them. Warmth and food might be a problem, though. For a moment Molly felt despair drag her down, but she dismissed it. She had to do this, and she had to do it now. She would lie to Trixie and say she was going to the ARP's wife. Well, it wouldn't really be a lie, as she would do that once she was better. She'd ask Dolly to pack her some food up – enough to last a couple of days, just in case.

'What're yer thinking about, Molly?'

'More than I can cope with at the moment. Look, initially we're going to need each other. I want you to find something to strap me up with, so that I can walk. Then help me to dress. I need to put several layers on. And I need a blanket.'

295

'None of that's a problem. We can rip the sheet to strap you up and take the–'

'If that's the way you think, then we have a big problem. How's it going to look, if one of the girls comes in and finds the bed wrecked, eh? Where are the others, anyway?'

'Out. Despite what happened last time they went out without Eva knowing, they've done it again. They didn't say where.'

'They wouldn't, would they? They know what you're like. I'm surprised they've even taken the chance of you knowing what they've done.'

'They said they would kill me if I told, and they meant it. That Elsie scares me. She held a knife to me throat as she threatened me. They seemed satisfied that I was telling the truth, when I promised I wouldn't breathe a word.'

'Good. So the coast is clear. Get a sheet and blanket from the store cupboard. And hurry.'

Stepping outside gave Molly the full impact of the dreadful night of the 29th. Utter and complete destruction met her. Blackened buildings teetered, bricks and debris lined the road and the path. The smell of smouldering fires choked her. Placing her handkerchief over her nose and mouth, she lowered her head and, with the help of Delilah, set off for Dolly's cafe.

Trixie stood outside Dolly's. She waved to Molly in what seemed like an excited, hurry-up kind of way. Molly thought she'd never be able to hurry again. When she reached her, Trixie burst out, 'I've heard from Ruby. She's in Scotland, and all settled. Having the bleedin' time of her life she is, mate.'

The words drained Molly. It was all she'd been waiting to hear, and now that she had, it was as if her last strength left her.

'Here, have they been at you again, girl? You look a mess. Let's get yer inside.'

'Ooh, don't hold me there, Trixie, I think me ribs are broken.'

As if she was experiencing it for the first time, the smell that had become familiar to her – sweaty bodies and cheap perfume, mingled with the cooking of low-cost cuts of meat and fried stale bread – turned her stomach.

'Sit down, lav, you look at the end of your tether.'

'I am, but you've cheered me. Good old Ruby. I'm so glad she's safe.'

Dolly brought two steaming mugs of tea over, and put one in front of Molly and one in front of Trixie. 'Here, get this down yer. Yer look awful, Molly. Has some bleeder clocked yer one, then?' Without waiting for an answer Dolly turned to Delilah. 'You can fetch yer own bleedin' tea, and pay for it.'

Delilah didn't protest, but got up and went to the counter. Dolly didn't follow her. 'She can bleedin' wait. What happened, girl?'

'I bumped into a wall, Dolly.'

Dolly turned away, the remark she made said more in jest than showing she was offended. 'Yeah, pull the other one – it's got bleedin' bells on it. But I get the idea, and I'll say no more.'

Molly caught hold of Dolly's apron and stopped her progress. 'You know how it is, Dolly. The less

297

you know, the better. Now, do me a favour and keep Delilah away from us for a while. I've things to talk to Trixie about.'

Dolly huffed.

'Don't mind her. Let's talk.'

'There's a lot I have to say. But, Trixie, I'm so pleased about Ruby. If I could, I'd jump for joy and scream out to the world that one of us has broken free, I would.'

'I know. I feel the same. So, what about Del? That was a turn-up for the books, weren't it? Fancy her turning out to be Martha Gardner, eh?'

'And you believe her, Trixie? Really believe her? Cos you know what she's like.'

'I do. I knew there was something about her, but could never put me finger on it. It's her all right. Me and her were best mates at school. That's when we turned up at school, of course.' Trixie's cackling laughter sounded good. Molly felt a sudden pang about leaving. She was going to miss Trixie.

When Trixie sobered, she asked Molly, 'What about you, eh? Are yer going or not, Molly?'

'I am, Trixie, and right now. I got me money, and a few more quid that Delilah has lent me. But you know she wants to go an' all?'

'Yes. And I think it's a good thing. Are yer willing to help her, like we did Ruby? I've already spoken to me mate in Scotland and she said she'll take one more, but that's it.'

'I was going to call me Aunt Bet, but I've thought better of it. Del will have to make her own way. She's got plenty of money. She'll have to stay in a bed-and-breakfast. I daren't take the chance. As it is, I'm afraid for me aunt. Eva mentioned her when she questioned me over Ruby, but I would only admit to helping Ruby get a taxi. With them not being sure, I don't think they'll try to find me aunt; but with me gone, they might. I'm not letting Delilah know anything about her, just in case.'

'Does Eva know Bet's in Birmingham?'

'I think so, but it's a big city, and travelling there ain't easy, so I'm hoping they won't pursue their search for any of us there. Eva and the others can't afford the time, anyway. And if Del keeps her word, then they'll be banged up before they can plan revenge for later on. I just have to take a chance on that.'

'Are you going there, Molly?'

'No.' She told Trixie of her own plans.

'Well, I can just see you in uniform, girl. Good luck to yer, and I hope yer find Flo. She were a good sort. Not sure about the ARP's missus that yer on about. If she was one of them we came across, she'll be a sour-faced bitch just doing what she has to. Not the angel her husband told yer she was.'

Trixie got up then and assured Molly that she'd do her part. She was to fetch the coat from the back of the cafe, organize the food from Dolly and contact her mate to bring his taxi round to the back, to take Molly and Delilah.

As she sat alone, Molly's nerves kicked in and her body began to shake. How would it all pan out? What would it be like sleeping rough? David came to her mind and she daydreamed about him. *I'll go to his house first. If he's there, he'll help*

299

me. She dared not even hope this would be true, but at least it gave her something to cling to. Then another thought occurred and she sent up a silent prayer: *Please let me find Flo.*

Somehow she knew that if she did, everything would be all right. Why she felt this, after only a few minutes with Flo, she didn't know. But just thinking about Flo's lovely smiling, concerned face gave her more hope than even thinking of trying to find David did.

Huddled in the taxi some forty minutes later, Molly asked the driver to take them to the station. On the way, her heart bled at the sight of the raging fires engulfing her beloved London. It seemed that it was almost razed to the ground, with more buildings in a state of collapse than standing. People milled around looking lost, where once they had been in a familiar place. Firemen still battled to douse the flames, and a newsboard proclaimed that fifteen of them had been killed, many trying to save St Paul's Cathedral. Alongside it was a picture of St Paul's dome standing out amidst the black smoke and flames. The headline, which was almost obscured, read: 'Churchill orders: Save St Paul's at all costs.' *But at what cost?*

Molly said goodbye to Delilah when they dropped her off at the station. Her voice held no emotion as she wished her good luck. Part of her still hated the woman and was untouched by her moving story. Yes, Delilah had been wronged, but what she'd caused had far outweighed that. Molly thought of the many beatings Ruby had endured, and of her own beating – and all because Delilah had wanted to save her own skin and ingratiate herself with the vile Gus. Her body shuddered at the appalling thought of the two murdered girls, and Delilah saying she was to blame. She didn't deserve any sympathy, but Molly didn't wish her harm, either; she just wanted her out of her life.

'Where to now, love?'

'Poland Street. Thanks.' If he reported back to Trixie, then Trixie would know it was near there that she'd met the ARP and that he lived nearby. The last thing she wanted was to raise Trixie's suspicions. She'd do anything to have her by her side, but this was something she had to do alone. As the taxi swung round, something that had been on Molly's mind caused her to change the instructions. 'Wait a minute. Before that, will you take me to Park Lane – it runs down the side of Pymmes Park in Edmonton? I know it's about nine miles away, but I'll pay you.'

'It'll be more than that, in this lot. Half the bleedin' roads are blocked. I'll have to make a few detours.'

'That's all right. I might drop off to sleep, but will you wake me when you're approaching Edmonton? Thanks.'

Snuggling down, Molly tried to quieten the butterflies in her stomach, but she couldn't deny the hope dancing around her body. It took a while for her to get into a position that gave her the least pain, but eventually she did and drifted off to sleep, dreaming of David.

The dream turned to a nightmare when Randy, the cab driver, woke her. Edmonton as she knew it had gone. She looked out at her town – because that's what those who lived there looked on it as: a town within the borough of London – to see it all broken. Hitler had all but destroyed it. Molly's heart pounded a plea around her mind: *Please let David's house be standing.* She thought the same of her own house and hoped that her dad, for all he'd done to her, was safe, but she dared not take a detour to Sebastopol Road to check.

Church Street and the shoe shop were mostly intact. As they passed by she read 'Phyllis's Shoes' on the sign that had once said 'Gould's'. This gave her a good feeling. *Good for you, Phyllis.*

Directing Randy away from the side of the park where dear Hettie had lost her life, Molly clenched her fists tightly together. She could hardly breathe. As the street came into full view, she gasped with the pain that tore through her. David's house lay in ruins. 'Oh God, no!'

'You all right, lav?'

'Stop a moment, Randy.' Molly knew that tears were soaking her face. They fell without her bidding. Her body was crying, but her heart was encased in stone.

'Can I do sommat for yer, lav?'

'Yes. Would you go to that house to the left of the ruined one and ask if they know where David Gould is, please?'

Randy didn't protest. Molly stared after him and watched the woman who answered shake her head. She felt her heart plummet and heard a cry escape from her own lips. *No, no – please … no!*

Getting back in the car and slamming the door before speaking, Randy turned towards her. His face told the story. 'Sorry, lav. David Gould is missing in action, presumed dead.'

Molly crumbled.

'Don't take it like that, lav – there's always hope, with the missing. That old girl said that he was hit over Italy. He could be in a prisoner-of-war camp. They get treated all right in them, they have to be – it's the rules of war. The old girl said she only knows about it because a telegram lad came next door, and the maid took the message. It was the maid that told the old girl what had happened. I asked where the maid was, and she said she'd sailed to America just after that, to be with the Gould family.'

Molly could only stare through tear-filled eyes.

'Look, lav, why don't you let me take you to the hospital? You're injured, and now with this shock.'

'No. I'll be all right. Just take me to Poland Street. Thanks.'

How she wished she could go to hospital. They'd tend to her, make her comfortable and give her a fresh bed to lie in, but they'd also want to know who she was and where she came from.

As darkness fell, the siren wailed. Molly curled up as best she could, wrapped in her blanket in the cellar of a bombed-out house. It was so close to the one she had been thrown out of on Christmas Eve that she worried, when she found out, that she would be seen by the man and he'd remember that she'd stolen a present from under his tree. But the house was the only one where she could access the inside and make her way to the cellar.

Cold seeped into her bones, but it couldn't touch the heart of her. That was wrapped in grief. Now she was alone and in darkness, her mind had fully taken in what she'd discovered. *Missing, presumed dead... Missing, presumed dead. No. Nooo!*

19

Flo

A Home of Their Own

The usual noises of the Garity family, in whose house she was billeted, filtered through the thin walls and wooden floor of Flo's bedroom. She looked at her watch: seven-thirty. She wasn't due to go on her shift until four this afternoon, having worked until midnight the night before. She was so tired, but now she doubted that she would sleep. The two boys, one twelve and the other ten, who never spoke to her, no matter how much she tried with them, didn't seem to care how much noise they made. She was sure one of them had kicked the door deliberately, and that had woken her. Now she could hear them arguing and their mother shouting at them, 'You'll wake that girl if you're not careful. Shut up!'

That girl. You would think, as this is me fifth week here, she'd use me name. Flo wondered if she would ever feel welcome, or be made welcome by this family. What she heard next made her cheeks flush. 'Why do we have to have her here anyway, Mum? She's common. Freddie's mum's got a posh girl who can talk proper.'

'Shut your mouth, Frank, or I'll clip your ear for you.'

'He's right, though, Mabel.' Her husband's deep voice carried just as far as his wife's high-pitched one. 'I can't understand a word she says. What's the navy doing, recruiting a girl like her?'

'Don't you start, Mick. I've enough with the boys. She's a nice girl, if you'd all just give her a chance. It's how them from up north speak – she can't help that.'

This soothed Flo a little, but the embarrassment she felt at being discussed in this manner made her not wish to leave her room until the male members of the family had gone out. That wasn't easy, though, as she was dying for the lavatory, and she'd need to go through the kitchen to get out to the back yard, where the only toilet was.

Through the gap where the curtains didn't meet, ice glinted on the windows. Flo shivered at the prospect of the bitter cold she would have to face, but she'd rather die of the cold than use the pot under the bed. Gathering her housecoat, she put it on over her pyjamas.

A feeling of utter misery and loneliness crept over her. If Mrs Leary knew how she was treated and the conditions she lived under, she'd be down here like a shot, wielding her frying pan to sort out the menfolk of this house. This thought made her smile, and suddenly her lot felt a bit brighter. *There's a war on, lass, so you've to get on with it.*

The kitchen door creaked as she opened it. The lively banter ceased. 'Eeh, I – I'm sorry, I didn't mean to interrupt or owt. I just need to go out the back.'

The boys giggled and their father lifted his newspaper to cover his face. Mabel Garity hurried over to open the door for her. 'Go on then, love, though mind yer don't slip. And don't worry if it don't flush, as it's frozen up. I'll put a bucket of water down it when you're done.'

The sound of their laughter as she closed the door cut through Flo. It was cruel and mocking, and even though Mabel had spoken up for her, hers was the loudest. *How am I to bear it here?*

Trying to keep warm under the bedcovers, after returning to her room, Flo got stuck into the crossword from the day before. She and Simon bought a copy each of *The Times* every day, and the next day competed as to who had filled in the most clues. At first Flo had won every time, but Simon was competitive and had redoubled his efforts, so now she had a job to beat him. Maybe, with the time she had on her hands today, she could complete it.

A knock on the door disturbed her. 'I've some porridge left, if you'd like some, love.'

Not really wanting any, Flo accepted, as she saw these small kindnesses on Mabel Garity's part as trying to compensate for her family's unfriendliness.

'Ooh, it's freezing in here, love. I've a fire lit downstairs and the menfolk have all gone. Come and park yourself down there and get warm, eh?'

'Are you sure I'll not be in your way?'

'No, I'm busy with the washing in the kitchen. You can sit in the parlour, if you like.'

'I'll give you a hand. I'm good with a mangle.'

The kitchen in this house was never a welcoming place, and that wasn't all down to three members of the household not wanting her here. The dark-green gloss paint of the walls resisted any water, and often ran with the droplets caused by condensation or steam from whatever was cooking. Today water ran off the walls as if it was raining inside, as Mabel's washing boiled away in a copper in the corner, causing a damp mist to fill the kitchen.

Against the opposite wall to the boiler, and between the door that led to the stairs and the back door, stood a scrubbed, dull wooden table, which would have benefited from being covered in a pretty cloth, as Mrs Leary's was. Its position prevented one side from being used, making it impossible for Flo to sit with the family to eat, so she was usually served on a tray, if her mealtimes coincided with theirs. The pot sink was a stone colour and rough to the touch, rather than gleaming white, as Flo was used to. The oilcloth on the floor and the two leather chairs, which stood each side of the cooking range, were dark brown, adding to the overall gloom.

'Eat your porridge first. Then, if you're sure you want to help, you can turn the mangle. I've sheets in the copper that are ready for rinsing.'

Flo had dressed quickly, donning a skirt and jumper of thick wool, and now felt hot and

307

clammy in the damp atmosphere. Porridge was the last thing she needed, but she somehow managed to eat the lumpy, half-warm stodge. Thoughts of lovely creamy porridge and warm buttered toast, which had been the normal breakfast at home – all served in a cheery and bright kitchen, with Mrs Leary telling tales of the dream she'd had the night before – gave Flo a pang of homesickness.

If it was just Mabel she had to cope with, Flo knew she could put up with everything else and even make a friend of the woman, but the rest of the family were never going to give her a chance. Somehow she had to find better lodgings for herself.

Sweat poured off her as she battled with the heavy handle of the mangle, which resisted the intrusion of the huge wet sheets with all its might, but Flo enjoyed the work and the chatter Mabel kept up throughout. It appeared that Mabel's husband worked for the gas board and was exempt from being called up, but was always moaning, as he didn't feel he was doing his bit and wanted to volunteer for the army. Mabel dreaded him doing so, but in a small way this lifted Mick Garity in Flo's eyes. 'Don't mind him, you know,' Mabel said. 'He don't seem friendly and welcoming, but he'll come round, and once he does, so will the boys. The boys follow whatever their dad does, and on top of that, they don't like sharing a bedroom and see you as the cause of them having to.'

'I might not stay long... Me mate is looking for someone to share one of them flats that's empty over the shops.' Where this fib came from, Flo didn't know. She'd seen a notice pinned to the board in the canteen at Bletchley that there was a flat going, but hadn't given it a second thought until now.

'Oh? Well, I can't blame you. I could scalp that lot of mine. They've not made you welcome.'

'By, I don't blame them. It can't be easy having a stranger thrust on you, especially one you can't understand.' Flo laughed and winked as she said this, and Mabel took it in jest.

'Ha, you heard that then. Well, for what it's worth, I like how you speak and could listen to you all day. I'm sorry you feel you can't settle, but I wish you well. God knows what goes on up at that Park, but whatever it is, you're doing your bit. You're away from your family and friends, and that can't be easy. I'm ashamed of my lot, but I don't have much influence over them.'

Cycling to Bletchley Park much earlier than she needed to, Flo realized how hungry she was. Though the stodgy porridge had lain in her for a while, it was five hours since she'd eaten it, and the hard work of the mangling had given her an appetite. She had a ride of six miles to complete, but would get there by 2 p.m. She had plenty of time, so she decided she'd go to the canteen to have lunch and finish the crossword while she ate.

As she passed the noticeboard she saw that the flat was still advertised and wrote down the telephone number. Glad that she'd broached the subject with Mabel, but feeling as though she'd burned her bridges, Flo felt apprehension settle in her. Her need to escape the unhappiness she endured in her billet had prompted her, but what had she been thinking of? She wouldn't be able to afford such a place on her own, and Simon seemed settled in his billet. Maybe she'd acted too hastily; after all, a few weeks were no time for a family to get used to another member joining them.

She made her mind up that she would decide about moving, or not, after she knew more about the flat and how much the rent was. This settled Flo. And solving three clues in quick succession, whilst eating a delicious lunch, cheered her. The Park was lucky with its food rations. According to Simon, Churchill had decreed that all the staff should be well fed and looked after, as their work was so vital and it was important to keep them fit and well. Tucking into chopped boiled eggs on a bed of spinach, topped with Béarnaise sauce and served with a chunk of home-made bread, was a treat for Flo.

By the time she'd finished eating, one or two of the previous shift were filtering in for a break. Kitty made a beeline for Flo. 'Can't you wait to be with lover-boy then, eh? It's only three o'clock – you're not on duty for an hour. Not a place to do your courting, you know.'

For the second time that day, Flo's cheeks burned with embarrassment, but this soon turned to anger as Kitty leaned closer to her and lowered her voice. 'You and that nancy boy don't fool me. So don't think you do. I reckon that bloke who was with you in the pub that day is his real lover. Dirty buggers. Ha, that's an apt saying, if ever there was one.'

310

'How dare you speak of a superior officer like that? By, you're a disgrace.'

Kitty jumped back, but soon recovered. 'I dare because it's the truth, and one of these days I'm going to prove it, so watch yourself, girl. And tell lover-boy to keep looking over his shoulder.'

Flo clenched her hands tightly by her side, as she feared she'd claw at Kitty if she spoke another word. A voice she knew saved her. The tension eased as she turned in the direction from which the sound came.

'Florence ... Flo, over here. Well, well, I didn't know you had landed here as well. How jolly.'

'Belinda!' Skirting round the amazed Kitty, Flo ran over to her friend. She hadn't seen Belinda since they had parted company after their training together had ended. The hug she received made up for all she'd endured this morning at her digs, and from Kitty. 'Eeh, it's grand to see you, lass. How long have you been here?'

'Just three days. One of them spent reading that damned Secrecy Act! Bloody thing was a mile long.'

'I know. I've been here weeks, and I'm still reeling from it. Were you stationed somewhere else at first? Or shouldn't I ask?'

'I caught a wretched bug and was confined to the sickbay after we parted. And you?'

'I came here immediately.'

'I see you've made friends and influenced people already. What's got her in a huff?' Belinda sat down and indicated that Flo should too, but before she had time to answer the first question, another came. 'You look altogether disgruntled,

311

Flo. What's it like here?'

'Oh, it's grand. At least, I enjoy my work. I have heard others grumbling about the repetitive nature of theirs, though. That's Kitty, as was speaking to me. She's the only bugbear. She has it in for me friend, Simon. She keeps trying to prove that he's ... well, that he likes men.'

'That wouldn't be Simon Fulworth, would it, by any chance?'

'Aye, it is. He's a reet nice bloke. Do you know him?'

'Knew his sister at university, and heard as soon as I got here what tragedy had befallen her, and that her brother worked here. There'd been rumours about Simon's persuasion in the past, but it's nobody's bloody business which way he swings. Though there's always those who are out to make trouble. It was someone like Kitty in my school who nearly got me expelled, for getting into another girl's bed and experimenting with her. Don't look so shocked, Flo – it goes on all the time in boarding school. Quite healthy really, I think. I liked it, and might end up with a woman partner myself.'

Flo wanted to giggle. Belinda had a way of saying things that was very direct, and she wasn't sure if she was making a joke or not. But then there was something about Belinda that suddenly made Flo realize this wasn't just her making fun; it was true.

'You're safe – don't worry, I don't fancy you. Nor any woman I've met. And I do have an eye for the men, so perhaps I'll go that way after all. By the way, do you sing or act?' Flo was taken aback by this change of direction in the conversation. 'Oh, don't answer the singing bit. I know you do. You have quite a powerful voice. I've heard you. Remember? That night down in the Underground?'

'Eeh, how could I forget – we had a grand time.' Flo hesitated for a moment. Talking of their time together in London presented her with an opportunity to tell the truth. 'Belinda, when we were in London, I told you a fib.'

'Oh, don't worry, I'm top-hole at fibbing. Is it important?'

Flo told her how she'd fibbed about coming to London with a schoolteacher as part of a school trip, when it was really Simon and his friend who'd taken her there; and why.

'Understandable. I never knew this place existed, and you were trying to protect yourself from blurting out the wrong thing. So, you knew Lucinda then? A lovely girl. Fell in love with a German student, you know. I thought their romance was really going places, but then the war and all that. She was killed in France, I believe, whilst on a journalistic mission. Very brave, and all very sad.'

Flo covered up her surprise at all this coming out. 'Aye, I knew her and loved her. We were good friends, even though we didn't know each other long.'

'I wouldn't think anyone has to know you long to be friends with you, Flo. I feel as though I have known you all my life, and yet, but for a war, our paths would never have crossed. Did Lucinda mention her German boyfriend?'

313

Hating having to lie a second time, Flo shook her head. 'No, we were never alone long enough for women's talk. Most visits centred around Simon and his friend. Anyroad, Belinda, why're you asking if I can sing and act?'

'I didn't tell you, but I'm a bit of a thespian ... an actress. Did it at university. A fellow thespian, Petulia Norden, is here. She was one of our set and a damned fine actor. She collared me the moment she knew I was here. She's getting a concert group together. Singers, musicians, actors – anyone who can entertain. She's been here for months and says it's jolly boring, with not much going on, so she decided to do something about it. She's going to put on shows. Would you be game for that, Flo?'

Excitement settled in Flo at the prospect of this. She loved to sing, and maybe it would be a way of her making some friends. She nodded, ignoring the nerves that were already kicking in at the thought of it.

'Right. I'm off-shift soon and meeting up with Petulia. I'll put your name forward. Ask Simon about joining us, if you see him. I'm sure Lucinda mentioned once that her brother acted in a play at university.'

'I'll talk to him today. But how will we contact each other? We can't just rely on bumping into one another?' She didn't ask which hut in the Park Belinda was working in, nor did she say that she worked with Simon; and Belinda didn't ask her. Even for those working at the Park, secrecy was of the essence, and the rules were that no one shared any information with anybody, not even

314

their closest friends.

'There'll be notices on the board about the concert group. But where are you billeted? I could leave a message there for you.'

Flo told her, and of her plans to move.

'I'm in Woburn Abbey. Sounds grand, doesn't it? But it's bloody freezing and bloody basic. I wouldn't mind sharing that flat with you, Flo. Would you consider it?'

'Aye, I reckon as I could put up with you, but no coming into me bed, mind.'

Belinda laughed out loud, a horsey kind of sound that caused a moment's hush in the room. This made Flo giggle. It felt good and lifted her spirits. Though they were worlds apart, she loved Belinda, and had felt on first meeting her that she was her equal – something that showed how nice Belinda was. This wasn't Flo's experience of toffs in general, as most of them wouldn't give her the time of day.

When they'd calmed down, Belinda said, 'Give me the number of the agents letting the flat, Flo. I'll contact them this afternoon. Better strike quickly, as I should think such places are snatched up. Shall I take it, no matter what it's like? We can make a home of it soon enough, as my parents will let us have some furniture. They have a lot in storage, as they had to empty a number of rooms when the government seconded half of our home to house officers who were training nearby.' Belinda puffed out her chest and gave a deep tone to her voice. '"Bloody barbaric, taking over people's homes in this way," Daddy said, but really you could see that he was proud to play his part.'

'That'd be grand. Ta, Belinda. I feel reet lifted now.'

'Yes, so do I, Flo. You're a great girl, you know. I like you very much.'

Flo couldn't have been given a better compliment and hugged Belinda again before saying goodbye to her. *By, Belinda's a good 'un. And that's what I'm finding, now I'm out in the world. There's good and bad in all folk, no matter what their station in life. Look at Pauline, struggling on her own and yet helping others; and Eunice, striving to better herself after the start she had. Please God, let Eunice's test results give her some hope. And that Molly, an' all. I've a feeling she was the lass the ARP talked to his wife about, as was forced to... Eeh, it doesn't bear thinking about. Poor lass, I wonder how she is?*

These thoughts didn't dampen the uplifting feeling Belinda had given her, as Flo told herself that Simon was right: she mustn't take the world on her shoulders, but just do what she could to help. She was determined to do that. She'd have to make sure this concert group didn't interfere with the time she could give to helping the Sallies with their work.

Looking at the clock as she crossed over to the cloakroom, Flo thought this was another day when Simon was likely to beat her at finishing the crossword, as she'd have to make tracks to Hut 6 soon.

The earlier encounter with Kitty was far from her mind, until Flo passed by her. She stopped in her tracks at Kitty's scathing tone. 'What are you up to, eh? Hobnobbing? Well, it won't get you anywhere.'

316

'By, Kitty, you never give up, do you? Get out of me way, please, I don't want to talk to you.'

'Ha, don't you realize that Simon Fulworth, and the set he and that girl you've just been talking to mixes with, don't want you really. You amuse them, that's all. They make fun of you and how you speak, when you're not around. You're different, and they take the rise out of you.'

'Well, that's where you're wrong. You know nowt about them, and never will. Belinda and me are friends. We met in training, and she doesn't have any side to her. And Simon's me friend, an' all. It's folk like you, Kitty, who don't have true friends. Nobody can stand your bigoted attitude.'

Kitty went red in the face, before recovering and counterattacking. 'You'll eat those words, you jumped-up cow. We'll see who's bigoted when your mate comes in front of a judge – because I'll make sure he does.'

Kitty stormed off, leaving Flo swallowed up in the fear that Kitty had instilled in her for Simon and Roland. What she had said could come true, and Kitty seemed on a mission to make it so.

The uneasy feeling stayed with Flo throughout the afternoon. There'd been no time to chat with Simon, as the coded messages were coming in thick and fast. Some were straightforward, and these Flo sent to the girls in the office, who would paraphrase them. But others needed Simon's expertise. With her help, he completed the extremely complicated and intricate work of enciphering a 'menu', and produced a 'crib' to be fed into the Bombe, a brilliant machine used in code-breaking.

By eight that evening, neither of them had taken a break. Out of the corner of her eye, Flo saw Simon stretch and heard him yawn. 'Ready for a cuppa, Flo? I'm going boggle-eyed here.'

'In a moment. I'm nearly there with this one.'

Flo found the work fascinating and never wanted to stop, once she had a hold on the key to whatever she was looking for. At last she'd completed it. Punching the air in exuberance had Simon laughing out loud. 'Well done, you. Ten minutes behind me, but still good.'

Flo threw a piece of chalk at him. It hit his shoulder and bounced off, pinging off the window before landing in the wastepaper basket.

'Great shot. Come on: race you to the canteen.'

'You go. I still have to despatch this. I won't be long.'

To see Simon sitting on his own in the canteen awoke in Flo the memory of what Kitty had said and, with it, the niggling worry over his safety. Simon was rarely welcomed into the groups of male workers who sat smoking, with a glass of wine or beer, and enjoying some easy banter together. This made Flo think of how lonely his life must have been before she arrived here, and all because of the wicked tongue and malicious ways of Kitty Hamlin.

Flo thought it more than likely that Kitty was responsible for her male colleagues seeming to view herself as a joke too, and that contributed to Simon being thought of as one. Flo didn't miss their smirks, and often heard their snide remarks to the tune that she and Simon deserved each other. How she wished Belinda was on the same shift, and hoped that eventually she would be. If Belinda saw how the men behaved towards her and Simon, she would soon sort them all out. Belinda had what folk in the North called 'clout' – a sort of standing in others' eyes that commanded respect.

'Penny for them, Simon. Eeh, you were deep in thought then.'

'Oh, nothing special. I've a few things to mull over.'

This mood usually meant he was thinking of Lucinda. There was nothing she could say to make things easier for him. He had a grieving process to go through, and although she longed to offer him comfort, to hold him to her and soothe his sadness, Flo knew she couldn't. Focusing his mind on other things was the only strategy open to her. 'A friend of mine has turned up here, a girl I trained with.'

'Oh?'

'By, I expected more interest than that. It ain't as though I've a hoard of friends.'

'I'm sorry, Flo. I was listening. Who is she?'

'Belinda Harper. I've just found out that she was a friend of Lucinda's at university.' Flo could have bitten the words back, as a flash of pain crossed Simon's face. 'I – I thought if you talked to her it might help. It can, you know. She could perhaps fill in some memories that you don't know of.'

'Did she mention Aldric? Good God, Flo, that's the last thing we need – someone who knew about that little episode!'

'Yes. But don't worry; it weren't much, just that she remembered Lucinda had a thing with one of the German students. She didn't go on about it. What she knew of Lucinda's death was what everyone as reads the papers knows. Someone here, who'd also been at university with Belinda and Lucinda, told her about it. It upset her deeply. I thought we could ask her along when we get round to having that memorial we talked of.'

Simon gave a little cough. It was a habit that Flo had noticed, when he'd been a bit hasty.

'I'll get me tea, as I have sommat else to tell you.' Choosing a thick, meaty stew and home-made bread, Flo glanced over and saw that Simon only had a cup of tea in front of him. She asked the canteen lady if he'd ordered. Finding that he hadn't, she doubled up on the order. Back at the table, she told him, 'I've mothered you and ordered you some stew. You don't eat enough to keep a fly alive.'

'Thanks, Flo. I just couldn't be bothered.'

More like he doesn't want to walk past that crowd. Or be in a position where he has to acknowledge them. Without remarking on this, but trying to keep up a conversation, she said, 'I've other news an' all, Simon, and it's reet exciting. I might be moving.' She told him of her plans.

'Well, thank you very much for asking me. I'd have thought you would have given me first choice.'

'Eeh, Simon, what's got into you? You're acting like a spoilt young 'un. How do you reckon it would look, me and you living together, eh?'

Simon laughed. 'It would quieten the gossipers.'

'Ha, more like feed them more to sneer over. Anyroad, I thought you were happy where you were.'

'I am, up to a point. I'm made welcome, and the people I lodge with are nice and interesting, but it's not like being independent.'

Flo had thought Simon very lucky to be put in with the local vicar and his family. The Reverend Jones was a really nice man. A lot of the folk of Simon's and Belinda's standing had been billeted with families whose standard of living was much lower than they were used to. Flo couldn't imagine how they coped. But she agreed that, whatever the people who took you in were like, it wasn't like living on your own, and in your own way. 'Let's see what Belinda comes back with. If it's a two-bedroomed flat, you could come, an' all. That'd be grand. You'll like Belinda. And the more of us there are, the more affordable it will be.'

Simon cheered up at this, and Flo hoped with all her heart that the flat was big enough. Having Belinda there would satisfy convention, and it would be grand to have Simon in the same house as herself. They'd proved, when they stayed together at his place in London, that they could live in harmony, despite the undercurrents that surfaced at times. Having Simon living that close to her all the time was probably all she was going to ever have of him.

Brushing these thoughts away, Flo told him about Belinda's plans for a drama and music society. 'She asked if you can sing or act. And, if so, would you be interested in joining them? I am.'

'Crikey, she's a girl who doesn't sit on her laurels long, isn't she? After three days she's sorted all this out? Good for her, though I hope she isn't a compulsive organizer who takes over our lives.'

'No, Belinda's nothing like that. She just gets on with things.'

'Good. Well, yes, I'll join in. Why not – it could be fun. I'm not a great singer, though I can hold a tune. But acting... I actually love acting, and really enjoyed the couple of roles I took on at university. I had great acclaim in the local press.'

'Eeh, that's grand.'

'Oh, Flo, I love how you say that. It makes everything seem a lot better than it is.'

'As Mrs Leary says, "life is what you make of it. If you're knocked down, you get up again – it's the only way."'

'Mrs Leary is a wise woman. By the way, Flo, what are you doing when we're off-duty for a couple of days next week? I thought I would go up and see Roland. Would you like to come?'

'Naw, but ta for asking. I want to go up to London and help out. I can't get that Molly out of me head. I'll call in on Pauline and see if I can help her. She might knaw sommat about Molly, or where she stays.'

'Ha, I doubt it. London's not Leeds, you know. You're funny, Flo. A mile and half in London is like a hundred elsewhere. People don't even know their next-door neighbours. I should think, at a guess, that Molly lives in and works out of somewhere in the Soho area, and that might as well be Timbuctoo, as far as people who live in my area are concerned.'

'By, that'd be a place to start, then. If I went

there I might find someone as knaws her.'

'No. I emphatically forbid you to go to that area looking for her.'

This pulled Flo up. 'You forbid me? Eeh, that's taking sommat on.'

'Beg of you, then. As someone who loves you very much, I beg you not to go to that district, Flo. You don't know Soho; it is notorious.'

The feeling that shot through Flo, at Simon saying this, had to be suppressed even to allow her to breathe. Luckily, their stew was delivered to the table at that moment, causing a distraction that allowed Flo to cover how she felt. 'I won't go there, I promise. But I will ask them as come to the van. Prostitutes, and the like. Someone must know Molly and could get a message to her. She needs help, and if I can give it, I will.'

'Yes, Florence.'

They both laughed at this and the mood between them lightened.

As it turned out, the flat did have two bedrooms, and large ones at that. Flo was seeing the inside for the first time and liked what she saw. 'Eeh, it's grand, and the station is just down the road, an' all. That'll be handy for trips to London.'

'Yes, and it's one of the reasons Bletchley Park was chosen for the purpose it has. Proximity to a railway means signals, which need lots of tele-phone wires. Hooking into them is jolly handy.'

There was a view of the rail track through the window of the room she and Belinda stood in and had earmarked as their bedroom. They'd already discussed the need for a third person to share, to make it viable for them. Flo broached the subject again, now that she'd seen the layout. The second bedroom was separated from this one by a hallway. A bathroom and the kitchen led off this, then at the other end of the flat was a sitting room.

'How would you feel if I asked Simon to be the third tenant, Belinda? I knaw as you've not met him yet, but he's easy to get on with, and given how this place is, with the bedrooms set apart, we'd still have privacy.'

Belinda liked the idea. 'A great choice. Three women might just be too many, though I don't fancy Simon's chances of bagging the bathroom.' They giggled at this. 'And, you know, it won't help his standing at the park, but I expect he's thought of that.'

Belinda has heard, then? Not that it seems to bother her, and she's heard similar before and it hasn't put her off.

At that moment, a whistle sounded from an approaching train, the noise of it as it rattled by filling the space around them.

'By, Belinda, we'll have to get used to that! Though I've heard tell that folk who live on a railway embankment soon don't notice the sounds.'

'Let's hope that's true. What if we were on midnight-to-eight and trying to sleep in the day?'

'I want to take a chance on it. What about you?' Flo crossed her fingers as she waited for Belinda to answer.

'I'm in. Anything has got to be better than Woburn. And if Simon doesn't like it, I have a friend who might.'

Flo prayed that Simon *would* like it, as she was unsure what this other friend of Belinda's might be like.

In the little cafe down the road they talked about furniture and other arrangements. Flo could hardly contain her excitement.

'That's all settled, then. We'll let the landlord know we'll take it and we'll pay our deposit on pay-day. Now, Flo, the concert group. Because of our work schedules, we can't make a set time to meet and rehearse every week, but we're arranging the first one for Monday evening after the four o'clock shift ends, and all interested parties should attend, if they can. Any chance you can?'

'Aye, I can make that, as I'm on the night-shift and then on leave, after I come off-shift that morning. I can have a rest, then come in and catch a train to London. I'll ask Simon to attend, but he might want to get off to Leeds earlier than that.'

'Right-o. Then we've decided that, after each meeting, we'll sort out which is the best time for the next one, by how many can attend at a specific time. Petulia has a production lined up for us, as she has enough musicians to form a small orchestra.'

'Ooh, it's exciting. What's she got lined up?'

'*The Wizard of Oz*. I've put you forward to play Dorothy.'

'What! No, I can't. I saw that at the flicks. Eeh, I'm too old to play Dorothy.'

'Well, we all are. But I've looked at all those that have volunteered and none looks anything like Dorothy, but you do, with your long hair and perky nose. And you can sing. Please say yes.'

With this, Belinda burst into singing the chorus of 'Somewhere over the rainbow'.

The few people in the cafe applauded her when she'd finished, and Belinda – being Belinda – bowed to her audience.

Flo thought her sides would burst with laughter. 'Eeh, you're a card. A real card.'

Somehow life in Bletchley, and in general, suddenly seemed better. Flo was full of hope. She had the prospect of a nice place to live; she loved her work; she had Belinda and Simon; and now this new interest. By, she never thought she'd be on the stage!

Her thoughts soon prodded her back to her worries, as she cycled back to her billet. How could she possibly keep Simon safe? And what about Eunice and Molly? If only she could make things right for them all. Because, no matter how much she told herself that she mustn't take everyone's plight on her own shoulders, she couldn't stop herself. As soon as she could, on Tuesday morning, she'd get in touch with Eunice and see if she had her results and what they were. What she would do if they were bad, she didn't know. After that she'd find Pauline and sort out working on the van with her, and she could only hope that somehow she would get in contact with Molly. Getting Molly off her mind was proving difficult, and she knew she had to try and help her somehow. Though God knew what she could do.

20

Molly

Finding Help

Was that a shooting star? Molly gazed up through the gaping hole in the roof of this bombed-out house, where she'd spent her time since escaping the brothel. The clear sky above, though wondrous, was like a sequinned blanket of fear, as on such a clear night as this the Luftwaffe were bound to visit. When would it end?

Easing her stiff body off the cold remains of an inner wall, Molly pulled her blanket around her. Though damp now, it still afforded some warmth. She didn't know how many days had passed. All of them had merged together. Most had been spent in a haze of crying when awake, and when asleep in terrifying dreams of ugly men with fat bodies plucking pieces of her until she was just a skeleton. Through it all, excruciating pain assailed her.

A fit of coughing seized her. Her chest hurt and she wondered if she was getting pneumonia, as poor Ruby had done. She didn't want to die. Somehow she must find the strength to get out of here and seek help.

Feeling her way back down into the cellar, where she'd spent most of her time, she groped around in the darkness, making for the corner where she'd hidden the money she'd brought with her. Nothing! *Oh God, where is it? I know I put it behind this broken pipe. I know I did.* Searching frantically along the wall to the opposite corner, she ran her fingers all round the area once more, thinking she might have the wrong corner, but there weren't even any pipes there. *Help me. Oh God, help me. I have to have money!*

Exhausted after finding nothing in any of the corners, Molly flopped down on the bottom step of the cellar. Defeated and in despair, she tried to think what could have happened to her stash. Even the cardigan she'd wrapped it in was gone. Someone must have sought shelter down here and found her money. Maybe they had even watched her come down here with her bag and gas mask. *My bag!*

Finding strength from somewhere, Molly renewed her search, shuffling over every inch of the small space in the hope of kicking against her bag. Tripping on some debris, she cried out in agony as she landed heavily on the ground. But then she knew a moment of hope as her hand landed on her gas mask. Pulling it to her, she patted the ground around it. At last she had to accept that her bag had gone, as the two had been together, next to where she'd lain down. Tears of frustration stung her eyes. Everything she had in the world had been taken.

After a moment of thinking through what she could do, she decided to go back up the steps to the ground floor of the house. She'd heard water running up there. At least she could get a drink and try to wash herself as best she could.

Once in the only part of the room that still stood, Molly could see better. The full moon lit the area around her. Taking stock of herself, she could see that at least the coat she had on still looked reasonable, if a little crumpled.

Walking carefully, she followed the sound of the water. Gushing from a broken pipe and sparkling in the moonlight, the flow resembled a waterfall. After drinking her fill and easing the discomfort of her dry, cracked lips, Molly braved putting her head under it, to rinse her hair and face. She felt as if she'd been plunged into an ice-bucket, and had to force herself to stay there long enough to remove the clinging dirt from her. When this was done, she took off her coat and other garments. Most had kept fairly clean, from being covered by the blanket, though she knew she couldn't wear her knickers again; she'd just have to go without. Luckily, the skirt Trixie had ready for her to change into, on the day she'd left, had been a long one that reached to her calves.

Stepping under the water was something she couldn't subject her shivering body to, but she did her best by catching handfuls of water to rub over herself, to freshen and clean herself as much as she could. Now she had to avoid touching anything, as everywhere was blackened and charred. It wasn't easy to get her clothes back over her wet body, or to squeeze her swollen feet back into her shoes, but she managed it, after a struggle. The effort warmed her and gave her some comfort. Once dressed, she ran her tongue over her coated teeth and thought to use the trick she'd told Ruby of: cleaning them with soot.

She only had her finger to use as a brush, but she wiped it along the nearest wall and used the residue to rub her teeth. The taste was of stale smoke, and it took several rinses to remove the tang. The effect was good, though, because now her teeth at least felt less coated.

Though weak with hunger, Molly climbed over the rubble and managed to get outside onto the pavement. A blacked-out world met her. The houses and skeletons of buildings showed no light, and no street lamps were lit, though a few cars passed by with dimmed lights, and there were still some people making their way in the moonlight to whatever destination summoned them. At last she arrived at the corner where she'd met the ARP warden and the firemen. She hoped against hope she would find the warden's house. But what she discovered was utter devastation.

A gaping hole a few yards into the road had a smashed bus protruding from it. The sight undid Molly, and she slumped against the bottom half of a ruined building and stared at what must have become a grave. Shock racked her body.

A voice penetrated her despair. 'Oi! What're yer up to, Miss? You shouldn't be out here, it's too dangerous.'

An ARP warden approached her, shining a powerful torch into her face. She cowered away from its beam. When he got up to her, he asked her again what she was doing, then said, 'Hey, you're all wet. What's happened to yer?'

When her eyes got used to the light, she could see that he wasn't the same man who had offered her help before. Remembering that day, and Derrick, the old man dressed as Santa, she said, 'I'm looking for the Copper Kettle Cafe.'

'Well, you'll look for a long time, as it's gone, lav. All round here went on the night of 29th December. What a night, eh? I thought London would be no more and we'd all perish. Hundreds did. Poor buggers.'

Molly remembered; of course, it'd been the night after she'd met Flo. A terrifying and intense attack had taken place, as if the Germans were throwing everything they had at them in one night. Telling the warden now that she had nowhere to go, she asked if he could direct her to the nearest Salvation Army depot.

'If yer go back to Poland Street, lav, yer bound to see one. But failing that, get yerself down the Underground. Good luck.'

Adjusting to the light once the warden had moved off, Molly turned round to retrace her steps. Back on the main road, she felt exposed. She was too near the brothel and Trixie's stamping ground, and might meet someone she knew at any moment.

Two uniformed male figures came towards her, although she couldn't quite make out which service they were in. But when one spoke, she knew they were Canadian; there were a lot of Canadian airmen stationed at Biggin Hill. 'Good evening, ma'am. We're in London looking for a good time. How about you tell us where to go, eh?'

His question gave her an idea. Repulsed by the thought of it, desperation made her carry it through. 'I can show you a good time, mate. I don't charge much. If you both have me, I'll ask for ten bob off each of you.'

'Done. Where can we go?'

'No. It's not done, Spike. Ignore him, ma'am.' The taller of the two, and the one supporting the drunken Spike, peered at her closely as he said this. He didn't show any disdain, only concern. 'Hey, you don't look well, ma'am. Can we be of assistance to you?'

Feeling embarrassed and lower than she'd ever been, Molly just wanted to get away from them. 'Thanks, but I'll manage. I'm just hungry and have nowhere to go – it's par for the course, for us Londoners. I'll be fine. I'll find some help.'

'We'll help you, ma'am. We won't leave you till you're settled somewhere.'

'Ha, we'll take you up an alley. You'll be settled there, when we've done with you.'

'Shut up, Spike. Excuse him, ma'am, he's not usually like this.'

'She said she'd show us a good time, Art. What's the matter with you? You said earlier that you needed a woman.'

Propping Spike against the wall, Art told him, 'Listen, Spike, I've had enough. I'm going for the train now, and I'm going to take this young lady with me and get her some goddamn help from that Salvation Army station we saw near there. Are you coming or not?'

'Hell, no, man. I ain't playing no guardian angel. I'm in London – Soho, the place of whores and drink – and I want a good time. We might be dead tomorrow.'

The fear of her proximity to Eva's place, and to

332

the area where the girls worked, was making Molly nervous. Without thinking of the consequences, she blurted out, 'There's a brothel in Beak Street, just around the corner from here. Only don't mention having seen me, as I'm trying to escape from there. It's above a tailor's shop. Just ring the bell of the shop.'

'That's where I'm headed, then. You can go to hell, Art. I'm going to have me a woman.' As if this thought had sobered him, Spike stood up straight and marched off.

'I'm torn, ma'am. I should go after him, but he's hard to handle when he's like this.'

'He's a grown man. If he gets into trouble, it's not your fault.' Molly was warming to Art. A big man and from what she could see a handsome one, he had a nice, caring way. Despite her appearance, he hadn't rejected her, nor had he taken up her offer or let Spike take it. She felt ashamed of acting the way she had. What must he think of her?

'You're right, ma'am. He can fend for himself. I have to make my way to Victoria station, to catch a train to Shoreham. Whenever I make the trip to the station from the Thames end, I see a Salvation Army van near Vauxhall Bridge. I've been that way today. I live near a river at home, and the Thames draws me to it. What say we get a cab and head there? I'd like to bet the Salvation Army are still there. They'll help you.'

Molly couldn't speak; it was as if her whole body let go, now that someone was going to help her.

Art managed to get a taxi. It seemed easy for

333

him. The Canadians had more money than they knew what to do with in broken-down London. They only had to raise their arms and they were tended to, wherever they went. Molly could imagine Eva rubbing her hands together in glee when Spike turned up there. Poor bloke would have nothing left in his pocket by the time he left. A small part of her was cheered by this. Spike was bent on paying to have a woman. If there weren't men such as him, there'd be no trade for those who exploited women.

The warmth of the cab soothed her. Art held her to him in a gentle hug. 'Rest against me, ma'am. We'll soon be there.'

It seemed no time at all before he told her they had arrived at Vauxhall. Molly opened her eyes. She hadn't remembered anything of the three miles or so they'd travelled, and yet she hadn't thought she'd dropped off to sleep.

'There – look, that's the van I told you about. Hold on to my arm.'

There was a queue at the van, but Molly didn't care. At last it was possible that she would have a connection to Flo. She only hoped that those who helped out on these vans knew of Flo, even though they were miles from where she'd met her.

Two women manned the van. One had a WRVS band on her arm. Molly felt a pang of guilt as she looked at her. Though she'd wanted to, she hadn't done anything for the war effort, and yet here was this woman doing her bit, and she must be sixty if she was a day.

The other one was a younger woman, smallish and hardly able to see over the counter, but with a nice, homely face. A real cockney, she was having plenty of banter with her customers.

'Last time I was here I saw a girl,' Art told Molly. 'She was tall and had chestnut hair and the bluest eyes, and a cute little chink in her nose. I sat over there and watched the girls working, and I fell in love with her and was hoping she'd be here again today.'

'Crikey, Art, I think that's the same girl I'm looking for. Her name's Flo. I'm hoping these women know where I can contact her because when I met her Flo said she'd be willing to help me, if I needed it. And I'm sure she meant it.'

'You know her? That's incredible! Gee, what's she like? I'd give my right arm to meet her.'

'You have got it bad, mate. But do you know what? I'd give my right arm, an' all, just to see her again. She's got a kindly way and makes you feel as everything will be all right, if she's helping you.'

'The queues are getting smaller. Go forward and ask.'

Molly started to go forward, but on letting go of Art's arm she found that her legs wouldn't hold her. Her body swayed. Everything near her swivelled round, as though she was on a merry-go-round.

'Blimey, girl, you're in a state. Let's help yer up.'

Molly knew she'd been carried somewhere, but was still disorientated. 'Where am I?'

'Yer in the back of the Salvation Army van. What's your name, lav?'

'Molly.'

'I'm Pauline. Yer all right now, Molly. We'll sort

yer out.'

'I – I want Flo.'

'I know yer do. That nice bloke who was with you told us. He's had to go and catch his train. But he said if ever yer need him, or if yer find Flo, you can write to Biggin Hill RAF station. He said to let him know where Flo is. What's he want with her, then?'

'He fancies her.'

'Blimey, he'd better get in the queue then, as she's smitten with another. Anyway, he left his name and address on a piece of paper for yer. Here, get a sip of this tea into yer. I've even managed to put some sugar in it. We had some given to us today, and I've been letting the neediest have it. It'll give you some energy.'

As Pauline had said, the energy seeped back into Molly, the more she drank of the delicious tea.

'Now then, we know what that bloke wants with Flo, but what is it you're after? Only she ain't here till tomorrow.'

'She said if ever I was in trouble, she'd help me. I've got nothing, and nowhere to go.'

'If Flo said that, then I'll help yer. I can do that much for Flo. Have yer been bombed out, lav?'

Molly hesitated. She didn't want to tell the woman why she was homeless and down on her luck.

'Makes no odds, lav. I'll sort yer out. I've to finish up here first, though. You sit there a mo. We close up in a bit, then you can come back to me house with me. I live on me own, so there's plenty of room. I'll make you up a nice clean bed – that's

336

if you don't mind sharing, as we only have one up and one down. And I'll soon have some hot water on the go, so yer can have a good wash down and put one of me winceyette nighties on. Then we'll see what's to be done. I've a nice bit of stew simmering on me stove as well. How does all that sound, eh?'

Molly was struck dumb. Her tears spoke for her as she smiled through them. Part of her smile was for the comfort that she felt coming from Pauline, and part of it was for the thought of that nightie. A feeling of being overwhelmed by the woman's kindness took hold of her. How things had changed. But for small pockets of communities, Londoners never used to give each other the time of day, and now they opened up their homes to strangers in need.

By the time Molly was tucking into the stew, she thought she'd landed in heaven. Pauline was lovely, and even though Molly had told Pauline her story, she didn't judge her.

'That's a lot for you to go through, girl. I've been at rock bottom, an' all, so I know what it feels like.'

Molly listened to how Pauline had been bombed out and had dealt with her husband being away, her mum living by the bottle, and now having her kids away somewhere in Wales.

'Flo helped me, yer know. She were standing on the bridge back there, when she saw me coming. Loaded up, I was. And she carried some of me things. She even gave me five bob. I couldn't believe it. I was bleedin' down, I can tell yer. I was ready for giving up. But that one kind gesture – and someone caring enough to make it – changed things for me. Me mum's all right now, and me kids are, an' all. And me old man: well, poor bloke has to take his chances, but I pray every day that he comes back to me. Anyway, after what Flo did for me, I vowed that once I could, I would help others.'

This fitted well with the Flo that Molly had in her mind, even though she'd only met her for a few moments.

'Flo reached out to me, an' all, only I couldn't take up her offer then. But thanks for what you've done for me, Pauline. I was desperate. And I feel the same, about helping others. I want to do war work. Sometimes, I have to admit, the idea of joining up was just an escape route, no matter where it took me. But now I really want to do me bit.'

Huddled up as she was by the roaring fire and with the lovely Pauline, Molly felt safe for the first time in many months. She loved the feel of the soft nightdress, and how it hung down to her feet and buttoned up to her neck. It seemed, to her, to wrap her in love and gave her a feeling that she really might have a chance at a new beginning. Well, she intended to take it. She prayed that Delilah would keep her promise and turn in Eva's evil gang.

With Delilah being on the list of reported missing, the police would have to listen to her. Especially as it would be away from London, where a lot of the coppers were in Eva's pay. Molly's thoughts turned to Eva now, and then to her dad.

Would he go to prison, too? She didn't want this to happen, but suddenly she didn't care any more. He'd turned his back on his own, in order to make money. He deserved to go to jail, and a big part of her wished that he would.

'Molly. Molly! Eeh, lass, wake up.'

Hearing Flo's voice made Molly feel that everything was going to be all right with her world. She opened her eyes and looked into Flo's huge blue ones.

'By, you're a sleepyhead, lass. I've been trying to wake you these five minutes since. I've brought you a cuppa and some breakfast. Can you sit up?'

It wasn't easy to, but Molly managed to sit up enough for Flo to put the tray she was carrying in front of her.

'There, lass. I hope you like porridge, as that's all there is.'

'Flo! Oh, Flo, it's good to see you.'

'And you. You got away then? By, I was reet glad when I called round this morning and Pauline told me you were here. It were like a miracle, as I'd made up me mind to find you, no matter what it took. I couldn't get you out of me head.'

'I wanted to take up your offer that night, but Trixie didn't trust the bloke with you.'

'Simon? He's one of the best blokes you'll ever meet. He was a bit on his guard that night, as he was being overprotective of me. He thinks I act on what me heart tells me to do, without thinking things through. He's reet as well, but it's never landed me in trouble yet.'

'I hope your heart thinks me worthy of you

339

helping me, Flo, as I've no other options at the moment. I will have, once I'm well, as I'm going to join up.'

'Aye, Pauline's been telling me. It'll be the best thing for you. You'll be taken care of, and out of the clutches of them as have done this to you. Me and Pauline have been having a natter, and Pauline's willing for you to stay here with her. I'll help her by paying towards your keep. How's that sound, eh?'

'I don't know what to say. I can't thank you enough. I'll pay you back, Flo. Every penny.'

'We'll see.'

'Flo, I have to tell you something. No one must know I'm here. That gang I told you of, they'll be looking for me. Me life's in danger. I did a daft thing last night, but I wasn't thinking right.'

Molly told Flo about the Canadian airmen, Art and Spike, and how she'd sent one of them to Eva's. 'If he tells them a woman sent him, they'll be curious and will ask what I looked like.'

'Eeh, Molly, it's a frightening world you live in. Are you sure they'll be asking him? And even if they do, how could it lead them here?'

'Because they'd know that all of their girls are in the house, so a woman sending a man to their brothel at that time in the evening would raise their suspicions as to who it was. They're always on their guard, but will be even more so, as two of us have now absconded. If they asked Spike if he knew where I was, he would know that I was heading for the Salvation Army van, as Art told him.'

'Don't worry, love. I'm sure nowt will happen.

340

Though it were an amazing coincidence that you were brought to the very van Pauline was working in, and where I'm to work today. Eeh, I'm reet glad, though.'

Molly laughed, then winced at the pain it caused her. 'Not such a coincidence as you might think. Art's seen you working there and took a fancy to you. He was hoping to see you again. They've been past the van when they've come up to London, as Art always makes for the Thames from Victoria station, before they go anywhere.'

Flo blushed. 'Eeh, go on with you! Though, I can remember two Canadians stopping by to say hello, when Simon and me worked with Pauline. It was our first time helping out in her van. I remember that the tall one asked how they could donate some money to help our cause; he was reet good-looking. Pauline showed him the box we keep for contributions and he put a whole pound note in it.'

'That'll be Art. I reckon you've made a conquest there.'

'Ha-ha. Not such an ugly duckling then.'

'Course you're not – you're beautiful, Flo.'

Flo blushed again, then changed the subject. 'Anyroad, try not to worry. The woman as took care of me from when I was a youngster allus says that half of what you worry about has already happened, and the other half will probably never happen. I'll have a word with Pauline. I'm sure she won't be changing her mind about you staying with her, but like you say, it's better that we knaw. Now, eat up your porridge. As much as you might not like it, it's good for you.'

341

As Flo left the room, Molly felt glad she'd found Flo. Even if it was in the most unlikely way. Flo was a good person, and Molly looked on her as the only one who could help her. But there was more to it than that. Molly felt an affinity with Flo, as if she'd known her all her life – and hoped she would do for the rest of it.

21

Simon & Roland

Devastation

Simon stretched out his legs. By jingo, he'd be glad to get off the train. There'd been a delay when he'd changed at Crewe. His welcome to Leeds had been hailed by the dawn, as the pale-blue sky gave way to a spectacular fire-red splash that bathed the tops of the snow-covered buildings.

A flurry of snow was still falling as he alighted. Roland should be waiting for him. He'd been on duty all night with the ARP. They planned to have a good breakfast together in a cafe that Roland often used, then go to bed for a few hours to catch up on their sleep. Simon couldn't wait to cuddle up, and wondered to himself how he could ever have thought he might be different from the way he'd always known himself to be. But then he had a confusion of feelings; when he thought of Flo, he knew he loved her with an intensity that sometimes hurt and, yes, he did fancy her.

Banishing these thoughts from his mind, as they didn't do him any good and felt disloyal to Roland, Simon collected his bag from the luggage rack and went out into the corridor to wait for the train to pull into the station.

A figure caught his eye. A man looked at Simon emerging from the train, and jumped back into the carriage just along the corridor. His movement seemed furtive. Strange. But then he might have forgotten something.

As the snow crunched under his feet, Simon soon forgot the incident and hurried for shelter, hoping that Roland wasn't delayed.

'You're here at last.' Roland stepped out of the waiting room and shook Simon's hand. Simon so wanted to hug him. 'Good to see you. I heard you had a diversion due to the weather. Well, at least you got through.'

'Yes, though I'm a bit nervous about getting back in time tomorrow. I might try to change my ticket and go early in the morning.'

'Might be prudent, but disappointing, as it will cut down our time together. Anyway, how are you? And how's Flo?'

They chatted in a light manner as if there was no emotional, invisible thread tugging at them both.

Outside the station the snow was even deeper. 'Hope you've brought your wellies. We'll need to clear a path to my door.' Roland's laugh was superficial. Simon knew that beneath the small talk and throwaway remarks Roland felt just as he did: frustrated that they couldn't show how much they'd missed each other.

'I'll crank the engine. You get in the car, Simon.'

Simon watched Roland's tall elegance and knew he would always love and desire him. The other feelings he had couldn't interfere with that. As soon as Roland got into the car, Simon reached for his hand. 'I've missed you.'

They held each other's eyes. 'Christmas seems a long time ago. I can't believe it's only a few weeks.' Roland's voice showed his feelings. 'I've missed you, too. I love you, Simon.'

The words provoked a nice feeling, though it was tinged with guilt. For a moment Simon felt as though he had betrayed Roland with the love he'd expressed for Flo.

The squeeze on his hand seemed to say 'Don't worry', before Roland released him and took off his glasses to wipe them clear of condensation. Before he set off, he smiled his lovely smile. It was as if he was saying that he knew, and understood. Simon relaxed.

The cafe gave off an aura of welcome. Bright red-and-white-checked cloths covered the tables and looked well against the mustard-coloured walls and cream linoleum. Lots of pictures completed the look and were of peaceful English country-side scenes. Simon felt a longing to go back to those times, and visions of picnics and long walks assailed him.

Silver cruets stood proudly on each table, which was laid with shining stainless-steel cutlery. The atmosphere drew you in, as if you'd entered a homely living room. The fire crackling in the huge fireplace added to that sense. The other occupants were all gentlemen, some reading papers, others tucking into eggs and drinking from china cups. Most were smoking.

'Mmm, real eggs. That will do for me.'

'They have a garden out the back and grow a lot of produce, as well as keeping chickens. Very fertile chickens, apparently.' Roland laughed at his own joke.

The over-loud bell clanged as the door opened behind them. A cold wind blew in from outside. As Simon turned, he recognized the man who entered as the one he'd seen on the train. Telling himself that he was being silly, he followed Roland and sat at a table in the window. He knew that his job, his encounter with Aldric, and Kitty Hamlin's threats had all contributed to him being more on edge than usual.

There was no reason in the world why the man should be a threat to him.

As Simon thought of Kitty, Flo's words telling him what Kitty had said came to him. Flo had seemed to take them seriously and had warned him to be careful. He looked over towards the man. Simon was relieved to see that he wasn't paying any attention whatsoever to him and Roland, but sat reading his newspaper.

'Is anything wrong, Simon?'

'No. Sorry. Well, I do have things to tell you. I couldn't write about them, or speak of them on the telephone. It's concerning Lucinda.'

'Oh, I thought you were going to say Flo.' Roland sounded relieved. 'I think of Lucinda all

345

the time. I still can't believe she won't be waiting to greet me when I come down next time.' He took a huge white hanky from his pocket and blew his nose.

Simon lowered his eyes. Just the mention of Lucinda caused him hurt. Would the pain of her loss never lessen?

'I hope to get down to London soon,' Roland continued, 'so we can go ahead with the service that we have planned. I think we'll all feel better after that, and maybe begin to accept it really happened.'

'I know. I think that, too. But there have been developments as to why she really went to France.'

Roland showed the same shock Simon had felt, when he'd first learned the truth of Lucinda's boyfriend's identity.

'I'll give you all the detail when we get back to yours. Our voices might carry in here, and it's quite sensitive.'

They ate in silence for a moment, as both gave their attention to enjoying the rare treat of real, not powdered, eggs. Roland spoke first. 'When I asked if you were all right, for a moment I thought you knew that man who came in. His appearance seemed to upset you, or shouldn't I ask?'

'Oh no. I don't know him; and yes, you can ask. He was on the same train as me. What's he doing now?'

'Ha, whatever it is you do at Bletchley gives you an overactive imagination. I bet there were a hundred people on the train, and most would want breakfast when they arrived. He's looking quite innocent, and is eating his eggs. He did glance

346

over here a couple of times and I caught his eye once, but he didn't look away in a guilty way.'

'It's just me, then. Well, I'm glad about that. You might understand, when I tell you what Lucinda's boyfriend was up to, and how that nasty piece of work you met in the pub in London has been threatening me again. She didn't do it to my face, but she has been dropping snide, threatening remarks to Flo. Anyway, talking of Flo, I can at least discuss something with you in here that isn't top-secret. We're moving in together.'

'Ooh?'

'Don't say it like that, as if you're suspicious or jealous or something.'

'But I am. I know how you feel about each other. And I'm jealous that it isn't me moving in with you.'

Simon felt an uncomfortable feeling creep up his spine. It wasn't unlike the one he'd felt as a boy, if caught out in a misdeed.

'Hey, I'm only pulling your leg. But be careful, Simon. Flo doesn't really understand how we are. The whole concept is very new to her. She isn't worldly-wise, and she could imagine herself in love with you and think you capable of returning those feelings.'

What Roland said was so near the truth that Simon felt his colour rising. Thinking that to protest would make things worse, he agreed. 'Yes, I'm aware of that, and I think it has happened to a certain extent. I am trying to be careful.' *A lie. I want Flo to love me… Oh God, what am I thinking?* 'We have a housemate. A horsey type, a jolly-hockey-sticks kind of girl. I like her very much.

347

She'll keep us both grounded.' He laughed at this as if it was a light-hearted remark, but inside, while part of him welcomed the fact that Belinda was going to be living in the flat with them, he really wished it was just going to be him and Flo.

'Good. But I mean it, Simon, don't hurt Flo. She's the best thing to come into both our lives, even though I didn't know it for five long years. And I, for one, would miss her terribly if we lost her friendship. Shall we go? I need to be alone with you and forget all about this outside world where we have to be so restrained with each other.'

Simon thrilled at these words, which set up an eager anticipation inside him. 'Me too, darling.'

The endearment was whispered, but Roland had heard. The pleasure the words gave him showed in his face.

Wrapped up in their love and desire for each other, neither noticed the man they'd been wary of quickly finish his tea and follow them out.

They held hands in the car, before driving off. 'Tell me about Lucinda, as I don't want anything to get in the way of our time at home... Oh, I didn't mean that to sound how it did. I'm sorry, Simon.'

'I know what you mean, and I know you would never be callous about Lucinda. You're right, and I feel the same way – our time together is precious.' Roland gave him a sideways look and squeezed his knee. His touch sent sensations travelling though Simon. 'Better not do anything like that or I'll risk being caught and will make you stop the car right now.'

Though they both smiled at this, the air

between them was fraught with the frustration of the love they had to deny until they were behind closed doors. Their look told each other how they felt. Simon knew he had to break the spell. If they were a man and woman, they could hold each other, kiss...

'That was a big sigh.'

Simon just smiled again. 'Well, anyway, what I have to tell you is quite shocking.' He explained how what had happened to Lucinda and Aldric was no different from what happened to them all the time. 'We can't choose who we fall in love with, and it's others who put obstacles in our way.'

'Poor Lucinda. Poor, poor Lucinda. In a way–'

'No, don't say it. There is nothing that would make her passing a good thing.'

Roland apologized once again.

Simon begged him not to. 'Lucinda wouldn't want us to be at odds on her account. She made her decision and it went horribly wrong for her, but like us, she had the courage to follow her heart, whatever the consequences might be.'

They were both silent then and didn't speak again until they were inside Roland's house. And then only to declare their love as they clung to each other.

Simon took longer to fall asleep. He snuggled up to Roland, content to feel the rise and fall of his gentle, restful breathing as he slept. It was enough just to be together. To him, it felt as though his heart pounded a rhythm of happiness around him. This was where he belonged. There would be time enough later to express their love fully. He thought of Flo, and wondered what it would be like to snuggle up to her in this way. But instead of confusing him, he knew with a clarity that gave him peace that it would never match what he felt for Roland. He must do all he could to help Flo see that. To help her understand that for a time he'd been lost, caught in a deeply sad world, and she had been there for him. This had made him misinterpret his feelings of deep friendship-love for the kind of passion that lovers need to share. He deeply regretted that and knew he must make it right somehow.

Before he drifted into a peaceful sleep he felt a longing for the war to be over, so that he and Roland could go abroad together. He thought of their holiday in Paris two years ago, and how liberated the arty set there were. The freedom that he and Roland had experienced, in being able to express themselves publicly, had been exhilarating. The poor Parisians – what must life be like for them now, imprisoned and shackled by the Germans?

A crashing sound catapulted Simon from sleep. Beside him, Roland shot up to a sitting position at the same moment, responding to the shock of the noise and the sudden emergence from sleep to wide-awake terror. The flash of a powerful camera bulb blinded them both. Each reacted the same way, by covering their eyes with their arm.

'Police!'

Simon uncovered his eyes to see someone he thought for a moment was Oliver Hardy, of Laurel and Hardy fame. *Is this a joke? Please God, let it be.*

The large man with a bulging stomach, blacker-than-black hair protruding from a bowler hat and sporting a moustache held up a leather wallet and flashed a police identity badge. Beside him stood a thin, poker-faced man of small stature, pointing a camera at Simon and Roland. He was engaged in taking photos from all angles. Of them, of their clothes left hanging over a chair and of the room.

'Now then, gentlemen, what do we have here? Get out of that bed and get dressed – you're coming with me.'

Realization that this was happening dawned on Simon. 'No. No... We weren't doing anything.'

'I think yes, sir. You have been caught in an act of gross indecency. You are both under arrest.'

'Oh God!'

This gasp of fear from Roland compounded Simon's terror. His mind wouldn't work properly. He couldn't rationalize anything that was happening. The only feeling he registered was fear. *We'll go to prison. Oh God, I can't. No!*

'Get dressed, you're coming with me to the station. There you will be charged. Tomorrow you will come before a judge. You're looking at an easy war, gentlemen. One spent behind bars. Though it doesn't look as if either of you has done anything to help the war effort so far.'

This incensed Simon. 'I am a serving officer in the Royal Navy, sir. Roland is too old for conscription and is a volunteer ARP.'

'Well, I beg your pardon. In that case, once at the station we will contact the Military Police and give them our evidence on you, and they will deal with you. But you, sir, will be dealt with in

351

the civil court, and I can tell you now: you face a good few years behind bars. Now both of you, get out of that pit of degradation and get dressed!'

'What're you in here for, then? You don't look like no thief or owt.'

Simon looked warily at his cellmate. But for the presence of this rough-looking, hard man with whom he shared the windowless, dingy police cell, smelling of urine and body odour, he knew that he'd be weeping his heart out. For Roland, more than for himself. He held hope inside him, at having to face a military court. They would recognize the extreme importance of his work and would probably allow him to return to it, with a sentence of no leave for a year, and hard labour to be undertaken at the times when he should have been on leave. But for Roland, there was no such hope. Simon couldn't see any alternative to him going to prison.

'I take it you don't want to tell me. You ain't one of them shirt-lifters, are you? You look like one. If you are, don't even think of coming near me, man. I'll snap every bone in your bleedin' body, if you do.'

Disgust and despair clothed Simon. *Will there ever come a day when love between two consenting adults, such as me and Roland, will be accepted? Why can't people realize that we were born different? We aren't perverts.*

'Obviously, being the age you are, and fit and strong, I don't have to ask you why you're here.'

'What? What're you saying? Talk straight, man.'

'I'd say you're either a conscientious objector or

352

an avoider who has been hiding from conscription. A coward, who's been caught and faces being brought to justice.'

The man's movement was swift. Simon had no time to defend himself. The blow caught him on his chin and sent him reeling backwards, hitting his head on the brick-exposed wall. Dazed, he saw the next punch coming; it was aimed at his stomach. Somehow he managed to roll out of the way. Caught off-balance, mid-punch, the man fell onto the bed. Something snapped in Simon – it wasn't going to happen again.

He grabbed the man's arm, twisted it up his back, hooked his foot around his ankle and rendered him incapable of being able to stand up. The man's hollering resounded around the walls of the cell and echoed down the corridor outside. The sound of keys jangling and chains rattling gave Simon a sense that help was at hand. Releasing the man, he thought he would only need to report his aggression to the police officer, who would surely attend and then he would be safe.

It was an assumption he regretted immediately, as a crushing blow caught him in his kidney area, bringing him to his knees. Large, rough hands grabbed each side of his head and jerked him forward in a violent movement that smashed his face onto the man's bent knee. His nose cracked, his front tooth left its socket and dug into his tongue. Pain seared through every part of him.

The sound of a key in the door offered a morsel of relief. Help was at hand. The door creaked open, but closed within seconds. *God, they aren't going to help me!*

With this realization came a sense of his own life being in danger. Survival instinct gave Simon strength. Grabbing the man's legs, he jerked them forward with all the power he could muster. The man crashed backwards, and his back jarred on the brick base of the bed. His head smashed into the wall. His body slumped to the ground. He landed on his knees, his lifeless eyes staring into Simon's.

The scream started deep inside him and rose to come from his mouth in a blood-curdling sound that had many feet running towards the cell. The door opened. 'Christ, he's killed him!'

Another voice shouted, 'Get the doctor, now!'

A hand pulled Simon roughly to his feet. Other hands grabbed his arms and yanked them painfully behind him, then snapped on tight-fitting handcuffs.

Blood blurred his vision, ran from his nose and dripped into his mouth, but the police handling him showed no mercy to his screams of agony as they dragged him backwards down the corridor. Roland's voice came to him, muffled but full of anguish. 'Simon, Simon, what's going on? Are you hurt? SIMON!'

He couldn't answer, but could only moan his agony through a rasping throat.

'Shove him in the solitary cell till the doctor gets here. Branyard, you were the first on the scene: charge him with murder and read him his rights. Wright, have you contacted the Military Police yet?' To the man saying that he'd not been able to get through, the voice barked, 'Do it, man – and do it now. This is a civil matter and we need

354

to establish that.'

As the men dragging Simon lifted him roughly onto a bed in a cell that he could just make out had padded walls, the voice came to him again. Only this time it was very close to his ear and full of malice: 'Bloody queer-boy, we've got you now. You deliberately killed a man. Witnessed by one of me own coppers, it was. You're a dead man, Nancy boy. Dead on the end of a rope is where you're going to end up. And rightly deserved – ponce.'

The door closed, leaving Simon in a blackness like none he'd ever experienced in his life. Not one beam of light showed from anywhere to relieve the impenetrable darkness. Thoughts of it being like a coffin had him shivering with the sheer horror of the situation he found himself in, until a pain in his head devoured all thoughts, taking his body and mind to the limits of his endurance, and he went into a swirling blackness. Different from the blackness of the cell, this place he was floating in had beams of light that caused an intangible feeling of happiness to bathe him. It lifted him and twisted and turned him, as if playing with him. He must go and tell Roland about it. Get him to join him here.

'Come with me, Roland. Come on, we can be happy here.' *Why isn't Roland answering me? Why does he keep saying my name?* 'Roland! I'm here.'

Another voice came to him. 'Lucinda?' Turning from Roland, Simon looked upon his beautiful sister. Her hand was outstretched. He took it and felt euphoria pass through his weightless body. 'Come, Simon.'

355

He couldn't refuse. He didn't want to refuse. An earthly voice called him, desperation clear in the tone. 'Simon. Simon!' Now it sounded as though Roland was shouting into a hollow pipe, as his voice echoed and faded. But it didn't matter. Nothing mattered. He was free... Free.

Roland sat up straight, trying to take in what had happened. How had Simon visited him? Where had he gone? His logical mind wouldn't let in the truth. *No one can float through walls. It must have been a figment of my imagination. The fact that I was thinking of him and in an extreme state of anxiety, and in fear of my own situation, must have caused me to hallucinate. It's the only explanation.*

The sound of footsteps coming nearer, and then stopping further up the corridor, had him listening intently. 'He's in here, Doctor. You'd better take a look at him first, and then attend the dead man.'

Roland heard the keys jangle once more and a lock snap back, then a heavy door creaked open. 'Good God, he's dead!'

The rasp of agony that coursed through Roland's body and forced itself through his throat was a release from the pain that kicked him in the gut and strangled his heart. 'No! God, no, no, no. *No!*' Tears streamed down his face, mingled with snot, without him being able to stop them. His strength left him. He slumped off the edge of his bed and sank onto his knees. 'No, God. No, please don't do this. Simon! SIMON.'

A policeman appeared at the bars of his cell. 'Shut up, queer-boy. We've enough to contend with. Your filthy, murdering lover-boy is dead, so put that in your pipe and smoke it!'

Shocked into silence, Roland heard the doctor's authoritative voice: 'Officer, that isn't called for. Now I need to examine both bodies. Despite what you saw, this man has been so badly injured that he has died from his wounds. I'm only a doctor, not an investigative officer, but even to me this smacks of a fight having taken place between two men, and not an incident where one man has wantonly killed another. Who started the fight, I don't know, but as neither of the victims can be questioned, I think logic tells us one was the aggressor and the other was defending himself. I would put my bet on this man not being the aggressor. You say he is an officer of His Majesty's Forces. And yes, he may have tendencies that you don't like or agree with, but–'

'Tendencies, as you put it, Doctor, that are against the law.'

'Quite, but on the other hand you have a known criminal, whom I have attended here on many occasions, who is capable of extreme violence and who, to me, seems more likely to be the perpetrator of any crime committed here.' Roland knew the solace of some relief slicing through his extreme pain, as the doctor went on: 'Therefore, no matter what your officer said he saw, I would not be so quick to judge. An autopsy will tell us how each of them died, and will more than likely solve the mystery. In the meantime, open up this man's cell. He is in shock and needs to be attended to.'

Roland felt some hope on hearing this. The

police officer turned towards him. 'Get away from the door – sit on your bed.' A simple command, but one holding intense hate and disgust. The doctor whom he'd only heard speaking and hadn't been able to see through the barred window of his cell door, entered the room. Roland looked up into a kindly face that was known to him.

'Roland! My dear fellow. I – I... Officer, help this gentleman up onto the bed, and don't hurt him. My God, Roland, how on earth have you landed up here?'

Roland couldn't answer. How had he not recognized Peter's voice? Tears clogged his throat.

'Officer, what is this man doing in here?'

Roland cringed as the sergeant stepped forward. 'Gross indecent act with the deceased you have just been attending to, Doctor. He is to face the judge in the morning.'

'Oh, Roland, I'm so sorry. You know that your friend has passed away, don't you? I'm so sorry.'

'Help me, Peter, help me.'

'Of course I will. Dear, dear, what sad circumstances you find yourself in. I'll give you some medication that will put you out for a while... No, don't refuse it, Roland. You've had a massive shock, on top of the shock you sustained by whatever circumstances brought you here. I need to shut that off for you and give your body time to recover. I'll contact Frazer for you. I'll get him to come and see you first thing in the morning. As you know, he is the finest lawyer going. Have you had a drink since you arrived?'

Roland shook his head.

'Officer, fetch this man a hot, sweet tea, please.'

Roland didn't want tea, but he didn't want to hurt his kind friend. All he wanted was answers. Everything Peter spoke about – Simon being dead, himself needing to be under sedation and requiring another friend, Frazer, to help him – was alien to him. *How did all this happen?* 'How?'

'How, what? How did your friend die?'

'All of it? We – we were asleep, that's all. Innocently resting after being up all night – Simon to travel here, and me after being on duty all night.'

'In the same bed?'

Roland just nodded. 'But how did the police know? Why did they burst into my house? It was my own private sanctuary. I wasn't doing anything wrong. There's no law about sleeping in the day with a friend by your side.'

'Rest your mind now. Drink this tea and swallow down these pills. We'll try to make sense of everything in the morning.'

'Peter, they were trying to fix Simon up as a murderer. Don't let them. Simon wouldn't hurt anyone.'

'I'll do what I have to do, Roland. The evidence will speak up for Simon, without any help from me. Not that I would do anything to make it lean either way, whoever I am dealing with.'

'Oh, Peter, I didn't mean that. I meant: don't let them bend the truth. They have made up their bigoted minds about us and want to get us, no matter what it takes. I just wanted you not to let that happen.'

'Of course I won't, my dear fellow. Don't worry. Now that they have called me in, I am in charge of both bodies. They cannot even move them without my say-so. I'm going to have them taken immediately to the mortuary and will do the autopsies myself. It's usually me or Dr Clinton who does them now. Medical staff of all disciplines are very short on the ground, as so many are abroad or working in specialized hospitals for the wounded.'

Most of this merged into a haze, as the sedative took effect and Roland drifted off. His last thoughts, before finally succumbing to a deep slumber, were to beg of God that when he awoke, his nightmare would be over and all this wouldn't have happened.

22

Flo

Trying to Grasp Reality

Her bike ride to Bletchley the first morning after her rest days exhilarated Flo. She'd managed to change her shift pattern from the night-shift to the 8 a.m. till 4 p.m., the one she liked most.

A hunting owl, fooled by the darkness into thinking it was still night-time, hooted from his hideout in the tree, no doubt thinking her a competitor. The eerie sound in the stillness around her increased the feeling deep inside her that all wasn't well. *Why didn't Simon ring at all over the two-day break? He promised he would.*

Although she'd been really busy, she'd missed him so much. The two days had been good, and she'd wanted to share that with Simon. Twice she'd got as far as lifting the receiver and starting to dial Roland's number, but had stopped herself. She had to get used to being apart from Simon. He'd made his choice, she was sure of it, and she had to allow him that, just as she said she would. But although she'd told herself this over and over again, she'd still wanted to hear his voice and let him know what was happening. That Molly was safe; that Pauline was well and had taken Molly in; and that the afternoon working on the van had been fun. But deep inside, she knew, she'd wanted more. Maybe to hear him say that he'd missed her, or that he had chosen her... *Stop it, Flo.* How was she to get better from this state of being in love? Simon was constantly on her mind. She couldn't wait to see him.

The thought of doing so enhanced the enjoyment of her journey. Pedalling faster, she marvelled at how her bicycle-light lit the lightly snow-covered ground, turning it into a diamond-encrusted carpet.

Today was going to be exciting, for more reasons than simply seeing Simon again. Belinda had left a hand-delivered letter for Flo at her billet, in which she'd said she would remain on the eight-till-four shift a while longer and would be at Bletchley Park at the same time as Flo this week. Flo had heard that this new system was under discussion and was glad it had been put into action.

The note asked if Flo and Simon, who were always on the same shift as each other, would like to meet her after work at the new flat. *We need to finalize things, Flo,* Belinda had written, and had gone on to ask if she and Simon could bring their share of the first month's rent. Flo had hers tucked safely into her bra, along with enough to cover Simon's, as she thought he was unlikely to be able to get to his bank in time.

Keeping her excess money somewhere safe had been a concern to her. She really needed to ask Simon to help her to open a bank account, as she hadn't a clue how to do so, or even if folk such as her were considered good enough to have one.

The last thing Belinda had asked for was whether they had any connections to anyone who had a van or a trailer, as that would be handy, too. Flo hadn't, at least not down in this neck of the woods. She had plenty of folk to call on in Leeds, but it was too far for them to travel. She hoped Simon might be able to help out with that problem.

Belinda had said they would need a trailer, as she'd asked her parents about letting her have some of their surplus furniture, and they had invited all three of them down to their home to choose what they wanted. Though they had stipulated that they themselves had to arrange transport for whatever they took. Belinda's note had ended, *I'll explain when I see you.* And was signed: *Belinda x.*

Just thinking of how her life was going to change spurred Flo on.

Pedalling through the wrought-iron gates, she

was surprised to be stopped by the guard. 'Sorry, Miss, but I have a message for you. You're to report to General Pradstow.'

Her heart dropped. She had a feeling that this summons had something to do with Simon. No one was ever called to the general's office unless they were in deep trouble or he had received bad news for them. *Oh God, don't let anything have happened to Simon. Please... Please!*

She knew something had happened, the moment she entered the general's office. Belinda sat in a chair in front of his desk and turned her head towards Flo. Her expression told her something Flo didn't want to hear. Without taking any notice of protocol, Flo blurted out, 'No! Not Simon? Please tell me it ain't Simon, Belinda?'

Belinda stood and came towards her. Part of Flo wanted to knock her away, as accepting her would mean accepting what she was going to say; and she didn't want to, so she stood still. Her body stiffened, and an invisible shield formed a barrier around her heart. Whatever Belinda said, it wouldn't hurt her – she wouldn't let it.

Belinda must have known that an attempt to hold and hug her wouldn't work, as she stopped her progress and stood within arm's distance. 'Flo, I'm sorry. I – I... It's Simon. He's been killed.'

Flo took in a deep breath that she never thought she would release again. When she did, questions came with it. 'What? How? Why?'

'I – I'm afraid it's a sorry story, love. Come and sit down.'

Flo looked from Belinda to the general. He hadn't spoken, other than to ask her into his office, but now he nodded. His face had a haggard expression, his countenance one of someone calling upon his inner self-control. And yet he was leaving everything to Belinda.

'Naw, Belinda. Naw! It ain't true, it ain't – not Simon!'

Belinda just looked at her and nodded. Something about the command she had over the situation, and the empathy she showed, made Flo do as she said and sit down.

'It is true, Flo. What I have to tell you is a very sad reflection on our society.' The general coughed. Belinda looked over at him, her look defiant.

Obviously the general doesn't agree with Belinda's thinking. 'It was to do with him being homosexual then, Belinda?'

Flo listened in horror as Belinda told her exactly what had happened. Shock held her in a vice-like grip. She couldn't react. She wanted to scream and scream, but all she could do was stare. But as the truth dawned on her, she pulled herself up. 'This will all be Kitty Hamlin's doing. She told me only the other day that she was going to get Simon put in prison.'

'But surely she wouldn't actually do anything about her threats. I mean, how?' Belinda asked.

Though her voice shook, Flo stated her reasons. 'She followed Simon to London once and turned up in the same pub where we were having a drink. Simon felt intimidated. You see, not only did she hate what Simon was, but she wanted to

364

destroy him, because he knew she's having an affair with a married officer, John Perry. Simon caught them having sexual relations around the back of one of the huts. He didn't report them, but he was beaten up for mentioning it.' Unable to understand how calm she felt, Flo told the general just what had taken place, as Simon had reported it to her and Roland.

The general didn't react. She shouldn't have expected him to. Whether he had a mind to do anything or not, he wouldn't share his thoughts with her, or even appear to believe her. But that didn't stop her raising her voice to him, as the frustration of it all made her want to hit out at somebody. 'You have to do something, sir. Kitty has caused the death of two people with her spite. And – and is responsible for another good man going to prison.' Flo knew she was screeching, but couldn't stop herself. 'Please, General – sir, *please.*'

'Wren Harper, please fetch the doctor in.'

'I don't need the doctor. I – I... Oh, Simon.' Flo could contain her grief no longer. A deluge of sobbing seized her body and rendered her like a rag doll. She slumped onto her arms on the general's desk.

'Wren Kilgallon, I'm so sorry. I thought a lot of Officer Fulworth. I knew his family a long time ago. This is going to be devastating for his mother, who, as you know, has only recently lost her only daughter. How she is going to come to terms with the circumstances around her son's death, I do not know. I will write to his parents, of course, but I wonder if you will consider doing so, too? Wren

Harper tells me you were also a friend of Simon's sister, so I know this is a double-blow for you, as well. But, as such, you will have so much to tell their parents that would be a comfort to them, whereas I can only relate the sordid facts.'

'They weren't sordid, sir. At least, Simon's love for Roland wasn't. Theirs was a good love. A loyal love, and a strong, binding love. Simon was dedicated to his work here an' all, and gifted in finding the right menus and cribs for the Bombe. He was kind and thoughtful, if extremely lonely, due to his treatment here. He deserves that you think more of this part of his life, and concentrate on his good points, as you would any other officer; and don't pay as much attention to your own bigoted ideas about his private life. Aye, and Roland deserves some consideration an' all, as you'd give naturally to a widow or widower. A small letter of condolence wouldn't go amiss, but I doubt it will ever be sent!'

'Wren Kilgallon. I must ask you to rein in your tirade of abuse. I understand how you feel, but it does not give you the right to speak to your commanding officer in the way you are doing. Please consider your own position. I would very much regret having to put you on a charge, but mark my words, any more of this and I will.'

Flo couldn't apologize. Nothing mattered to her any longer. Her world had collapsed at her feet.

'As you say, Wren Kilgallon, Fulworth was gifted, but so are you... A lot of vital information may be lost, if you cannot carry on. You know how much the war effort depends on us here. The other code-breakers are stretched as far as they can be. You know this without me telling you. To have two down would be a disaster. Already, with both of you having a break this week, there is a backlog. Somewhere amongst it may be information that will save us losing one of our ships and all the men aboard her, or will give advance warning of an attack, so that our army generals can work at a counter-attack.'

'I know, sir. I don't intend to have time off. Simon wouldn't want that of me, and I couldn't cope – I need to work. But, I can't do so with that Kitty–'

'Don't say any more. I will deal with that subject. As soon as I can, I will get you a new partner to work with. I'll ask some of the boffins if they know of anyone. If not, we'll have to approach Oxford or Cambridge for their bright stars – or have them directed.'

Flo was shocked to hear the general discuss these things with her, but supposed his strategy was to take her mind off everything that was happening and focus it elsewhere. She'd used the same tactics with Simon, to help him with his grief over Lucinda. *Well, darling Simon, now you are with Lucinda. At least, I hope you are. There'd be no justice in God if He didn't arrange that, as I can't bear to think of you carrying on being lonely. Oh, Simon... Simon.*

A knock on the door saw the doctor entering with Belinda.

'I'm all right, ta, Doctor. I've work to do. I've to carry on, for Simon's sake. I'll get over to me office now, sir.' This last she directed at the general

367

and managed a smart salute.

'No, not straight away, Flo. Go with Wren Harper and have a hot drink, and take the tablets with you that the doctor has brought for you. You can always fall back on them if you need them.'

'Thank you, sir.' Wanting to escape, Flo saluted again, turned smartly and marched towards the doctor.

He gave her a strip of tablets. 'Take one at a time, and allow four hours in between. Only take them when you can rest afterwards. And don't hesitate to get in touch with me if you feel ill in any way. Shock can cause many things to happen to you.'

'Thank you, Doctor.'

Not trusting herself to do any different, Flo walked through the door and along the corridor, her head held high, her walk precise, as if she was on parade.

'Hey, slow down, love. Flo?'

'Sorry, Belinda, I daren't. I've to get to the canteen, then I knaw as I'll be reet.'

Belinda didn't try to persuade her again, but fell into step with Flo. When they reached the canteen, it was mercifully empty. Flo slumped into a chair. Everything about herself felt unreal. Everything she'd been told and had done seemed to have no meaning. *By, did I really shout at the general?*

'Flo? Look, I'll get you a cup of strong tea. Though I doubt there's any sugar again – goodness knows where it goes; it certainly isn't rationed amongst us all.'

'I don't need sugar. A saccharine will do.' When

Belinda came back to the table, Flo blurted out, 'I can't go back to me billet, Belinda, not tonight – I can't. Oh, Belinda, what will I do?'

'We'll stay at the flat. The shop up the road will still be open when we leave here. The landlord's agent is meeting us at five. Once we've paid a month's rent, the place is ours. Have you brought some money with you, Flo?'

'Aye, I brought two-thirds of it, as I thought as Simon ... he might not have the cash on him. I were going to lend it to him.'

'That's top-hole, well done, my dear. Now we'll have the full rent. I'll get us some supplies, as I brought extra money for that. I was planning that we might cook our dinner and eat it on our knees, whilst sitting on the floor. A good ice-breaker between me and ... well, anyway–'

'Don't do that, Belinda. Don't *not* talk of Simon, I couldn't bear it. You're me only friend here now, and I have to be able to talk to you about him or I'll go mad.'

'Right. Just as you want it. I'm a good listener, Flo. And if it helps to talk, I won't mind.'

'Ta, Belinda.' Flo marvelled at how she could make these arrangements with Belinda, and at how calm she felt. *Not calm – detached.* That was it; none of it had really touched her yet. Not even Roland's plight. She couldn't give her mind to him. There was too much to take in.

'Our only problem is: how are we going to sleep? We'll have warmth, as we have electrics and there's an electric fire, and then the oven and cooker rings – we can turn the whole blooming lot on. And there are blackout curtains up already. But that's it.'

Flo couldn't think of a solution. Her mind was a blank.

'Leave it to me. It may not be the most comfortable night we've ever had, but it has to be better than not being together. I'd never sleep, thinking of you alone in your room at that house you're billeted in. Only thing is: we do need to let them know not to expect you.'

'I'll cycle back there as soon as the agent has left. Mabel, the woman of the house, knaws that I'm planning to leave, and she don't blame me. I'll fetch some of me things back. Me pyjamas and me toothbrush, that sort of thing. I'll tie them to me handlebars in a bundle. It's best that I go – I owe her that much – rather than just leaving, as this *is* me leaving, Belinda. I knaw I can't ever go back there, except for the rest of me things. I couldn't deal with owt stuck up in that bedroom. And that's what happens, more often than not.'

'Oh, Flo, it must have been lonely and very difficult, but it's one thing that will change for the better today, for you. I'll do the same. Petulia brought me in in her car this morning; she's billeted at Woburn Abbey with me. I'll beg her to wait until I've seen the landlord, then to take me back. I'll do my best to sneak out a couple of blankets, as well as some night-things and toiletries. Ooh, it's going to be a real adventure, Flo.'

'I hope so, Belinda. I hope I don't dampen it for you, because at the moment I just need to curl up somewhere private and cry me eyes out.'

'Well, you can do that, love. You can do as much of that as you need to. I know how you felt about

Simon and Lucinda, and I know you must be worried sick about your friend Roland. You have a lot on your plate, and I really admire how you're determined to carry on. Talk about "Your Country Needs You", as Kitchener spouted in the last war. Our country doesn't even know they have us, and probably never will.'

They sat silently for a moment. Flo's limbs had stopped shaking. She couldn't drink much of the tea, but was grateful for the respite she'd had. Standing up, she excused herself and made her way to Hut 6. Every step held the dread that Kitty would be there, sneering more than usual. Even if it was never proved, no one would ever convince Flo otherwise than that Kitty and her lover-boy were responsible for what had happened to Simon.

The door opened silently, and yet the babble of noise, which was usual for the hut, ceased as if someone had switched off every machine and shushed all the women. Flo took a deep breath and walked through, towards her office. Jane Downing stood as Flo approached her desk. 'Flo, we want you to know that we're very sorry. Devastated, in fact. The general sent round a communication about ten minutes ago. He told us that Simon was murdered. How? Oh, Flo, were you with him?'

'Naw, Jane, I weren't. I wish I had been, but we went our separate ways this time. Simon visited a mutual friend of ours, and I went to London. So I knaw as much as you all do. I'm devastated an' all, but we have to carry on; it is what Simon would want us to do, and it's what our country

expects. Ta, though, for saying sommat. It helps.'
As she finished talking, Flo found the courage to
look around at Kitty's desk. It stood empty.

'She was marched out at the same time as the
communication arrived. Is she involved, Flo?'

'It wouldn't surprise me, but we'll never knaw.
I'm glad she's gone; I couldn't have worked with
her being here. She had it in for Simon, as you all
knaw. But he felt safe with the rest of you. I thank
you all for that. Now, the best thing we can do is
get our heads down and turn out the best day
we've ever had. We have to help to win the war.'

Turning from Jane, Flo felt herself gaining in
strength by the minute. Every time she thought
of what Simon would want of her and she carried
it through, she felt a little bit better. A sound surprised her. It began very slowly, then increased as
more joined in. The women were clapping her.
These women – who'd hardly given her the time
of day and hadn't included her in anything, or
made any effort even to greet her sometimes –
were clapping her. She turned and smiled at
them, bowed her head towards them, then went
into her office and closed the door.

Leaning against it, she let out a huge sigh, took
a deep breath and blew it out in an exaggerated
fashion. Somehow she had to stop the flow of
tears; if she didn't, she would open the floodgates
for all the tears tied in a knot in her chest to be
released, and she couldn't do that yet. Not here.

Simon's desk stood like a lonely monument to
him, his pen still where he'd thrown it down, in
his glee that at last the time had come for him to
leave the office and make for the station. Going

over to his desk, Flo picked up the pen. From now on, she would use it. And she would sit in his chair. Little things, but they would bring him closer to her. Not that he would ever leave her. He was bound into the very fibre of her, and always would be.

By the time Flo had ridden back to the flat, she felt exhausted. Parking her bike, she noticed a car outside that she'd seen many times recently. *Petulia must still be here. Blast, I'm not up to meeting anyone.* She rubbed the base of her neck; the tension there jarred through her body. Her legs felt like jelly. Sitting on the step for a moment, she watched a cat crawl under Petulia's car. That's what she'd like to do: crawl under something where no one could see her and curl up in a ball. She wasn't sure she could cry. She felt empty of tears, but wanted just to be alone and to think everything through. Try to make it all a reality, then she might be able to deal with it.

The door at the top of the steps opened. 'Flo, how long have you been there – you'll freeze to death! Come up.'

Flo stood and looked upwards, and the light from the open door dazzled her for a moment. 'I were just resting a mo. It was some bike ride, with me bundle on me handlebars, it took it out of me.'

Belinda didn't protest. Instead she stepped aside and beckoned Flo up. The door led into their kitchen, a small but functional room with all the utilities along one wall and a small wooden table at the other. Flo could see that Belinda had been shopping, as there were a few items on the work surface: a bag of potatoes and a couple of sausages were dwarfed by a huge winter cabbage. Other than that, there was some salt and a loaf of bread. No butter, and only a very small bottle of milk – one-third of a pint, Flo would guess. She'd only ever seen this size of bottle down here in the south, but it did seem to be an area of people living on their own, especially in London.

Flo went through to the front room. A young woman sat cross-legged on the floor.

'Hello, I'm Petulia – Pet for short. I won't stay long, but I just wanted to wait for you to tell you how sorry I am about what has happened. I knew Lucinda, and met Simon once when he came to the university to see her. He was jolly nice, and very handsome. It's all tragic, and I can't imagine how you're feeling. If I can do anything at all, you only have to send a message through Belinda for me.'

'Ta. That's kind of you.' Suddenly Flo felt tongue-tied and unsure what to do next. Everyone she met at Bletchley had so much confidence and spoke with such a posh accent, it intimidated her. Pet was a pretty girl with a mound of curly fair hair and big brown eyes. When she smiled, her cheeks dimpled.

'Look, I'll go. We can meet up and get to know one another some other time. Belinda told me you're interested in joining my group. I'd love that. We'll be holding auditions for Dorothy soon. I hope you feel up to coming – that would be spiffing.'

Flo nodded. She so wanted to be nice to Pet.

She liked her; Pet didn't look like Lucinda, but her manner reminded Flo of her.

Pet stood and walked towards Flo. Flo wanted to run. She couldn't understand this feeling of wanting to be as far as possible inside her own body and not have anyone touch her. But touch her Pet did. As if on impulse, she held Flo and kissed her cheek. And then was gone. The gesture embarrassed Flo, but at the same time made her think she was right to like Pet and knew they would become friends.

When Belinda came back in, she laughed off the incident. 'Don't mind Pet, she's an arty-farty type – they kiss everybody.'

A giggle bubbled up in Flo.

Belinda joined her, although hers was a nervous giggle. She covered it up by being her usual matter-of-fact self. 'Well, Flo, we're here! Let's get down to work. Can you cook? I didn't think, when I said about making a meal. I haven't got a blooming idea how to boil an egg, let alone anything else.'

This made Flo giggle even more. The giggle turned to a laugh, a real belly-aching laugh that she couldn't control. Her already-weak legs became weaker. Her voice echoed around the empty room.

'Flo – Flo, stop it. Flo, what's got into you? Flo!'

These words seemed to be coming down a long tunnel. She was hurting now, real physical pain from the stretching of her throat and her stomach muscles, but there was a hurt far greater than that and it threatened to swallow her up.

A sharp sting on her cheek shocked Flo into

silence and she stared back at Belinda.

'I'm sorry, love, but you were hysterical. I had to do that.'

Flo tried to say it was all right, but no words would form, only sobs. Huge, screaming sobs. Her body gave way under the weight of them and she sank to the floor.

Belinda wrapped her in a blanket and held her. But no one could hold her world together, or put it back the way it was.

Roland came to her mind. And for the first time since hearing the news, she cried for him, too. What he must be going through, she couldn't imagine. The thought helped her pain a little, as she knew that no matter how much she was hurting, Roland would be going through twice as much. Lonely, fearful and grieving beyond endurance. She calmed enough to be able to sit up. Belinda handed her a towel.

'I've a big kettle of water on, love. Why not go and have a wash and put your pyjamas on, eh? You could do with a soak in the bath, but I don't know what the chances are of me filling that boiler, let alone setting a fire under it.'

'I'll be all right with a wash. Ta ever so much for your kindness, Belinda.' The reflex sobs made it difficult for Flo to speak, but she managed to say, 'I like your friend. She's nice.'

'Come on – don't start me off again about Pet. I don't want to make you laugh, but when you feel more able, I have some funny stories about her. She's lovely, but a minx. She can get you into trouble with her pranks.'

Flo didn't really want to have a conversation.

She didn't know what she wanted, except to have things back the way they were. Now she was consumed with worry and quizzed Belinda frantically. She needed to know where Simon's body was and who would see to the arrangements – would that person contact her?

'I'm not sure, in the case of someone being murdered. But it won't be possible, I should imagine, for his parents to get over from India – no waters are safe enough to travel that distance. Leave it with me. I'll speak to General Pradstow and see what he will do for us. And I'll ring my father's solicitor tomorrow and see if he can help, with information about what will happen to Simon's friend; he is a brilliant solicitor and I'm sure he can find out if Simon's family has a solicitor, and can liaise with him. Don't worry; we'll do our best to make sure everything is sorted out and that you are kept informed. But, Flo, try to prepare yourself for the fact that Simon's friend may go to prison. I'm sorry, and I wish it was different, but the way the story was told to the general and he told me, it looks bad for him.'

'Which is all the more reason why I must try to cope with it all. Roland's going to need me. I knaw he has a lot of friends and is well regarded, but how many of them will come to his defence or his aid, when they hear what he was arrested for? Not many, I should think. I have to be able to contact him somehow. Could you ask your solicitor if he would get a message to Roland for me?'

'I will. As long as this way of coping is going to make you fit to cook some dinner for us – I'm starving!' Belinda smiled and hugged Flo as she said this. Flo didn't reject her.

The crying had released her from the barrier that had made it feel as though she was encased in a cocoon of ice. She'd been afraid of it melting and exposing her to a hurt she couldn't let in, but the ice had gone now, and Flo could feel the reality of it all and knew she had to call on all her courage to get through. She was needed at Bletchley, where her expertise could help the war effort; she was needed by Molly; and she would be needed by Roland. She had to be strong for all of them. Simon would expect nothing less of her. And she would give nothing less.

23

Flo & Molly

A Meaningful Encounter

Ten days had passed – some of them in a haze for Flo. But there had been so much work to do, which had given her a distraction, though times without number she'd lifted her head whilst deeply engrossed in a difficult equation to ask Simon for help. These had been painful moments.

On hearing what had happened, Belinda's parents had changed their mind about making the girls choose what furniture they wanted and transporting it themselves, and had sent them a vanload of furniture and two men to place it all, as well as bedding, towels and kitchen utensils – all they would need really.

The flat looked lovely, if a little imposing, with the grand furniture gracing it. The beds weren't just iron-sprung ones, as Flo was used to, but had carved wooden headboards and frames, and latticework cords to hold the deep, feather-filled mattresses in place. There were four in all and these had been assembled, two in each bedroom.

The front-room furniture didn't quite look at home in the square, plain surroundings it was placed in, but to Flo it seemed as if she lived in a palace. The deep-maroon velvet chaise-longue and the two gold velvet high-backed chairs were fit for a queen and were set off by the mahogany occasional tables and bureau, all of which had intricately carved legs. But it was the Persian rug that added the touch of pure magnificence to the room. Stretching to within a foot of each of the walls, it brought together the golds and maroons in a pattern of flowers so beautifully woven that it gave Flo the feeling of standing in a glorious garden.

The flat had become a home, and a haven, in such a short space of time; and Flo had been glad that Belinda had decided still to sleep in the same room as her. It had been good to have her near in those moments when everything became too much for her, or a bad dream woke her.

The news about Roland had been another terrible blow. Roland had pleaded guilty and had been dealt with by a magistrate within two days. In his distraught state, he hadn't listened to the lawyer who was willing to fight for him, and had been sentenced to two years in prison for gross indecency with another man. This had compounded Flo's pain and completed the shattering of her world.

With all that was going on, Flo found herself torn as to what to do next. She had two rest days to take and felt pulled in so many directions, she didn't know which way to turn. London tugged, as she desperately wanted to find out how Eunice was and what her results were, and to catch up with Molly and Pauline; but she also needed to go home, to be hugged by Mrs Leary and to do childlike things with Kathy, to feel their love for her protect her and soothe the pain she was cocooned in. But then there was Roland, too. She knew he was in Wandsworth Prison and she had asked about visiting him, only to be told he wouldn't be allowed any visitors for at least a month. His plight tore at her heart. All she'd been able to do was send a message through Belinda's solicitor to tell Roland of her love for him and to talk of their shared grief. She asked him to stay strong, and promised she would come and see him the moment they allowed her to. She'd also written the letter to Simon's parents that the general had suggested she do.

At times her tears had smudged the ink and she'd had to start again, but she'd managed to include as many happy memories as she could. Doing so had helped, and made her feel as if she'd known Simon and Lucinda for a lifetime. She'd spoken of their love for one another and how they had cared for each other, and of the special love she and Simon had shared, and how they had all loved Roland. She'd also included a small paragraph on the love Simon and Roland had shared. Though she'd found it very difficult to put into words, in her heart she knew it was right to tell them where Roland was, and the reason he was there. She expressed her opinion of Roland feeling immense grief and guilt at Simon's death, and asked if they would find it in their hearts to write to him:

What happened wasn't his fault. Roland is only guilty of loving your son and of giving him, and sharing in, the happiness that shone from them both when they were together. I know it is difficult to understand the kind of love they had for each other – I found it difficult at first – but just being with them gave one an understanding and a sense that it was right that they should be together. Both believed in God and practised their faith, and I firmly believe that God would not have denied their love and that Simon is resting in Heaven and at peace, with dear Lucinda. I hope that, for the peace of your own hearts, you can come to think of their union in this way, too.

Although the sentiments were her own, Belinda had helped Flo to write them in this eloquent way, as she hadn't wanted the meaning distorted, as might have happened with her northern twist of the language confusing them. In reality she'd wanted to put her arms around them and say, 'Eeh, you had a grand lad there, in your Simon, there were none better. He were a loving, kind and thoughtful man and he shared that with me, making me the luckiest lass in the world to have known him. And I loved him, with me all.'

The general had read the letter. He'd hesitated over it for a while, but in the end he'd looked up at her and nodded, then dismissed her without a word. This had given Flo confidence and helped her to know she'd chosen the right words, even though something she'd written had unsettled the general for a moment – probably her references to Roland. And so now all she could do was wait for the outcome of the inquest into Simon's death and hope, with everything in her, that he was cleared of the murder of the vicious man who'd taken his life. She also hoped very much that Simon's mother and stepfather would write back to her, as that, she knew, would help to settle her mind and might go some way to soothe the pain of her broken heart.

Still torn apart by her decision to deny herself the comfort of Mrs Leary's and Kathy's loving presence, Flo stood at the reception desk of the military hospital in Endell Street, waiting to be told where Eunice was.

'Here you are, love: Ward Twelve. Nurse Eunice Dirkham. That's the one, ain't it?'

'Aye, it is. Do you reckon as I could see her now?'

'I don't see why not. We don't stand on the ceremony of specific visiting times for our nurses. Hang on, while I contact the sister of the ward for you.'

Flo's stomach muscles tightened with fear about what she might discover. No wonder Eunice hadn't been in touch. She wouldn't want to worry Flo. With Eunice being in a ward, Flo could only surmise that the news wasn't good.

As Flo walked the corridors to the ward, the squeaking of her shoes on the polished lino increased her trepidation. Each footstep seemed to count down to doom. But when she saw a sign pointing in the direction of Ward 12, she took a deep breath and told herself, *Be strong, lass. Put all you're going through to the back of your mind and be strong for Eunice.*

This helped, but didn't save her altogether, as she opened the door to find herself in a small private room with its only occupant looking nothing like Eunice, but a shadow of the person she'd been just a short time ago.

'Eeh, lass. Eeh, love, what's to do?'

'It's all right, Flo. Honestly, don't take on. I'm going to get well. They operated the moment they found the tumour. It was in my lower bowel, and they're confident they have it all. I'm sorry I didn't contact you, but it all happened so quickly.'

This good news did to Flo what bad news couldn't have done. She no longer had to be strong, and so her weak, vulnerable heart came to the fore and she collapsed onto the chair next to the bed, buried her head in Eunice's pillow and wept.

Gradually she became aware of Eunice's hand stroking her hair, allowing Flo to empty her heart of tears, not trying to stop her and not asking her any questions. With this soothing of her pain, Flo was able to control the outpouring of emotions and calm herself. 'Eeh, I'm sorry, lass, that's the last thing you needed.'

'No. It was the first. I know what happened – I had a letter from Mrs Leary. And all I've wanted to do was to hold you, Flo.'

'Ta, love. I ... it was the relief. It seemed to say that now I could take some comfort. Not that I haven't been offered any, but there's nowt like it coming from your own.'

Eunice smiled at her. A weak smile, but one that held hope.

'Tell me it's reet, lass, you're really going to be all right?'

'I am, Flo. I've nothing to worry about. The tumour was contained, but they've had to take away part of my lower bowel. I can live without it. But the main thing is that they feel certain they have all of the cancer and it hasn't spread any-where.'

'Eeh, I can't tell you how glad I am.'

'And I can't tell you how sorry I am for what's happened – it's tragic. How are you coping, Flo?'

Flo sat holding Eunice's tiny hand and poured her heart out to her.

When she'd finished, Eunice just said, 'I guessed you'd given your heart to Simon, love. It was a love that might not have gone anywhere, but I suppose you always had hope that it would, but now...'

'That's it. That is part of my desolation. If Simon had lived, I could have hoped. And even come to accept if that love wasn't to be, as I could still have him in my life as a friend, but now there is nothing.'

'Not nothing, Flo. You have your memories. You have that Simon told you he loved you in a way that he loved no other, and wanted to deepen that by making love to you. That's a precious memory to have.'

'Aye, it is. And one I shall treasure. I have to think of them as are living and need me. That'll bring me through all of this. Oh, Eunice, I'm so glad you're not going to be one of them.'

'Well, that's a nice thing to say!'

They both laughed, and the feeling was a good one. 'Eeh, lass, I didn't mean it like that. I'm so glad as you're going to get better. I couldn't bear the thought of owt happening to you.'

'No, me neither, and I'm looking forward to being strong enough to be able to leave here. Lucky me, I get to spend three months back home.'

'By, lass, that's the best news I've ever heard. Lucky you. These last days I've longed for the uncomplicated days of home.'

'Flo, well, have you ever thought of Mrs Leary as your mam?'

'Aye, I have. She's the only mam I remember having. And she's the best one we could ever have, an' all.'

'Well, I've made my mind up. I'm going to ask her if I can call her "Mam". I've wanted to for a long time.'

'It's funny you should say that, as I've thought about asking her, an' all. I reckon it was fear that she might not like me doing so that's held me back. I worried because she's never asked us to call her "Mam".'

'We won't know, if we don't ask, will we? So I'm going to. I mean, I want to. I want her to know what she means to me.'

'I'll tell you what: I'll write a note for you to give to her, telling her it's what I want, an' all. Otherwise, she might think I'm just saying it because you have.'

'No. We'll do it together. Come up to see us as soon as you can, Flo. Let's all be a family together, eh? Me, you, little Kathy and Mr and Mrs Leary.'

'Aye, that'd be grand, lass. And I hope they won't mind us asking, because I reckon we should ask Mr Leary to let us call him "Dad", as that's what he has been to us. A quiet but loving and stable influence in our lives.'

'That will be lovely. I don't think they'll say no. I think they have always left it to us, and not tried to replace our own mams, but to be a substitute for them. And they've done a wonderful job of it.'

Flo had no answer to this other than to gently hold Eunice to her.

The cold March wind whipped Flo's coat around her legs, causing her to shiver as she left the hospital. Looking up at the heavy, cloud-laden sky, she hoped the weather would worsen, then there would be little chance of an air raid. This thought lifted her already-lightened heart even further. There was still a life to live, and one that was enriched with wonderful people who loved her. They would be her prop. She would get through all this misery. She'd do it with the help of these loved ones, and by doing all she could for those who needed her.

With this thought, she walked tall, making her way to the station to catch the train that would take her to Pauline and Molly. She would call at the Sallies' van to see if Pauline was on duty. She had a favour to ask; she needed a bed for the night, otherwise she'd have to find a guesthouse, as she wasn't going to miss staying over. She wanted to offer her services to man one of the soup kitchens later that afternoon.

Pauline's smile held concern. 'They been working you hard, love? Yer look done in. Give me a mo and I'll be with yer.'

This was the worst part for Flo, the telling of Simon's death and all that had happened over and over again, and having to deal with the emotions it conjured up in those who loved her, as much as it did her own emotions. 'I'm fine, though in need of a bed for the neet.'

'Oh? Not using Simo– Has sommat happened, Flo?'

'Aye, it has. I'll tell yer when we get to your house. Is Molly all right?'

'Sort of, but not well yet.' Pauline handed a bowl of steaming soup to her next customer, gave a word of comfort and asked if there was anything else she needed. Once she'd dealt with her, she stepped out of the van. 'Course yer can stay, love – be glad to have yer. I've only got to do another hour and I'll be with yer. Make yer way to the house and see Molly, eh?'

'I'll go and check in at the depot first, to offer me services for this evening. I need to keep busy. I'll see you later, Pauline. And ta, lass, I'm reet

387

glad as you can have me for the neet.'

As soon as Flo opened the door to Pauline's house she knew the reason for Pauline's less-than-enthusiastic response to her question about how Molly was doing. There was a gaunt, lost expression on Molly's face, and one of fear.

'Eeh, Molly, it's good to see you, but I expected to find you much improved in your health, lass.'

'Oh, Flo... Flo!'

Molly collapsed in her arms. Flo helped her to the sofa underneath the window. The room was much as she expected, though she'd never stepped inside before. Brown was the dominant colour, with a horsehair sofa in a dark-brown material shedding some of its stuffing around the arms, and a brown brushed-velvet cloth covering the wooden table that stood in the centre of the room. A fire spat sparks onto the rag rug, which was already pockmarked with burns. That, too, was brown. Only the yellow curtains brought some relief to the overall shabby look of the place. But although every corner and every piece of furniture showed wear and tear, the room was spotless and gave the feel of being a home.

The clamminess of Molly's skin, as Flo held her to her, worried Flo. 'So, you're not feeling much better, lass? Have you a lot of pain?'

Molly's breath laboured as she answered yes to this.

'Eeh, love, we're going to have to get medical help. I can pay the callout fee a doctor would charge.'

'No, Flo. I told you: they'll be looking for me. I

dread a knock on the door, for fear it'll be one of them. If I'm sent to a hospital, they'll find me.'

'But ten days have gone by.'

'I know, and that will have increased their determination.' Molly sighed as she leaned back. 'Flo, I know of a good doctor. A quack who looks after the working girls. He'll come and he won't say a word about where I am to nobody. He's a good bloke and knows how it is for us working girls.'

'I'll fetch him. Where...?'

'No. You mustn't go to that area – sommat might happen to you. We'll ask Pauline if she has someone she trusts who can take a message. I haven't done so up to now as I haven't got money to pay him with, but if you're sure you can pay, Flo, I think I do need help. I'm scared. Me lungs hurt when I breathe in, and I get a sharp pain under me shoulder.'

'All right, love, don't worry. It'll be sorted. Let me make you a drop of tea. The cure for all ills.'

'Ta, Flo. But I haven't asked how you are, and I can see you have sommat on your mind.'

'I don't mind telling you, lass, I've been through the mill, and am still going through it, but ... well, the telling about it can wait till Pauline gets here. I can't go over it twice.'

Molly didn't press her and Flo was glad of that, as she busied herself putting the kettle onto the grate-plate and swinging it over the flames to boil. Finding the tea and mugs, Flo soon had them a hot drink and felt comforted, as the sipping of it brought colour to Molly's pale cheeks.

Their small talk covered a lot, and yet nothing

389

at all really. The underlying fear of unburdening herself was always there for Flo. Eventually Molly showed signs of weariness and Flo helped her to lie down. Covering her with a woollen blanket that she found folded over one arm of the sofa gave Flo the feeling that getting the doctor was urgent. 'Tell me where this doctor is, Molly, just in case you fall asleep. I can give the directions to Pauline then.' Molly didn't protest, but gave her the street and house number. Her eyes closed once she'd done this.

Flo stood for a few moments looking around the room for a likely place to find some notepaper and a pencil. At home such things were kept in the bureau drawer, but there wasn't anything in this room that resembled that kind of furniture. As her gaze fell on the table, she remembered how Mrs Leary's table, which wasn't dissimilar to this one, had drawers in it. Maybe that was a good place to start.

Finding what she needed, she wrote down the address and then penned a note to Pauline, saying that she was going for a doctor. Looking at her watch, Flo realized she had very little time left. The director of operations at the Salvation Army depot had asked her to man the same van that she and Simon had last manned, at the bombsite of St Anne's Church. She'd to be there by five and it was already a quarter past three.

Deciding that the two destinations – the doctor's house and the soup van – must be very close to one another, as that was where she'd first met Molly, Flo added to her note that she might not come back until after she'd done her shift, but would make sure the doctor came in any case.

'Here, lav, what the bleedin' 'ell are yer doing here?'

Flo jumped. The voice had come from inside the cafe she was passing and stopped her in her tracks. Relief entered her as she recognized Trixie, who'd been with Molly the first time they'd met.

'Flo, ain't it? If yer looking for Molly, yer out of luck; she's been gone a good while now, thank goodness, though I wish I could hear from her. I'm worried sick over her.'

Torn as to whether to trust Trixie with where Molly was, Flo stammered her reply. 'I – I were told as there were a doctor around here.'

'You know where Molly is, don't yer?' Trixie said this in hushed tones, looking this way and that as she did so.

'N-naw, I were just–'

'Yer can trust me, lav. I'd not do anything to hurt Molly. I helped her get two of them away from that place she was in. Besides, I have news for her, and it's vital it gets to her. I've been out of me mind. Look, give me a penny or sommat: make yourself look like a do-gooder who's stopped to help me. Then walk on. I'll meet yer somewhere later. There's eyes and ears everywhere.'

Flo took her purse out and gave a few coins to Trixie. 'I'm going to be at St Anne's Church the neet. Try to come to see me there. I start at five.'

'The neet? Oh, you mean tonight? Ha, that's a good one. But I will. Do you know where you're going now?'

'Aye. I got me taxi driver to drop me a few

391

streets from where I were told as it was, then I asked a passer-by. I were afraid to be taken there, just in case the taxi driver was too curious.'

'Good girl. You're learning. Get off then. And give me love to Molly.'

Trixie turned from her and went back towards the cafe. The incident had frightened Flo. She looked around her, before moving off.

As she was about to turn into Winnett Street she had the sensation of someone following her. Sweat broke out over her body. Not daring to look round, she crossed the road instead of taking the route she wanted. There were plenty of people around, and she'd scream if anyone touched her.

The feeling persisted. Once she stepped onto the kerb, she turned quickly and almost bumped into a large man. Shock registered on his face. 'It *is* you, ma'am!'

His accent was American or Canadian, Flo couldn't be sure, but her fear left her. 'Eeh, you gave me a fright. What're you doing? Were you following me?'

'I was, ma'am, begging your pardon. Let me introduce myself: my name is Art and, well, I've been taken with you for a long time.'

This astounded Flo. No one had ever spoken so openly to her before. 'Aye, I know who you are now.' So this was the man who'd helped Molly, and yes, she could remember him.

'I'm stationed at Biggin Hill. I'm in the Canadian air force. I saw you working in a Salvation Army soup kitchen and I fell in love with you, ma'am.'

Flo laughed. 'Don't be daft.'

'I'm telling the truth. I've not been able to get you out of my mind. Will you do me the honour of having tea with me? Though not anywhere here – we'll go to the Savoy. What's a nice girl like you doing in this area, anyways?'

Flo couldn't help but giggle. Art's forward manner took her breath away. But there was something about him and his ways that lit a spark in her, which she never thought ever to feel again. 'I'd ask you the same, as there seems to me to be only one reason why men frequent these streets.' Saying this, a blush crept over Flo's face. *Does he think I'm here doing business?* Flustered, she blurted out, 'I can't go with you. I don't know you, and anyroad I'm on a mission to get a doctor for a sick person. And then I've to get to the soup kitchen, as I'm to help out.'

'I'll come with you. Where's this doctor live? Will your friends be at the soup kitchen? I can help out, if you like. I'm on a twenty-four-hour pass.'

He was like a whirlwind. One that took no heed of niceties or propriety, but barged straight to the point. In a small way, it was refreshing. All of a sudden, Flo felt she could trust Art, whatever his reason was for being here. 'Alreet. You can come with me. I'd be glad to have you, as I'm nervous being around here. We need to go back across the road. I dashed over here because the street I needed looked deserted, and I thought you... Well, anyroad, we'd better get going.'

As they crossed back over, he held her arm. 'To tell the truth, ma'am, I'm on a mercy mission myself. You're Flo, aren't you?'

Molly must have told him her name. They'd reached the doctor's house, but the nervous feeling that had overcome Flo made her wary of knocking on the door. She nodded to Art. 'Aye, that's me. Ta for helping me friend. I – I've to... I mean, I'm here now.'

'Is there something wrong, Flo? May I call you Flo, by the way?'

Flo knew now that the impression she'd formed of Art – from the time he'd put some money in their collection tin to support them in some way, and from what Molly had said about him – had been the right one. He was just a nice man. She still found it strange that he should say he loved her, but she supposed that was the way of folk where he came from. 'Aye, that'd be grand. You calling me "ma'am" makes me think above me station, as them as are high up in this country are addressed in that way, not ordinary folk like me. Anyroad, Molly – the girl you helped – is still not well, and it's for her that I need the doctor.'

With this, Flo found the courage that had deserted her and knocked on the door of the house. Her nerves jangled, as she couldn't dispel the feeling she was dealing in something that wasn't legal. After all, this man wasn't a practising doctor and could be anybody, for all she knew. But needs must.

The doctor immediately agreed to go to Molly. 'I know the young woman, and I know the area you say she is in. And yes, I understand the need for secrecy, don't worry.'

Despite her earlier misgivings, Flo was flooded

394

with relief, as the doctor instilled confidence in her that all would be right with Molly now.

As she and Art walked away from the house, Flo felt a knot in her stomach. Art was a stranger to her really, and yet he didn't feel like one. It was weird how he'd come up behind her, but she supposed she did stick out amongst the women in this area, dressed as she was in her calf-length dark-grey coat and felt hat and sporting leather ankle boots – clothes that distinguished her from the scantily dressed women offering their services, and that would make her easy to spot. Especially to someone who was deliberately looking for a particular person and so was scrutinizing every passer-by.

She had to admit that something about Art felt right and she wanted to get to know him. No, it was more than that; she felt compelled to know more about him, and to have him in her life, not for a fleeting time, but as a friend.

'You knaw, I'd like it very much if you wanted to come with me to help me on the van. It's more than likely as I were going to have to man it on me own. But we'd better go and see the organizer first, as I couldn't just let you help me without his approval.'

'I'd love that, ma'– Flo. In any case, I wasn't going to leave you until my train was due. I was going to sit on the nearest wall and watch you.'

'Eeh, you're a funny one.' The giggle that came out with this had a depth to it. To Flo, it seemed like the first time she'd really felt like giggling since... But she'd not think of that, not now. She'd plenty of time to revisit her grief when she was with Molly and Pauline later on. She had to face telling them all about it yet. *By, that's going to be an ordeal for me, as it is. Better that I get on with things.* And, strangely, Flo knew for certain that being with Art would help her to do that.

24

Flo

Fears for Molly

Flo marched beside Jane Downing, the only person who'd agreed to attend Simon's funeral. The general had asked for four volunteers from the workers in Hut 6, but none of the others who were on a shift that would enable them to attend had come forward. This had hurt Flo. Thinking of those who worked in Hut 6 brought Kitty to mind, and she felt glad she'd never had to encounter her presence again. She wouldn't have been able to bear her smirks.

Kitty had never appeared back on duty again, and they'd all been told that she'd gone on long-term sick leave. This was a source of relief to Flo. She had so much anger in her that she was afraid it would spill over, if she had to deal with Kitty on a daily basis, and she'd not want to taint Simon's memory in that way.

If only Belinda had been able to be here, but although she'd wanted to come, the hut that she worked in couldn't release her from her shift.

Seeing the coffin pass by as she stood to attention, forming part of the guard of honour – such as it was, with just herself, Jane, the general and one other navy person whom she didn't know – Flo's heart broke in two. When she fell in behind the mourners, none of whom she knew, her legs threatened to give way, but she'd got this far with dignity, and she would go the whole way.

It was a comfort to see Art standing in full uniform on the side of the path leading into the church. Next to him was Pauline. Pauline had remembered Art when she'd seen him again, and they had got on as if they'd known each other forever. Now he'd visit her van and help out for an hour or two, whenever he could.

Three weeks had passed since that day Flo had met Art, and during that time she'd been beset with fear for Molly's safety. The doctor had diagnosed Molly as having pleurisy and had treated her with some potion or other that he'd concocted himself; whatever it was, it had worked like a miracle, and Molly was now recovered and was getting stronger than Flo had ever seen her, although she was in imminent and constant danger.

Trixie had relayed the news that one of the girls she and Molly had helped to escape had gone to the police. Delilah her name was, or rather Martha, as she was really called. Hers was an incredible story of kidnap and murder, which Flo remembered had been headline news and had shocked the nation at the time. It seemed unbelievable that Martha was now found, after all these years.

According to Trixie, Martha had let Molly down, as she'd promised not to go to the police until she was informed that Molly was safe. Trixie had been waiting to hear from Molly about that being so. Poor Trixie, she'd been shocked to learn what Molly had gone through since she'd last seen her. She'd imagined that Molly was getting well and would soon be joining up.

Trixie had told Flo that the girls who worked for the same gang as Molly had reported that Eva was desperate to find Molly, to stop her from talking, and that her connections were searching everywhere for her. Many of these connections were police officers whom Eva had in her pay. They were keeping Eva informed about any news that came in, concerning Martha's case.

Flo lived in perpetual fear of the gang finding Molly.

The sound of the choir brought Flo back to what was happening. They were inside the church, and the thought came to her that this was where they had meant to have a service for Lucinda, but now Simon's body lay before the altar.

Simon's parents hadn't made it over to England. Flo's heart went out to them. She'd received a lovely letter from them, thanking her for writing to them and saying they would write to Roland eventually, but in the meantime they would be grateful if she would keep them informed about his welfare. Contacting him was a step too far for them at the moment, as they coped with losing both of their children.

The next hour passed in a daze. Inside her body was a cold, locked place. Flo wouldn't allow herself to cry, but stood to attention as the procession left the church. A feeling of being lost overwhelmed her as she came out into the open. Her eyes followed the receding coffin on its way to be placed in the hearse. Simon's final journey was to be with his family and close mourners. *Simon, me love. Oh, Simon.*

'Take my arm, Flo.'

Art's voice gave Flo some strength. He had become a solid, dependable rock to her, in such a short time.

Jane touched her other arm. 'I'll have to go, Wren Kilgallon... Flo.'

Flo smiled at Jane, glad that she'd found it in her to use her Christian name. 'Thank you, Jane. I'll not forget your kindness.'

'I liked Simon. I'm sorry he ... well, I'll see you in a couple of days when you return to camp.'

Someone coughed beside Flo. She turned to see a man a few inches taller than herself. For a moment she froze in shock, as his eyes were Simon's eyes. 'I'm a cousin of Simon's. I understand from the general that you were his friend. Wren Kilgallon, isn't it?'

'Aye. Simon was me best friend. I can't come to terms with him going.'

'Quite. I came to say that, as a family, we would like to thank you. I ... we – that is, my sister and I – knew about him. We were never allowed to speak of it in the family, and gradually, as Simon lived his life how he wanted to, the ties between us became very thin, as it was never approved that we mixed with him. We're younger than him, you see, so we had very little say. This is dreadful, really dreadful, and I regret not defying my parents and staying in touch with Simon. My father is a brother of Simon's father. He's not here today. Too ashamed.'

Flo saw a tear trickle down the young man's face and felt compassion for him, even though he epitomized what Simon had to endure. But this seemed even worse, as it was a member of his own family admitting that he'd ostracized Simon. 'By, I'm sorry for you – you missed knowing one of the kindest, funniest and grandest blokes that ever walked the earth.'

'I – I know. Is there anything I can do for you?'

'Naw, not me, but you could make up a bit for your absence from Simon's life by making sure his friend Roland is given something of Simon's to remember him by.'

'You mean the man who was sent to prison?'

'Aye, I do. He should never be there. He's not a criminal.'

The man coughed again and felt in his breast pocket. 'Here is my card. Will you contact me with details about where Roland is, please? I will see what I can do. Simon's mother is the executor of his will; she was made so by Simon when poor Lucinda... Well, anyway, she has appointed me to act in her absence. I promise you, I will see that Roland does get something. Thank you. I have to go now. Will you come to the graveside?'

'Naw. I couldn't bear it, but ta for asking me – it means a lot. I'll write to you once I have proper details about Roland.'

The man doffed his hat and left. Flo stood still, gazing after the carriage as it drew slowly away, taking Simon from her. She thought of the rose bush they'd bought together for Lucinda, and it came to her that it should be planted on Simon's grave in memory of them both. She'd ask that of the cousin, when she wrote to him. He'd seemed nice, and Flo felt sure he'd do right by Simon in death, even if he hadn't in life.

Once the cortège was out of sight, she turned to Art. 'Ta for coming, Art. I didn't knaw as you were on your rest day.'

'I swapped. There weren't any raids planned, and a few of the guys wanted the dates that were set out on my rota. I have a forty-eight-hour pass. Where do you want to go, Flo? I could take you anywhere. I've bought a car in the last few days, so that I can visit you more often. That's it over there – the big black one.'

Flo looked over and saw a large car, making all the others look like little boxes. She'd only ever seen one like it before, and that had stood on the drive of Belinda's house. 'Is it a Rolls-Royce? By, it looks grand as owt.'

'It is. Some lord or other, who lives not far from Biggin Hill, sold it to me. It's hardly been out of his garage. I got it for a snip!'

Flo doubted that, but money never seemed to be any object to Art. He'd talked in the two letters he'd sent her about his family in Ontario being the owners of a printing firm, and of their large estate, where he loved to ride his horses.

His letters had been a salve to her, although she was embarrassed at how he declared his love for her in them. She knew it was possible to fall in love as quickly as Art said he had, because it had happened to her with Simon, but she wasn't ready to let Art be anything other than a friend. She was afraid to misinterpret her feelings for him. He wasn't like any other person she'd ever known and he'd come into her life after Simon had died, so he helped her in a different way from the way those who had known Simon could. This made her wonder if she might value just that: the chance to talk to someone who didn't know him, and couldn't relate back all of the time. *Oh, I don't knaw. I only knaw I feel comfortable with him.*

And that comfortable feeling allowed her to let go of her emotions, once she sank into the soft, welcoming ruby-red leather seats of Art's car. The smell of the leather reminded her of Simon's car interior. *I'll never again sit next to Simon, chatting away as he drives me through the countryside in Bells.*

The tears Flo had held back spilled over, as the car roared into life and sped her away.

'Gee, honey, I'll pull over. We're near to the Thames; we can sit on the bank and you can let it all out.'

'Naw, it'll be too cold. Besides, I'm in uniform.' Dabbing her eyes, Flo wished she could release the knot of pain inside her. If only she could be alone, just for an hour, so that she could scream and hit things and unleash her agony. But always there was someone by her side, comforting and loving her, so that she had to seek composure rather than vent her grief.

'I'll be reet; just drive around a bit and let me

compose meself, then take me to Pauline's. When did she leave the church, by the way? We could have given her a lift.'

'She said she needed to get back; she seemed anxious about something. She left before the service, and said she just wanted you to see that she was there and then she had to leave.'

This pulled Flo up short. Always alert to the fear she held for Molly, her tears dried instantly. 'I don't like the sound of that, Art. Forget driving around. Will you take me straight to Pauline's, please?'

'Oh, Flo, I'm glad yer back. Are you all right?'

'Aye, I am, lass, though a bit worried as to why you left so sudden. What's to do – where's Molly?'

'She's upstairs in the bedroom. Sommat has happened. It was last night. I was followed. A car pulled up by the van where I was working, a sleek black, American-looking thing it was, and there was a blond-haired man at the wheel. One or two of me customers slinked away when they saw it, and another said, "Blimey, that's that gang from the East End." Everyone in me queue seemed frightened. I didn't know what to do, as it was still there when I left. In the end I went back to the depot, and they followed, driving a bit and stopping just in front of me.' Pauline's body shook and her face paled. 'I were scared out of me wits.'

Flo took her hand. 'Sit down, lass. Did they follow you back here?'

'No, I lost them. I stayed in the depot a while, then slipped out the back way into the alley. Then I cut up through there and walked along the bank

403

of the river till I got to Vauxhall Bridge again. When I crossed over the bridge, they were nowhere to be seen. But I'm scared, Flo. What if they come back when I do me shift tonight?'

Molly came through the door to the stairs. She ran into Flo's arms. Flo could feel the trembling of her body. Her own fear deepened, with all she'd heard and the terror shown by these two women, who had become her beloved friends. She looked over at Art. He too showed a concern verging on fear. What had she got him into? He was a pilot with the Canadian air force, from an upstanding family, and she'd dragged him down into the sleazy world of gangsters.

'You go, Art. We'll sort this. I've a mind, from what's been said, that the gang Molly escaped from have an idea she's with Pauline – or at least that Pauline is involved in some way. It's not reet for you to be party to owt like this. I'll write to you as soon as I can.'

'Neither can you be involved, Flo. You're a Wren. You have a lot at stake, too. If you're getting involved, then I am, too. Besides, I got myself into this. I went willingly to Soho with...Wait a minute, that must be it! The fellow airman I was with – Spike – you remember, Molly? He must have told them where I was going to take you that night.'

'I've thought of that, and it's the only answer. God, I was such a damn fool to send him to Eva's brothel, but I was angry. Angry at all men, as I saw them as the cause of what happened to me. Their need – well, you know what I mean. I–'

'I reckon as there's nowt to be served by apportioning blame. We're all in danger, we knaw that, so we have to think straight and sort sommat out.'

'There seems only one solution: we have to get Molly and Pauline away from here, but where to?'

'You're reet, Art, we do. What about the aunt in Birmingham you told me about, Molly?'

'It's more than likely the gang have already been there looking for me. I'm worried sick over her safety. They're ruthless. What if they've hurt her? Oh God, what have I done to you all?'

'They don't know about the place in Wales, where me mam is and me kids are. We could go there.'

'But that's just it, we can't. None of you know them like me. Now that Delilah is pointing the finger at them, they have to find me, to stop me giving evidence as well. Oh, they can cover up, pay enough bribes to the police, kill someone as an example; and they will do so, to wriggle out of what is being said by Delilah. But I have a lot more recent evidence, with the operation going on at me dad's. And Ruby, she'll be in danger an' all, as she can back up most of what Delilah knows. I'm so sorry, Pauline, but if they have an inkling that it is you who has helped me – and it seems they do – then they will find out everything about you.'

'No! No, Molly, not ... me kids? Oh God!'

'I'm sorry, I'm so sorry. It's how they work – they're evil. I have to give meself up to them, it's the only way.'

'Naw!' But as she said this, Flo was filled with

despair as to what alternative there was.

Art voiced her confusion. 'I'm lost. How can Pauline's kids be in danger, if they're living in Wales with their grandmother?'

'Because, Art, if Eva's gang want information from you, they will make threats about what they will do to someone you love. They'll stop at nothing. They'd use Pauline's kids to frighten her into revealing where I was. It was the threats that kept me doing everything they wanted me to. I couldn't go to me dad for help, for he's in up to his neck with them; and going to the police wasn't an option, as the top brass are all in Eva's pay.' Molly told them how she and Trixie had helped Ruby to escape, and how they'd never been able to trust Delilah, but had only helped her when they knew her story about who she really was. 'Once Ruby was safe, I could then make me break and get away. But it all went wrong for me. They beat me up so badly... Well, you all know the rest.'

As Flo listened to it all, she felt more and more afraid and just stood transfixed as Molly ended by saying, 'Oh, why did Delilah do this? She was supposed to wait until I was in the forces. She's such a selfish cow!'

Flo saw Art raise his shoulders and hands in an action that said he didn't understand. She felt the same herself, for this was a world she knew nothing about and thought existed only in films. Even after her terrifying conversation with Trixie, when she'd been told that the gang Molly had been forced to work for were after Molly, she hadn't taken in the full implications. *Murder, bribes, threats to life, black-market operations, prostitution –*

my God!

At this moment Flo couldn't think straight, but the real terror of their situation was beginning to seep into her. They should just be able to go to the police, but from what she knew now, even they couldn't be trusted. She had the feeling of being trapped in a nightmare. Stranded, with no one to help them and nowhere to turn without being in danger. She sank into the chair behind her. *I have to think: there must be a solution. I've a logical brain, and I solve codes others can't begin to get a handle on. There has to be a way that I can solve this problem.*

'Pauline, Molly, I need peace for a moment. Aye, we're in a frightening situation. But I need you all to calm down. I need to think it through.'

Whether her voice had come out like a command or not, Flo didn't know, but what she called for happened. Pauline, Molly and Art sat down. Their fearful eyes were on her. She leaned back and closed hers, shutting them all out. She had to think.

After a moment, a clear plan began to form. She needed to get an idea of which police force was dealing with the case. They would be the ones to go to with the information they had. Molly would be invaluable to them as a second witness. If they could get hold of more evidence, then their efforts to bring a conclusion to the case surely wouldn't be hampered by the corrupt police in Soho, as must be happening now. And there was Ruby, too. Maybe she has been too afraid to talk, as she would know the gang had Delilah's whereabouts from the local police, and

407

that they might conclude she was there, too. Flo needed to know where this was. 'Molly, where is Delilah? Can you contact her? Are she and Ruby in the same place?'

'Yes, they're in Scotland. I have a telephone number and an address. They're with a woman who's a friend of Trixie's. Trixie gave me the number so that I could get in touch with Ruby, once I was settled. It's in with me gas mask, thank goodness, as me bag was stolen.'

'Scotland? Eeh, no wonder this is all taking such a time. The distance and the communication difficulties will be causing delays, without the possible lack of cooperation from the police in Soho. Besides, I doubt that the Scottish police have any jurisdiction in England.' Flo knew these things through her own work. Outposts had to be manned in these areas to pick up any coded messages being relayed to, and between, ships in the North Sea and the Atlantic. Often getting these messages by wireless telecommunication proved difficult, as the signals were weak and so had to be delivered by hand through a trusted chain of couriers, causing crucial delays. If that was so for the largest and most technological operation in Britain, as Bletchley was, then what chance did a small police force have? 'As I see it, we need to get them back into England.'

'What, Ruby an' all?'

'Aye. The more witnesses to the gang's activities there are together, the better. Besides, Delilah's – Martha's – case is known here. There will be records to corroborate her story, and evidence that can be matched to her. Even to timing, as you said Gus was in prison for a long time, and yet he was involved in her kidnap. The Scottish police won't have any of this. I'd like to bet a case such as hers, that was of massive countrywide interest, was dealt with by Scotland Yard, so that's where we must take her.'

No one spoke for a moment. Flo frantically tried to form more of a plan to bring together all they had to do, and yet make sure everyone was kept safe. *But how? Where?* Bletchley? No. What if everything got out of hand? What if the gang found them and the actions they took compromised her work at Bletchley? Or, God forbid, put Bletchley on the map, jeopardizing the secrecy about what went on there?

At the thought of this, and her involvement in something that had even the remotest possibility of connecting this sordid business to Bletchley, Flo's fear intensified. Sweat broke out over her body. A trickle ran down her face and plopped in a cold bead on her neck. Art's hand reached out to her. His gentle touch on her tightly clasped hands helped. She calmed her mind. None of that must happen. Panic-mode had given her all the scenarios, and now she must avoid any involvement with Bletchley at all costs. Nevertheless, she needed to do something.

'Are you all right, Flo?'

'Aye. I am, Art, ta.' She took her hand away from Art's and fumbled for her hanky. Wiping her face, Flo took a deep breath. 'We have no other choice than to go to Scotland Yard.'

The silence deepened for a moment. Molly broke it. 'But you can't just go up to Scotland

Yard as you can to a police station, Flo. It's not open to the public to wander in with all sorts of complaints. It's an investigative operation within a building.'

For a moment this floored Flo. She'd had no idea, and thought they could go in and present what they had to a desk sergeant and all would be well. But the fact that this wasn't possible didn't put her off. She needed to get help to bring the gang to justice and make everyone safe. Her mind took a moment to come up with a solution. 'Whitehall 1212! That's it: that's the number we all know for Scotland Yard. You have to telephone that number, Molly, and say that you know where Martha Gardner is and that you have information about a gang operating in London. Tell them you are in danger and need protection. Tell them everything. We'll all move to a hotel tonight – somewhere very public, so that even if the gang finds out where you are, which ain't likely, they won't want to act until you leave. But by that time you will have been in touch with Scotland Yard and, hopefully, everything will be sorted.'

'The Savoy.'

'Eeh, Art, naw. The likes of us can't stay there!'

'It's where I'm staying, and I'll pick up the bill. There's a motley crew staying there – deposed royalty amongst them – but the hotel can always find rooms, because apart from Europe's un-wanted, not many people wish to stay in London, with the nightly air raids going on.'

Molly didn't discount this, but came out with the practicalities of how she would look there. 'But I ain't got any clothes, only me ... well, you know, them as I came in.'

Flo went into action. Her quick-thinking brain had her accepting Art's wild suggestion as a solution. Yes, they would be safe in such a place, and would have access to telephones. 'I have a frock in me bag as would fit you, Molly. And you can wear me nice coat, an' all. I'll stay in me uniform. What about you, Pauline?'

Pauline hadn't said much the whole time they had been locked in fear about what to do. Flo looked at her and felt the pity of everything this kindly lady had been drawn into, through no fault of her own. *And, aye, I have to admit, through actions I took in offering help to Molly.* But then Pauline would have done the same, if she'd been the one to meet Molly first. They were alike in nature, she and Pauline.

'It's a chance, Pauline. If we can get somewhere safe and get Scotland Yard involved, we can keep your kids and mam safe, an' all.'

'Right-o, Flo. It ain't what I ever thought I'd do, staying at the bleedin' Savoy, but needs must. I've slummed it before.'

The burst of spontaneous laughter at this unexpected joke from Pauline lightened the tension in the room. 'Good old Pauline, I knew you'd take it in your stride.'

'I'm a Londoner, Flo. And yer know what? Us and you northerners are made of grit. We'll cope, no matter what is thrown at us. I have to say I was knocked off me axle to think of me kids in danger, but I think your plan is a good one and I'm ready to go through with it. I'll put on me Sunday-best frock. It's done me proud for weddings and

411

funerals, and it's good enough for the bleedin' Savoy, an' all.'

'That's the spirit, ladies. Everyone will think you're all royalty in your posh frocks, and being driven up in my Rolls. Let's show this gang that they don't mess with Art Tendray of Ontario and his ladies.'

Again they laughed. Flo wondered if Art would have made the joke if he'd known the implications of calling them 'his ladies', but knew he was too decent even to think in such a way and meant to imply just what he'd said: that they were ladies, in his eyes, and his friends.

The offer by Art to foot the bill worried her, but she would make sure she gave him whatever she could; in the meantime, she had no alternative other than to accept his generosity. Outrageous and unbelievable as it was for her, Pauline and Molly ever to contemplate staying at the Savoy, it was the only solution to their problem that they had at this moment in time.

Once they were all in the car, Flo found her own body trembling. She'd kept strong for Pauline and Molly, but the enormity of it all was now having an impact on her. She was involved in bringing one of the most notorious gangs in London to justice, and yet she held a position of trust and secrecy that had to be protected at all costs. Thinking about this, she knew she had to call a halt to her involvement.

'Art, I can't go to the Savoy. I – I have to...' Flo felt her voice tightening as the atmosphere in the car tensed once more.

'What's wrong, Flo? Is it to do with your job?'

'I – I can't say. Art, I just–'

'Leave it at that, then.'

Flo felt relief at Art saying this. She glanced back at Molly and Pauline. Both looked lost, sunk in the deep leather back seat of the car. 'By, me lasses, I feel as though I'm abandoning you, and it ain't in me power to be able to explain, but I can't do owt as might implicate me in something as big as this. And nor can you, Art, if the truth be known.'

'What are we going to do then, Flo? It was such a good plan. I felt safe for the first time since I can remember.'

'It still is a good plan, Molly. And it's one you have to go through with. But as military person-nel, me and Art can't be involved. You have to be strong and go through with this on your own. Do exactly as we planned. We'll book you into the Savoy, and you must ring Scotland Yard. Then stay put until plans are made to make you safe. Me and Art'll foot the bill. I – I mean, I'll pay you back every penny, Art, but if you can, you'll have to stand the cost for a little while. I don't reckon they'll be there for many days.'

'I can and I will, no worry about that. But, girls, Flo is right. If we stay with you, we'll be involved, and neither of us can be.'

'By, if things were different I wouldn't leave your side, Molly. But I've no choice. Just tell the police whatever it is they need to hear. Then as soon as I see in the papers that the gang's been arrested, I'll be at your door like a shot, Pauline.'

'And that's where you'll find Molly an' all, Flo. I'll take care of her. And don't worry, we know

413

you wouldn't leave us if you had a choice. There's a lot we don't know about what you do, but whatever it is, I can see you have to protect it above all other considerations.'

'I do, Pauline. Molly, I–'

'I understand, Flo. Please don't worry. You've done more than anyone could expect of you. I'll never be able to thank you. You've given me courage, too. I was trying to think of a way of keeping me dad out of this, but I realize I can't. He has to take what's coming to him. Once they're all behind bars, I'll have a home again. Me own home, where I was brought up.'

This further relaxed Flo. She didn't know how it would all pan out for Molly, but she knew she'd done all she could. She had to stop now and leave Molly to go forward on her own. Once Molly had done what she had to do, Pauline's family would be safe, and Pauline could return to her home and carry on as normal. She was just the kindly lady who'd taken Molly in, and the police wouldn't be interested in her. They'd know to keep her name out of everything, to ensure her safety for life. This thought was provoked by a worry Flo hadn't voiced, but one that her keen mind had visited: the prospect of the younger members of the gang coming back from war one day and maybe seeking revenge. But that was all in the future. A future where none of them knew the outcome.

Through the dim light of the car interior, Flo looked over at Art. It had felt nice when he'd held her hand. What she'd have done today without him by her side, she didn't know. Simon would

414

have liked him, too, she knew that.

This thought, instead of sending her into the deep pit of her grief, sat well with her. She had to accept that she'd always live like that. Referring back to Simon. He'd never leave her. She needed time to heal, but she knew she could go forward with her life. Simon would want that for her.

25

Roland & Flo

Coming to Terms

Roland sat opposite Frazer. His mind took many turns as he listened to his friend and lawyer drone on about how they could lodge an appeal.

'I don't want to appeal, Frazer. I know I was upset when I pleaded guilty, but I can't go through all that again.'

'But look at you – and your face. I can't protect you in here. I've tried, but the wardens just say that you fell over. You're being mistreated, and I can't bear it.'

'Don't worry. I have four months under my belt now and it's getting easier. I've started to hold a class for those who can't read and write, and some of them are warming to me. Besides, there's talk of a few of the younger ones, who are the worst aggressors, being released to active service, so that will improve things for me, too.'

'Roland, you can't keep punishing yourself for Simon's death – it wasn't your fault. You said yourself how careful you were in public. What happened is more than likely down to that person you spoke about who worked for Simon.'

Pain stabbed at Roland's heart at the mention of Simon's name. Frazer must have seen it, as he hung his head for a moment.

'My dear friend, I can't bear to see you like this. You know how I feel about you, and it breaks me in two to see you here and in this state.'

'Don't ... I'm not ready. I don't know if I ever will be. Nor will I ever feel safe again. I'd rather stay single and live a bachelor's life. I can't even think about another relationship.'

'I'm sorry. I never meant to mention my feelings. I... Don't shut me out because of them, Roland. They have been there since we were at school together, you know that. I have carried on all these years, and I can shut down and carry on forever, if I have to.'

'Why don't you find someone else, Frazer? Don't wait for me. You may wait forever.'

'If that's what it takes. Anyway, a solicitor from down south has been in touch again. Your friend, Florence, is desperate to come and see you. Why don't you let her?'

'All right. When I'm next allowed a visitor, I will see her. I think I'm ready to deal with doing so now.'

'Good. It will do you good to see someone other than me, and will let me off the hook. Seeing you, and not being able to be more to you, is tearing me in half.'

'Oh, Frazer, I'm sorry. Who knows what will happen in the future?'

'Is that you offering me the crumbs off your table?'

'Maybe. I don't know.'

When Frazer had left, Roland went back to his cell. Life was complicated. Over these last months the only person from outside the prison that he'd see had been Frazer, and he did have some small feeling for him, but he had to be sure that feeling was worth nurturing. Maybe it was just a thread of the lifeline that Frazer offered to him and would snap the moment he tried to grasp it fully. He didn't know.

'Here, nancy boy, my shoes want cleaning. But no, you're not fit to spit on them, so I won't bother you after all.' A hideous laughter echoed down the corridor. Something snapped in Roland; he'd had enough. Max Brown, the prison bully, had made the remark and had come out of his cell to bar his way.

'Move out of my way.'

'Huh, ponce – are you going to make me, then?' The huge man stomped towards Roland, fists clenched, aggression and hate making his ugly face uglier.

Roland stood his ground, wishing he'd taken more notice of the martial-arts classes offered at his school. But he had enjoyed boxing and had been rather good at it. He raised his fists. Max stopped in his tracks. His head went back, and his laughter echoed once more off the walls. Sweat rolled down Roland's back. Heads appeared out of open cell doors. Roland attacked, catching Max off-guard and landing a heavy punch to his stomach. Max leaned forward, staring Roland out, his mouth twisted. The punch had hardly tickled him. Roland hated his own next move, but saw no other way. He lifted his foot and sunk it deep into Max's groin. Max's huge body curled and fell onto the floor. Squeals that a woman would be proud of emitted from his slobbering mouth. Roland stepped over him and walked, with as much dignity as he could muster, towards his cell.

A cheer went up that deafened Roland. The sound scared him rather than lifted him. Max would want revenge and there would be reprisals, but whatever they were, he'd have to take them and deal with them as they happened. Though the men showing appreciation would make things worse, for Max had his pride to regain. Roland shivered with fear as to how that would happen.

Sitting on his bed, he held his head in his hands. His thoughts took on the guise of a flickering film, as events from the past visited him, then left him before he had time to grasp hold of any. Most of them held Simon. And Lucinda and Flo. Now there was only him and Flo left. Seeing her would be so painful. How had she coped? How had Simon's family coped?

The click of his cell door woke him, when he hadn't been aware of falling asleep. A strange silence pervaded the usually noisy, echoing prison. Roland saw a pair of knees first. His eyes travelled up the huge body standing close to his bed. *Max. Oh God!*

418

'Think yourself the big man, do yer? Think you can mess with the likes of me, eh?'

Roland thought quickly as he stood up and faced Max. 'No, I don't. I'm no match for you and I apologize for using such underhand tactics, which are against the Queensberry Rules, but I hope you will understand that, although weaker than you, I had to fight back. And as that makes us even, maybe we can put all animosity behind us and try to get on together.'

To Roland's surprise, Max put out his hand. Wary of taking it for a moment, Roland froze. 'Take me hand, and take me heart, man. Anyone who can fight back like you did deserves some respect. I ain't liking what you are, but we've both got our time to do and we can do it in peace, if you'll take me hand.'

Nervous to do so, but nervous not to, Roland took Max's hand and gave it a firm shake.

Then he was surprised as Max said, 'You teach folk to read, don't yer?'

'I do, Max, and I'll gladly teach you, if you would like me to.'

'I would. And I'll offer you protection, as payment for your trouble. I envy them as can get a book out of the library and lose themselves in it for a few hours a day. It must make the time go more quickly.'

'Sit down, Max.' Roland indicated the end of his bed. He could do with sitting down himself as his legs were shaking. Taking a seat next to Max, he noticed the big man move further away. He smiled inwardly at this and wanted to say, *Don't worry, I don't fancy you, mate*. But instead he

419

outlined what the lessons entailed and explained that he only had a Friday afternoon free to fit Max in.

After Max had left, the bell rang out for the evening meal. It was a time Roland had dreaded every day of his incarceration. A time when he was prodded with forks, tripped up or had his head shoved into his food. Or, even worse than that, on occasions had his food spat into. However, he had no choice but to attend the dining hall. Such events were compulsory and were supervised by more than one bully of a warden.

As he entered the hall, a hush descended. Keeping his head down – to make eye contact was considered the worst of the bad sins you could commit in this place – Roland made it to the counter. A good-sized portion of mashed potato was slapped onto his tin plate, followed by a good helping of hot stew, more food than he'd ever been given before. As he walked down the aisle between the long wooden tables, no one stopped his progress or tried to hurt him, and when he sat down in his allotted place, none of those already seated moved away or began making snide remarks. Relief flooded through Roland. So much so that his guard slipped and for a moment he struggled not to cry.

Though no one spoke directly to him, he had the feeling that he could join in with the conversation if he wanted to. He didn't. The discussion was about the marine engineer, George Johnson Armstrong. It seemed he'd lost his appeal against his sentence to hang, and a date in early July, almost three weeks from now, had been set for his execution. The general opinion was that no one was going to remain silent, as was usual when these events took place, as the convicted man had been in contact with the Germans and had offered them assistance. He'd been found guilty of treachery.

This repulsed Roland, and he felt glad the man was getting his just deserts, though a part of him felt some compassion about how the fellow was feeling tonight, as he pondered on his last weeks on earth. The thought sent a shudder through his body.

Life at the prison settled down and Roland was at last feeling that he could cope. Two weeks had now passed – a time during which, true to his word, Max hid given him protection and not a single incident had occurred. Roland was feeling better health-wise, too, as he ate regular meals that hadn't been interfered with, and he hadn't endured any painful punishments for being who he was. At last he felt able to see Flo.

The men in the line of prisoners waiting for visitors stood to attention. Though they were quiet, as none wanted to risk being sent back to their cell without having their visit, there was a tangible air of excitement that Roland felt he could almost touch. He was experiencing it himself, and a surge went through him as the line moved forward and through the open door into the visiting hall.

Flo stood looking anxious, scrutinizing each face as the line of men came through. Roland saw her before she saw him. When her eyes alighted on him, her face lit up. By the time they sat down, her eyes were glistening with tears. Roland swallowed hard.

'Oh, Roland, how are you?'

'I'm fine,' he lied. He wanted so much to hold her. To sit by her and lay his head on her chest and weep. He swallowed again.

'You look well. Better than I expected.' Stilted, nervous conversation. *Oh, where has the easy rapport that we used to have gone?*

'Flo...'

'Roland...'

They spoke together. Flo giggled. 'Eeh, we're acting like two strangers.'

'I know. Tell me what you've been doing, or is all your life happening within four walls of secrecy?'

'Naw, I've been mixed up with gangsters!'

'What?' It was Roland's turn to be amused. Though that amusement turned to worry as Flo related her story.

'My God, Flo, can I not leave you for a few months that you don't get into trouble?'

'Ha, it doesn't look like it. But all's well now. The gang are on remand in Brixton, and we've been told that none of them will see the light of day again. Sadly, Molly's dad is also on remand and looking at ten years at least, but he isn't well. He did redeem himself a bit, though, as he had already signed over his property to Molly. There wasn't much money, as that was all seized, but at least she has a home and she's given one to Ruby, an' all. They've to decide what war work they want to do before they're directed somewhere. They don't want to be separated again.'

'Good, I'm glad your friends are settled. Now what about you? I've heard enough about the waifs and strays you've been picking up and assisting. What about your life?'

'Oh, I've been doing some amateur dramatics, with me mate. She and I share a flat. She's lovely. And... Well, I – I think I'm in love.'

'But that's wonderful. Tell me.' Roland saw Flo's face light up. His heart bled the agony of the love he'd lost, but he squashed that feeling and concentrated on being happy for Flo. 'Well, he sounds nice. I might pinch him from you when I get out of here.'

Flo laughed, a lovely sound that reverberated around the room and had many eyes falling upon them. A silence fell, when she composed herself. Both knew they were skirting around what they so wanted to talk about – Simon – but both knew they daren't, not here. That had to wait until Roland was released.

A bell rang. Roland's heart sank. Somehow, now that he'd been with Flo, he didn't know how he was going to face the next eighteen months. 'Come again soon, Flo.'

'I will. I'm off up to Leeds after I leave here. Art is taking me. I haven't seen Mrs Leary for such a long time. All me time's been taken up with Molly and Pauline, and Ruby. But they're all safe now, so I can come on me next leave, if you can arrange it for me.'

'Thank you, Flo. I'll talk to my lawyer. You may know him, Frazer Turner, of Turner and Turner, in Leeds?'

'Naw. I knaw of him, but I don't mix in them

423

circles. Or at least I didn't until you introduced me to... Oh, I'm sorry, I–'

Roland ignored this. 'Will you write to me? I've been given the privilege of receiving one letter a month. I – I have no one else'

'Eeh, I'd love to. I've a lot I can tell you.'

'Don't talk about – well, you know. I can only deal with it by locking it all away. If I gave way in here, it... Let's just say this is a place where everyone has to be manly to survive.'

'I won't. I can't. I'm the same. I haven't let all that surface. I know it has to one day. But...'

'I understand. Goodbye, Flo. Please come again soon.'

As she turned from him, Roland wanted to run after her and hold her to him. Instead, he took a deep breath and waited to hear the command to file out.

Flo didn't speak when she got into the car. Her feelings were jangled, some tied in a knot she thought she would never undo, whilst others were ones of relief to see Roland looking so well. And yet another part of her felt a deep sadness at seeing him in such a place. All of these emotions mixed with an excitement that at last, after months of not going home to Leeds, she was finally going to see her beloved family. Eunice would be there, too. Having now recovered, Eunice had returned to work, but was on leave from the hospital. *Ooh, it will be so good to see them all.*

Art touched her hand. It was enough. A comfort, but not an intrusion. Turning to him, she smiled. His nod said that he understood, without her having to explain or delve into words to express how the visit had been for her.

The engine was already running. Art must have cranked it ready for the off once she came out of the prison gates. He selected a gear and drove away from the prison. Flo relaxed back in her seat and closed her eyes. They had a long drive north, four hours or more, but had arranged that they might not arrive this evening, depending on how the journey went and how Art coped with it. As though at last the Blitz on London had come to an end, Art and his fellow squadron members were now engaged in flying their new Spitfire aircraft on missions across the Channel to engage in small bombing raids and fighter sweeps – harassing the enemy and increasing morale at home. The RAF were everyone's heroes and when they reported successes, everyone felt happier, but the toll on the men themselves was plain to see in the deepening lines around Art's eyes.

By the time they reached the countryside the sun was still dancing off the buttercups in the fields, birds were sweeping down and flying off with a prize worm or two, and trees swayed in the slight breeze. 'Shall we stop for our picnic, Flo? I'm hungry.'

'Aye, so am I. Look for a gateway to pull into, then we can climb over and sit on the grass to eat.'

With the cloth laid out and their sandwiches and lemonade ready to tuck into, Art spread a rug for them to sit on. A peace settled around them. War and all of its demands seemed a million miles away, and Flo felt the stress of seeing Roland melt away from her as Art's body, so close, awakened feelings she'd never thought to experience again. When his hand rested on her thigh, it was as if she'd received an electric shock. Looking up into his hazel eyes, she was met with a raw passion that she couldn't resist. Her body leaned into his without her bidding it to do so. The solid feel of his chest pressing against hers, as his lips brushed her lips, ignited a deep sensation she could no longer deny.

As Art drew out of the kiss, his breath fanned her cheek with his whispered, 'My Flo, I love you.'

To Flo, the moment released her from the pain of the past that had held her feelings trapped as if in iron chains, and she knew she loved this man. Loved him with a passion she'd never touched before. It surmounted all she'd felt for Simon. In this moment a crystal-clear certainty came to her. Simon had been a first love, a sweet and yet painful love, an awakening. What she felt for Art was a deep binding of souls. 'I love you, Art.' She held his cheeks and looked deep into his eyes, till she felt their souls connect. 'I love you with all that is me, my heart and my soul. Aye, me heart's been touched afore, but never me soul, and that's as deep as you are in me feelings, Art. You're part of me.'

Her fingers wiped away the glistening teardrops that had formed as she spoke and had now trickled down his cheeks. His words held all he was for her. 'Oh, Flo, my Flo – my love.'

Their bodies swayed together. The wool rug accepted them as they lay back, still entwined, holding onto each other, because now that Flo had opened to Art's love and let her own seep from her, she never wanted to let go of him again.

There was no resistance, only complete acceptance of her man as his hands caressed parts of her that no one had touched before, gently teasing sensations that had her moaning the pleasure that her body was being transported into. Shyly at first, but finding such joy in discovering the feel of him, she explored her man. Loved the feeling of his strong body and every curly hair on his chest.

Without permission having to be asked, their clothes were discarded. This was so right. Flo knew the time had come to lie with her man and give herself to him, and accept him in a union that nothing could ever break. Art's gentle handling of her, his concern and his loving, helped her through as he slowly entered her, easing himself out again if she cried out with pain, until at last he could make her fully his.

Heaven descended around them as she drowned in the ecstasy of becoming Art's. Truly his, and he truly hers. This was a giving of love, not a taking; this was happiness beyond measure, abandonment of her very spirit as she gave it up and embraced Art's spirit as her own.

Suddenly something happened deep inside her. A feeling that threatened to be bigger than her. Part of her denied it happening, but then it overwhelmed her and she heard her own voice hollering as the exquisite sensations took over her body. When it was over, she lay beneath Art, shivering, crying, completely spent. His hand stroked her hair, his lips kissed every part of her face, and his words were of love, forever-love and devotion. 'You are my woman, Flo. I'll treasure you all of my life. I give all of me to you.' Words that tinkled, like music. Words that made her his forever.

When his thrusting became more urgent, Flo could only lie beneath him and allow him whatever he needed. When his moment of completion came, she wanted to wrap her legs around him and take all of him into her, but he quickly took himself out of her, gasping and calling her name as he held her close. A feeling of missing something seized Flo for a second, but she realized as a dampness covered her thighs that Art was thinking only of her, of them both. And what he had given her was enough for now. More than enough.

'I'm sorry, darling, so sorry.'

'Don't be. Please, never be sorry. I – I...' A shyness came over her, but she had to tell him, had to put his mind at ease. 'I've been to heaven and back. I've never experienced such feelings – it was wonderful. I love you. I'm yours, Art, truly yours. If you will have me, I want to marry you, to have your children and to live forever in your arms.'

His already-flushed cheeks deepened a shade, and the sweat trickling from his forehead shone in the sun, but his eyes lit as if a torch shone from them. 'Are you proposing to me, Flo?'

'I am.'

'Yes, yes, yes, yes.' They were rolling together down the bank, laughing and shouting. When they reached the bottom, Art held her to him. Flo could hear his heart beating, and hoped that it would never stop. That nothing would ever happen to him. For she knew she couldn't live without him.

They giggled as they dressed, and talked silly talk as they ate, before Art became serious. 'We're not going to make it to Leeds tonight, do you mind, darling?'

'Naw, I'd not have it any different.'

'Mr and Mrs Smith in a hotel, then?'

Flo giggled her consent.

'Come on then, let's pack this up. I can't wait to get you in a big comfy bed, have my wicked way again and curl up around you to go to sleep.'

'Ha, you're taking a lot on yourself. I might have my wicked way with you!'

Art laughed out loud. It was a sound that gladdened Flo's heart. How had it happened that in London – a place that had been alien to her when she was growing up – she'd met a man who'd been brought up on the other side of the world, and yet was the one meant for her?

Though war in all its forms was evil, but for this war happening, she might never have met Art. *Eeh, it's like as is said: good can come from bad.*

When the car pulled up outside Mrs Leary's, Flo felt exhausted, and at the same time elated. After Art's loving of her for most of the night, they had slept late, curled up together, and had taken breakfast on the run, making a sandwich out of the dried spam and eating it on the way. Their happiness gave them energy.

As the door opened and a squealing Kathy

429

emerged with arms in the air, and behind her Eunice, Mrs Leary and even Mr Leary, the thought came to Flo: *I'm home.*

Through the noise of the greeting, Art whispered, 'I hope they like me,' just before the welcoming committee swept her up.

He needn't have worried. He received hugs almost as enthusiastic as the ones Flo was given. Mrs Leary took charge. 'Come on, away with you, let Flo get inside. Will you calm down, the lot of you?'

Flo felt a lump rise to her throat. She swallowed hard. It had been so long, so very long, but she was home.

When all had quietened and they were in what Flo thought of as the beautiful kitchen, Flo said, 'This is Art, my fiancé.'

The squeals set up again, with everyone asking questions at once. Flo answered as best she could. 'Naw, we aren't getting married yet a while. By, we've a war to win first.' And to Kathy, 'Yes, Art had better be at buying me a ring, or I'll be calling it all off.'

Mrs Leary's gaze made Flo blush as her response to this was, 'So, it is that you've sealed your love for one another, but haven't been at announcing it to the world.' There was so much meaning in her words, but they were said with a twinkle in her eye.

'Aye, sommat like that. Now stop all of your nosy parkering and put the kettle on. What kind of a welcome is this?'

Mr Leary surprised her then. 'Ha, you be telling her, Flo. It's a good day, so it is, to have you back in our family. You not being here has been a powerful feeling of loss. And you're for being more than welcome in our humble home, Art. It's good to meet you.'

As Mr Leary shook Art's hand, Flo thought that never before had Mr Leary uttered words of love to her, and these were words of love. She swallowed once more the feeling of wanting to cry. 'Ta, Mr Leary, I've been at missing the pair of you, an' all. All of you.' She ruffled the hair of a clinging Kathy. 'By, lass, let me go. I need to cuddle Eunice. Oh, Eunice, it's good to see you, an' all, lass.'

Eunice crossed the room and hugged Flo to her. Flo filled with joy as she clung on to her fleshy body. Eunice truly was well again. As she released Flo, she went into Art's arms. 'Lovely to meet you, Art.' The pair hugged.

Art, who hadn't spoken till now, said, 'Well, I've heard a lot about you all, and now I find it's all true. That was a welcome I would only get from my folks back home.' Flo saw his emotions visible on his face. Eunice left his side, and Flo went into Art's arms. All of the family cheered. A warm happiness glowed inside Flo.

'Flo, I think the time is right for what we want to ask.' This, from Eunice, jelled with how Flo felt.

'Aye, I think it is an' all, Eunice.'

'You say it, Flo.'

'What? What is it you girls are cooking up now, then?'

Flo stood straight, and her hand found Art's. 'Mr and Mrs Leary, Eunice and I, we need to be

431

at thanking you, and want to tell you that you've been like a mam and dad to us. Eeh, we couldn't have had the life we've had without you. We want you to let us call you "Mam" and "Dad" from now on.'

Mrs Leary sat on the chair that had been pulled out from under the table, and Mr Leary put his arm around her shoulder. She looked up into his face. Flo saw him nod. Mrs Leary nodded back.

It was Mr Leary who spoke. His voice croaked. 'Sure, you'll both be doing us the greatest honour we could be asking for. And I am for thanking you from the bottom of me heart. We've always been for looking on you as ours. All three of yous.'

'Does that mean you're me mummy and daddy now, forever and ever?'

The seriousness of the way Kathy asked this question had Flo holding her breath.

'Aye, if it is as you're ready for us to be, me little lass.' Mr Leary smiled a gentle smile as he said this to Kathy.

Kathy thought for a moment. 'Aye, I'm ready. I didn't think you wanted to be, but I've been saying me prayers this good while that you would.'

Eunice acted first. She moved over to Mr and Mrs Leary and put her arms around them. 'Thanks, Mam and Dad. I feel as though I've just been born.' Her grin had them all laughing.

Flo moved over to them and joined in the hug. 'Aye, I do, an' all. And to the best mam and dad in the world.'

If she lived to be a hundred, Flo thought she would never forget this moment. Love flowed between her family, as Kathy clung to her. 'And do I have two sisters now, Flo? Is Eunice me sister, an' all?'

'She is, me little lass. And soon you'll have a brother-in-law to top it all.'

'Art can be me brother *now*, if he wants to be?'

Flo looked over at Art. Her heart filled to bursting as he nodded his head, and Kathy ran and jumped into his arms. Art swung her round, and the action showed his joy. But his joy and that of everyone in the room couldn't match hers, for Flo was bursting with it. *By, I'm the happiest woman in the whole wide world.*

The thought came that the world was a dangerous place and all of this could be shattered in an instant, as had happened to her before when she'd lost her darling Simon. But then something very strange happened. An image of Simon floated above the dresser. He was smiling, and a feeling entered Flo that told her he was always by her side, that he was happy for her and that he'd never let anything hurt her again.

She smiled back.

Art squeezed her arm. 'Are you all right, darling?'

'Aye, I am. I've never been more all right in me life.' And she meant it. With Simon looking out for them, she and Art were going to come through this war, she was sure of it.

26

Molly

Finding a Way

The tea burned Molly's lips. She sipped slowly, tentatively, blowing the steam away and making whirlpools in the top of her cup. Her thoughts were far away from the little kitchen in which she'd suffered so much abuse from her dad, but which now looked different as she'd painted it a bright yellow and had accessorized in blue. She'd been lucky to get the roll of yellow material covered in blue flowers, which had run to making curtains and a cloth for the table. The decor spoke of happiness and gaiety, but Molly felt neither.

The news that her dad had died in prison from a sudden heart attack was playing with her emotions. Part of her felt glad she'd never see him again, but the little girl inside her remembered the jolly, handsome, kind man who always had time for her, and had cared for her in a gentle way after her mama had died. *How did he turn into the monster he became?*

A tear plopped onto her cheek for the lost dad of her young days, though her heart was full of hate for the one who lay on a cold slab in the prison mortuary.

She'd refused to take charge of his body. They could do with it whatever they wanted to. She wanted none of the pretence of a funeral, where mourners gathered just for the food and drink.

Her thoughts went to David. How often that had happened since she'd been back home. How often her walks had taken her past the ruin of his house, and through into the park. It was a different feel from talking to Hettie. Hettie was gone – really gone – and Molly could connect with her spirit, but was David dead? She didn't know. There was plenty of talk of concentration camps, so maybe he was in one of those? The thought of the treatment of the Jews, which David had told her about, shuddered through her. *If David's alive, please God, keep him safe.* Funny how much she prayed these days. And how much store she now set by doing so; after all, prayers had become a solace to her at times, and she could say they were answered. Hadn't she prayed for release from the clutches of Eva, Gus and Lofty? And for an end to the Blitz? And for the safety of Ruby? All had happened; now all she needed was for God to bring David home.

Sighing, Molly picked up the Registration for Employment form. She and Ruby had both been issued with one, now that the welfare officers who'd been taking care of them and Martha, throughout the trial and since it ended, had finally declared them mentally able to cope, and their doctor had said they were strong enough physically.

They rarely saw or heard of Martha. It seemed that her parents' estate, which hadn't amounted to much at the time of their deaths, had been astutely taken care of by their solicitor, in the hope that one day Martha would turn up. Now that she had, she was a wealthy young woman and had taken an apartment in the West End. Molly doubted whether Martha would ever be called upon to take up war work, as the trauma she'd been through was considered to be far worse than that of Molly and Ruby. Another sigh escaped her as she thought of the hard-faced Martha. *Trauma? I doubt that lady knows the meaning of the word!*

Filling in the form, Molly put her preference down as the ATS. She knew this force was the least popular among women, as the conditions were said to be inferior to the other forces and ATS women had a name for being promiscuous, but she'd always fancied the army.

Just as she was signing it, Ruby burst through the door. 'Guess what? Trixie's here!' Ruby's excitement gave Molly a pang of jealousy – Ruby had always adored Trixie. Oh, Ruby returned the love Molly had for her, but theirs was just a friendship, whereas the feeling Ruby showed for Trixie seemed to be a lot more.

Trixie followed Ruby through the door. Molly noticed but didn't comment on the suitcase she placed at her feet. Standing up, Molly opened her arms to Trixie. 'What's wrong, love?'

Trixie's sobs filled the room, distressing Ruby enough to make her cry, too. 'Refill the kettle, Ruby. Come on, Trixie, let's go through to the parlour and you can tell us all about it.'

Molly and Ruby sat staring at Trixie. Molly could see that Ruby couldn't take in what she was hearing, no more than she could herself. They knew Peggy hadn't been well, but for her to have gone and died just didn't seem believable.

'We all took care of her. All of her girls, and there was a funeral to be proud of, with all the street workers – no matter who they worked for – turning out. It was like a bleedin' carnival, a right good send-off.'

'Oh, Trixie, I'm sorry. I always envied you having Peggy to look after you, when me and Ruby ... well, you know. More than most, you know what I mean. But for you, we'd still be there. If there's anything you need, no matter what it is, we're here for you, love.'

A tearful Ruby nodded.

'I'll be all right. I've had enough of working the streets. To tell the truth, I've had enough of men, an' all. I've volunteered for the Land Army.'

'What!' This was such a shock, and nothing Molly had ever dreamed of happening, that it caused her to giggle. 'What about that house you were always going to run, eh? I can't see you getting your hands dirty, Trixie.'

'I told yer, I've had enough. And if *I* have, I can't expect others to do the work for me, can I? Anyway, I'm capable, you know; you needn't bleedin' laugh at me.'

'I'm not. Oh, Trixie, you have to see the funny side, though. I can just picture you in wellies and dungarees,' Molly spluttered, then laughed uncontrollably. The others hesitated, but were joining in before long. It felt good. As if they were truly healed.

'Well, I'm joining them, an' all, then. And if

they don't send me to the same place as you, Trixie, I'll refuse to pick up a bloody spade!'

This, from Ruby, had them in stitches once more. 'Oh God. Help! Me sides are splitting.'

No one could help Molly as they were all in the same predicament. It was as if the world had gone mad, and it took a while for them to calm down. Each time they tried they would look at each other and burst out again.

When at last the bout of laughter passed, Molly asked Trixie to tell them all about it and what she'd done so far. 'Not a bleedin' lot. I went to the exchange to register me interest in war work, and the cow behind the desk looked me up and down and said, "Don't you think it's about time?" I told her to mind her own, and give me the bleedin' forms. She had the cheek to say, "I think you'd be more suited to one of the factories." And that's when the Land Girls popped into me head. It was a poster on the wall that did it – a jolly-hockey-sticks type waving a pitchfork. I wished I had one of them and could jab the miserable cow with it, so I thought: That'll do me. Every time I stuck a bale of hay with me pitchfork, I could imagine I was sticking it through all the men who've taken advantage of me.'

Molly wanted to laugh at this, but she'd exhausted her ability to and was only able to manage a giggle.

'So I'm fully signed up and awaiting me deployment. I've given this address, Molly, I hope yer don't mind. And if I could beg a bed till it happens, I'll be grateful to yer.'

'Yer can share mine, Trixie.' Ruby said this with

such enthusiasm that Molly found herself blushing.

But Trixie surprised her. She looked at Ruby with love in her eyes and, much as a lover might, answered, 'I'd like that, girl. I would.'

Molly didn't know what to make of everything.

'Molly, me and Ruby might as well tell yer. I expect yer'll be shocked, but we realized, when we were forced apart, just how much we meant to each other – and that it was more than in the way friends are close. We started writing to each other, and our letters turned to love letters. And since Ruby's been back, we've met up a few times and, well, we both know our love is different, but it's real. We want to be together for the rest of our days.'

'I – I had no idea! I don't know what to say.'

'Yer could bleedin' say yer pleased for us.'

'Trixie, don't talk to Molly like that. She's me best friend, and it's been a shock to her, that's all. Yer have to give her time to get used to it.'

'No, it's fine. I – I'm pleased for you. I am. Really pleased. Two of me best mates becoming a couple. It's wonderful. Like Ruby says, it's just so unexpected, that's all. Come here, let's give you both a big hug.'

The three huddled together. Molly couldn't really take in what they had told her, but these women had been her life for so long, and she knew she wouldn't have made it through without them, so no matter what made them happy, she was happy to accept it and allow their happiness.

'Well, get your stuff moved in then, Trixie, love. You're very welcome. And you move yours too,

Ruby. You two can have the room with the double bed in. When you're ready, we'll have a bite to eat. We can sit out in the back yard. It no longer smells of rotting meat. I had a couple of blokes come and clean it all down.' *And in doing so I've finally erased the smell of Foggy. May he rot in jail, the rotten sod!*

As Trixie and Ruby went through the door giggling together, Molly wondered if she'd ever get used to this turn of events. It embarrassed her, if she was truthful, but she was happy that these two dear people were at last safe and joyous. She'd try to celebrate that for their sake, and for the sake of the friendship she couldn't live without.

The situation wasn't without its irony. Ha, that'd make her dad turn on the cold slab: two lesbians in his bed! Molly nearly laughed out loud, but the photo of her dad and mum caught her eye. She picked it up off the top of the piano and for a moment wanted to take it out of its frame and rip it in half, keeping just the half with her mum on. But no. Her dad was her dad. She remembered him how he used to be. And for the sake of her mum, and any regrets that she herself might have in the future, she would contact the prison and tell them she'd changed her mind. She wouldn't have a big funeral for him; in fact she'd not tell anybody about it, but she'd have him brought to the church down the road and buried next to her mum. She could do that much for her mum, couldn't she?

On her way home from the church two weeks later, Molly felt a sadness in her that she couldn't explain. It wasn't for her dad, not altogether; but for everything – broken London, the lives lost, her own experiences, her mum, David; oh, just everything. She wished she could scream and scream, as that seemed the only thing that would give her release.

Turning into Sebastopol Road, she was taken aback for a moment. A large car, black and sleek, stood outside her house. It took a few seconds to register that it wasn't the car of her nightmares, but a Rolls-Royce... Flo! *Oh God, Flo and Art are here.*

Breaking into a run, Molly was out of breath by the time she arrived at her house. She banged the knocker, as if her life depended on someone opening the door, before she remembered she had her key. The door swung open and she was in Flo's arms.

'Oh, Flo, why didn't you tell me you were coming? Oh, I'm so pleased to see you.'

'Eeh, lass, I'm pleased to see you, an' all. Pauline's here, and Art, and we've met your mate, Ruby, and Trixie of course.'

'Oh, Flo. You're really here.'

'Aye, I am. And you're looking well, love. Though a bit on the tired side. Are you all right?'

Molly burst into tears.

'Eeh, lass, what's to do?'

Feeling stupid, Molly blurted out, 'I've just buried me dad.' But instead of the tears continuing, laughter bubbled up. 'He's gone, Flo. It's over. Over.' The tears took over once more, crumpling her body, draining her.

'Eeh, Molly, let's get you to a chair. Move,

everyone, let Molly come through.'

Molly saw a sea of faces lining the entrance hall. She couldn't distinguish who was who, but they all moved to let her into the parlour. Once there, they came into focus, and she smiled weakly at each of them.

'I'm sorry to intrude on your grief, lav. Here, take me hanky.'

'Thanks, Pauline. It's good to see you, love. And you're not intruding and this ain't grief – at least, not for me dad, it's not. I think seeing Flo just released a knot that needed shifting, though it will never go until I know what's happened to David.'

Why she said that, she didn't know. Only Ruby knew anything of David, and she doubted she'd remember the early days, when Molly had talked of trying to get a message to him.

'The kettle's hot, and I was just going to make a cuppa. Me and Trixie will bring it through – the tray's all ready. I've told Trixie about David, so you tell the others while we're busy in the kitchen, eh, love?'

'So you remember then, Ruby?'

'Of course I do. How could I forget the pain I knew that you, me best mate, was suffering.'

'Ta, Ruby. I could do with unburdening meself. Everyone, find a pew.'

Flo sat next to her and Molly felt her arm come round her. When Molly had finished telling them about David, Art was the first one to speak. 'You say he was a pilot, lost over Italy? I've heard of a list that is kept of servicemen in concentration camps. It's part of the Geneva Convention that

442

all prisoners have to be reported to their own countries. That's how they are able to let families know that loved ones are prisoners of war. I'll try to find out for you, especially with David being in the RAF – he's one of our own. Write David's full name down for me, and I'll do what I can.'

'Aye, and me an' all. Me mate who I live with, she's from top-drawer folk and they have their own solicitor. He's been helpful to me in getting information about Roland. You know, me friend as is in prison. I could ask this solicitor to help, an' all.'

Hope surged through Molly. She looked from one to the other. In a way, she didn't want to know, in case David's name wasn't on this list they were talking about and she had to finally face the truth of his death. But neither could she stop them from trying, as a big part of her wanted to know. Had to know.

'Reet, we have news for you, an' all, Molly. Me and Art are engaged – look!'

Molly felt her heart fill with warmth, shutting all the cold fear from her. This was such good news. 'Oh, Flo, Art, congratulations, I'm so pleased. We knew you loved him, didn't we, Pauline?'

Pauline nodded. She seemed a bit overcome, but then she had her own troubles. But, Molly decided, she wouldn't ask about them now, for there was a celebration to be had. 'Right, hold the tea. That lot who raided this place left behind an opened bottle of whisky, as they said they couldn't be sure it hadn't been bought legitimately by me dad. I think this calls for us all having a drop.' Glad to have the distraction, she jumped up and went to the cabinet in the corner of the room. 'Here it is. Ruby, get some glasses, there's a love.'

With the glasses filled, Molly lifted hers high. 'Here's to Flo and Art: may they have a long and happy life together.'

Everyone clinked glasses and murmured, 'Flo and Art', before taking a sip. Amidst the coughing that followed from the women, as none of them were used to such fiery liquid, the chatter started up, mostly questions: When would the wedding be? Where? And would they live in England?

'Eeh, hold on, let me get me breath,' Flo laughed, as she told them how the wedding wasn't being planned until the end of the war. Though she sobered as she said they had discussed where they would live, and she would be going to Canada.

Art broke the silence that followed this. 'I'm sorry to take your Flo away from you, but I have a business that I will inherit. I have to be there to run it. But we have plenty of room, and you're all welcome to come and visit, any time.'

Even knowing this, Molly felt a lump of sadness.

Flo lightened the moment. 'By, girls, why the long faces? We have a war to win first. This is 1941 and the world is in turmoil. Sadly, it could be years before all this is over, so I'm not going just yet.'

'But we are, Flo.' Molly told of the plans they all had; and how she was to go for a medical in a few days and if found to be fit would be despatched to goodness knows where for training.

And how Ruby and Trixie would be both going to a farm in the Midlands to work as Land Girls.

Molly could see all of this had an impact on Flo, but she soon brightened. 'Well, we will all get together when we can. We'll all have leave to take. We can write to each other, and make arrangements to see each other whenever it's possible.'

'That's right, we can. And, Flo, we have news for you all, an' all. Me and Trixie are a couple!'

Molly watched Flo, but there was no sign of shock or embarrassment on her face, only joy. 'By, I'm so glad as you've found happiness together. No one deserves it more than you two, after all you've been through. I knaw we hadn't met until today, Ruby, but you've been in me mind ever since Molly told me about you. I'm reet happy for you.' Flo hugged and kissed Ruby and Trixie, and at that moment and for the first time, Molly really accepted them herself.

She'd never told them any different or showed how she felt about their union, but there had been dissent in her. Now that had gone. She rose and joined in the hugging, finally hugging Pauline to her. This kindly little woman had saved her life, and had been with her through some of the worst moments of it. She hadn't spoken much since being here, but now she said, 'And I have happy news an' all. Me mam and me kids are coming home.'

Everyone clapped, even though Trixie and Ruby hadn't got much idea what Pauline was talking about.

'Play the piano, Molly. Let's have a jig.'

'I will, Ruby, yes. I feel like a jig meself. Fill the

445

glasses up again. I didn't say, but I have another bottle stashed away. Let's have a party. Bugger the war. We're going to celebrate.'

As she lifted the lid to the piano, she wished with all her heart that she had something to celebrate herself. But she'd hide that feeling. She wouldn't spoil the day. These were her friends; they had saved her life between them and she'd rejoice in the good news they all had to celebrate, and would leave her own sorrow until she was in her room at night, as she'd always tried to. And she'd hang on to the hope that Flo and Art had given her.

As she started playing 'Show me the way to go home', they all joined in singing and laughing. When the song came to an end, Art said, 'Play one that Flo can sing to. What about one from the musical you're in rehearsals for, with your amateur theatrical group, Flo?'

'Eeh, they don't want to listen to me.'

A chorus of 'We do' set up around the room. 'Come on, Flo, you say we can't come and watch you on the stage, but we'd love to be part of it.'

'All right. How about "Follow the Yellow Brick Road". That's in keeping with the mood we're all in, and I can do a comic version of each animal and the Tin Man's part.'

'Give me a mo.' Molly could play by ear, but always needed to play a few notes until she got the music into her. She hummed the tune to herself as she picked out the notes. 'Right, I've got it. Off we go.'

The atmosphere that followed was like the pantomime that Molly's mum had taken her to years and years ago, and she felt her heart lifting. She was so glad Flo hadn't chosen 'Somewhere over the rainbow', as she didn't think she could have stood the lyrics of that. As she looked around the room at the happy, smiling faces of those she loved, and watched Flo's hilarious antics as she mimicked the movements of the Tin Man, a smile spread across her face. No matter what she'd been through, without doing so she would never have met these folk, and they had enriched her life. Yes, she was lucky, but she wished with all her heart that the wonderful things the Wizard of Oz could do included bringing her David back to her.

27

Molly

1943 – Inspiration Strikes

Molly slumped down on her bed. The other beds in the Nissen hut were empty and she felt glad to have a short respite, before more of the spotters and telegraph operators came in, after their celebrations with the gunners ended.

Trained as a spotter and stationed just outside Reading for the last two years, Molly did most of her work on the cold embankment, training her sights on the sky, searching for incoming German aircraft. Usually, thank goodness, it was a fruitless operation, but tonight an aircraft had been spotted and she had been one of the two ATS who had fixed the height and range. A direct hit had occurred, but Molly couldn't find it in her to cheer as the rest of the team had, or to join in the revelry that followed. Her imagination had shown her David's plane being hit, and the Germans cheering as he fell to his fate.

One thing had lifted her. The German pilot in the plane tonight had bailed out and she'd just heard he'd been taken prisoner. *Please let it have been so for David.*

Digging out her mail from where she'd tucked it under her pillow when it arrived, she settled down to read it. Just seeing the envelopes cheered her, as she could tell by the writing and the postmarks that one was from Flo and the other from Ruby. Not that she received mail from anyone else, but to have them both write to her at the same time was unusual.

Flo told her how Roland was now out of prison, but was finding life very difficult. His old college had snubbed him, and though he'd tried to revive his private night-school, he'd had no takers:

He's not short of money, mind, but getting more and more depressed as he feels rejected by the society he was once an upstanding member of. Eeh, Molly, I just don't know how to help him.

There's something else as well. He has this friend, Frazer. Roland has told me they have fallen in love, but that they don't have a relationship, as Roland is afraid, which is understandable. But he is denying himself any happiness.

Frazer is a lawyer, and his father is in banking and investments. He has an office in Brighton and has offered Roland a job, but Roland won't hear of it, even though Frazer lives there, having set up a practice that handles a lot of his father's clients. Roland tells me that Frazer thinks they could have a good life there together, but no. Roland's fear holds him back and their only contact is by letter.

I just don't know how his life will work out, and am afraid he'll end up old and lonely, as Frazer may get fed up and meet someone else. And I will be thousands of miles away, and Roland has no one but me. When I speak to him about this, he gets very upset, but just can't see a way he can change things.

Anyroad, how are you doing? I hope you're still happy. I'm getting increasingly worried as 'A' is away on business more and more.

Molly knew this meant Art was flying more and more missions. Something she knew already, as many times she watched the RAF squadrons going out. It had become the norm for the ATS spotters on duty to count the planes out and then count them in again. If the same number came back, they celebrated; but if any were missing, the mood was very sombre. At those times Molly dreaded being called to the sergeant's office to take a call from Flo. Such was the daily fear of their lives.

Flo never spoke of the official work she did, only of her work with the Salvation Army, which was mostly with the homeless now; and of her social life, cither with Art, if he had leave at the same time as her, or with her friends Belinda and

Petulia. Molly hadn't met these ladies, though she did have a photo of Flo with them. They were all wearing the costumes from one of their concerts. They both sounded fun-loving girls and really nice and caring of Flo, but then that was a measure of Flo's personality: she was accepted and loved by people from all walks of life. They only had to meet her to love her.

Molly missed her so much between the times when they could meet up, usually in London with Pauline for a cup of tea in a cafe. Though once Molly had been able to stay over and they'd gone to His Majesty's Theatre and watched a hilarious comedy called *Lady Behave!*, about a billionaire getting drunk at a party and marrying a fellow partygoer. It had been a wonderful night. London was full of Americans and the atmosphere was electric. One day she would take Ruby and Trixie there.

Opening Ruby's letter, Molly expected it to be full of the fun they were having: going to village dances where the only men were too old to fight and were with their wives, so it was acceptable for the girls to dance together – something that suited Ruby and Trixie. But what she found alarmed and distressed her.

Trixie had been involved in an accident when they were doing something Ruby called threshing, and it looked likely she might lose the use of most of her arm. Oh God!

Molly read on with increasing concern:

Oh, Molly, I just don't know what to do. At best, the arm is going to be very weak; at worst, they may have to amputate. Please try to come and visit us.

We're worried an' all about our future. We've been thinking of trying to get a place together and getting jobs to support us. It has been so exciting planning it, as our private moments together are so few and far between. Now Trixie may not be able to work. I'm really scared, as she is depressed and said something about going back to her old life, if there is nothing else she can do.

This shocked and frightened Molly. Sitting up, she tried to blot out the image of Trixie once more walking the sleazy streets of Soho; the danger she would be in, and the depths she might have to sink to, as a prostitute who would be considered a cripple. Somehow Molly had to prevent that.

The idea came to Molly a few days later, when she overheard a conversation between two of her colleagues. One asked the other what she was planning to do when the war was over. The other replied that her mum was selling the guesthouse she had in Brighton, and the family were planning to emigrate to Australia.

It was hearing Brighton mentioned that brought Roland to her mind, and how his friend lived down there, and how there seemed no future for them.

This wasn't the first time she'd been thinking about how difficult it was for couples like Roland and Frazer and Trixie and Ruby to live together and sustain a lifestyle. The predicament Trixie and Ruby were in meant that she'd pondered the problem, looking for solutions, for most of her free time. Though she knew it must be easier for women, as it was acceptable for two girls to live together, just as it was for women at any age, even old maids. But now, with Trixie possibly unable to earn a living, the prospects for Ruby and Trixie seemed really limited.

Offering her friends a permanent home wasn't an option. Though Molly loved them, she would be forever embroiled in what they were doing. Besides, she'd been thinking lately of selling up herself and starting a new life in another country after the war – probably Canada, to be near Flo.

But what if two homosexual couples, two men and two women, had a pretend marriage between the men and the women? That would give them a 'normal' life to present to the world. Then, if both couples lived together, who would know who slept with whom? And to make it happen for Roland and Frazer and Ruby and Trixie, she could sell her property, buy this guesthouse from her colleague's mother, and make part of it into two flats with some letting room. The girls could have one flat and run the business, and the men could have their own flat and live a completely separate life from the girls and continue in their careers. No one would ever know. No one who didn't know and accept them, that is. *It's the answer. It has to be.*

Thinking her plan through, Molly realized she'd need some capital investment from the men; they'd have to be equal partners, but by all accounts they were both well off, and Ruby and Trixie could pay rent from their business. *Perfect.*

She'd write this minute to Flo to see what she thought. *Oh, I feel really excited. This is a solution, a real possibility.* The thought came to her of what she'd wear to the double wedding, and she laughed. *Me and Flo could be bridesmaids.*

The whole idea had lifted her so much; she couldn't wait to put it to all concerned. She could help them to fool the world, while they lived the life they wanted to and, hopefully, found lasting happiness together. The more she thought about it, the more she hoped it would all happen.

28

Flo

1946 – The Wedding and Putting on *The Wizard of Oz*

Flo twirled round in front of the long mirror in her bedroom. The happiness that clothed her was epitomized by the ivory-coloured, beautiful calf-length damask wedding dress she wore. Art had sent the material over from Canada. It had been devastating when he had been posted back home after the war ended. But now he was demobbed and working back in the family business. At last he was here in England again, and this was their wedding day.

After the end of the war Flo had stayed on at Bletchley for a few months with Belinda and

Petulia. There was still work to do in the Japanese section, as that war hadn't ended at the time Germany surrendered, and there was sensitive material to categorize, ready for it to be archived by the government, as everything had to remain secret for the next thirty years. Soon after Hiroshima, her work came to an end and it wasn't long before she, too, was demobbed.

Not ready to go back to her old life in Leeds, Flo had gone to London for a while. She'd taken a job in an office and rented a flat, but it had only been temporary, until Art could come back to her and this day, which they'd waited so long for, could be arranged. Once plans could be made, Flo had gone home.

Whilst in London she'd met up often with Pauline, and had met her Fred, who'd returned all in one piece and was a jolly soul. Pauline had looked so happy. They were soon to move into a council house of their own, as was Fred's right. Molly, Belinda and Petulia had also been regular visitors, but she hadn't seen Ruby and Trixie, or Roland and Frazer, as they were now all living in Brighton. That would change today, though. Happiness warmed her at the thought of having all her friends around her on her special day.

Belinda and Petulia had taken on the task of making Flo's beautiful wedding gown. The bodice fitted to her waist and had a heart-shaped neckline, prettily edged with lace. The back of the bodice had a row of pearl buttons from her neck to her waist, and a string of pearls formed a plaited band where the buttons ended, making the back view as pretty as the front. The skirt flowed to a hem of lace. She loved it, and felt special wearing it. Belinda had even made her a hat to go with it. She'd used an old straw summer hat with a large floppy brim, and moulded it into shape with fine wire, so that one side stood up and the other draped down to Flo's shoulder. The whole hat was then covered with swathes of damask and with netting of the same shade, which extended over the brim to drape over Flo's face; it felt as though she was wearing a veil. Where the materials were fastened to the hat, they were cleverly held in place and disguised on the lower side of the brim by a bunch of forget-me-nots that Belinda had made out of blue silk. 'Something borrowed and something blue,' she'd said. 'The forget-me-nots will be your blue, and here – these pearls my grandmother left me will be something borrowed.'

The pearls were exquisite, a single row with a much larger pearl in the centre. Flo picked up the gold box that contained them and stood for a moment, looking down at them as they lay on their bed of black velvet. She hardly dared touch them; they must be so valuable.

Everything Belinda and Petulia had done for her was perfect, even down to the soft ivory satin shoes they'd found for her, with a little heel and a strap across her foot, which looked so dainty; and the white silk stockings, which added a lovely touch and felt heavenly on her legs.

At times she'd had to rein in their ideas, as you would think they were making a costume for one of their theatrical productions, the way they wanted to add sequins and bows to the bodice and flounces to the skirt. But it had all been fun, and she'd been so grateful to them for taking time away from the theatrical-costume business they'd set up.

Both had found that they had talent and a vivid imagination to put into such work, during their time of producing various plays and musicals at Bletchley. And both were skilled seamstresses, as sewing and embroidery had been a huge part of their education to turn them into capable women for marriage. Not that she could see either of them marrying for a long time, though both of them had a suitor now. Belinda's was the son of her solicitor, and Petulia's was an actor, apparently much disapproved of by her family. But both girls declared they were too tied up in building their careers to think about marriage. So their poor young men had to hang around a lot and often found themselves roped into delivering costumes across London.

The door to Flo's bedroom opened and Molly walked in. She looked a picture, in her blue bridesmaid's frock. She, Eunice and Kathy were to be in attendance today. Their dresses were of satin, and of a similar style to Flo's, their hair held in a band of forget-me-nots. All of their outfits had been made by Belinda and Petulia, too, and her own forget-me-nots had been made out of remnants of the material used for the bridesmaids' dresses. Flo didn't know how to thank them.

'Oh, Flo, you look beautiful.' Molly wiped away a tear. Flo hoped it was put there by joy and not sadness. Molly covered it up by using a mockcrossness in her tone. 'But you're being very slow – come on, time's getting on. Here, let me fasten those pearls for you.'

'Ta, Molly. Eeh, I'm so happy and excited. I've been like that since I helped you arrange Roland and Ruby's and Frazer and Trixie's double wedding. I couldn't wait for me own, and now it's here. By, we pulled that wedding off, though, didn't we?'

'Ha, Frazer's distant relatives and his friends were funny. The whole plan had come together so well, but they were very shocked by what they discovered. Their faces at the wedding reception were a picture – and their comments! They couldn't accept Frazer marrying an East Ender, or understand him having a double wedding with Roland. But then coming to terms with the staid type they'd all known Roland to be, and him also marrying an East Ender, was beyond them. They left soon after the wedding breakfast. We all partied then, didn't we? We had a ball.'

'We did, but I think it was as much for the end of the war as anything else. I can't believe that was eighteen months ago.'

'No, nor me. It's all working out for the best, an' all. Trixie manages well with her withered arm, and helped by the love and support of Ruby she does most of the cooking for their guests, and for the cafe. That was a great idea of Ruby's to open the street-level rooms of the guesthouse as a cafe; it's very popular and looks set to bring them an income all year round.'

'It was a new beginning for them all, and put my mind at rest – it's wonderful for me to think of Roland feeling happy and settled. You did a wonderful thing for him.'

'Flo, you reached out to me in my darkest hour. You saved my life. I wanted to give something back to you. Helping your friend was my way of doing that.'

'It was a good day when you came to the Sallies' van. You're a great friend, Molly. And I'm glad as you had enough money over to help you have this respite, after your own demob. Have you settled into your new flat?'

'I manage. It's a bit lonely... Flo, would you mind if I emigrated and came to live in Canada, somewhere near to you and Art? I could do with a new beginning. A complete change.'

'Oh, Molly, I'd love that. Oh, I hope you do. We'll help you to find somewhere, and Art will be really happy, as he's worrying about me settling down. Eeh, you've made me day.'

'Ha, getting married is supposed to make your day, love, so let's get going. I know a bride can keep her fiancé waiting at the altar, but not for long. Everyone's ready.'

As Flo swept down the stairs she was met by Eunice and an excited Kathy, both looking so lovely. Both screamed with delight on seeing Flo, and Kathy hugged her. 'You're like a fairy, Flo. A princess.'

Flo eased Kathy away from her. 'Eeh, me little lass.' She still thought of Kathy as this, even though she was now fifteen, almost sixteen. 'Let go of me – you'll crush me dress, and yours, an' all. You look so lovely, my Kathy. And you, Eunice. I am blessed to have such beautiful sisters.

Where's Mam and Dad?'

'Mam had to leave. We told her to come up and see you first, but we think she was too overcome. Besides, the car taking her to the church has to pick up your friends, Belinda and Petulia, from their guesthouse and then come back for us bridesmaids before you can set off with Dad.'

'Eeh, I've made everyone late. I've been daydreaming, and I wanted to get everything reet.'

A hooter sounding had Molly, Eunice and Kathy running to the door. They waved as they left. Molly turned and smiled and said, 'See you at the church, love. Good luck.'

For the first time, Flo felt nerves clutch at her stomach. The last years had been tough, but they'd all come through – all her 'waifs and strays', as Roland called them. Everyone was settled in the life they wanted, though perhaps not Molly, but she was making the best of things; and a new start might be just the thing for her. And now to see that Eunice was so well and happy; and Kathy too, working with the lovely Mr Godfern and his daughter, now that their business had picked up and was thriving again. Kathy was looking forward to following in Eunice's footsteps to become a nurse, when she was old enough. Though Eunice would soon be giving up that work, when her junior doctor qualified and they could marry. By, that was a day Flo would come home for, as she would as often as she could.

Her mind went to Simon and Lucinda. If only they were here, too. That would be so wonderful, but she knew they were here by her side in spirit. She sent a little greeting up to them. *Eeh, me friends, I miss you. I hope as you're together and happy. Thanks for all you did for me, in accepting me. And, Simon, I loved it at Bletchley. By, we cracked some codes and foiled them Germans, just like you taught us to. And we had fun, an' all, with the theatrical group. You'd have loved that. Well, wish me luck, the pair of you. Here goes.*

'Is that you ready now, Flo?'

'Aye, Dad, I'm ready.'

'For sure you look a picture. Your mam's going to be crying enough tears to put hell's fire out.'

Flo smiled. 'Thanks for being me dad. I've never said, but I love you, and Mam, and I'm going to miss you. You'll come over to Canada to see me, won't you?'

Mr Leary nodded. Flo could see he didn't trust himself to say any more. He put out his arm and she took it. When she stepped outside the little cottage, a roar went up. All the neighbours stood cheering her. She waved and smiled. She was truly ready to go to her Art. All the ghosts had been laid to rest.

The day had passed in a dream. Art had never left her side. And his mam and dad weren't far behind him. Flo loved his mam, and couldn't think how this little woman could have given birth to a son who would tower over her, as he did. Though she showed a strength of character that belied her height. Art took after his dad, who, although not as tall as Art, had the same hair and hazel eyes. He had a way of making you feel you were in a conspiracy with him against Art's mam, but it was all done in a joking manner that had Flo giggling.

There'd been time during the afternoon to spend with Ruby and Trixie and Roland and Frazer, and with Pauline and Fred and their boys, and Pauline's mum. But at last Flo had found a quiet moment with her own mam. Mrs Leary looked lovely in her cream suit with a lemon blouse and navy hat. 'This is a grand day, so it is, Flo. And I'm for being very happy. Your Art is a fine fellow. He'll be for looking after you, so he will.'

'He will, Mam.' Flo took her mam's hand and held it. Sometimes words weren't needed and this was one of those times. Her mam broke the silence between them. 'Well, me darling, go forward with me blessing and be happy. I'm at working on Mr Leary; he can be spending his savings on paying for a trip to Canada for me, and he's for knowing he'll have to give in to me wishes. We'll be with you afore you know it.'

Flo had been amused to hear a slur in her mam's words. Everyone was having such a wonderful time, and the bar was making a good profit.

The time was coming when she and Art would have to leave. They were honeymooning in a remote cottage in the Lake District and that was a few hours' drive away. Though Art had said that maybe they would stop in a hotel on the way, depending on how they felt. Flo didn't mind, either way; she just wanted to begin her married life with the love of her life, her beloved Art.

There was just Belinda and Petulia to say goodbye to, before everyone followed them outside. Belinda caught hold of Flo's arm. 'We've had a wonderful day, Flo. I'm so glad you came to Bletchley. I'm that glad I'm almost thanking Hitler. You'll keep in touch, won't you?'

'She'll do more than that, Belinda. Flo, I've a proposition to put to you.'

'Petulia, you can't – not here, not today.'

'I have to, for when else can I? You sail to Canada in a month's time, don't you, Flo?'

'I do. Me and Art come back here for a while, to spend time with me family, and as you know, we spend our last week in London afore we sail. But I don't think I'll have time to visit you both.'

'You won't have to. I'm planning a reunion of the Bletchley Theatrical Club. I have everyone on board – I just need you. We want to put on a production of *The Wizard of Oz* to raise funds for the homeless of the East End. I've found a venue, one of the few church halls that's still standing near the dock, St Mary's. And it's all arranged for the week you're in London.'

'Eeh, it sounds grand. But what about rehearsals and costumes? By, it's all making me nervous, just thinking about it.'

'Just say yes, and leave the rest to us. We need you as Dorothy. You'll only have to run through the positions on the stage. Besides, most people can only travel to London on the day, so we're just going to ad-lib. It'll be fun. I'm staying in London with Betsy Randell – you know, the one who played the Glass Cat and a host of other bit-parts. And me and Belinda will make all the costumes – we have all your sizes. It's not as if there's a cast of thousands; there's only twenty of us, and we'll use the same script of the adaptation that Captain Gregory did for our production

462

at Bletchley. I've given a copy to your mother to hold till you come back, so you can refresh your memory then. We did them on a printing machine we bought recently.'

'Eeh, it sounds grand. We'll be staying at the Savoy.' Flo just had time to give Petulia the date they were to arrive in London, before Art called out to her.

As she kissed Belinda and Petulia, it struck her how strange life had turned out to be. Here she was, mixing with the likes of ex-debutantes and posh folk, and staying in places like the Savoy, as if she was used to doing such things all her life. By, war changed people's lives in so many ways. And sometimes for the better, though if she could bring back all those who'd lost their lives, she'd gladly have stayed as she was. She caught sight of Art beckoning her forward, and she knew that wasn't altogether true. She wouldn't have missed meeting him for the world.

They drove away to the clatter of tins and old boots that had been tied to their car, and the sound of cheering and shouts of 'Good luck'.

Flo snuggled up to Art.

'All comfortable, Mrs Tendray?'

The sound of her new name rang in her ears. Yes, she was comfortable, and happy, and knew that she would be for the rest of her life.

The week passed by so quickly, and it didn't seem any time at all until Flo and Art were back in Leeds. They'd booked into the Parkland Hotel, and on arrival had a message to ring Belinda's solicitor.

Intrigued, Flo dialled his number.

'Flo, congratulations on your wedding. I hope you'll be very happy.'

She didn't know what to say. She'd never been on close terms with Mr Westbury, though he'd been very helpful in getting her to see Roland that time he was in prison. The memory shuddered through her as she thanked him.

'I hope you don't mind me finding out from Belinda what you were up to and where you were staying, only I have news.'

'Oh no, Mr Westbury. It's grand to hear from you. What news?'

'Do you remember you were asking after a Mr Gould – David Gould, a pilot in the RAF?'

Flo drew in a deep breath and waited.

'Well, my friend in the Ministry of Defence office has just contacted me. He'd kept my request on file for further information, and there's someone who's turned up who may be your man.'

'What! Oh God, where? Is he all right? Eeh, Mr Westbury, I do hope as it is him.'

'He's in hospital; well, not hospital as such, but one of those convalescent places for exservicemen. It's called St Joseph's and is in Maidstone. He found his way to England from Italy, but didn't know who he was or why he was here. It appears that he wasn't captured, but was cared for by some remote farmers. They helped him to get back here. He gave his name as George Black, which we think is an assumed name that he must have been living under. He came back in his pilot's uniform; the farmer's wife had patched

464

and cleaned it. And although there is no record of a George Black ever serving in the RAF, this fellow had obviously lost his memory and could only give the investigators a letter that the farmer had given him. It was in Italian and had to be translated.'

Flo swallowed, and a part of her was praying as she listened.

'It appears that his plane came .down. The Italians had written down when that happened, and how they managed to get him out of the wreckage and nursed him over a long time back to health. They buried what was left of his aircraft, so that anyone snooping around couldn't detect that he'd ever been there, and nothing could be seen from the air. When enough time went by and he'd recovered, they put him to work on their farm and passed him off as a relative. Though they never knew his name, as he couldn't remember it. Anyway, investigations have now determined who he really is and apparently, on being told, some of his memory is coming back.'

'Eeh, that's a grand story. Ta, Mr Westbury. Ta ever so much. Can we go and see him, do you reckon?'

'That depends. I can ask, of course, but if I remember correctly, you don't know him and he doesn't know you. You were trying to find out for a friend who was engaged to him, weren't you?'

'Aye, but ... well, I don't want her hurt. What if he don't remember her, or doesn't want to? I'd rather me husband and I visited him first, to see how the land lies.'

'I'll ask. But do you know anything about him

that would help the investigators? They know he lived in Edmonton.'

'Me friend told me his parents went to America. They're Jews and were afraid of England being invaded, but I don't think she knows where they went. They owned a shoe shop, and David was a lawyer.'

'Right-o, leave it with me. You're going to be in Leeds for a couple of weeks, aren't you?'

'Aye, I am. But we would travel from here to visit David. Eeh, do your best, Mr Westbury. Me friend has never stopped loving David, or hoping that one day he'll return, and she deserves a chance at being reunited with him. I'd like to try to pave the way for that to happen.'

'I will, Flo. Funny you and I have never met, and yet I feel as though I know you. You strike me as a kind person, with everyone's interest at heart.'

'Aye, and you do me, an' all. I've never paid for your services, but you've allus helped me. Ta for that. I'm really grateful.'

'Ha, don't forget my prospective daughter-in-law in all this. Whatever Belinda says, we all jump to and get done!'

Flo laughed with him about this, before putting the telephone down.

Molly arrived at St Joseph's, a monastery-type building outside Maidstone, surrounded by fields, trees and tranquillity. This was all so surreal to her.

Flo had paved the way for this visit. She and Art had been to see David and talked to him. It ap-

466

peared he was still fuzzy about his past, and was very frail in his mind. Flo had warned her that David shuffled around a lot. But the amazing thing was: he remembered Molly. At least he'd said he had a picture of a beautiful girl in his mind, and he'd described her. He'd also said that he knew this girl was very precious to him and that he wanted to find her.

Flo had said David didn't appear to remember the circumstances that he knew Molly under, or mention anything about her leaving, before he'd made that fateful flight.

Walking through the gates of St Joseph's took all her strength. Compelled by her love for David and yet afraid of what she would find, Molly felt sick with nerves.

She saw him before he saw her, even though he was sitting on a bench facing the gate. Was he waiting for her, and did he even remember that she was coming?

His head was down, his feet shuffling the pebbles beneath him.

'David?'

He looked up. He was beautiful. 'Oh, David.'

'M-Molly?'

He knew her name! 'Oh yes, David, my love, it's me – Molly.'

David stood. His slouching body gradually straightened.

Molly waited. They were feet apart, and she wanted to run to him and feel his arms around her. The moment seemed to stretch to eternity. Tears wet her face. 'My David.'

His arms opened. She went into them. Not in

the rushed way she wanted to, as David seemed afraid. Fragile.

They stood for a moment holding each other, their bodies swaying, David's tears wetting her hair, her own tears soaking her face.

'Sit down, my love. Let's talk, eh?'

As if he were a child, David sat down. His hand had taken hers and he held onto it. The years rolled away as he said, 'You're beautiful, Molly.'

'Do you remember me, David?'

'I remember that I love you, and always have.'

Her body shivered. The woman he'd loved in the pure way they had known was no more. So much had happened to her. She felt dirty, and unworthy of him. Part of her wanted to run back through those gates she'd come through, and keep on running till she dropped down dead. But she had to remember what Flo had said to her, when she'd been speaking to her on the phone: 'None of that was your doing, Molly. Please don't let the sins of others ruin the rest of your life, as they did while they had you in their clutches.'

Flo was right. The road to David's recovery was going to be a long one, but she was going to be with him every step of the way. Maybe one day she would tell David the truth, but that was for the future. For now, she had him back with her, and she was never going to let him go.

'David, would you like to come and stay with me? I can look after you, and whatever treatment you need, I can bring you back here for. I have a car now and I drive.'

David looked at her, and his eyes – his lovely blue eyes – bored into hers. 'Molly, I – I remember some things. My house, my family. Each day, pieces come back to me, and that has been happening since I came in here and they told me who I was; and more so since your friend came and told me about you. With you, I think I can get better, but I don't know if the doctor here will let me come with you. I want to. I want that more than anything in the world. I know we belong to each other. We do, don't we, Molly? You and me, we belong to each other.'

'We do, darling. We do.'

Flo heard the music. It was her big moment, her favourite in the whole production, the moment she sang 'Somewhere over the rainbow'. As she began the first lyrics, the hall was hushed. A sea of faces looked up at her. Amongst them she could see Ruby and Trixie, and Roland and Frazer, and Pauline and Fred and their family – all looking at her with love in their expressions. And next to them her darling Art, and his parents, who'd been touring England and had now joined her and Art in London in readiness to go to Southampton, where they would all board the ship for Canada. Her 'somewhere' – where her happiness lay.

The door at the back of the hall opened.

For a moment she couldn't believe her eyes, then a deep happiness entered her as she gazed at Molly and David standing in the open doorway, smiling at her, their arms linked, their bodies close.

Though tears of joy choked her, Flo raised her voice and sang the next line, putting all her heart and soul into it.

469

And their dreams had come true, as the song said they could. She'd dreamed of the day Molly would be reunited with her David, and now that had happened.

And she'd dreamed for so long of the day when she and Art could be together forever. And that had happened, too.

War had torn them all apart in one way or another, and had shattered so many lives, but that terrible time had enabled Flo to reach out to Pauline and Molly.

Together, they had come through it all.

Author's Note

I am the proud owner of a wonderful book written by a remarkable lady, and personally signed by her – *Secret Postings: Bletchley Park to the Pentagon* by Charlotte Webb.

Charlotte, in her late eighties, still works at Bletchley Park, the code-breaking centre of England, where, in strict secrecy, she was stationed during the war and helped to make a great contribution towards victory and the saving of thousands of lives.

Through my friend, the author Kate Thompson, who facilitated a telephone call to Charlotte – known by the short version of her second Christian name, Betty – I experienced first-hand the 'coming to life' of this mysterious place.

Betty spoke of the long hours she worked and of the sometimes boring life she led at Bletchley, but she spoke with pride in her voice, as time has made her aware of the great importance of the work she was involved in. I got the impression, though, that the work she does now – welcoming guests, answering questions, giving talks and writing her memoir – is a much more interesting existence than code-breaking was.

One of the things that comes through when researching Bletchley Park is the secrecy. Very few people knew the place existed during the war, and it wasn't until thirty years after the event that the real activity that took place there was revealed.

I visited Bletchley Park as part of my research for *Brighter Days Ahead*. It is a fascinating place, needing more than a day to absorb everything there is to see and experience. But for what I needed, as my story was only to have the Park as a background setting as very few scenes actually take place there, my visit furnished me with a clear understanding of the atmosphere and the conditions the people worked under, and also acquainted me with the machinery and some of the terms used at the time. In just one day, I was steeped in the knowledge of how life was for the code-breakers, and the girls who sat for hours feeding machines with words that meant nothing to them, but which had a massive impact on wartime decisions.

Brighter Days Ahead is a gritty tale set around the private lives of a few fictitious characters who worked at the Park. Although we know that the wonderful Alan Turing, one of the men based at Bletchley Park who contributed so much with his work developing the Enigma Machine, did have homosexual tendencies, Simon, one of my main characters, is not based on him. Nor are any of the events that happened to Simon in any way related to anyone who ever worked at the Park. They are a figment of my imagination, based on my knowledge of how homosexuality was perceived at the time; as a criminal offence, punishable by imprisonment, according to the law of the land.

The secrecy surrounding Bletchley both during the war years and after was held with pride and honour, and I hope that comes across in my novel. Although the people who lived in the area were aware that something went on there, most thought that it was an administrative hub of the war. However, I have taken poetic licence in going a little further than that as it is very difficult not to mention the place and the function it serves when writing a novel and setting it in a certain place. And so, although I have allowed the friends and family of the characters who work at the Park to know where their loved ones were based – which didn't happen during the war – I have not allowed them to know what went on at Bletchley. I hope that veterans will forgive me for this and recognize that I had no choice if my story was to have any substance.

I highly recommend a visit to Bletchley Park. There is so much to see and wonder over. Those who run the Park strive to keep the memory of the vital work carried out there alive in such a way as to make the experience an enjoyable and informative one. I will never forget my visit.

I hope you enjoyed *Brighter Days Ahead*. I would love to hear your thoughts and can be contacted through my website:-

www.authormarywood.com.

Much love to all, Mary.

Acknowledgements

My grateful thanks to Charlotte 'Betty' Webb, a remarkable woman, for the help given towards my research. Betty was one of the many women who were stationed at Bletchley Park during the war, and she still works there to this day. Thank you so much, Betty.

And to author Kate Thompson, who selflessly shared her research into the work of the women of Bletchley and kindly facilitated a phone call between myself and Betty. Thank you. I highly recommend your books to all my readers!

To one of my readers, and now my friend Pauline Totten, for her support in entering a competition on my Facebook page to have her name used in the book. I hope that you like the lovely character named after you in *Brighter Days Ahead*, Pauline, and that she does you proud. Thank you.

As always, my eternal thanks to the Pan Macmillan team who work tirelessly on my behalf: my editor Victoria Hughes-Williams and her assistant Jayne Osborne, for always being in my corner, praising and encouraging me, and for 'getting me' and my work. To Laura Carr and her editing team, especially Mandy Greenfield, for their insightful and sensitive edits that make my work sing off the page and yet keep my voice and imagination central. To Kate Green, my publicist, for the exciting events you arrange to promote me and my work, and the special care you give to my well-being whilst I am on tour. To all the members of the sales team, especially Stuart Dwyer, for believing in me and working so hard to make my books available. To the designers, for the wonderful covers that always tell the story. To Wayne Brookes, for the joy you bring to me when you report you are signing off more reprints, and for your belief in me. Thank you all, from the bottom of my heart. Not forgetting the many who work in the background, too. You all help me achieve my dream.

My thanks, too, to my wonderful agent, Judith Murdoch, for your efforts on my behalf. For seeing something in me and my work that others have overlooked and for bringing that out and standing firmly by my side as you took me on the journey to traditional publishing. For your continued encouragement and foresight, and for the support you give me – always there for me. I am forever grateful.

No acknowledgement can be complete without mentioning my wonderful husband, Roy. Holding my hand and holding my love. Without you there is nothing.

And my wonderful family, especially my children, Christine, Julie, Rachel and James. You are my support and my world. A special thank-you to James for the hours you give to reading my draft manuscripts over and over. And for your honesty in pointing out flaws as I go. Your contribution keeps me on the right track as I can get very carried away as I write.

I love you all very much.

And last but not least, to all my readers – you are so important to me, especially those of you who follow me on Facebook and on my website, as you have become my friends. You encourage me and support me, and I am so very grateful to have you in my life. Love to you all.

The publishers hope that this book has given you enjoyable reading. Large Print Books are especially designed to be as easy to see and hold as possible. If you wish a complete list of our books please ask at your local library or write directly to:

Magna Large Print Books
Magna House, Long Preston,
Skipton, North Yorkshire.
BD23 4ND

This Large Print Book for the partially sighted, who cannot read normal print, is published under the auspices of

THE ULVERSCROFT FOUNDATION